I0586061

AUSTRALIAN HERITAGE
Courage, Pride, and Honour

AUSTRALIAN HERITAGE
Courage, Pride, and Honour

Nigel Clayton

First published in Australia by
Zuytdorp Press in 2021

ISBN: 978-0-6452540-0-6

BISAC

FIC014000	FICTION / Historical / General
DRA012000	DRAMA / Australian & Oceanian
NAT019000	NATURE / Animals / Mammals

Epic poems by this author:

Afghan - Song of the Desert
Orcinus Orca - Song of the Ocean
Hollandia Nova - Song of the Coast
Kibeho - An Epic Poem
Song of the Templar
Songs of Australia - A Poetic Trilogy
1453 - Constantinople

Other titles by this author:

The Long Road to Rwanda
The Templar: and the City of God [Part 1]
The Templar: and the Temple of Káros [Part 2]
The Templar: and the Cross of Christ [Part 3]
Amazon [Part 4 of The Templar series]
Chivalry [Omnibus]
Underworld
Templar, Assassination, Trial & Torture
Dreamtime - An Aboriginal Odyssey
The Zuytdorp Survivors
Afghan Camel Strings and the Australian Outback
Tom of Twofold Bay

PART ONE

Courage

THE ZUYTDORP SURVIVORS

HISTORY

The Dutch United East India Company (Vereenigde Oost-Indische Compagnie – VOC) was the most powerful company at the time of the Zuytdorp, and the Zuytdorp was one of their largest ships. A great monopoly stretched from Holland to Asia – namely Batavia (Jakarta) where the VOC headquarters was established – and other countries, which were a source of great wealth and commodity. Within time the VOC boasted settlements in Java, Sumatra, Borneo, India, Ceylon, Arabia, Persia, Bengal, Malacca, Celebs, Timor, China and Japan. Trade between these centres was also of strategic importance where trade and wealth was concerned, copper, tin, spices, opium and dyes being basic requisites of commerce.

Spices were something that was new to Europe, tantalizing fragments, granules and flakes, or powered, that inspired great satisfaction within all across the country, each and every one tired of the tasteless morsels dished out at dinner time and turning to spices en masse.

In more cases than not the ideal time for departing on these grand ventures across the seas, where it was usual for more than one ship to be in the company on another, was in December or April, eight months forecast for the voyage ahead, and this after being provided the mandatory and rather necessary rest stop at the Cape of Good Hope, Table Bay, for a period of ten days, a period of time which had been cut drastically from an extravagant three to four weeks. There was a fort here, established in 1652 for the sole purpose of providing medical aid and stores. A hospital of 200 beds saw many stationed upon the seafaring ships take harbour within the facility to fight that dreaded scourge of the seas, scurvy, and it was common knowledge that many hands would exchange places, those that had commenced a journey from Holland not necessarily completing the trip with that posting; it was another sad fact that all had to face and that was the death rate for those on such a long voyage, for quite a large portion of the ship's company would come to grief and be launched into the sea covered in sacking; savoury morsels for the fishes.

To avoid the dangers of the coast, from Table Bay to Batavia, at a time when the Portuguese were an enemy to be avoided, an alternate route was discovered: which also alleviated the problems in regards to wind direction. The ships would travel due west for approximately

1,000 Dutch miles before turning north. It was unfortunate, however, that there was no means by which to accurately determine longitude at sea, latitude on the other hand was quite reliable. Eventually land was encountered and this then became the accepted method of voyage: to seek the sight of land and then head north towards the coast of Sumatra. For almost a hundred years some were lucky enough to cast their eyes upon the west coast of a great mass of land, thought to have been part of New Guinea. Many names were cast upon the landmass, eventually Nova Hollandia taking hold: or as the age-wearied maps prove, Hollandia Nova. Only one real warning of impending danger was forecast to the captains of these ships and that was to avoid the Triall Rocks [the spelling is misconstrued for Trial comes from Tryall, sometimes spelled as Tryal, so Triall could essentially be correct, as seen recorded on numerous occasions] as the submerged capacity of the hidden encumbrance was enough to see a ship easily bashed, sliced, and quartered.

The Zuytdorp was considered by many as the largest ship within the VOC and only two others were of equal size. It was built between 23 Dec 1700 and 22 June 1701, being 160 feet long, 40 feet wide, and the depth of the hold was 17 feet (283 millimetres to the Amsterdam foot). She was capable of carrying 250 lasts (500 tons) which towards the latter portion of her life was increased on paper and task: the Zuytdorp in 1712 carried in the vicinity of 576 lasts.

The Zuytdorp, due to the situation with war and pirates, carried ten 12-pound guns, twenty-two 8-pound guns and eight 4-pound guns (swivel cannons). The swivel and two 8-pounders were made of bronze; all others were iron muzzle loaders.

The Zuytdorp and Belvliet had set sail for the Cape of Good Hope, to journey for most of the voyage within sight of one another, but there were instances where they were to become separated, for one reason or another. The voyage was treacherous to say the least; a longer than expected journey being suffered as the ships had to sail up and around Scotland in order to avoid English ships of the sea patrolling the Channel.

The Zuytdorp arrived at the Cape of Good Hope on 23rd March 1712, and of the original 286 crew had lost 112 men and had 22 sick on board; eight having deserted at São Tomé; most deaths are attributed to scurvy but others of tropical malaria from São Tomé itself. The Belvliet fared little better, percentage wise, and arrived on

27th March, and from a crew of 164 had lost 60 dead and 18 sick, with two desertions at São Tomé.

Much time was then spent at the Cape to replenish men and stores when finally, on 22 April 1712, the Zuytdorp departed the Cape with the ship Kockenge; the Belvliet departing several weeks later on the 9th May.

The Zuytdorp pulled ahead of the Kockenge due to her being a much larger and faster vessel, a vessel of the first class, 200 'eaters' (people) on board, 80-90 of them being new to the ship. Due to the departure being in April, opposed to the favourable March, the captain decided to sail until sighting land before turning north for Sunda Strait, to take good advantage of the winds from the west and the voyage then to the north.

But catastrophe is all they meet, no success in voyage to be celebrated. This is their story, the story of the survivors of the Zuytdorp, a part of history that is known by few, and those few are none other than the survivors, and their legacy.

GENERAL NOTE

There was no single, homogeneous Aboriginal society, but around 250 different tribes and well in excess of 100 different dialects spoken, the difference between the languages in some cases were as comparable to English and Portuguese. With such a vast network of tribal backgrounds and varying ceremonial beliefs, where interaction between groups was a common occurrence, it is not surprising to understand how members of a tribe were multilingual and able to quite effectively speak 10 different dialects or more.

The differences between tribes were as different as chalk and cheese: their language was different; their customs, kinship systems, ceremonial music and dance... all had its place, but some were used as tools of trade.

Where subtle interaction was sought between the different clans in order to pursue marriage, partners for boys coming of adulthood and of girls ready to enter into sacred ceremony, groups were bonded by belief and enactment. New myths could hence be strung, beliefs exchanged, strategies of the hunt and food gathering techniques discussed. A cycle of life and survival was maintained and the gene pool stirred well to prevent the curse-of-ancestors from rising from the dead.

There is also one other aspect of aboriginal life which must be made quite clear, and it certainly isn't considered normal, but quite the opposite, and that is in respect to the genes. There is evidence [in the 20th Century] to show that Aboriginals of the Shark Bay area suffer from Porphyria Variegate, a gene mutation that is traceable to the Dutch, as is the disease in South Africa where 1 in 300 persons suffer from it. It is uncommon and rare, and there is no reason, other than the coupling of an Aboriginal with a survivor of the Zuytdorp, that currently explains the disease being discovered in Australia.

But for the most part there was peace amongst the Aboriginals, right across the land.

In 1623, Jan Carstenz put colourful descriptions to several armed encounters with the Aboriginals. He spoke of how arid the land was, of how inhospitable and barren the entire place was, where no such horrid place existed anywhere else on earth. He spoke of the inhabitants as the most wretched and poorest that he had ever seen.

These comments were carried quite literally back to the Netherlands, and the Dutch government decided that the land was not suitable for colonisation and no benefit could be won from seeking such an endeavour.

It is not surprising therefore that all the men and women that saw the land from far out to sea felt the fear build up within them, a fear suddenly drowned by the so deeply satisfying and secure feeling within, in both knowledge and thought, that they would never have to set foot upon such a miserable place.

And then one day a ship approached this horrid place, its crew unaware of what was about to become of them, for the Zuytdorp had ventured too close to land....

PROLOGUE

The Swan River Colony was founded in 1829, a community no different than any other found on the east Australian coast. The land was bountiful, gifts ready for the plucking. The name Swan River was derived from that which it was christened, by the Dutch, many decades before, when black swans upon the river evoked a stirring of affection and beauty within the men that saw them. So beautiful they were that several were taken back to the Netherlands as somewhat of a gift to the people and the government.

It was just five short years after this 'founding' when two aboriginals could be seen within the district, walking with such a leisurely pace that they seemed to carry but not a single worry, not a single hurt within them; not a care in the world.

They were Tonquin and Weenat, tall men of darkened flesh, rather beautiful when it comes down to the point of characteristics. Their faces were alive, a living script to the lives they had so-far lived. The very structure of the skin and bone, their faces of undulating skin and large noses that appeared to sit flat and a little crooked, were but testimony to a life well lived, a life shared with nature and what the land had to offer them.

They had come to terms with the white men from afar, the way in which they settled upon the land, and wondered what they could do in order to share common courtesy, where food and tobacco might replace their friendly gesture and information on the shipwreck that had come their way. Such information must be worth something for it was a white man's ship, one that had been bashed against the rocks about forty miles north of Kalbarri. But the information they had was somewhat misconstrued, hazy to say the least, passed down from tribe to tribe, elder to young, carried from meeting to meeting, from corroboree to sacred ceremony.

The police officer sat rigid behind his desk before relaxing a little, listening with great effort to the story pressed upon him, the sentences delivered his ears missing words here and there, but the main gist of the story was noted for what it was. There was a shipwreck some thirty days walk to the north in the land of the Malgana, where the tribe Wayle lived off the land in pleasant solitude.

There was much money that had been washed upon the rocks, silver coins that were so thick in the water that it was ankle deep in places. The ship had broken up into three main parts, a three-mast ship that no longer resemble anything more than the remnants of a pile of rubble in places, covered by ocean waves.

Tonquin and Weenat looked the officer up and down as he took his notes, writing upon a sheet of paper the points that he needed to remember the most. They then continued with their story of how the tall white men were taken in by the aboriginals, where courtesy was exchanged with courtesy; and the relationship between the two became good.

The officer displayed a frown, missing a little of the interpretation, thinking that the wreck had just recently occurred, not considering for a moment that the information being delivered to him was 122 years old.

And further still, both Tonquin and Weenat advised that the white men lived in little houses, around three fires, each made of wood and canvas, and not so very far from the face of the cliff.

The police officer decided that he must act quickly, provide aid to those in need, and so a rescue was prepared, a rescue that was 122 years too late, and nothing would be found of any survivor - unless one was to dig and conduct a thorough examination of the site.

CHAPTER ONE

Today, the 5th of June, 1712, and on board the Zuytdorp are 286 souls: 174 seamen including those of higher rank, 100 soldiers, 4 tradesmen and 8 passengers. Almost all will perish.

It came upon the men, women and children without warning, a great calamity that fell upon them in the dark of the night. The sky above was as dark as one had ever known it, only intermittent sparks of light throwing themselves upon the world and decking around as lightning struck its cord with the savagery of wind and rain.

The thunder rolled all around them as the wind stole their breath away, little voice being herald to safe ear, for the strength of the gale broke up the shouts for all to pull their weight, remnants of garbled speech not being heard. Crew members on deck however were throwing themselves to duty as though it were the last thing they would ever do, and it would be the last if they were not successful in their endeavours.

The eight passengers below deck huddled together, bound by the horror which had culminated their fear to the highest point in this journey of theirs to Batavia. Their sight of the situation fared a little better as several small oil lamps were alight, swaying back and forth as the ship rocked like a cork in a tub. Three were wives heading to Batavia, a child in each of their arms, upon a voyage to lay visits upon husbands and fathers of high and important stations. The other was a man, neither brave nor cowardly, neither weak nor strong. He was heading to Batavia to fill a position advertised back at home, a position which would see the skills of his profession as a bookkeeper taxed to the limits. And there was one other, a child of fourteen, older than the others cradled safely close to mothers' breasts, and he was alone; in fact, the only keeper he had was the bookkeeper, for the bookkeeper had sworn to maintain a vigil on the boy during the long and frightful journey.

The boy's name was Willem Steyns, cast upon whichever way the wind would carry him, to take him far and wide until the limits of the earth had been reached; or so it seemed. He had been set forth by a poor mother, a drunken wretch worthy of nothing except the little money she carried in her purse. He had been cast aside by her, for him to be attended to by his father, a merchant in Batavia, and a man of lean living and completely unaware of the poor state in which his wife of England had founded for herself. In fact, he wasn't even aware that Willem was on his way to seek him out for the letter his wife did dispatch was carried by the boy himself.

The man, as tall as he was fair, tried with all his might to comfort the small group of seven as the calamity above deck continued unabated, fifty per cent of the crew seeking to right what was wrong and to ensure that the ship they sailed upon would see the light of day once more. His name was Pieter Pelsaert, 34 years of age.

Pieter had come to know the three women and Willem rather well, having spent the entire voyage strapped to their every yarn and piece of gossip, heralded to hear of what they would say about the captain of the ship or a member of his crew. They were thrown together in an area away from the main body of seamen whose job it was to see them and the ship's cargo safely ported to dock in Batavia.

Pieter saw one of the women fall, atop her baby of just 14 months, its face as blue and crimson as any darkened sky and heated furnace. He helped her up then.

"My God," Pieter bellowed into the woman's ear as he pulled her up from the sopping floor. "What manner of transgression forced you to attend this voyage with one so young? What are you running from?"

He picked the two up and noticed soon enough that he had scolded her in the face, a torment which was yet to be fully revealed, for without realising it the woman sobbed as she looked at the man and then down into the lifeless eyes of the one she held in her arms.

Pieter's mouth dropped.

"My boy; he's dead," said Willemtgen. She looked down upon the form of flesh that she pulled into her, a tightened grip that could not be pried loose. The tears streamed from her face and Pieter put an arm around her and she shifted upon the floor. The other ladies looked upon the scene and then to their own young; Ariaantje with her 18 month old girl and Willemyntje with her 4 year old daughter.

Suddenly the door burst open and a seaman by the name of Ariaen Leyden looked into the parlour of darkness flaked with the fluctuating light of the lamps, shadows moving around abruptly as the Zuytdorp creaked and groaned, bellowed and cried.

"Pieter, quick man, we need you! All hands to deck, now Pieter!" and with more suddenness than the man had employed as he entered, the entire ship shuddered that unthinkable shudder, a noise from beneath her hull, and the entire vessel shifted on its axis, the stern trying with all its might to overtake the bow by moving out to the port. She had hit a rocky seabed that loans no remorse.

She first hits rock at one hundred and twenty feet from the shoreline platform, a platform which is dwarfed by the cliff either side. It is swivelled around parallel to the coast, stern to north-west, and bow to south-east, driven sideways upon the shore of rock upon rock, upon rock.

The fear within the eyes of the women were of the sheerest grief, their distorted faces of horror painting a picture of little doubt. Each clutched ever more the little ones so close to them, even Willemtgen embraced hers as though he was still full of life and vigour.

"We're going!" yelled Ariaen as he fell heavily away from the doorway, knocking his head heavily upon the mast of the ship that penetrated deep into the Zuytdorp, and with great ease and horrible wrenching the mast from just above the deck did snap and fell away with the rigging, the little sail currently on loan to the wind falling with it, tearing here and ripping there.

The Zuytdorp was under short sail and in the midst of an early winter storm. This big, square-rigged ship was unable to move effectively, and the pending disaster was unavoidable.

Men upon the deck were thrown overboard, presented to the mercy of the sea, but little mercy was received this night. Barrels and cannons rolled around the decking killing men as quickly as a trail of ants became trodden on by a heavy foot.

The cargo in the hold shifted suddenly, aiding the abrupt shifting of the Zuytdorp upon its current course, barrels and sacks of all variety, much of the merchandise tearing open for the rats below deck to avoid in their rush for safer quarters.

The Zuytdorp carried within her a great quantity of merchandise including precious metals, wealth in the form of silver coins being its largest hoard. Coins in their thousands; Dutch ducatons, guilders, rix dollars, schillings, double stuivers and stuivers; Spanish pieces of eight, pieces of four and pieces of two; Spanish-Netherlands ducatons and patagons. There was also Gold which came in the form of Dutch ducats and ingots of silver too. The great quantities of wealth were carried in chests, packed and secured to prevent movement. Two locks saw to it that each chest was bolted secure, each chest then nailed down secure with sail cloth within the captain's cabin below the poop; silver coins to the value of 248,886 guilders, 100,000 guilders of which were newly minted schillings and double stuivers. But she also carried other commodities; lead, linseed, bacon, needles, muskets and blunderbusses. She was filled to the brim with barrels of wine and beer; butter, 1,813 pounds of fresh meat, ten live sheep, vegetables, potherbs, 2 hundredweight of beans, 2 hundredweight of peas, 300 pounds of rice, bacon, oils, cloth, rope, sulphur, pitch, canvas, paper, leather, copper, salt, sail yarn, window panes, medical stores, iron hoops and plates. And what good was all of this? It was ambition, enterprise and above all money to be made. Not only was there wealth to be sanctioned from the hull of this grand ship but the Zuytdorp was to return to Europe with an even bigger catch; Spices, salt, pepper, textiles, china, cotton, silks, tea, coffee, nutmeg, cloves, cinnamon, mace, and anything else that could be tied down, or locked away in chests and barrels.

Damn it; damn it all. It was all loose, being thrown around here and there; impossible to avoid whether below deck or upon it. Men were being killed. Broken bones made their appearance; broken arms, broken noses, and a sudden call was snatched by the wind, a call of 'every man for himself', and no sooner had it be called then the man responsible was speared in the gut by flying debris as another of the ship's masts snapped and fell upon the decking, the ship pitching further off its bearings and being forced upon the unforgivable shoreline of rock.

The Zuytdorp gave way to sudden bouts of lurching, enormous waves of terror thrashing out upon the starboard side of the ship, water commencing to flow freely within the hull, the vessel taking on water, everyone trying with all their effort to save themselves from the torments of the sea. It was not a time to reflect upon anything except all manner of escape, but one thing was clear within every single one of those still alive and able to think, and that was that the ship was wrecked.

Pieter took this as a call for him to act, a call to duty which was not his to answer but the last thing he wished to do was leave anyone behind, in particular an helpless woman with child, be it dead or alive, or the boy known as Willem.

"Quickly, Willem; you have to help me," and Pieter stumbled with the shifting of the ship as it grinded itself upon the bottom, further groans of mayhem being voiced from the very fibre of the ship's core, wood commencing to split, the sound of cracking wood reaching their ears, so loud that it could hardly be believed.

"What do I do," came Willem's reply, the fright upon his face written in bold, the bulging eyes giving rise to the frantic state of his mind and nerve. "Tell me, Pieter."

Pieter could not deny that the boy's frame of mind scared him to wit's end, but the boy must be forced to endure and provide assistance, for only then would he forget the fear within him and commence to crawl from the abyss in which he had fallen.

"Give aid to Willemtgen and her son, I'll attend Ariaantje and Willemyntje," said Pieter in haste, as Willem's mouth began to open. "Quickly, now!"

"Please, Willemtgen," said Willem as he set to his task. "Take hold of my arm and we'll scale the steps together."

Willemtgen's face showed a glare of hope then, even with her dead son still in her arms, as she reached out to grab hold of the boy. It was just then that the worst thing that could possibly happen did occur.

The entire ship broke into three pieces as a huge wave with frightening force behind it hit hard the starboard side of the Zuytdorp. The bow broke away, 22 feet of her, and shifted 60 feet towards the shoreline platform where many large boulders with bone-breaking knobs and points awaited its delivery, to gnaw upon it as a man gnaws upon a bone. The stern headed in a forward motion towards the nearest portion of shoreline, just 28 feet away from the main bulk of the ship, breaking up just a little but steadying herself upon the rocks, 53 feet of her in which all the treasure on board was stowed. The centre most portion, all 85 feet of that which remained, rammed home against the platform, the fallen mast upon the deck crushing several men as it shifted position.

Those few men that remained upon, or within, the bow portion of the vessel, died quick and slow deaths, broken bones and concussion; drowning and knocked unconscious, trapped within the rigging and skewered by the wood of the ship, large splitters delivering death as though she, the Zuytdorp, was filled with a cursed evil. And those of the stern fared little better, the portion of the ship in which Pieter and Willem were housed, alongside their female companions and other members of the crew.

The higher the station a sailor of the sea held and the closer he could find himself to the door of the captain's quarters, and other than the captain himself were the following: the uppersteersman, senior carpenter, master surgeon, second carpenter, understeersman, comforter of the sick, third carpenter, undersurgeon, clerk, master gunner and bosun; the stockmaker, bricklayer, coppersmith and firelock maker... all were dead, spread out through the ship, cast out upon the sea, dashed upon the rocks of the coast, pulled beneath the waves by the surmounting weight of wave upon wave as they crashed upon their victims without a shred of effort or remorse.

But Pieter broke free from the ferocity of the sea as it swelled in upon him, spluttering and gasping for breath as he tried with all his effort to gain some form of initiative against his predicament. He saw a baby floating close by and then the body of a woman, and then another, and finally the third. And Willem suddenly clawed his way from the bottom, breaching the surface of the sea with an outstretched arm reaching for the sky. They were surrounded on three sides by the interior of the ship which they had called home, the fourth side was now wide open to the dark night air. And with as much astonishment as they could perceive the glory of God cast down upon them the opportunity of a lifetime, the hands of glory pushing aside a small opening in the sky, just enough to allow a little light to make its way down to earth, to light up the scene around them. With the accompaniment of the lightning strikes the two, both man and boy, could see one another and the silhouette of the cliff that looked like doom peering down upon them.

"Are you okay, Willem? Are you hurt!" shouted Pieter at the top of his lungs, the open side of the stern becoming an open invitation for more noise to envelope them both.

"Yes; yes! I'm okay," came the reply and Pieter moved closer to the boy, the one he had grown a little fond of, the one that had kept him company on occasion and had lifted his spirits when they were down. Now it was Pieter's job to see to it that the favour was returned by saving the child's life and remaining by his side in this, their hour of need. Pieter, the bookkeeper, was to fulfil his duty as carer, to provide all the support he could to the boy of fourteen.

There was a small gap between the stern and the shoreline, the platform of rock which was vacant of sand. There was no soft landing, no offering of support from nature. The gap had to be breached by them without their being thrust against the rocky talons of that which stood before them.

To speak more than what was required was wasteful. When gasps for air were called upon, and energy reserves within were the only means by which to climb to safety, all else mattered little. Instinct took over and together the two bodies of flesh and bone acted as one.

Pieter closed the small gap towards the boy and grabbed hold of his arm, each then reached for buoyancy which came in the form of a large piece of debris, and then an upturned barrel. But the barrel fell from their grip and filled with water. They grabbed hold of a chest, a foot locker with air trapped within it, offering to provide sufficient support for them to make their way towards the rocky platform which was now within view below the cracking brilliance of piercing light delivered by another lightning strike, different shades of darkness outlining the scene before them.

The energy within them peaked quite rapidly to such a degree that within as little as half a minute both found themselves so near the edge of the platform that they could almost touch it, the platform which was covered in crashing waves and ebbing surf. It was like being upon the surface of a giant cauldron at the boil, and without warning a tidal surge of water lifted them both up and over the danger of the jagged lip, a miraculous salvation from harm which they were most grateful for.

"Quickly! Willem; to me; grab my hand!" yelled Pieter, his voice penetrating the cold of the night where the wind and spray from the sea stung at his unprotected face.

Willem reached for Pieter, stretching beyond his doubt until fingertip touched fingertip and then their hands were clasped together like welded metal. Pieter pulled the boy to him and in the fury of gut-deep surges, where the platform made itself visible from time to time, its undulating surface offering itself as just another obstacle, the two scrambled to a temporary safe haven behind a large boulder: a small pinnacle or nubbin, being part of the rock formation itself.

The sea continued to lap up around them and another freak wave forced itself up and over their protection, the man and boy gasping for air as the water ebbed back into the fury of the sea in readiness for another opportunity to beat itself against the platform of rock and the Zuytdorp.

Pieter looked up and saw his opportunity for salvation, a rampart of sorts, a mass of crumbling rock, detritus in all its glory which was steep but passable; rock, stone and boulders having fallen away from the cliff, a way to the summit of the cliff face before him being revealed, the height of the cliff still obscured from knowledge due to the inaccuracy of perception in the current light and surrounding misery.

"Willem; with me; come with me, now," ordered the tall bookkeeper, and together they scrambled up the gradient of detritus as best they could, losing two steps to every three that they took but making such good progress considering the position and condition that they were both in.

Each must have slipped at least ten times in the short trek to the top, their fingernails splintered, caked in mud, cuts and abrasions upon their skin, muscles torn in the effort applied. There was not a single part of their body which was not working itself hard; all the tissue, ligaments, muscle; both physical and mental; all was worked to the brink of collapse. Every thought but that of survival was shaken from their minds as they continued on up the slope.

Salvation wasn't far ahead, they could see and feel it, looking up momentarily to see what was ahead, to try and visualise how far they needed to climb before victory was won. And on reaching the top a little more cloud moved aside and more light lit up the night as both of them fell onto all fours at the edge of the cliff, exhausted beyond all realisation, Pieter and Willem then collapsing upon the rock of the cliff that was little more than 115 feet high.

They gasped for air where they lay, a great wave of relief empowering both to sit up and look around, both open mouthed and in disbelief, shock taking momentary hold prior to another surge of adrenalin embracing the sanity they still had within them.

It was now, with the providence offered them that they could see out across the scene of destruction, the Zuytdorp ripped apart into three main parts, her cargo spread far and wide, planks of wood being thrown through the air alongside barrels and other matter, each a lethal weapon that lashed upon the unwary. But what could they do? These two skeletons of humanity, starved in the course of the voyage, tired from the conditions on board ship, tired from the swim to shore, the climb to higher station, and exhausted beyond all imagination.

There was nothing they could do for the others, those below in the surf, still aboard ship and attempting to pull themselves to safety and away from harm.

Many men could be seen, dashed against rocks, hit hard by an unsuspecting barrel, drowned by the viciousness of a wave and the surges of water coming down upon them one after the other without a moment's stay.

"Hey, up here; we're up here!" shouted Willem as he waved his arms in a frantic attempt to help those below, the rain falling hard upon him, stinging at his numbed face, the pain hardly felt due to the calamity of the situation.

Pieter lifted an arm and made Willem lower his by grabbing a gentle hold of his wrist.

"Save yourself, Willem," said Pieter with angel eyes looking upon the boy of fourteen, the boy looking back, their stares locked momentarily. "They can't see nor hear you."

"Then what are we to do, just sit here and do nothing?"

"Avert your eyes, Willem. That's all you can do," advised Pieter.

"But we must do something to help."

Pieter looked down upon the scene and then back to the boy who he could see was now in fact a man.

"Then do as I do, Willem. Keep your eyes open. Ignore the pain you see; ignore the horrors of this night, of the devil at play. Watch, Willem; watch with your entire might and keep a mental record of where people lay. Keep a note on where they may be found on the break of this viciousness in order for us to venture down and pull all ashore. There will be survivors, Willem, as we have survived, but all we can do now is watch... but ignore the suffering you see, do not allow their suffering to plague your mind."

And Willem nodded acceptance of the task set before him and both cast their eyes upon the horrors of the shipwreck as it continued to develop into a betrayal that was cast down from heaven above, and the cold of the storm penetrated deep, the panic that had overridden the effect of the cold having dissipated. He began to shiver.

"Here, Willem," said Pieter. "Sit in front of me, between my legs. We can gain a little warmth." He looked around into the dark and saw nothing behind him but frequent exposures of an open land with no apparent cover available.

"I see nothing at all," continued Pieter. "Nothing but open ground." Willem was now seated in front of the man. "We must remain strong; stay as warm as possible until the storm has abated. From our experiences on ship I think I can safely surmise that this cold spell is not something that is common for this land."

"I've heard many stories," said Willem as his teeth chattered and his body convulsed a little with shudders of pain, "that this land is as cold in the winter months as it is hot in the summer."

"No one has been around long enough to tell the difference," voiced Pieter above the storm and thrashing waves from below, spray from the sea reaching them with little difficulty. "This job of ours will be a hard one," added Pieter. "I don't know if we should remain aloft the wreck for too long. I feel the pain of this bitter cold within you as I feel it within me, you there, shivering like a nervous wreck." He looked around himself once more. "Willem; I don't think we'll find adequate shelter but we can't remain here. We must find a hollow in the least, something to shelter us from the wind."

Without a further word the two stood up, and stooped lower than normal proceeded away from the cliff face and into the unknown.

It wasn't long before they came across a small re-entrant, a small stream with banks of little concern. They followed this for some distance before coming upon a band of scrub; thick and seemingly impenetrable.

"Maybe we should turn back," said Willem with growing concern.

"Up here, Willem. I see several boulders. Come; follow me."

They stepped out of the low ground and halted next to several large rocks, and behind them, away from the blast of the wind and soaking of the rain, sought shelter for the remainder of the night, curled up and holding each other close. They did not sleep whilst the storm continued in its fury, but the rest they attained was better than nothing at all, their thoughts on any possible survivors and how they would be able to help come morning.

By the time the storm had blown itself clear of the coast the sun was almost upon them, and it was at this time that they fell asleep.

CHAPTER TWO

Birdsong was filling the air from some distance away, a medley of choruses that seemed to have suffered little, uninhibited by the night's misery, and as the mellow sounds from many species filled the air the two fragile forms of human existence woke up to be greeted by the arrival of the sun. The bite of the cold was easily felt upon them, though now there was not a cloud in the sky, and the cold of the morning had less effect on them than the night before, where they were covered in the spray of the ocean and rain from the sky; but with their clothes still being very wet and their combined body heat less effective than they would have liked, the chill teased them when they moved from their tight embrace.

Willem was the first to sit up and was followed shortly by Pieter, both shivering and fighting to open their heavy eyelids.

Suddenly a vibration hit them both, a sound unfamiliar and a long way off, a penetrating sound that was mystifying to say the least.

"Did you hear that, Pieter?"

"I did, Willem," the man answered as he stood up upon his feet, looking out towards the north-east, from where the sound made its unwavering approach. "And I think I know what it is."

"What?" asked Willem as he looked up into the tall man's eyes, seeing the reflection of humanity still alive in the sodden form that stood before him, a man with scratches and bruises covering his arms and face, his clothes torn and tattered, his trousers ripped down one entire side baring the flesh of his leg to the world, his shoes missing and socks soaked.

"I think it's the men of this world."

"Wretched souls of humanity," replied Willem, casting his eyes upon the earth.

"There has been much talk; much hearsay, which may be untrue," corrected Pieter.

"Do you think they'll eat us?"

A small smile caressed Pieter's face, "No. But let's forget that for the moment. We must get back to the cliff, view the damage, and find what survivors we can."

Leading the way back to the cliff face, Pieter looked behind him from time to time during the short trek to ensure that Willem was close by and at hand, and before they knew it they were stepping up towards the edge of the cliff and looking down upon the site of the shipwreck.

Such a site could never be explained; the feelings of despair and depression, the horror of seeing the bodies lying upon the now exposed platform of rock. There was debris everywhere, not a single foot of ground bare to a part of the wreck, be it a plank of wood, a barrel, cannon, cloth or body. Every single item of commerce transported within the Zuytdorp seemed to be free of its holdings, splashed upon the scene as though in reckless doubt, doubt as in whether to stay or be swept out to sea, the former glory of the ship itself torn apart into three parts, each wedged up tight against the shoreline platform. It was sheer misery that enveloped them both and as they perused the tragedy a voice came from behind them.

"Pieter, is that you?" asked a weary voice, a man by the name of Ariaen Leyden.

The bookkeeper turned, half startled to death by the broken silence.

"My God, Ariaen; thank God... you're alive," said an exuberant Pieter, stepping towards the man of 28 years, a man of the sea, a common sailor who had made the voyage to Batavia on three separate occasions as well of many years travelling between the countries of Asia under the keeping of the VOC.

"I'm well."

And from behind the man came further hope, a mass of people, twelve all told, each as weathered as the first, dressed as lepers, steeped in rags, and a majority without footwear upon their feet, feet that had been lacerated by rocks. Some of those present were in shock, had been soaking wet all night long, cold from the early winter storm and the face of the wind.

"How many of you are there?" asked Pieter.

"We're seventeen, including me, but several of them are injured."

"What kind of injuries? Asked Pieter as those from behind Ariaen closed the gap, sunken faces worn by them all, the life gone from their eyes like the embers disappear from the remnants of a blazing fire, turning stone cold as on a winter's morning.

"Broken bones, mostly; and some of the walking, as you can see behind me, carry many cuts and abrasions."

Pieter looked upon his friend and saw a gash on his forehead, a deep wound that had clearly removed some bone.

"You too are hurt."

"It appears so. It hurts like hell to tell you the truth but there is more suffering here today than could ever be suffered by me in a lifetime of suffering."

"We need to move down to the wreck," started Pieter before looking upon the others and raising his voice, "to the wreck we must go, to look for survivors; others that may be trapped and require our assistance."

"No, Pieter," said Ariaen. "We've been down there already, me and two other men. We've searched everywhere and not another soul has survived."

"Are you sure...? Maybe you missed someone; maybe there is hope left for some unfortunate soul left stranded below this cliff."

Ariaen grabbed his friend upon the upper arms, "No, Pieter. We've tried. There is no one else."

"Then what's to be done?"

"Supplies. We need water the most. Drinking water and food; bandages and medicine for the sick. We need tools for cutting splints."

"And a cannon," voiced Cornelis Lieffers, a young man of 19 years, and a seaman of vast experience for having joined the VOC so young, "to signal a passing ship."

"Shoes," voiced another from behind, "we also need shoes."

Pieter looked down at the man's feet and then to his own. Yes, indeed, there was much to be sought.

Pieter looked to the others and quickly realised that they were like lambs, flocking around a single soul. It seemed that Ariaen had adopted the leadership role for all concerned but Pieter felt he had more to offer.

"I am a bookkeeper and some of you know me. I have exercised my ambition and expertise upon many stations of the sea and visited many ports, all of this before my 29th birthday when, soon after, I decided upon remaining sure-footed and comforted upon dry land. In time I grew to change once more and decided to work elsewhere. I have many degrees and sound knowledge on navigation. It would honour me if you'd all allow me the opportunity to help in this predicament of ours."

A man took a few steps forward and the others around him also stirred, "I am Hendrik Blaauw. Ariaen knows me. I am 47 years old and have spent most of my life upon the sea. Why should the task of command and rescue go to one as you?"

"I have—."

"Yes, yes; you have degrees," Hendrik announced sarcastically as he turned to look at the others around. "Does a common piece of paper hold more authority than experience?"

"I am simply offering my hand," said Pieter in defence. "It's for you to decide what to make of it."

"I say that we make-of-it right now," voiced Hendrik. "Who shall be in command of this shipwrecked crew? Let's vote!"

"Aye!" shouted one; "here, here," came another.

"All of those in favour of me taking command place your hands up in the air," commanded Hendrik.

With Ariaen and his twelve, then Pieter and Willem, there stood to be cast a total of fifteen votes, from there upon that very spot.

Eight hands showed themselves after a little hesitation, including Hendrik's.

"The tally has spoken," said Hendrik. "I have eight votes, including mine; the remaining seven will be yours."

"What of the lame, the ones with broken bones?" asked Ariaen in defence of his trusted friend. "Don't they have a vote?"

"I have spent many years at sea and know that gangrene will visit them all. A dead man can't vote."

Ariaen then considered the situation, instantly deciding upon something more: "And what of me?" stated Ariaen. "I wish to make a stand. I am from a higher station than most."

"There's no rank here," came a voice from the back.

"That's right," confirmed Hendrik. "We're no longer on the sea. Our survival depends on being able to live off the land until a ship comes to the rescue."

"Which won't be long now," said Ariaen to all those listening to the argument unfold. "I know that the Kockenge will pass by these shores soon... within the week. When we were at Table Bay I also heard of others. We can expect such ships as the Oostersteyn, the Zuyderbeeck, Belvliet, Popkensburg, Corsloot and the Oude Zyp; all of these to come past this way over the next four to five weeks. Not all will be seen by us; not all will come within range to our waving arms. We need to build a signal fire and prepare it for immediate ignition when the time is right... we need to get a cannon," said Ariaen as he lay his eyes upon Cornelis Lieffers, the 19 year old with the idea to save them all. "We must bury the dead and collect rations where possible, and much, much more."

"Here, here," yelled Dirck Fret from the rear. "All those that vote for Ariaen put your hand in the air," and to the astonishment of Hendrik a show of nine hands could be seen, including those of Willem and Pieter.

"Not counting the soon-to-be-dead," added Pieter to the insult.

"So let it be done," said Hendrik in defeat, the evil in his eyes brewing something against what appeared to be nothing less than a conspiracy against him, ignoring the comment against those injured by the storm, by allowing them a vote.

CHAPTER THREE

The storm had done its job well, the pounding surf having smashed the hull, driving it into shallow water three to ten feet deep beside the shoreline platform.

It was easy to see how many of the survivors had reached safety, a large tangle of rigging alongside a fallen mast connecting the ship with the shore. It was precariously unstable at the moment and wouldn't stay long where it currently lay. It was a devastating site and beyond belief.

The cliff was limestone and only around 90 feet high at the actual wreck site. The area before the cliff was a jumble of boulders and jagged rock, no sand. The stretch of rock before the cliff was approximately 65 feet wide and 6.5 feet above sea level.

To all of those now looking upon the scene, from atop the smallest portion of cliff along the entire coast [for 155 miles], an unbroken stretch of cliff disappeared into the horizon; so daunting to say the least, it was nothing less than a devastating blow to morale.

A carpet of silver could be seen far below, glimmering in the early morning sunlight, every single chest of treasure seemingly revealed to the world. The biggest decision was where to start.

"We need to be systematic about our salvage," announced Ariaen as all of those present gathered around. "I see the wonder in some of you, the glittering of the silver below lighting up your eyes. Listen to me; the money will do nothing for you if you're dead. It'll all still be there next week and the week after that. Help yourself if you wish but remember one thing; whatever you salvage of the silver is the property of the VOC and when we're rescued it will have to be returned. You'll receive no special favour, so leave it. Some of you need shoes; that is priority. We need wood for shelter, a cannon if possible, just the one will serve our purpose. Breech blocks will help the most, the more we can salvage the better. Food and fresh water, barrels for storage and anything else you think appropriate. This is the calm after the storm and we don't know what the future holds. We may not get another opportunity to gather supplies so let us make the most of it."

Ariaen then waved his hand frantically about his face, trying with great effort to release himself of the bondage that the flies around him had subjected him to... there were thousands of them.

There were nods of agreement and the men commenced to lower themselves towards the platform, slipping upon the steep bank as they made for what remained of the good ship Zuytdorp.

Little was said during the task, shoes being pulled from the dead, bodies collected and moved towards the cliff where they could be pulled to dry land by ropes and rigging, for the corpses would rot and create all manner of disease and if the shipwreck was to be made a constant visiting pleasure for those in search of different items then the threat of disease must surely be extinguished... besides, didn't the dead also deserve a decent burial.

Several men tried to get one of the smaller bronze swivel guns ashore along with the breech blocks for it, guns mounted on the poop deck, the highest part of the ship and currently quite accessible. Eight breech blocks altogether were taken ashore but the swivel guns were too cumbersome and heavy, unable to be moved. No other guns could be taken ashore.

The breech blocks were 12-18 inches high, weighing approximately 28 pounds each and looked remarkably like large jugs, drinking cups with handles, and a pair of callipers were also taken ashore along with brass dividers to aid in navigation should they later decide to make a boat in an effort to launch it and make for Batavia, even though no map was secured from the wreck.

Others concentrated on gathering food and it wasn't beyond Willem, of all those that were scampering around looking for salvage that would be of some use, to find that the area was encrusted with oysters, abalone, whelks, periwinkles, rock barnacles, mussels and other shellfish. Whether or not they could survive solely upon shellfish was another concern, something that Willem was too young to consider... and how long would the supply last the totally-combined, nineteen survivors, especially in the face of the impending difficulty where many were on the brink of gangrene and death?

One of the searchers found dry powder for a musket, but no musket, and sheets of lead, and all manner of the wreck was deposited upon the base of the cliff and out to where the wreck lay in three parts. A figurehead of a pregnant women had been dislodged from the Zuytdorp and thrown against rocks, this was carried into a cavern below the cliff face for safe keeping, too large to worry about carrying to the cliff top at present as there were more important things to do, the figurehead a possible memento of little worth other than a reminder that could be made into a memorial of some description when the time was right. The figure was from the stern of the ship; she had a small plump face and bore a placid expression; she was the only woman amongst them, though mute and carved of wood.

One by one, in their two's and three's, men appeared briefly upon the cliff top to place down their salvage before returning to the work; bodies too were accumulated on the platform below, stacked precariously, shoes taken by those that needed them, a quick prayer accompanying the removal of the footwear.

The ship's sails were torn apart – what was left of them – and taken to those with broken limbs, several men providing their special ability to give aid to the suffering, knowing a little on the subject of broken bones. It was a horrid sight, frantic yells for help reaching for the sky, even after the administering of alcohol, for many green bottles, square in shape and full to the brim with gin, were handed out willingly to those in need.

Some of the more fragile-of-mind, sought to carry many bottles off to a station upon the cliff face overlooking the sea. Here sat Gerrit Jongbloet, Jacob Albertsz, Jacobus Nuyts and Cornelius Brouwer. They had wandered off from their duty not long after it had commenced, drawing their bottles close into their chests, wrapping their arms around the necks of the bottles and caressing them as though they were wives. They suckled off the bottles as though being milked by their mothers, weaning the glass bottles of every drop, becoming drunk and loud amidst the misfortune that had fallen upon them all.

The four men with broken limbs lay not so far away, clutching at their ears to prevent the awful sound, for the drunken slander of those above the cliff face were as horrid as the screams that were emitted by those with broken bones.

Dirck Fret, 35 years old, and Wiebbe Leuftink, 29 years old, assisted those in need, the strain of their task being very real and unparalleled. Never before had either of them provided medical assistance without the aid of someone of sufficient knowledge beside them, but for what they achieved the victims were most grateful. But this, the degradation of the drunken swines not so far away, making a mockery of the survival situation; it was beyond belief. The two men could only look over their patients and talk to them with passion as the gin took its effect and the pain from their injuries commenced to evaporate for a while.

Francisco Roelofsz had a broken leg and a punctured gut wound, Johannes Snitquer a broken arm and fractured skull, Marinus Leynsen had a broken arm and several broken ribs, and Hayman Jorisz had two broken legs.

Dirck looked to Wiebbe as the noise from the drunks drifted upon the breeze to where they had set up temporary shelter for the wounded, several planks tied together by rope and some of the ship's sail placed over the top of this to act as shade and protection from the wind and rain. It wasn't the grandest attempt anyone had made at pitching a shelter but for the time they had been allowed they fared reasonably well.

Out of earshot, Dirck said to Wiebbe, "I fear that Hayman won't last the week. He's in much pain and by morning the gin would have lost its effect."

"Hmmm," acknowledged Wiebbe. "I fear for Francisco. I'll go and see Ariaen, and ask him what he thinks."

"Don't give him too much credit, Wiebbe. He's just a man like us. Give him too much satisfaction and his position of command will go to his head."

"Then will be the time to change the leadership of this group," said Wiebbe and moved off without further word from Dirck being voiced.

Dirck pulled a sopping piece of cloth from a damaged bucket and wiped the sweat from Johannes' forehead, the bruising upon his skull being very evident, a large swelling and mostly red. There was much pressure beneath the skull and the worst was feared for his well-being, for his fever was very strong.

CHAPTER FOUR

Wiebbe approached Ariaen who had just appeared at the lip of the cliff carrying one end of a plank, Pieter coming up from the rear. They placed the plank down, and Willem, waiting patiently for his chance to perform his duty, lifted one end of the plank and pulled it with great effort over to a pile that he had growing rather large.

"The boy works well," noted Wiebbe, smiling at the boy and waving away flies.

"He's a man now," said Ariaen, seeing Willem's mouth erupt into a smile.

Wiebbe reflected briefly on the boy before announcing his reason for his running errand.

"The wounded are in a bad way... as I have said, the gin worked well but won't last the whole night. There'll be much suffering tonight."

"What about those drunken bums over near the cliff?" asked Pieter. "Can't we seize the bottles they have, give them to those in need?"

"Oh, they have more than you think," added Wiebbe. "They've taken a great quantity of bottles and have them close at hand; some hidden and others beside them."

"Take them," said Pieter as he looked to Ariaen and then Wiebbe.

"They have knives..." commenced Wiebbe. "What is it to us that they choose to crawl inside a bottle; really?"

"Inflicted by the devil. It will be to their own demise," said Pieter.

"What is it that we can do for you anyway?" asked Ariaen.

"The wounded, as I have said; they're all in a bad way, but some more than others. Most of us have something to remember the storm by, but those four... I think their time is short. Francisco has a punctured gut as well as a broken leg. We can't do anything for the wound except bandage it. It will become infected soon unless it can be cleaned and closed."

"Can we attain anything from the ship's doctor?" asked Pieter of Ariaen.

"His cabin isn't far from the captain's. You were in there, Pieter. What was it like?"

"Last night it was like hell; this morning I searched for some personal belongings but found nothing. Most of the quarters are below the surface and I would hazard a good guess that the cabinet in which the medicine is kept would have been spoiled as much by the storm as the medicine would have been spoiled by the sea and rocks. I don't think we'll find anything there."

"Isn't it worth a try?" asked Wiebbe.

"I'll have another look," volunteered Pieter, none too confident that anything would come of the effort, and to that he was correct, for nothing could be salvaged from the doctor's belongings or the medicine under his charge.

"Meanwhile the only alternative is to comfort them," said Ariaen.

"And with that I'll return to my station," concluded Wiebbe.

Another man then appeared upon the cliff, a regular seaman as ever could be found. Jan Wysvliet put down an empty bucket and Willem came in from the side and removed it to his stockpile.

"Jan, can I ask something of you?" queried Ariaen.

"Certainly. What is it?"

"Take another man with you and find a campsite, somewhere not too far away from the cliff but far enough to be away from the drunks over by the cliff just there."

"Sure," acknowledged Jan, tired reflection showing upon his face and the way in which he held himself. "I'll take Harmen with me."

CHAPTER FIVE

Harmen Akkerman and Jan pushed themselves on into the unknown, and having quickly established a site for a camp, where the waters of the Indian Ocean could be seen both far and wide, decided to continue with their reconnaissance, for it wasn't enough for these two men of the sea to be satisfied with such a small accomplishment.

They commenced upon their reconnaissance of the area, in particular towards where they had heard the same sound that Pieter had heard earlier that morning, the flies going along to keep them company, thick upon their backs, licking at the saturation upon them both.

From the edge of the cliff inwards for about 1,300 feet was void of anything except a little low heath vegetation but after that there existed very dense scrub for two miles, made up of tea-tree and eucalyptus. The trees themselves were well spaced and would provide ample opportunity for the making of a small raft or shelter should the need arise; as it was, however, there was plenty of salvage from the wreck that would currently serve all of their purposes, including material for a fire, once the planks had dried sufficiently.

The going was tough on the men for they were already exhausted from the salvage operation, not to mention that they had gone without food passing their lips since the day before, but they continued on. The sky was a beautiful blue and there was not a cloud to be seen. Both felt as though winter was fast approaching the area, if not already in place, and felt that the clear sky was not to be a common occurrence over the coming months.

Several gullies presented themselves, each several hundred meters apart, stretching out from the land and towards the coast, being quite deep and several miles long. Like small streams during winter after heavy rain but dry for the remainder of the year. Harmen and Jan knelt down and drew handfuls of fresh water into their mouths, the tiny trickle of water from the night's storm refreshing them of what they had lost, the feeling lasting them for just a few minutes.

Small rock holes were also found to hold up to 12 gallons of water but these were scarce and not altogether a reliable source of water. It would seem that they would make a good source during the winter months only.

Further inland there was a great expanse of undulating sandplain stunted with low scrub, like a sea dotted with acacias, eucalypts and banksias. To these men of the sea, used to the sights and smells of home, where land was bound by cities in their fullest glory, the scene before them was devastating to say the least. The heat of the afternoon had built up quite dramatically, as it does at sea on long voyages, and their feet were swelling up with the effort of the walk, even though winter had well and truly started and the migration of some birds was already complete.

As they continued on into the clearing, Harmen came to a stop.

"Look, Jan. Over there," said Harmen, pointing with his head low as though trying to aim his finger with great accuracy, as though it were a weapon ready to be discharged.

"What do you see?" asked Jan as he looked off into the distance.

"A head, I'm sure of it. It moved, look... there it is again!" Harmen said hurriedly.

"Ah; yes. I see it too. It's not moving now. It has great ears and a long snout."

"A dog," concluded Harmen.

"No," disagreed Jan, looking his friend with lowered eyebrows, signifying his puzzlement at such a stupid suggestion. "Look around you, Harmen. This grass is almost chest high in places. If that is a dog then it'll be the largest damn dog I've ever seen."

"It could be standing upon a recent kill, or a dirt mound, searching for prey," suggested Harmen.

And then it moved, dashing off in leaps and bounds, against the open plains of grass-filled expanse, a kangaroo as never seen by the eyes of a white man before. Harmen and Jan cowered in the long grass, holding palm to chest, the fright of the animal moving with such rapid action catching them completely by surprise.

"Did you see that?" asked Harmen, and then another fifteen animals picked up their heads and followed the previous.

"My God. I don't believe it."

"We must get back with the news, Jan."

"No, not yet," Jan looked at Harmen and saw the anxiousness within him. "They're just animals, Harmen. We should look further, beyond where they stood."

"But not too far, Jan. We don't want to get lost."

"Lost," scoffed Jan. "We just head west, simple as that. Come; let's look some more."

Before they knew it the day was drawing to a close, and by the end of the day they felt exhausted. There was no time for a meal of any sort... it was missed; the sun commenced to disappear over the horizon, their eyes watching that stunning sight, the appearance of a myriad of colours cast across the sky and the stars came out in all their glory, giving enough light for them both to see out in all directions. The cool night air was comfortable enough to keep them from freezing and the sounds of the night reached their ears, but still they huddled together like man and wife: it wasn't until the early hours of the morning that the vacuum of cold left by the evaporated heat of the day hit them hard. It was all new to them, completely strange. Being too tired the night before and in the midst of a ferocious storm, they had missed the chorus of songs offered by the bush. And then out of the distance, seemingly not as far as they first thought, came the sounds that reverberated across the land, a ceremony taking place upon this strange land, a tune of drumming notes that brought the fear within them to surface.

There could be cannibals in the area and they were mightily concerned.

CHAPTER SIX

The salvage operation had gone quite well and before the sun disappeared below the horizon, all that could be carried to the top of the cliff, before the waves moved it out to sea, had been moved. There was still a lot of material to be had but it wouldn't be going far; too heavy to be carried out by the waves or still attached, even if precariously so, to the main hulk of the Zuytdorp. All of the barrels of wine and beer, the butter, ten sheep, rice, bacon and oils had been lost, as too, were much of the other stores. They were fortunate enough to have rescued a little of the vegetable – namely peas – and cloth; rope, canvas, salt and plates; this and just 128 pounds of meat, over 1,600 pounds having been lost to the hungry sea or simply ruined beyond contemplation, and the last thing the survivors needed was illness adding to their ruin.

The meat had salt rubbed into it but even so wasn't expected to last long; they would need to make the most of what they had and early on, hoping to secure more food as the days unfolded before them.

The bodies of the dead had been piled as delicately as possible to one corner of the shoreline platform, ready to be moved over the next few days to a fire which they intended to build, a fire which would not only act as a point from which to cremate all the dead but to signal any passing ship that might be within range of the coast. With the calculations suggested of the ships in port at Table Bay, and of the ship that accompanied them from that harbour, it was quite reasonable for Kockenge to be past their way over the coming six to seven days; and all knew that she was a slower vessel than the Zuytdorp.

The four men, drunk and beyond comprehension, lay near the edge of the cliff, their sorrows drowned to the point where they were literally oblivious to anything that was going on around them. Empty bottles of gin sat around them, some broken, some in one piece.

Away from the drunks a temporary fire had been lit by way of several lamps full of oil and a tinderbox procured by Ariaen, for he secretly held within his possession a small tobacco box of dry tobacco and the fire-starter. But his secret did not last, for although the average seaman displayed little intelligence, they weren't halfwits incapable of summing an answer from two plus two. He had come clean with his possession of the tinderbox but remained tight-lipped in regards to the little tobacco that he carried, and until such time that a suitable device for smoking could be secured he would have to content himself with sniffing his moistened weed of delectable perfume. Water was then brought to the boil, for a dry satchel of tea had been found along with a single tumbler rescued from the captain's cabin, but the tea was too little for the handful of survivors; a large quantity of meat was also cooked within a pot found on the shoreline platform, enough to feed everyone present. The fire was heaven to them but wouldn't last. They hadn't gathered much wood and that which had been retrieved was still quite wet from the storm the night before. Pieter picked up the last of the lamps and shook it in inspection, seeing that it was quite empty. He stood up and threw it as far as he could towards the sea, temporarily jolted by the anger within him.

The injured had been moved to be right beside them in order for them to be provided assurance and comfort in their time of need, but it was too late for one. Johannes Snitquer, the man with the broken arm and fractured skull had passed away. His brain had hemorrhaged and death was like a dream, his thoughts fading away, drifting off to nowhere as he fell into a sleep from which he would not return. He was moved towards where the fire was to be built, a portion of the sail draped across him, for the blankets retrieved from the ship would serve a better purpose than to be discarded as a covering for the dead.

Seebaer Phillipse and Joannes Spandaun sat to one side of the small fire, talking between themselves and glancing at Ariaen from time to time. Ariaen responded.

"You have something to say," said Ariaen, kindly. "I see it by the way you are looking over at me."

Dirck and Wiebbe continued to examine the injured as the others shifted their eyes over to the two young friends, young seamen who were on their first voyage; never before had they been to sea.

"We think the fire should be bigger," answered Seebaer for the two. "No passing ship is going to see this... little thing."

"Have you been past this way before, in front of the coast of this strange land?" asked Ariaen as he rubbed his head wound, a thick broad bandage now covering his forehead and tied neatly at the side, courtesy of Wiebbe and his learning.

"We are both new to the sea," answered Seebaer as he shifted slightly upon his spot, a little embarrassed by his inexperience.

"I have been this way many times, and many times I have seen the shore from far out to sea," said Ariaen. "At this point, just off the coast, a ship will turn to the north and head towards its destination. Only during certain months of the year will one travel so far east that they will come into decent eye contact with this land. In all my time, traversing the coast from here and to the Sunda Strait, I have seen many fires. This land is inhabited by black men. They wear nothing upon their bodies and carry spears and shields. From my knowledge they are very ready for war and must skirmish with others from this land on a regular basis. A small fire will not do anything to encourage assistance of any description, but to do nothing will not satisfy everyone here. So I shall do as I think is best. When the dead are ready for burial and the fire built up as high as she can be built, we will cast a flame upon it and cremate all those that have perished... we can't bury them, there are far too many and we don't have the manpower or tools. I hope that the Kockenge will be near at that time to see something of our attempt to draw their attention to us but I don't expect it to be a success." Ariaen looked around the camp fire to all those that had survived, all except the drunks, and Harmen and Jan. "If we don't see a ship within the next five weeks then it will be time to consider our next move," a solid coughing spell then concluded his views on the subject, a fly being swallowed.

"What shall we do?" asked Seebaer.

"A ship arriving at Batavia will learn of our disappearance soon enough. It is possible that they might link our fire with those that are missing. I give it five weeks of signalling, conserving as best we can our fuel, linking our attempts to the time table I offered earlier. Ships will be past this way but their precise day of passing is simply a guess derived from what I heard before leaving Table Bay. After the fifth week we will wait until the approach of next summer and then make an attempt at launching our own boat, unless winter proves acceptable and not too ambitious. I have no idea at this stage how successful we will be... the first thing to do is find a good launching pad from which to set sail."

"I shall set out tomorrow," volunteered Seebaer. "I shall go south for one day and then return." He looked at his friend. "I'll take Joannes with me."

"Good," said Ariaen cheerfully. "Who will go north?"

Silence dominated the scene.

"Seebaer and I will go," volunteered Joannes, "once we've returned from the south and have found... nothing."

"You may well find nothing, but even if you find something of value you should still take a look further afield," advised Pieter. "You might find something better in the north. And be sure to take some cooked meat, the driest portions; shellfish can also be obtained from the platform... if it extends that far south and north... and for God's sake, be careful."

Joannes nodded approval, "Very well. We shall look to the south and then the north."

"There are some blankets where Willem has been placing our stores. Take some with you," finished Pieter, Joannes nodding acceptance with a smile.

"Is there anything else that concerns anyone?" asked Ariaen. "I don't wish to command, as much as organise. We are all good seamen, even if young and out of our element for the first time, so no one here is any better than another, simply more experienced. It is this experience which we need to collaborate with in order to survive this ordeal."

The faces around the fireplace were filled with agreement for what was said.

Willem stood up and sat down again beside Ariaen.

"Shall I take some meat to the others?"

"You're a good lad, Willem... thinking of others when they have done no work this day."

"We shouldn't turn our back on them," said Willem. "I overheard one of the other men saying that they too wished they were drunk."

"Wishing to be drunk, and getting drunk, are two completely different things," said Ariaen, "but you give me an idea." He stood up. "We shall both deliver them some meat and whilst we are amongst them, if they appear incapable, or asleep as I expect, we will throw what they have of their stash into the sea."

"I'll come with you," said Hendrik. "Throwing evil drink into the sea will be my honour."

As expected the four drunk men were flat on their backs and sleeping heavily, drowned of all reality until the morning brought clarity to their pitiful lives once more. It took quite a while to find the spare bottles of gin that had been hidden, but in the stupor of their mindless action the four men had failed to hide their tracks and the source of their drunkenness was found. Willem too, enjoyed throwing the bottles as far as he could into the night air, the noise of the breaking waves upon the platform below a pleasantness that he hadn't expected, and on return to their fireplace they all drift off into sleep, a well-deserved rest from their arduous task being delivered and not for a second did they realise that the gin could have been used to their advantage when aiding the sick.

CHAPTER SEVEN

6th June, 1712.

None of the survivors awoke until the sun started to make its appearance. The day was a little cloudy but it was quite cold on this, their second morning in a strange land. It was at this same time that Harmen and Jan woke to be greeted by a noise in the bush not very far from their position.

Jan shook his friend and got up upon his knees, his head lifted high enough to see across the top of the expanse of grass, for as far as the eye could see, and where the grass died out there was nothing but a scorched earth to replace it, a prairie of softly undulating ground dotted here and there with eucalyptus to break up the monotony of the view.

"What is it?" asked Harmen as a rumble came from within him, rubbing his eyes as he spoke. "What do you see?"

"I don't know... my God! Quick, Harmen," yelled Jan, being up on his feet and running in the opposite direction as quickly as his feet could carry him.

The fright within Harmen was so high that his heart missed a beat and stole his breath for the briefest of seconds as he too shot up and looked out towards where Jan had glanced. There before him, just one hundred feet away, was a naked man with shield and spear, standing firm upon his ground and looking upon him as though mystified by the appearance, as though half astonished but unafraid.

Harmen was quick on his friend's heels and they continued at a fast pace for several hundred feet before coming to a stop and looking behind them, to see once again the dark flesh of the naked man looking upon them as though they were spirits from another world.

"Who do you think it is?" asked Harmen.

"I don't know and I don't care," answered Jan with scepticism taking strong hold upon him. "He's a savage; possibly a maneater."

"Shall we try and communicate with him?"

Jan looked at the man as he stood there, some three hundred feet away and doing nothing but glancing in their direction.

"I think we should leave him be. There's no telling how many others are nearby," and with that said, Jan looked around to make sure that none other was trying to move to his rear, to cut off his withdrawal.

"I think he's alone," said Harmen.

"Yes, probably."

"He doesn't seem to be too concerned about us," added Harmen. "He has a weapon—."

"He's hunting for food," concluded Jan. "That creature we saw the other day, hopping across the ground in great stride." He looked his friend in the eyes. "The others won't believe any of it."

"Shall we return now?"

"Yes. Let's go and tell the others."

As they commenced the short journey back to the site of their misfortune they continued to shoot glances back over their shoulders to ensure that they weren't being followed, and although mightily concerned for the encounter which they had experienced, they didn't fail to take note of their surroundings.

Several gullies were crossed, the same as they had passed the day before. Several rock holes presented themselves for closer scrutiny, sources of water that would supply the survivors well over the coming months, and before long the undulating sandplain was well behind them and almost forgotten as the pair continued their painstaking walk back to the others, their stomachs feeling less empty than they had the night before, the pain of hunger dissipating slightly.

At around a thousand feet from the sandplains they came across a site which drew their attention.

It was on a higher elevation than the surrounding ground and reasonably good vigil could be maintained upon all directions even though the tea-tree scrub further afield prevented them from seeing the waters of the Indian Ocean.

There was an old camp fire and some bare spots where people had slept, and an old lean-to was laid flat upon the ground. A large tree provided shading and a large rock with a smooth concave surface – a grindstone made of basalt – sat next to the fire.

"It looks like our friend used this site," said Jan. "But it hasn't been used for a while."

"A summer camp," suggested Harmen. "That shelter isn't much to keep out the weather."

"Do you think he, or possibly they… that they'll return?"

"I don't know; but we'll have to keep an eye open," said Harmen as he moved over towards the fallen shelter where sheets of bark from the tree acted as part of the shelter. He bent down and lifted it up to see what else he could find. "Maybe they left some tools behind... a spear or something..."

"What is it...?" Jan said as he turned to the silence. He then froze.

Beneath the shelter, hiding coiled and peaceful beneath was a snake which was quick to lift its head and taste the air with its forked tongue.

Harmen had held himself well for the fright he had received, holding onto the shelter in his left hand and half stooped to look beneath the layers of bark. He was in easy striking distance of the reptile and quite at a loss as to what he should do.

The yellow scales of the six foot snake gave it a menacing look, not to mention the position it held, ready to lash out with a bite to Harmen's leg or arm.

Jan could see that Harmen wasn't going to move and considered the situation most briefly before arriving at a sound conclusion.

"I'm going to pick up a fallen branch, Harmen, to try and distract it. Don't move; for God's sake... keep still.

Jan moved around towards the rear of the snake, taking a long branch from upon the ground and preparing it for action. The snake turned its head to look upon Jan and as it did so, Harmen allowed himself to move his foot a little further from reach. Within an instant the snake turned and struck out at the movement, sinking its fangs into the flesh of the calf before retracting the dripping fangs and heading off into the scrub as Jan's empty effort to beat down upon it missed and he hit the hard earth instead.

Harmen bent over in more shock than pain, grabbing hold of the wound with the palm of his hand before removing it and taking a probing look with shaking fingers.

"Damn; damn that thing!" cursed Harmen as he fell upon his arse. "Of all the blasted luck. Shipwrecked upon this worthless land and now bitten by God knows what."

"I never saw such a thing," a shocked Jan said in reply, open-mouthed and looking out towards where the snake had slivered before turning his gaze upon the frightful look of his friend.

"What am I to do?" shrieked Harmen.

"The poison... we have to suck it out."

"Quickly," prompted Harmen. "Get a knife."

"I don't have one, Harmen."

"At the camp; get Dirck or Wiebbe," ordered Harmen. "Quickly, Jan, or I'll die. Run for your life, get them, quick."

"Should you come with me? I can help by carrying you."

"No; but you're right... I can walk. Quickly; let's go."

Harmen got to his feet and started to run as fast as he could behind his friend Jan, running to be saved before the poison had time to react with his weakened body and spirit.

They weaved in and out of the scrub, pushing through the tea-tree which was very thick in places. There was more than a mile to go, over rough terrain and in a direction that was not guaranteed to bring them out on top of the others.

The sweat commenced to pour from them both as the water from the rock holes that had been drawn into their mouths through lips forming a tight circle, escaped their pores, and as the distance grew behind them, from the scene where the snakebite had occurred, Harmen suddenly halted and drew his hands to his heart. He fell suddenly like a sack of potatoes, straight to the ground in an instant, death overriding his will to live, a grotesque contortion painted upon his face.

CHAPTER EIGHT

Seebaer and Joannes had commenced their exploration of the south on morning's first light, taking nothing more with them other than some small portions of burnt meat procured from the meal the night before and a belly full of water. The intention was for them to return by last light, in this way they would be afforded a full stomach prior to setting out upon another exploration, this time to the north of the coastline.

The two had only travelled less than half a mile when they came across what appeared to be a small beach fronted by gentle sloping ground, which extended out onto a rocky sea floor. They took note of the area for the importance that it offered, not so much for the ability to launch a boat, in the case that they were able to make one, but for the sake of landing a boat from a rescue ship if one was to see their signal fire and come in close enough to the coast to rescue them.

They spent little time here as they were concerned in covering as much ground as possible and by midday their feet were rather tender; the effect of wet feet shoved either loosely or tightly into the shoes of its previous owner offering little comfort but much protection.

The way south, as too, was presumed for the north, was full of many species of wildlife, mostly of the feather, whistling, squawking, and fluttering upon the breeze. Creatures upon the ground were also numerous, with ants, centipedes, lizards and beetles foraging for food.

"The food at camp won't last long, Seebaer," said Joannes out of the blue, trying to provoke a new conversation as they continued on their exploration.

"No. But time will be our reward."

"Certainly, and there's plenty of that to be had."

"If a ship doesn't pass our way soon, more time than we can bear will come our way."

"I was thinking," said Seebaer as a few more steps were taken, looking out upon the sea and in towards the land unknown to them both, "if these beetles and other insects we see all around us are edible."

Joannes screwed up his face for a second as he considered the idea of crunching into a beetle, pressing it between his teeth until its innards came rushing out of its arse and onto his tongue.

"I mean to say," continued Seebaer, "if the savages upon this land have learnt to survive, then why can't we?"

Joannes considered this for a moment.

"You might have something there, Seebaer. Yes indeed; struck a chord you have," congratulated Joannes in his round-about way, nodding his head in approval of the consideration. "And what better way to learn than from the savages themselves."

Seebaer stopped dead in his tracks, "What? You can't be serious?" said Seebaer.

"Why not?" said Joannes as his shoulders shrugged up and down. "They've lived on this land for as long as any ship came into view of the coast; even longer. They survive day to day. This is a strange land, an entirely new environment to what we are used to. The savages haven't attacked us."

"But we haven't come into any contact as yet," said Seebaer, not knowing of the sighting that Jan and Harmen had experienced. "What if they're hostile?"

"If they're hostile then we are dead already. The only way is to befriend them, search them out, share in their secrets in order to survive."

"Look, the sun is directly above us," indicated Seebaer. "What says we return with what news we have and then make suggestions."

"I honestly believe it's our only way. If a ship doesn't find us within the next few months then we will have to trust the savages of this land like the VOC trusts in those of Batavia and beyond." It was by these words that Seebaer seemed to be convinced.

They were both in agreement and turned on the spot, and commenced the trek back to where they had begun.

CHAPTER NINE

It was a little after midday when the survivors upon the cliff gave into their urges for something to eat. They gathered at the place which had been transformed into a temporary campsite, a small fire burning dull with embers cooled but still alive. Kindling was quickly added and the flames stirred into motion as a pot of water, filled from a nearby rock hole, was placed upon it, its base buried into the ash and charcoal. What meat remained was wrapped well and stored back in a barrel with a cover, before being placed in the shade, away from the flies.

Gerrit Jongbloet, one for the drinkers from nearer the cliff face, walked over and stood there next to those that were seated upon the earth.

"I've come to see if I can get something for the others to eat," said Gerrit, a shameful look of despair upon his face.

All of the others looked upon him and then to one another, before finally shifting their view to Ariaen.

"You'll have to wait, Gerrit," said Ariaen. "The sick must come first."

Hayman, the man with two broken legs, quickly voiced his opinion, "Give them nothing, I say; nothing at all."

"What is it to you, old man?" scolded Gerrit. "You'll be dead soon."

"Damn you to hell!" cursed Hayman.

"Enough!" and Ariaen was upon his feet in an instant. "You will have enough to eat," continued Ariaen, "but be warned; you and your friends must make amends and help with the work. There will be no more drinks for any of you."

"Yes," said Gerrit. "Our supply is missing, only several bottles left from what we had secured aside... for a rainy day."

"Every day would be raining in your eyes," scoffed Hayman.

"Okay, so I was wrong, but I am hungry, too," defended Gerrit. "We are part of the crew, we deserve to get something to eat."

"Be warned, Gerrit, there are no other bottles left for you, every bottle found below has been opened and thrown into the sea. You must all help with what needs to be done or there will be nothing for you," said Ariaen. "And, Gerrit; we are more than you, it would be wise to help."

"Is that a threat, Ariaen?"

"Make of it what you will, but discipline must remain if we are to be successful in our plight."

"Very well," said Gerrit after a few seconds of silence. "I shall tell the others, but please give me some food so that I can go back with a full hand. The others... they are still very hungover. We can commence work in a few hours or more. Is this acceptable?"

"It is, Gerrit, but advise them first and then they can have some food. We're also going to have some rest, for the work is hard. The salvage is almost complete. A signal fire will be our next concern and the dead will have to be cremated... to stop the spread of disease."

"I understand," said Gerrit. "I'll go and tell the others and return shortly for some rations."

"Fine; you do that."

Gerrit turned and departed, leaving the main group to continue with their rest and cooking. A noise then came from beyond, a voice that sounded familiar.

"It's Jan," said Dirck. "I'd know his voice anywhere."

They all listened carefully and it came again, muffled by the background noise of the sea and the natural barrier of the thick scrub of tea-tree.

"Jan, over here," yelled Dirck.

"Help me. I need help," came the voice.

"Did he say 'help'?" asked Dirck of what he had heard.

"Yes," replied Pieter as he, too, stood. "Quickly, follow me."

Dirck and Pieter raced off through the scrub as fast as they dared, calling out every few seconds, closing the gap between themselves and Jan. When they finally fell upon him they saw that Harmen was upon his shoulder, draped over him like a rag doll, a dead weight with most of the colour drained from his face. Jan let the body fall as he fell to his knees and sobbed lightly.

"He was a good friend. There was nothing I could do," defended Jan.

"What happened?" asked Dirck.

"A snake bite," said Jan, and with the word came two looks of despair, for they had been completely void of thought on such dangers, but now more than ever, they needed to tread warily, wherever they went.

"Come, Jan, you aren't to blame for anything," comforted Dirck.

"There's nothing that could be done."

"If only I had a knife, I could have cut his wound, sucked the poison from within him."

"It's finished now," said Dirck. "Come. We'll carry Harmen back to the fireplace. You take a rest. None of this is your fault."

"No," protested Jan. "I'll carry him, too. I was his friend, the best in the world."

"We'll all help," said Pieter.

CHAPTER TEN

"Help, come quickly," came the voice.

"What now?" said Wiebbe, looking up towards where the two men had moved.

"No, Wiebbe," said Willem, pointing towards the cliff. "Over there; it's Gerrit."

"Quickly, help," gasped Gerrit as he raced towards the fireplace.

"What's wrong, Gerrit?" asked Wiebbe, only slightly concerned, feeling as though an injustice had been served by Gerrit and the other three.

"Cornelius Brouwer has fallen off the cliff and down the slope. I think he hit his head. He isn't moving."

Wiebbe looked down to the three men in his care, "I can't leave these men. Quickly, take someone with you Gerrit... someone capable, not your friends; and see if he's hurt."

"I'll help," said Willem, standing up and preparing himself for duty.

"You stay there, Willem, and cook the food. We all need nourishment. Hendrik, you and Gerrit go and see what can be done."

"Aye," obeyed Hendrik without as much as a batter of the eyelids, grabbing Gerrit by the arm to help him upon his feet. The two men took off towards the scene of the accident.

Willem sat back down and stirred the meat and peas within the pot that he had under his control as Wiebbe looked down upon the open-eyed threesome, the wounded under his care.

"This is a fine mess, Willem. Two calls for help, three wounded... that's me and you, boy; that's it... just the two of us," Wiebbe turned to look at the boy. "I don't mind telling you that this very minute, right here and now, is the loneliest I have ever felt before in my entire life."

CHAPTER ELEVEN

Pieter, Dirck and Jan could be heard moving back through the scrub and no sooner did they fall upon the fireplace and Wiebbe was at their side ready to assist wherever he could.

They laid the body of Harmen upon the ground and in full sight of the three wounded, who in their state of misery could only contemplate their near future as being the same. Of the three that lay upon the ground with bandages and splints in place only one didn't consider himself as being familiar with Harmen, but he had come to know him during that first morning after the Zuytdorp had wrecked.

The body of Harmen was laid upon the ground and Wiebbe knelt down beside him, Dirk opposite and looking rather solemn, for Dirk knew that he was beyond saving.

"It's times like this that I wish we had a priest with us," said Wiebbe, "a man of comfort, a comforter of the sick."

"We had such a man," said Dirk.

"I know," replied Wiebbe.

"But he died in the wreck, during the storm."

Wiebbe looked Dirk in the eyes and understood his frustration too, for neither of them was a doctor but both had intelligence enough to understand the rudiments of providing aid to the sick. It comes naturally after many years at sea where men fall victim to scurvy and diseases of the tropics, where the shells of men fall victim of God's own vengeance... or so it would seem.

The split second silence was then pushed aside as Jan, standing there with something to say, opened his mouth and gave the news which all were dreading to hear.

"I saw a savage, a naked man with a spear and shield."

The others hanging around those injured and laying upon the ground, and even the breeze itself, stopped what was being done or talked about, to listen with great dread to what was to be said.

"I saw one of them, and Harmen saw him too," and after the incident with the snake he had come to change his mind on the circumstances of their arrival in hell. "He was dark and stood erect, holding his ground and eyeing us with hunger in his eyes. I could see and hear his mind in play, his wish to boil my flesh for eating, or to roast it above a fire. His thin shell showed how hungry he was, his eyebrows providing shelter to those dark eyes of his, the evil that they cast in our direction. If it wasn't for the fact that he was alone, he would have been after us."

"Was he all of that, Jan?" asked Pieter, still standing beside him.

"He was indeed, and much, much more," concluded Jan.

"Then we must prepare for the worst," said Ariaen. "Several knives have been salvaged."

"They'll do little against the thrust of a spear," said Dirk. "And what other weapons does he have: do 'they' have?"

"They're savages," reminded Wiebbe. "What can they have?"

"They have survived here, haven't they?" advised Pieter. "Lived upon this land, naked to the world, and survived the elements."

"And the damnation of God," said Marinus from his place upon the dirt, rubbing his palm across his broken ribs, the pain of speaking cast upon his face like the marks of a sculpture's chisel made upon rock.

"They're God's creatures too," said Willem, voicing his opinion.

"Savages like them don't have religion," said Jan. "I saw him both plain and simple, and saw his intentions. He was evil, very evil, and I wouldn't wish to confront a group of them for fear of death."

Gerrit and Hendrik then returned with bad news. Cornelius had died in the fall from the cliff, having hit his head hard upon a boulder before coming to an abrupt stop just half way down the slope of detritus.

"We dragged his body to where the others lay waiting," said Hendrik as he looked upon the form of Harmen. "What happened?"

"He was bitten by a snake and died," said Jan and all of those around quickly scanned the ground around them for their fear of snakes was as real as their fear of being stranded upon this land for the remainder of their miserable lives.

CHAPTER TWELVE

Before dusk had arrived upon the scene of the wreck and the survivors in the temporary campsite, Seebaer and Joannes had returned to their friends, smiles cast upon their faces, happy to be back after such a short time away. It was a miracle in itself, the safety they felt being amongst the group of other survivors, all of whom were in the same predicament and shared the same fears. It wasn't as if they'd be absent for any great length of time, or returning into the arms of a loved one. It was the comradeship that they needed, the comfort of another that shared the same will to live.

Both men listened intently to the story told, of how Cornelius had fallen to his death, how Harmen came to grief, of the savage seen beyond the scrub where the land was like a motionless sea of undulating plains, bare of life other than trees which sucked the land dry of all its moisture.

All of the survivors were now around the fire, a small yet necessary commodity, the centrepiece of their communion, two of the drunks, Jacob Albertsz and Jacobus Nuyts, still out cold, unconscious from there sucking on the last of the bottles of gin that had been hidden so well, five bottles between them which now lay smashed upon the ground, remnants of their poor discipline, empty bottles that only now could join the other bottles drained the night before. It was surprising that they were still alive. But it appeared that they had already been forgiven for blankets had been placed over them, to keep them warm as the cold of the night came rolling in from over the sea, where another cloudless night sucked the warmth from their very surroundings. How on earth did the savages survive such weather, walking around naked as they did?

Cornelis Lieffers then appeared from his work, his devotion to keeping busy, bringing another bucket with him filled with fresh water, water scooped by hand from a rock hole not far away.

"Cornelis, young friend," said Ariaen to the young man. "You work too hard and need to rest."

"I fear the thoughts that linger within me will surface and explode," said Cornelis, seemingly ashamed, willingly letting his guard down, his emotions betraying him, his exhaustion taking hold upon his very being.

"You need to rest, nevertheless," continued Ariaen. "There have been too many deaths already, and I don't wish to see another." Ariaen looked at the man still coming of age. "Will you sit and join us? Seebaer and Joannes have returned with news."

"Is it good news?" asked Cornelis.

"We've found somewhere that will accept a rescue boat, just to the south," offered Seebaer.

"But not to sail one?"

"We don't think so, Cornelis, no," said Seebaer with a downturned eye. "But we intend to go to the north, to search for another place from which to launch a boat. The work you've achieved alone will provide us with enough wood for a small boat; I'm sure of it."

"Yes," said Cornelis, his heart lifted. "Enough to make two boats. All we need to do is drag the wood from the platform and up the embankment."

"Yes, indeed," said Ariaen. "We'll do just that tomorrow morning. But we want you to go with Seebaer and Joannes tomorrow, to support them."

"They'd be faster with two," said Cornelis. "Wouldn't they? And what of the work here?"

"We are plenty," added Ariaen. Gerrit, Jacob and Jacobus will be joining us tomorrow; to be put to work... isn't that right, Gerrit?"

"Yes," said Gerrit, looking up into the eyes of Cornelis. "The other two will have sore heads but with a little food and water they will do just fine."

Cornelis smiled and nodded, "Okay, I'll go."

"Great," said Ariaen. "Now sit down and have something to eat; rest those weary bones of yours, for tomorrow you will journey far."

"It's just a day trip, isn't it?" asked Cornelis.

"You didn't hear?" prompted Pieter.

"Hear?"

"Of Jan and the savage?" said Gerrit.

"No," said Cornelis. "What savage?" and the ordeal with the remnants of the land were provided to Cornelis to the very last detail.

"So you see, we need at least three, and armed with weapons, too," said Ariaen.

Cornelis nodded acceptance for the last thing he wished to do was let down the other men. Willem thought how proud he would be to take after Cornelis, to be willing to do whatever it takes to survive, to relish any task handed down, to devote himself to any given opportunity.

"And I think we should stop thinking of them as savages," said Joannes. "If a ship fails to be drawn to our presence then they might be the only way to survive, the only avenue open to us. They are natives, not savages."

"Only time will tell, Joannes," said Ariaen. "For the time being we need to explore towards the north where much coastline is known to exist. Many ships have used the coast to mark their progress, almost three hundred miles of it... if my calculations are correct."

"And I'll go too," said Jan. He looked at the others. "I can't stay here, not with my friend having departed from this world."

"We'll be saying our goodbyes soon enough, Jan," said Ariaen. "Don't you want to stay and say farewell?"

"I have said my farewell, carrying him upon my back for many hours in the heat of the day. I sometimes wish that winter was here already," and he kicked at the dirt.

"It's upon us, just not as severe as we're used to," said Ariaen, scratching at the bandage covering the gash in his head and looking out over the sea towards the west. "It has just begun."

"If it wasn't for the heat, that snake might not even exist."

"There is much we don't know about this land. Everything needs to be learnt. The ways of one snake isn't necessarily the same as another. Take that creature, for example, the one you say was jumping in great bounds across the ground... that in itself is unbelievable. How can such a thing exist?"

"But it does," said Jan.

"And we believe you," confirmed Ariaen. "If you wish to go north then go, we won't stop you," and to change the subject he looked to Willem. "How's the meat and peas?"

"Ready," said Willem.

It seemed that death was all around them and that it couldn't be avoided. It was one mishap after the next. Some drew on the situation as a condemned ending to a sadly shortened existence whilst others looked upon it as an opportunity to shake the defeat from within them and to pour on the courage to continue as best they could, moulding a new life for themselves upon a land that they simply did not know. They would do as Joannes and Seebaer had suggested and try to make friends with the natives, people of the land, no longer savages of the mind.

The bounds of survival were commencing to surface and for those with the courage to take it all into an open palm... for them the future was ready to be written.

Of the man that had fallen from the edge of the cliff; he had fallen to his death and was left there at the bottom, simply dragged over to the pile of dead that currently existed on the shoreline platform. The mass of flesh was beyond them all, hard to fathom such wasted life, the deaths of both young and old, those of command and structure, seamen, women, and boys that had enlisted to do a man's job at sea. Of the little children, only one was found and placed at the pile as it grew in size, the others had been lost by way of the sea, the waves taking the fragile forms of human remains to a burial site which would never be discovered.

That evening there was much to reflect upon and reflect they did, but mostly in silence. They were all too tired to do much about anything; so they lay there, asleep, half asleep, or simply contemplating the future, but rest was the order of the night and so rest was quickly secured by all, whether it be a little slumber or a lot, and every single one of them was appreciative of the meat and the peas, stomachs silent for the night.

CHAPTER THIRTEEN

7th June.

The drunken men were now sober and their heads completely clear by the following morning's first light, to see the errors of their ways, but not to admit them, and along with the sunlight came a fresh wind from the west, a steadily increasing wind which dragged along with it a mass of cloud. With broken bottles left to remain as a memorial to those that had perished at this site, the shards and pieces reflected light, there in the rays of the sun, to just sit there undisturbed, unmoving, to be clambered upon by ants, to remain mostly undisturbed for the future, a future which had not yet been set for those that remained. And of all the futures that would greet the drunkards as they woke from the misery that they had created for themselves, was another body, a body now relinquished of his ghostly spirit, for Francisco Roelofsz, the man with the broken leg and punctured gut, had died. But of all the things that mattered most was the fact that they had now all come together, to be as one community.

And the damn flies, they were nothing less than a plague, not to mention the growing concern over the ants that clambered over the sick without remorse.

Hayman Jorisz pulled his fingers from his bandage and placed them beneath his nose, withdrawing them quickly for the smell upon his fingers was disgusting, the most horrid thing he'd ever smelt in his life before. It smelt of decayed meat, of death. He was gangrenous. He looked over to the others, Seebaer, Joannes, Cornelis and Jan having departed already for the north.

With an upturned nose he was about to request help; some water in which to wash his fingers when he heard two men approaching; Jacob and Jacobus. Hayman simply watched them in silence, his hatred for them written upon his face. He knew deep inside of him that his legs would have to be amputated, cut off from above the knee. What was there to help him with the pain, the torture of having himself mutilated? There was no gin... it was gone, every drop, wasted upon drunkards who weren't strong enough to handle the horrors of the shipwreck that had seen them cast upon this land like the forgotten choruses of an unfamiliar song heard but once, drained from the head, like the waters of a river so hastily spilled into the sea. He would have to show that he was man enough to accept the disfigurement, to hold back his cries of pain, to show that he was a man of men and as strong as any of them that had survived.

And the two men walked past him, glancing down but briefly as they took several more steps towards the congregation, Willem, Pieter, Ariaen, Hendrik, Dirck, Wiebbe and Gerrit, not to mention the two soon-to-be-dead.

"Sit down," said Ariaen in invitation. "Have something to eat. There isn't much but we are hoping to secure food later on today; some shellfish and maybe other supplies."

"Thank you," said Jacob as he sat and pulled a slightly curved piece of bark into his chest, a little meat and peas sitting there upon the piece of bark, several ants already having a go at the meagre pickings, waiting for him to shovel the meal down his gullet.

"And for you, too, Jacobus."

"Thank you."

Gerrit looked upon his so-called friends, those that had successfully corrupted him into accepting the gin, "How do you both feel?"

"I'm fine," said Jacob.

"Me too," said Jacobus with a mouthful of food.

"And why wouldn't you be, you scum!" cursed Hayman, thinking of the pain to be endured. "You take all the gin and scoff it down, and now you come here, not having done a single days work other than a few minutes, from what I hear, and now you partake of our sustenance as though you have worked hard since our shipwreck here upon this horrid place."

"It's for all of us," said Ariaen, indicating the little food they had, but understanding the hate, but not the inability to forgive. "Let's hear no more of it."

"It's easy for you to say," said Hayman, a tear slowly filling his eye before drying in the breeze that blew in from beyond the sea and across the land. "I'm to be amputated and there is no gin left; no wine; no beer; no medicine."

Gerrit stirred and spoke softly to the man in anguish, "I have a bottle, saved for you."

The two drunks shot a glance apiece at Gerrit.

"Where is it," stabbed Jacob.

"Enough! You swine! Damn you to hell!"

"Sit still, Hayman," ordered Wiebbe as he raced over to the man as he tried in vain to claw his way to Jacob, to kill him.

"You have sinned," said Gerrit, stabbing a glance of pure hatred at Jacob.

"And so have you," answered Jacobus for his off-sider.

"Gerrit is one of us," spoke Ariaen. "You two men have been given food and water, and this is how you repay your debt, by illustrating a growing need for gin, to satisfy your weakness."

Jacob held out his hand for all to see, shaking out of control, unable to stop the tremors from within.

"I'm not a doctor; you can't be helped," said Ariaen. "You helped yourself to the gin, now help yourself to overcome your wicked desire."

"I can't," said Jacob in all sincerity and regret, a look of terror upon his face as the juice from the peas and meat dribbled from the corners of his mouth and down his chin. "I must have it; please. There was plenty on the Zuytdorp before she was wrecked and my desire is still strong."

"There are others in need of it more than you," said Wiebbe as he leant forward and smelt the wound, sorrow filling his face as he stroked with great compassion the forehead of Hayman.

"Pieter; Dirck... will you help me?"

"What is it, Wiebbe?" asked Dirck.

"It's time," answered Wiebbe with a plain face, undefined and solemn. "Time to take these legs off; the sooner the better."

The sorrow within Hayman's eyes was like the look of an innocent child, a hideous crime about to be committed; the look upon Jacobs was similar, but filled with deceit.

Silence... the men moved to the task in silence, forgetting their food and water, forgetting their comfort, thinking only of the poor man about to be operated upon.

They moved Hayman, sobbing, away from the others, towards the south where the screams would not be heard; Ariaen went too. Embers were carried by Willem, for he had been asked to help raise a small fire, a fire which was to be employed in preparing the cutting tool – a knife. It was large enough to be handled as a cutting device and could be used to chop, to chop through the bone.

Willem returned to get some cloth, some rope, and a little extra kindling for the fire, several small logs not going astray, and as he returned he passed Gerrit who stepped off to retrieve the hidden bottle of gin, and behind him, close enough to see but far enough so not to be heard, followed Jacob. Willem ignored what he saw, not thinking anything of it, focussing only upon his task and his task alone, to try and take his mind away from what was about to happen: all he needed to do was to ready the fire and bandages.

CHAPTER FOURTEEN

Gerrit stepped out amidst the broken bottles and saw the place where he had hidden the last of the gin, behind a small tea-tree and beneath a large rock, where a hidden lair had been scraped from beneath it.

He got down upon his knees and commenced to excavate the pain-killer when a noise caught his ear. He turned his head and saw Jacob standing over him, and Jacob's face screwed up tight as he brought a large rock down upon the man's head, killing him instantly, grabbing for the bottle which had been revealed, the neck sticking out like a sore thumb, the best sight Jacob had seen in his entire life.

He wasted no time at all and soon had it open, swallowing in great gulps all that he could fit into his mouth. Before long it was empty, as though it was nothing but a flagon of water, drained of every last drop.

Jacob suddenly turned and saw Jacobus standing there, having followed soon after, seeing that Jacob was up to no good.

"You bastard," scolded Jacobus. "What have you done?"

Jacob looked down at the deceased Gerrit, but Jacobus was referring to the gin, not the deceased.

"It's gone, every damn drop. You took it for yourself," said Jacobus before the reality of the situation hit him hard. "You've killed Gerrit, killed him for a bottle of gin; the last to be had. My God, what have you done?"

"I had to... I..." stammered Jacob, seemingly drunk already from what he had administered to himself.

CHAPTER FIFTEEN

Back at the fireplace, where Willem had returned to secure more bandages, Hendrik looked to the boy for confirmation on something he'd heard in the distance.

"Did you hear that, Willem?"

Willem stared off into the distance and then back to Hendrik, realising full well what it was.

"It's Jacob, and Jacobus; they've gone after Gerrit."

Hendrik looked down upon the sleeping form of Marinus, out cold and oblivious to what was going on, having been awake and in pain for most of the night.

"Stay here, Willem, I'm going to see what's going on."

"Here," urged Willem, thinking straight from the top of his head, "take this," and handed the knife to him before moving towards where Wiebbe and the others were waiting.

Hendrik took the knife without second thought and raced towards the commotion, upon the scene in what seemed to be a moment's notice, to see Jacob and Jacobus fighting, rolling around upon the ground, Gerrit unmoving where he laid, blood running freely from the wound upon the top of his head.

"What have you done?" Hendrik said in disbelief of the struggle between the two men, and Jacobus fell from the ledge, clawing at the earth as he slipped and fell, the short fall upon rocks below seeing to his own demise.

Jacob turned, his eyes blazed over by the gin, his mouth in a snarl, all manner of civilization gone from his face. He was no longer a man but the devil possessed and with the bloodied rock still in his hand he circled Hendrik, motioning him to fight, trying to corner him closer to the edge of the cliff.

"I have a knife, Jacob," advised Hendrik. "You don't stand a chance. Put the rock down, forget all of this. We're here to help, all of us; I am... here. Let me help you."

"I curse you... damned, bloody fool. I got more than you," stammered Jacob and held up his hand, high above his head, rock clenched in his fist. "I have the rock." He looked back down into Hendrik's eyes and raced towards him, the rock in motion, an extension of Jacob's arm, a weapon with which he was prepared to kill, but he stumbled and Hendrik stepped aside, Jacob falling to his death, too.

Hendrik just stood there, disbelief within him, his mind unable to calculate what the hell was going on. This was not how man was supposed to survive. What manner of evil could possess another to commit such heinous crimes against his fellow man? It then suddenly dawned upon him that he too had plenty to repent, for his vicious treatment of others before now was not to be forgotten. He had tried to become leader, to have the ability to sway judgement over those under his command, but now... he didn't want it. He was glad that Ariaen had received more votes than he, he was happy to have lost to a better man, for Ariaen was proving, day in and day out, that he was a good man with a clear vision for the future. It's what was needed, a strong man to lead a volatile group, a bunch of men who would have trouble finding their way in this new world, where the devil played with the souls of those unfortunate enough to be cast upon a land with little water and seemingly nothing to eat.

Hendrik could only whimper to himself, feelings of sorrow filling him like a carafe filled with water. He would have to come to grips with it all or come undone at the seams. He had but little choice.

CHAPTER SIXTEEN

By the time Hendrik had returned to where Pieter, Dirck and Wiebbe were readied for amputation, Willem tending the fire and checked over the supplies he had placed neatly beside Wiebbe, Ariaen sat silently at Hayman's head, ready to assist where possible, ready to obey orders as they were given to him.

"Willem," said Wiebbe, "Thank you, but it's time for you to go back to the main fire."

"But I can help——."

"No, you have done enough," concurred Pieter as he smiled at the boy. "Go and get yourself something more to eat, or better still, prepare something for all of us, for we'll be hungry after the job is done."

Willem nodded acceptance of the task and turned to depart, bumping into Hendrik as he stepped away, forgetful of Hendrik's intervention upon the two drunk men. No sooner was he out of earshot and the others asked Hendrik what had happened, swayed more by the look upon the man's face.

"They're dead," said Hendrik in a half daze, not quite believing the words as they stumbled from his mouth.

"Dead?" repeated Dirck.

"All three," nodded Hendrik.

Pieter stood, "Maybe you're wrong, maybe we should have another look."

A hand lashed out and grabbed at Pieter's leg; it was Hayman.

"The bastards deserved to die," said Hayman

"No one deserves to die in this place," said Pieter, looking down upon the man to be operated on, "no matter what their faults."

"They are dead," repeated Hendrik. "I saw two fall to their death and Gerrit has a wound to his head, a deathblow severe enough to kill him outright."

"Where's his body?" asked Pieter.

"At the cliff where he was killed."

"No, Pieter," said Dirck. "Don't go now, leave him. He's dead," Dirck looked at Hendrik, "there's nothing that can be done. Our task now is to help Hayman."

"You're right," said Pieter as he took his position beside the man to prepare for the task of holding the man down.

And that was the last of the words for a while as Hayman's legs were unbandage, the smell of defeat hitting them all, the mass of swelling revealed to them all, the discolouration taking full effect upon their hidden emotions, and the wound where the bone had, not so long ago, broken the skin and was open to the air.

Wiebbe was to do the cutting, and Dirck and Pieter were to hold Hayman's arms and upper body as motionless as possible, Dirck next to Wiebbe so that he could take over the task of hacking through the bone if the need arose. Hendrik sat at the ready at Hayman's feet, feet that were soon to be separated from the whole.

"No, Hendrik," said Dirck, cautioning the man to the requirement. "Get beside Pieter and help with restricting the upper leg... the thigh; keep it still.

'It'... a part of the body, not of Hayman, referred to an object, not of flesh. Hayman noted the course of words and the procedure to be conducted, Wiebbe's manner of expression. Wiebbe had already separated the task and his friend, the body to his front no more familiar to him than a sack of potatoes, for the way in which he was to deliver this man's pain was beyond contemplation, beyond belief. The last thing Wiebbe wished to do was to think of Hayman, as Hayman. No distraction was needed in this, Hayman's time of need. No manner of yelling or screaming, no amount of struggling or demand, nothing at all would stop Wiebbe in his tracks as he operated upon the legs to be removed. Once started it could not be stopped. It must be done in the shortest amount of time.

Willem was sitting beside the fire, cooking as he sat, thinking about what was to unfold not so far through the scrub. His only wish was for Hayman to survive the surgery; but that soon changed. Once the screaming started, the thick piece of leather between Hayman's jaws having served little of its purpose, Willem could only wish for silence to reign around him. It was shear torture, the sounds of pain and torment, the screams coming in unbroken cycle, filling the air with horror. Tears then welled up within Willem's eyes, the noise too much to bear, and he rolled over on his side, rolled up in a tiny ball, clutching his palms tightly upon his ears, and still the screams came reverberating through him as though the devil himself was standing beside him and holding back the cushion of his palms against his ears. There was nothing that could compare with those fifteen long minutes, the screams finally coming to an end.

Willem removed his palms from his ears, thankful that it was over, praising the Lord that he had stopped the torment, thanking God for answering his prayers, for bringing him silence. He wiped his eyes and sat back up.

It was only minutes later that Pieter appeared at the fire and stopped as he stepped next to the hearth, a look of solemnity about him.

"What is it?" asked Willem, thinking he knew the answer but afraid to say it out loud.

"Hayman is dead," answered Pieter. "The pain was too much for him."

And Willem began to cry once more for it was his fault. It was he, Willem, that had requested an end to the screaming; it was his prayers to God, for him to put an end to the torturous noise; yes indeed, it was he, Willem, that had asked for Hayman's death to be delivered this day. And his prayers were answered.

"What? What was that?" came a tired voice as Marinus awoke from his slumber, having missed all that had happened. "Who's dead?"

The wind commenced to pick up a little, blowing fiercer now than it had some twenty minutes before, Pieter's words a little muffled by the growing ferocity of the storm as it made its way in from the coast.

CHAPTER SEVENTEEN

Seebaer, Joannes, Cornelis and Jan were making seemingly good progress as they continued towards the north when their attention had been diverted to the growing tension within them all.

The basic lay of the land was similar as it was to the south and also the west; though the further west one proceeded the more there was for the eye to see... an almost barren wasteland of semi-desert, a rainfall average of just eight inches per year being cast upon the land.

It was most inhospitable, from the limestone cliffs and in towards undulating and featureless sandplains of virtual monotony where thickets of acacia and banksia could be found, the bush acting like little islands of shade from the sun where birds could park and enjoy the tranquillity of their surrounds. As for the margin between this barren landscape and the limestone cliffs, it was little more than a boundary of coastal dunes of chalky earth covered in salt-tolerant coastal heath and acacia scrub.

The limestone platform continued along the coast, as it was near the shipwreck of the Zuytdorp, the size of the platform ranging in width, rolling in similar contrast to the waves forming a wavering line upon any beach.

There appeared to be no permanent water source in the area, from what the men could see, but the aboriginals knew where the rock holes and soaks were, wells of life-sustaining water, the liquid gold needed in order to preserve life, but such soaks were almost five miles away and not on the coastal fringe.

The approaching storm had been building up over the past several hours and it wasn't long before they decided upon taking some form of action against the foul weather which would undoubtedly fall upon them.

"We'll have to make shelter, soon," said Joannes to the others. "This storm isn't going to relent nor pass-us-by."

"I agree,' said Cornelis, shifting the blanket upon his shoulder, it being tied with a single strand of rope with a loop, it being slung up and over his left arm.

"Where to, that's the question," stated Seebaer. "This cloth we have with us isn't going to do much against this wind, and the blankets we have are going to be useless unless we can find shelter."

"How far do you think we've come?" asked Jan.

"Why? Do you want to turn back already," said a joking Cornelis, unafraid of a little bad weather and hard work.

Jan was seen to take the comment the wrong way, interpreting it as an insult, "You think I'm scared; lazy perhaps?"

"No," winced Cornelis. "I was simply commenting... look, it doesn't matter. I too would prefer to accept any option; but even at the camp, there's little to no shelter."

"You're right," accepted Jan, "I'm, sorry."

"Well, we need to find somewhere," said Seebaer, "and the sooner, the better."

"We've come about ten miles is my guess," answered Cornelis, a quick calculation of time and pace being considered. "But it's so hard to tell when there isn't any sun by which to tell the time."

"My feet are as sore as hell," said Seebaer.

"Mine too," added Jan.

"Courtesy of the shipwreck and these damn conditions," concluded Cornelis for them all. "Let's try heading inland," he said to Seebaer. "There will be trees there, will there not?"

"Yes," answered Seebaer with little emotion, hunched over and shielding his face with an open palm as the heavens opened up and the downpour commenced, an opening to a storm which would rage for many hours, the suddenness of the downpour precipitated by a lightning strike that shook the earth they were standing upon.

"Come, let's go; quickly," voiced Cornelis as he led the way into the unknown.

CHAPTER EIGHTEEN

The rain fell in buckets, the gullies filling up temporarily as they led the water away from the undulating ground of the open sandplains and into the sea, small torrents of water falling over the cliff of limestone.

Willem was hunched over and seemed very pale, the shelter they had struck providing sufficient shelter from the pouring rain but not from the penetrating cold. The boy was shaking like a leaf and he looked like hell, sweat started to fall from him freely.

All of the men had managed to gather together, endeavouring with all their ability to harness the body heat as a tool of survival; only Dirck and Marinus remained apart, just several feet away and laying beside each other, a large rock pile at their head where red hot embers from the fire had been placed in an effort to keep them from being completely doused by the rain, a similar construction amidst the others who now looked upon Willem with concern.

The symptoms had come out from nowhere, one minute he seemed fine and the next he seemed to be suffering.

Wiebbe held his palm against the boy's head and shook his head, "He has a fever, but from what I don't know."

"This damn land and the savages upon it," said Hendrik, obviously concerned for his own health as he pushed away to the farthest corner of their small shelter, the sail above his head leaking slightly, several drops of rain penetrating the fabric and falling upon him. He wrapped the blanket he held tightly around him.

"No," said Ariaen. "I don't believe that. No one else is suffering."

"So he's the first," said Hendrik, "that's all; the first to suffer."

Willem was clutching rather hard at his stomach. He was in much pain and seemingly a little delusional, looking here and there, but not at anything in particular. It was then that he vomited all he'd eaten that day, the meat, the peas, and the little shellfish he'd managed to consume.

"Poisoned by his own hand," said Hendrik. "Greed it is, that's the answer; his greed has seen to this torment being delivered. God knows when one is being greedy."

"It has nothing to do with poison," said Pieter, holding onto the boy's arm in an effort to offer some comfort.

"Too much food, you fool," said Hendrik sarcastically.

"I know what you mean, Hendrik," spat Pieter out of character, "but the boy has had nothing more or less than any of us. We have all had the same."

"Did anyone notice anything strange?" asked Wiebbe of the others. All shook their heads. "Dirck; Marinus; did you notice anything wrong with the boy?"

"What?" came Dirck's reply, he in a daydream, contemplating his death from where he lay farthest away, seeing with sudden surety that Willem was in further difficulty, clutching at his stomach. "What's that? What else is wrong with Willem?"

"You tell me," answered Wiebbe. "Did you see anything wrong with the boy earlier on?"

"Not, not a thing," said Dirck. "What are his symptoms?"

"He's vomiting, has a fever and is in a lot of pain."

"Maybe it's something he ate," came the reply from Dirck.

A smirk fell upon Hendrik as he looked Pieter and Ariaen in the eye, "Told you, didn't I?"

Wiebbe tried to gain Willem's attention, lifting his head and staring directly into him, finding nothing but clear vision and nil response.

"Willem; do you hear me?" asked Wiebbe.

"Of course he hears—."

"Shut up, Hendrik," and the death stare from Wiebbe shut Hendrik's mouth for the remainder of their discomfort, sitting there beneath the shelter so hastily made. "Willem, look into my eyes. Do you hear me?"

"Nothing," said Pieter. "Let's put him down and make him as comfortable as possible, explore this later."

"There may not be a later," confided Wiebbe. "Whatever it is that Willem is suffering might very well be the end of him."

"It might very well be the end of all of us," added Ariaen.

"I pray not," concluded Pieter.

CHAPTER NINETEEN

8th June.

Later in the night, when the stars came out to greet life on earth, the clouds having passed and the waters of the storm having drained away via gully and simply having been swallowed up by the dry land, invisible creatures could be heard giving their songs freely for all to hear. There was pleasantness about the sounds that stretched out through the night, over the folds in the ground, mating calls amongst them, disparate to anything the men of the Zuytdorp had heard before.

Dirck and Marinus were asleep on the far side of the hearth, Ariaen and Pieter fast asleep, as was Willem, seemingly over his spout of misfortune. Wiebbe, on the other hand, was wide awake and listening to the sounds all around him, trying to decipher what he could of the beatles, grubs, insects and nocturnal animals, species he'd never known existed, let alone seen with his own eyes.

It seemed to him that the boy, Willem, had recovered sufficiently to be left unattended, a little colour having returned to his cheeks, his pulse seemingly normal, the fever gone and no sweat to speak of being present; the boy was even sleeping comfortably and with his arms loose across his body... no longer was he crunched up in a ball and holding for dear life to his stomach. Whatever was wrong with the lad had been put right... he was out of danger.

Wiebbe wasn't an educated man, but neither was he stupid. He'd learnt a little of medicine and of comforting the sick and could tell rather well the time of night by looking to the heavens above. It was in this way that he could see that the morning would be upon them in three to four hours, the storm having passed them by without too much of a problem being encountered.

He stood up and stepped from the shelter and headed towards the higher ground, through some thick scrub and following his intuition, some scratching noises coming from not too far away.

He'd gone several hundred feet when he came across what he considered might have been the proposed campsite suggested by Jan earlier on, for the ocean could be seen quite clearly from it. He continued on his way. Within minutes he fell upon a little bare ground, a good site for a camp although only a little more rewarding when compared to the other, except for the fact that it would serve well as a makeshift camp for any sick. Many thoughts then travelled his mind, on life and death, disease and cure, medicine, food and water. The scratching noise had been forgotten and he continued to wander around as he made his way back to the campsite and bedded down once more, unable to sleep with his mind full of theory and consideration.

CHAPTER TWENTY

The early morning had brought Ariaen and Pieter to the fire, Wiebbe stoking it with a stick, getting it ready for a breakfast of peas and shellfish, the meat, what was left of it, to be saved for later on.

"Have you been up long?" asked Pieter of Wiebbe as he and Ariaen sat down upon the ground, a little damp but not overly uncomfortable.

"Not long," answered Wiebbe. "I couldn't sleep and so went for a walk and thought to get the fire started. We don't have much dry wood left."

"There should be plenty," remarked Adriane. "Enough for several days, at least until we can gather more."

"I was thinking," said Wiebbe, "we might need to make another campsite, further away from where we are."

"What in God's name, for?" queried Ariaen.

"The edge of the cliff is a dangerous place, in particular if Willem is to fall into another dream-state. We also have to consider the added discomfort of the spray from the ocean during unsavoury storms."

"But that's not the only reason, is it?" added Pieter. "I see the look in your eye, Wiebbe."

Wiebbe couldn't put it any other way, none other than to come clean with his idea, "I've had a look further inland, towards where Jan and Harmen ventured the other day. I came across a great spot which offered a little protection from the wet and the rise in elevation was enough to see the ocean. It would be rather easy to maintain a watch from the comfort of a warm fire and we could make it ready with a signal fire as proposed earlier."

"And?" prodded Pieter.

"We could make another campsite just beyond that where the sick could be placed; like a hospital."

"You're concerned over Willem, aren't you?" asked Ariaen.

"Not just him. Look at Marinus. He seems well enough, but what if he turns gangrenous... should we have to suffer the smell?"

"Look," began Pieter, "I have no objection, but if we're going to have more than one camp then I think I should be with the sick, and remain permanently by their side."

"With Willem?" said Wiebbe.

"Yes, that's right."

"I see no problem with that," nodded Wiebbe. "Dirck and I will have to take turns in looking after any sick, regardless, and your assistance is no less appreciated. It's a duty which must be performed. But there is one other thing which I'm concerned about."

"And that is?" asked Ariaen, waving the flies away from his face.

"A lookout near where the sandplains begin. Just one thousand feet from the sandplains there's an old camp; Jan told me of it... told all of us."

"Where Harmen was bitten by that snake," said Pieter as he turned his face away, upset by the death of one of them.

"Yes, that's right. We can maintain a vigil on the natives, see what they do, and act as an early warning for the others if they should approach. It already has a large tree nearby for preparing food... hanging a dead carcass... and there's a large rock there, seemingly used for grinding corn or other substances. There must be food nearby, something we don't know about as yet. We must explore all options and keep our eyes open. Staying in one spot just won't do. We need to commence with the laying of traps for food; and we don't want a dead carcass attracting any wild animals."

"There aren't enough of us for three sites, Wiebbe," consoled Ariaen. "You've already condemned—."

"That's rather a strong word," protested Wiebbe.

"Nevertheless, you suggest placing the sick plus another, either yourself or Dirck, in a camp for the sick; that accounts for three of us, not to mention Pieter. That leaves seven others, including me."

"We would only need to place two men at a time near the sandplains; the others could maintain the camp nearest the sea, watching for a passing ship."

"I think he's right," agreed Pieter. "It's against my better judgement to separate Willem from the remainder, but I see the logic."

Ariaen was silent for a few seconds and then nodded acceptance, "Very well. We'll tell the others when they wake and commence immediately."

"There is one other thing," said Wiebbe. "We must burn the dead where they lay and as soon as possible, ensuring they burn. I don't see the point in dragging this out too much longer. We'll do what we can with the dead stacked near the cliff; place enough deadfall upon them so as to incinerate them all. It's the only way."

79

The others nodded in silent agreement for they all knew deep down that Wiebbe was right. They could not afford an epidemic, a flood of disease spreading through what remained of the precious cargo of flesh and bone... them. Their lives meant more to them than anything else and they were all sure in their minds that the dead would forgive their grievances against them.

CHAPTER TWENTY-ONE

Seebaer and his companions fared reasonably well in the conditions that had fallen upon them, considering that all they had was a little sailing cloth and several small blankets. The tinderbox they had carried with them was of little use as there was no dry material for which to start a fire at the time when they needed it the most. As for the food, that was all gone, their stomachs filled prior to departing the shipwreck and filling up again during the storm.

They were thankful that it hadn't lasted as long as they dread but now weighed up the options open to them.

In most places the cliff proved to be impassable and so the gathering of shellfish would be a major problem for them, and no other means of support availed itself, including the sighting of a rock hole from which to top up the only water-carrying device they had: an old pot with a loose piece of cloth as a lid.

Without fire, food, or water, they were already in dire straits.

The misery of the men wasn't so contagious, for all were suffering the same, but misery of such weight won't allow a man to continue on a journey that offered little reward.

Huddled around the old pot, now replenished due to the night's rain, and blankets draped around them, they considered the only option open.

"We have to return immediately," stated Seebaer without argument being voiced, only nods of the head being received.

"I think we can all agree to that," said Jan. "It's against my better judgement, but only as I volunteered for the task; but what choice do we have? Shall we start now?"

Seebaer nodded, "I'll lead the way if you wish and..." the sudden fall of silence attracted all eyes, ears intent on being the first to find out what it was that had drawn Seebaer's attention.

"What is it?" asked Joannes in a whisper.

Seebaer held his finger to his mouth and then the noise came again. There was something moving towards them, something close to the ground and seemingly dragging something along. It was a rustling noise of slow approach, the crunching and debris beneath a heavy weight.

Seebaer stood up, half crouched, and as he looked out in the direction his eyes popped out of his head and he sat again.

The others looked upon him in terror, afraid for what it might be, a savage, or a group of them, something heinous; who knew what this land held in secret ready to be unleashed against them.

"Seebaer, what is it?" Joannes asked again.

"A large creature with very small legs; it's almost as big as Willem," answered Seebaer as he placed his finger against his lip one more time.

"Listen to me carefully and trust in what I say," said Seebaer. "Do you trust me?"

Everyone nodded, yes.

"When I say go you must all stand and take up a stick or rock; kick with your foot if you must... throw a blanket upon it, all of you. Do what you can. He will be slow because his legs are small." Seebaer looked around once more and nodded, "Are you ready... now!"

And the four men rushed to their feet, three of which didn't know what they were up against.

Before them was a wombat, large and plump, a great mass of flesh ready to be made into stew.

Blankets were thrust upon the creature, stones taken from the ground and thrown, a large rock was then lifted by Cornelis and he delivered a shocking blow to the creature's neck as it moved, a blanket falling from it. It moved with great speed away from them as other blankets were thrown and then picked up, and the chase was on. The commotion of the hunt was in full swing, all in complete disbelief at something that looked like nothing they'd seen before, although Joannes had seen a picture of a badger once, a creature from England that looked remarkably similar: as far as he could tell.

Colourful language filled the air as orders flew from one to the other, the mass of energy now exerted by all four men beyond what they thought was within them, the adrenalin rush for fresh meat overwhelming them all.

The wombat was under great stress now, several blankets thrown upon him not budging, getting caught around him as he tried to step away from the vicious men that now surrounded him.

The men closed in on the creature and lashed out, several beats to the head connecting well and it was then that Seebaer fell upon it with the only knife that was carried between them all, penetrating the back of the animal. He withdrew it then and stabbed again, and again, and again; and before they knew it the creature was dead, and with the deed complete the animal was skewered from mouth to anus with one of the poles employed to hold up the sail cloth during inclement weather, sharpened at one end and pushed through with a great amount of effort.

The pole was carried between two of them as the group made their way back towards camp, exchanging positions from time to time, taking rest breaks as they grew more hungry and tired.

It was very tempting to bring their return to a momentary halt, in order for the four men to cut away a small portion of the beast they had captured, to cook it up and eat it fresh. They could already savour the fat of the meat, imagine it running down their faces, spoiling the rags on their backs that they called clothes. But the time they needed to find dry wood and then bring a fire to life was beyond their contemplations.

The trek back would have been considered as the most tiring, where the men were exhausted and without proper nourishment, but the fact that they had caught food for the first time gave them such an amazing uplift in spirits that they almost found themselves singing, and if it wasn't for a lack in energy they may very well have broken out into song.

And as the morning grew into early afternoon, Seebaer looked up and saw something to his front, something that gained his immediate attention, for he saw smoke.

"Do you see that?" shouted Seebaer for the rest to look, his arm pointing in the direction of where their camp was situated.

"A signal fire!" presumed Jan, breaking out into a run in order to see for himself the white sails of a ship coming towards the cliff - but there was none.

"Don't; Jan," yelled Seebaer. "No ship is expected until at least the eleventh of June... today's the eighth."

"Leave him, Seebaer," said Joannes. "Let him run. He'll find out soon enough."

"But maybe it is a ship," said Cornelis.

"No, Seebaer is right."

"Then what is it?" asked Cornelis.

Seebaer stopped in his tracks and turned to look at the pole bearers, "It must be the dead. They're torching the bodies, burning their decay, cleansing the air we breathe."

"So be it," added Joannes. "All the less work for us. It'll make a good fire for this prize we carry."

"Come on," encouraged Seebaer, "let's get moving."

Pieter moved up to the cliff as the fire raged, the bodies that remained after the storm beginning to burn, the fat within the bodies providing fuel for the flames and in an outstretched hand he offered Ariaen something which he did not expect. In his hand he held a pipe.

"For the tobacco you carry in that small box of yours," said Pieter half smiling, the dirty deed of setting light to the fire having been done. "You might like to clean it first."

"Thank you, Pieter," smiled Ariaen as he turned the pipe over in his hand, studying it closely, seeing whether or not it would hold up to being smoked. "It looks sound. I'll clean it tonight."

"You should consider yourself lucky that only a few other men amongst us smoke as you."

"I guess so," agreed Ariaen. "But share I must," and turned to glance upon the flames as they licked up the cliff's face and into the air.

Hendrik then stepped up from beyond some scrub and nonchalantly said, "It might concern some that the fire will attract the attention of the savages."

"My God," answered Ariaen with a little panic, "You're right."

"But if we are to signal a ship at a later date then I guess it's of little concern," and walked away, continuing on back to the campsite.

"That's the first, real, common sense thing I've heard him say," said Pieter, to Ariaen "and he just walked away before I could tell him so."

"Savage this, native that," shrugged Ariaen. "I guess we will encounter each other sooner or later. It won't make a great deal of difference... what do you think?"

"No, not really," answered Pieter. He looked over to where Wiebbe and Willem were standing. "They don't seem to care too much."

"Maybe they haven't given it much thought," replied Ariaen. "Or maybe they're concerned for one another. After all, Willem currently has needs, as does Wiebbe."

"Why, Wiebbe?"

"He and Dirck are our only real hope," said Ariaen. "They know more than the rest put together when it comes down to survival and the needs of the sick."

"Then maybe they should teach us."

Ariaen looked into Pieter's eyes, "Maybe we should be looking to the natives of this land. They've lived here for their entire lives. They're the ones that can save us; no one else."

"Hmmm, you're probably right," agreed Pieter.

"So... I know Hendrik smokes; I can see it in his teeth," stated Adrian. "Who's the other?"

"Dirck."

"What about Seebaer and the others?"

"I'm not too sure, but maybe you and I should just shut our mouths and keep it between just a few," said Pieter.

"No," said Ariaen. "I'll share... lead by example."

"It's a sorrowful sight... very depressing," said Pieter as he looked down upon the burning corpses, the flames leaping into the air.

"You're right," answered Hendrik and turned away, heading back to the small camp, to filter through what was left of the food, and he wasn't gone long before he screamed out a mass of obscenity in respect to what confronted him when he got there, for just beyond the fire, where the meat was supposed to be kept tightly bound with a cover and in the shade, he found it was bare to the air around.

The others came running, Willem following up the rear at a slow pace, feeling weak and mentally drained.

"What is it; what's the matter?" asked Ariaen as he drew alongside Hendrik, Marinus looking over from where he lay, half drowsed from slumber and finding it hard to see what was the matter.

"The meat," pointed Hendrik. "It's spoiled; every last chunk, strip, and bone."

A mass of flies of the likes they had not seen before had swarmed upon the meat, the cover to the prize having been dislodged by the wind earlier on and falling to the ground. There were ants in the thousands, lines upon lines of them, coming and going, a banquet ready for the taking.

"Maybe we can wash it," said Marinus, trying to help, hoping to contribute something to the group as opposed to laying there like a cripple, drawing his rations in water and food but performing no task or responsibility.

"Wash it!" cringed Hendrik. "Are you mad? It's contaminated."

"I'm afraid he's right," said Wiebbe.

"Of course I'm right," came Hendrik's familiar tone once more.

"We can't take a chance on it," said Wiebbe. "Willem has been bad and it could well be because of this meat. He's young and fragile, unable to take the abuses of disease as a fully grown man can. If nothing else, the sea has taught me that."

"Ah!" yelled Hendrik. "The boy, it's his fault. The meat was stored by his action, his responsibility. The fault is his."

Willem then stepped upon the small open area, the others surrounding the fire and the stored meat, the dislodged cover bearing all to the world, invitation for all the insects that roamed the land.

"It wasn't me," said Willem, a pleading look within his eyes. "I placed the cover upon it, I know I did."

"It's okay, Willem," consoled Pieter, "It's not your fault; it was the storm."

Hendrik fell upon his haunches and covered his face with his hands, "Blast, it. The boy should have checked it, thrice each morning, thrice each night; to double check is obviously not good enough."

"It's too late now," said Wiebbe.

"Yes," agreed Dirck as he moved over to Marinus, tired of the bickering. "Throw it into the sea and forget it. The last thing we need is to be divided by discontent, and to see this meat sitting there is a bad reminder."

CHAPTER TWENTY-THREE

Their faces were rather solemn, a little shellfish to be shared amongst them all. Hendrik stared at Willem from time to time, a snarl expressed, an upturned lip betraying his feelings, though little betrayal was required as Hendrik had offered his dissatisfaction earlier on.

The large fire was still burning although the flames were quite small when compared to before, the black smoke having subsided and the fat from the bodies, though little there seemed to be, turning the mass of flesh into a blackened mass of unrecognizable burnt bone and charcoal.

Seebaer was the first to be heard as he called out to the group, knowing he was close due to the disruption in the air caused by the heat from the fire. The others came suddenly after him, the wombat placed down for all to see.

"Seebaer," said Wiebbe, standing on his feet and greeting him with a slap on the shoulder, happy to see that all had returned safely, the fact that smiles upon their faces indicated good spirits, and he could see why.

"By, damn," said Ariaen. "What manner of creature is that?"

"I wish I knew," answered Seebaer. "We caught it this morning and have been carrying it ever since."

"We also saw the smoke from the fire," interrupted Jan, pushing into the conversation, cutting Ariaen off from making further comments. "I can only presume that Harmen was amongst those burnt in the fire; unless it was a signal for a passing ship, which I doubt considering that none of you are dancing upon the edge of the cliff."

"You're right," said Ariaen. "We burnt the dead; all of them."

"With or without sermon?"

"Without, Jan. Who here is a priest or other man of the cloth? No one, that's who."

"I would like to have said my goodbye before he was cast into the flame."

"It's never too late," said Ariaen, understanding the torments of friendship torn apart.

Jan looked around and stepped away, not another word passing his lips as he disappeared from view.

"So; what news do you have?" asked Pieter, changing the subject, bringing joy back into their world, even if briefly.

"No real news," said Seebaer. "We ran out of food and found it hard to continue under such trying conditions. We decided to return and have brought back this... thing, as you can see."

"We'll have to hang it," said Wiebbe.

"Not here," said Ariaen. "Seebaer, we've decided on a few changes to make our survival more comfortable and increase our chances of communication with the natives."

"Waste of time," said Hendrik, "if you ask me."

"It's necessary," said Adriane, standing up for Wiebbe and his plan. "We're going to maintain three campsites."

"Three," voiced Cornelis apprehensively. "We can't even manage to care for one; how are we going to manage three?"

"We have to try," said Wiebbe. "There's a good position a little further inland... not far. We can see the ocean from there; any passing ship will be easily spotted. A little past that and we'll have another, for the sick."

"The sick?" prodded Seebaer for confirmation.

"Willem fell ill last night," advised Wiebbe. "We don't know what caused it but it could have been the meat or something else he'd eaten."

Seebaer and the others having just returned looked to Willem who seemed well enough.

"He had a fever and stomach pain, felt very weak and seemed to forget himself for a while," continued Wiebbe. "He's better now, as you can see, so we know he doesn't have a disease or tropical fever."

Seebaer looked at Willem, "You look pale, too," he added.

"Even paler last night," said Wiebbe.

Seebaer took a pace forward, "Do you know what I think it is?"

Wiebbe was utterly flabbergasted, beside himself and in shock that Seebaer should happen upon the cause of Willem's discomfort and in a matter of seconds.

"I think he has Porphyria Variegate," concluded Seebaer. "I've seen it before, and it strikes mostly after childhood." He looked to Wiebbe and back to Willem. "Exactly as you say, the symptoms exactly. The more severe cases can suffer hallucinations, skin damage, diarrhoea, muscle weakness and seizures; sensitivity to sunlight, blistering of the skin and scarring. Fever and sweating is quite common. Willem; your family... does anyone suffer like this?"

"Yes," said Willem. "My mother suffers badly from hallucinations and pain, weakness and fever. She's a drunk and cares little for me. The doctors said what you just said... that name."

"Porphyria Variegate," said Seebaer.

"Yes, that's right," confirmed Willem.

"Well, I think that's your answer," said Seebaer.

"And what's the cure?" asked Wiebbe.

"There isn't one, but it can be helped," said Seebaer, though with little confidence.

"And how is that?" prodded Pieter for an answer, eager to help the boy under his care.

"Plenty of food."

Ariaen took no time in giving the orders, the overwhelming power of command flowing through him that second, to see to it that all was done to help Willem, "We do as suggested by Wiebbe. Wiebbe, show us all where the campsite is to be and then the hospital. Cornelis and Jan can carry Marinus, Dirck his things. Seebaer and Joannes, bring the... animal; we can set up the third sight and prepare our next meal immediately, for Willem's sake."

"Throw it on a fire as it is," interrupted Hendrik. "Why waste your energy cutting away the skin and draining the blood?"

"Because we know too little about the animals of this land and I see no good coming from supping on more blood than is necessary," advised Ariaen. "It's called farming, Hendrik, and besides, the skin can go towards making boots and a hat... or do you think we should throw all manner of material to the flame of a good fire?"

Hendrik didn't answer, he saw the error of his way and it was clear to him that the others had put more thought into the campsites than he had done, not to mention the preparation of the animal that he had overlooked.

"Let's get to work immediately and get Willem something good to eat," finished Ariaen. "We start trapping for more food as soon as we can but in the meantime we set up our campsites and get ready to eat."

Nothing further was said and the men set to duty, doing as they should do in order to survive. There was no more bickering, just hard work.

CHAPTER TWENTY-FOUR

By nightfall all had been secured: the three separate sites had been established, to some form of reasonable degree.

All of the survivors came together as darkness fell upon them, even Marinus was carried down to the main camp where the sea could be easily seen, carried upon a litter made from some wood from the Zuytdorp and some cloth.

The meat of the animal had been separated from the remains of the animal, innards discarded, thrown aside for the ants and flies to have their way with it, and the skin lay out upon the ground, pegged into place and stretched ready for further scraping. The ants clambered over it and they would remove all of the meat from the skin, and the stench of the remains would be buried later on when more time was made available for those manning the third site, but the time now was for a little celebration, to congratulate one another on what they had, so far, accomplished.

Each person held a plate of some description, whether it be made from wood or a large piece of bark, each filled with well cooked meat and fat. Willem wasted no time at all in having his fill and all around knew that from this day forth they would have to provide special care to Willem, to ensure he remained full of food and spared the more arduous chores availed by the group. Wiebbe could only think that the work the boy did earlier contributed to his falling sick, but he knew deep down that he wasn't to blame... Willem was simply unstoppable when it came to pulling his own weight but now that would have to change.

There was more eating than talking and for obvious reasons, for the group of survivors had been without a good meal for so long. Their main staple was shellfish of varying types, which was not always going to be available due to the weather – an alternative would have to be considered.

"Do you know something?" said Joannes. "I was thinking that we could build ourselves an oven, for smoking fish and drying meat. Jerky would serve us well at times when the weather proved too bad to scrounge. We can't stuff ourselves with food and then go days without."

"Especially not Willem," added Pieter.

"What about the natives?" prodded Dirck. "How do they survive?"

"Don't worry about them," said Jan. "They'd not go without."

"Which is why we should consider befriending them," said Ariaen.

"It's all well and good to be thinking along the lines of long-term survival," said Hendrik, "but I don't see how any of it is going to achieve anything. We should wait for a boat to come."

"And what if one doesn't?" said Dirck.

"Don't give me your defeatist attitude," spat Hendrik. "If a boat doesn't come then we build our own and set sail for Batavia."

"It's no good building a boat if it can't be launched, and we certainly can't build on the shoreline platform... the boat would be decimated within a day or two."

"But there is a site," said Hendrik. "I heard of it, just a few hundred yards away, to the south."

"Take a look, Hendrik," said Seebaer. "It's not good for launching. We're stuck here and that's all there is to it. Our only hope is that a ship will see our signal fire and launch a boat to save us. Other than that we are on our own."

Silence struck again and the meal was finished, it was then that Ariaen pulled a pipe from within his tattered shirt pocket, "Do you see what was found by Pieter earlier on."

"Not much use without tobacco," said Hendrik.

"Which I have with me," said Ariaen as he pulled his tobacco box from within his blanket on which he was seated, "right here."

"By God," said Hendrik, "Real tobacco.

"How much is there?" asked Cornelis.

"Not much," said Ariaen, "but enough to satisfy us each night this week and even the next. If we spare it properly I can see it lasting a good four weeks, at least. But it depends on one thing... who here would like to smoke?"

Voices were raised as were arms, five individuals offering themselves to their luxury of indescribable pleasure and relaxation; six including Ariaen.

"We shall have one pipe a night, to be shared between us, and no more," said Ariaen. "Do you agree?"

"Agreed, agreed!" came the response, all but Hendrik voicing his anxiousness to the restriction.

"Do you think you are in more need than another?" asked Ariaen.

"No," said Hendrik, his feathers ruffled. "I don't," and then, "just light the damn thing so that we can get it started."

And the joyous song of satisfaction went up again and a single pipe of tobacco was surrendered to its ashes, the last wisps of smoke filling the air around the camp, all breathing a sigh of relief in the feeling that it provided them. Even those that didn't smoke enjoyed the smell of smoke, the reminder that they were still a part of civilization, even if thousands of miles from home and shipwrecked upon a strange and seemingly uninhabitable land.

"Shall we consider our order of business?" asked Wiebbe of the others, looking at Ariaen for his input.

"Yes indeed, let's deliberate," said Ariaen. "From our earlier conversations it is clear that a ship may very well pass by this way in three days. We should make haste tomorrow and ensure that we are ready with a signal fire within two. Every able-bodied man should assist in this, except Willem and one other. These two should remain at the third camp and prepare traps, try and make a few weapons such as a spear; like we have seen the natives carry. We also need to consider what means of contact we intend to use with the natives."

"I don't think that will be a problem," said Jan. "They will show themselves soon enough; in that I'm quite confident. They won't shy away too long."

"I agree," said Pieter," but it wouldn't do any harm to keep our eyes open and to make the first approach towards friendship."

"We need a gift," said Joannes, "something to offer them."

"And what do you suggest?" asked Hendrik.

"I don't know."

"Food," said Willem. "Everyone here will need food, even if they are natives of this land. The others we have seen were carrying spears, so unless they feared others that they are at war with, they must be on the lookout for food."

"Stands to reason," said Pieter with a smile. "I think we should make an oven for drying meat as soon as we possibly can, and there is no better place than the third campsite, nearer the plains where the natives have been spotted earlier."

"And how do we know they're friendly?" asked Hendrik in his sour way once more.

"We don't," said Willem, "but we can smile and make an offering to them. If they were going to kill us then they would have done it already."

"Maybe," said Hendrik, "maybe not. Only time will tell. But I tell you all this, right now, that I don't care for these schemes of yours, none of them. I would much prefer to build a boat... and maybe tomorrow I'll start."

"Hendrik," said Ariaen, "so long as you don't take the wood we use on the signal fire, you can take what you want from the Zuytdorp."

"And when my boat is ready for the sea I shall only take those that make apologies and pay for their place," said Hendrik, full of spite.

"Maybe we should make you pay for the tobacco, Hendrik, and the place you keep beside the fire."

And seeing the error of his way, Hendrik moved off towards where the cliff top looked out over the sea, the clear of the night growing colder but the wind having died down to practically nothing.

CHAPTER TWENTY-FIVE

Over the next two days all went reasonably well. No natives had been spotted and Marinus appeared to be healing rather well, considering the manner by which the splints had been applied.

The traps made by those at the third campsite were rather petty and proved to be ineffective, so shellfish was the main source of their nourishment, although several large fish were caught on the shoreline platform, separated from the sea by small rock pools. But the sea was too dangerous to remain next to for too long, with waves casting themselves upon anyone who went down to the Zuytdorp to look for salvage and wood. Most of what was carried by the Zuytdorp was either washed out to sea or if heavy enough had sunk to the bottom and lay in wait for future treasure hunters. It was here that the coins were found, but as they offered little to the men who had survived they were left where they lay, only several handfuls taken as reminders of a world lost more than anything else.

Willem had prevented further attacks by remaining well fed when compared to the others, in spite of what Hendrik had to say in regards to having less, and his workload was down to non-essential duty where he performed menial tasks for those that were hard at work improving on their living condition such as sanitation, the gathering of fuel for the signal fire and in constant forage for food.

Two signal fires were made, the second not too close to the first so as to be ignited when one was put to flame, but close enough so that the second fire could be struck if the first failed to flare properly, or if it burnt out and further signalling was required.

Tinder was maintained at the main camp which could see far and wide across the expanse of the sea to the west, kept as dry as possible in a small barrel taken from the wreck, a shelter above the main fire provided sufficient protection against the wind and rain, though rain hadn't been seen since the last downpour, and each knew that the construction of the site might not stand up to a storm as ferocious as the one that had wrecked them upon the shore. For a better and more permanent construction the campsite would have to be moved in land, away from the cliff and wind, to a place where there was sufficient protection offered by tree trunks and other natural sources within the lay of the land.

The availability of water was also a concern for most as it was apparent that the gully to their flank, which drained into the sea, was not flowing. When rain was prevalent then it might flow substantially enough to provide a good source of fresh water, but this couldn't be guaranteed. In respect to this another barrel, damaged along the top third of its circumference, was used to store water, set up so that it would catch any rain that fell from the cloth that they used as part of their shelter, the barrel half buried in the ground to prevent it from toppling over.

It seemed that everything was in order until on the morning of the day that the Kockenge was expected to appear somewhere upon the horizon, for on this morning the unexpected occurred.

CHAPTER TWENTY-SIX

11th June.

Hendrik was hard at work, fighting against the thrashing sea as the waves threw themselves upon him, one after the other.

He had commenced to gather good wood for the building of a boat, a boat that would take him to Batavia, or in the least, towards any passing ship that neared the coast. It was simply a matter of time, or so he told himself, until a ship passed this way, and it was up to him to ensure that he survived.

He maintained a steady watch towards the west, keeping a fitful open eye for any sail that might break the horizon with squares of white, flapping cloth; not that it mattered any, for the boat he intended to throw into the sea wasn't even made yet, not even started; all he had was a mass of wood.

In the least he provided the other survivors with pieces of wood that didn't serve his purpose and although these were rather small and still quite soaked, it was the only way in which Hendrik felt he could make amends for his wretched way. He knew deep down that he was pushing the survivors to hate him more and more each passing day, but he couldn't help it; it was his way. So he cast his thoughts aside and continued with his work whilst above him, overlooking the sea to the west, the others continued to put together their signal fire, placing tinder and other small bushes, scrub and branches beneath a pyramid of heavier wood, with a barrel of drier material close at hand for the ignition of the fire when the time arose.

All felt that the calculations made earlier were correct and that today was the day that a sighting would be made, but how close the Kockenge was to sail was unknown; if it was day then it might stay far out to sea, and might not even be seen; if by night then they would have to rely on a good moon or noise from the ship itself to know it was even there.

The bells, bells upon the deck, that's what they would listen for. The lookout at night would most definitely hear any noise from the ship, surely, in particular when taking into consideration the direction of the wind.

Night, however, was a long time off as it was currently just after noon, lunch having been missed by all except Willem, who ate a small handful of shellfish, and didn't feel the better for it. It was his inner ambition to help the survivors, not to impede on their desperate plight; his being no less desperate. He was a child turning into a man, as indicated by his Porphyria Variegate. He knew full well that he had to eat as did the others that fed him, but he couldn't help feeling as though he was a burden upon them, just another inconvenience to be suffered on top of everything else that they had to suffer, and all the time that he put food into his mouth he felt worse and worse for it.

Dirck took time off from the parties at work during the day to check on Marinus, even though Willem had made this one of his sole duties. It was simply another stab in the heart for Willem who felt that he hadn't yet been fully accepted, for if he had been accepted then Dirck would have left Marinus in his care and not troubled himself with taking time off from the work that was urgently required.

Dirck knew there was no ulterior motive for his attending Marinus, though this was hard to prove to Willem. He'd been looking after the man since they first arrived, where Wiebbe commenced to undertake other duties and leaving him to attend to the sick as they dwindled in number before their very eyes. It would be too easy to ward off the responsibility to Willem, as Wiebbe had awarded the responsibility off to Dirck; he refused to allow this to happen. Dirck had sworn to himself that he would attend Marinus until he was fit and well, walking upon his own two feet and without need of further assistance; there was simply no way that Dirck was going to offload the pressure of the job to Willem. Dirck, a man of faith and great inspiration, sitting there and drawing a dirty sleeve across his lips, a little blood having come from his gums. He ignored the signature of blood and continued with his work.

As for Wiebbe, he felt more in command than a healer or comforter of the sick. To Wiebbe their very survival depended on good decisions being made. He looked at himself as being a part of the council, a council of several men that made the decisions for the remainder of their group. There was himself and Ariaen and Pieter, each and every one a good man with the brains to organise and see things through. With a council of three the others were more likely to listen and pay heed to the suggestions that were made and the decisions finally decided. The council weaved their magic rather masterfully, corrupting the minds of the others into accepting their judgement without even realising that judgement had been passed, and even more profound was the fact that the council didn't fully understand that they were indeed being manipulative... it was simply the way of the council, a system that was jostled into position and worked well. It was more a case of sheer luck than anything else.

Ariaen and Pieter were happy with their roles within the group, Ariaen as leader and Pieter as an advisor: a right-hand man with plenty of good ideas. Pieter had come from a good background where family issues were more important than most other things in life, a passion for living that his mother cast upon him, passions that his father seemed to wish see destroyed, proved by his pushing Pieter, as a child, into working his mind, to pry out an existence in an insane world, to make him stronger on the inside. Pieter never reflected upon it much, never deliberating on the subject openly, but had been rewarded by his parents actions by instilling self-confidence and the will to work a solution through and through until the end result was worthy to be praised. He was only held back by Ariaen whose very presence seemed to shower Pieter with an invisible blanket or shroud, Ariaen shining through as the decision maker of the group through the combined motion of the council. Ariaen: a man of distinction, a man of healing, a man of good standing when on board the Zuytdorp and now washed up on land. It was his easy-going nature that made it for him, his very character that showed all around him that he knew what he was talking about. How could such a man be refused an open ear, a friendly smile, and a nod of the head?

And what of Hendrik? He knew how to scoff and refuse.

And so Hendrik continued to plod away on the gathering of good wood until that hour after midday when a freak wave towered out of the sea and fell upon him, bashing him hard against a rock. His vision blurred with the knock to his head, a cloud moving across him, a permanent covering; death. It was almost immediately after that that the alarm was raised and men appeared upon the cliff to look down upon the body of the man they knew as an individual, being washed out to sea, a burial that would see his body eaten by creatures of the Indian Ocean.

Seebaer was just near the edge of the cliff when the incident occurred; all he could do was stand there and watch. It was as though his voice had been stolen from him, despite the fact that the wave was too loud, too large, and too fast. Hendrik was too busy to notice anything out of the ordinary and any effort on Seebaer's part to draw the attention of Hendrik to the wave would have been futile. His jaw simply dropped when he saw the wave bury Hendrik, the lifeless body coming to surface momentarily as the water then cascaded away from the shoreline platform, another coming in to carry the body beneath the surging waves, the body showing itself from time to time before finally disappearing for good, never to be seen again.

Hendrik wasn't that much of a friend to Seebaer, but he was a survivor and that meant they were brothers of the same ordeal. Each and every one of them needed to look out for the other, otherwise they were all doomed to the same fate, be it buried by the sea, bitten by a snake, or carried away by the natives of this barren land to be cooked upon an open fire and eaten.

Joannes, Cornelis and Jan were the first to be at Seebaer's side, looking down upon Hendrik for that last dying minute. What could be said? Very little. It was simply amazing how quickly the waves had grabbed hold of Hendrik and taken him away, as though he were connected to some invisible rope and being drawn away by an invisible ship.

But they continued to watch even after he'd disappeared as they scanned the ocean for a final glimpse of their friend, and then Cornelis, his young eye seeing something on the horizon, gave an emotional leap of joyous salvation, springing the news upon all around that a ship could be seen coming towards them, nothing more than a little scratch in the distance where the sea met the sky, and then it disappeared.

"I don't see anything," said Jan with such hope in his voice that he nearly fell over through careless shifting of his feet.

"It was there," came the exasperation from Cornelis. "I swear to God that I saw a ship."

"It must be the Kockenge," voiced Ariaen as he came running up, confused between the sad look of Joannes as he looked down into the surf and the overcrowded joy of the other three. "What's wrong, Joannes? If it's a ship, then we're saved."

"Hendrik has gone, taken by the sea," he answered.

"It's a miracle, is what it is," said Seebaer. "If it wasn't for the wave that took Hendrik's life then we wouldn't be looking at the ship at this moment."

"But I don't see it," repeated Jan.

"Nor do I," came Pieter's voice as he too moved up behind the others.

"Just look and wait," urged Cornelis. "It's disappeared... there it is!"

"I see it!" yelled Jan.

"Me too!" came a frantic call from Pieter.

And before they knew it everyone upon the cliff top had seen the ship in the distance, disappearing and then coming to view, the waves obscuring their sight of the ship from time to time.

It was sheer jubilation, a great relief, as though all of their burdens had been removed from them; but Ariaen was more sober in thought and gave the command to set light to the signal fire, his mind quite open to the reality of the situation and that the ship might not see them at all. It was so far away and could turn to the north at any minute.

Seebaer and his three closest companions set themselves to task and the signal fire was soon ablaze; Pieter had alerted the others to the rear of the approaching vessel and then returned to stand by Ariaen when he noticed that his expression was rather lax, not a crease to be seen, neither a smile nor a grim expression being painted, just a simple, sober look.

"What is it, Ariaen," asked Pieter.

"If we can see the ship then the ship can see the coast," he answered nonchalantly, "which means that they will turn to the north at any minute. I'm sure as sure can be that there will be many eyes cast in our direction, but the fire might not be seen. Men will be resting below deck or busy upon it. There is no navigational reference in this region that will confirm their position so the lookout will have his eyes on the north, looking for the bay which I've calculated as being around fifty miles to the north. Aye, I see the look in your eye. I've taken many notes on the layout of the stars, as others have done. You know as much as I do about our predicament. The way men work on the sea is one of question upon question, confirmation needed on their position; how deep is the sea; how much till they bottom out when approaching land; what's the best speed that can be maintained? Our best hope lies in the reality that the smoke might be seen, if we are lucky; but no call to action will be taken upon us until they reach Batavia. Only then will they learn of our disappearance; only then will they consider the signal we make today as a signal from the survivors of the good ship Zuytdorp."

Ariaen looked around at the others, some having stopped in their tracks to look upon him. "Light the second fire, immediately. Our only hope lies in the hope that they will see us and report it to the officials in Batavia on learning of our failure to show."

And the men worked as they had never worked before, setting light to the second signal fire, running for scrub and anything else that would burn and send plumes of smoke into the sky.

"If the natives don't know we're here," said Joannes, "they certainly do now."

The smoke was thick for a few minutes and then quickly died away, a thick haze of rising heat replacing the black clouds of the furnace below. Was it enough to alert the Kockenge; was it enough to kick a seaman in the head, to bring a rescue ship over the coming months? Only time would tell.

And that was the first and last ship they saw. The Oostersteyn on 15th June, Zuyderbeeck on 24th, Belvliet on 25th, Popkensburg on 29th, and then the Corsloot and Oude Zyp on 5th July; all had bypassed them, either by day or by night, too far out to be seen or passing too far to the north. Salvation wasn't to come their way, not to be a part of their lives. And so the signal fires sat at the ready until such a time that each pile was steadily reduced to help maintain the three fires in the campsites they had established.

CHAPTER TWENTY-SEVEN

12th July.

They all sat around the camp fire of the main site where vigil upon the sea wasn't made available during the day, the other two temporarily abandoned as their purpose was superseded by the requirement for comradeship and togetherness.

They were well into the winter months and although rain was not altogether a common occurrence it did provide them with the ability to maintain stock levels on their water supply. As for food, that was another story. They had learnt to set traps for the slower animals and never shied away from testing the stench of a reasonably fresh carcass for edibility. Shellfish was always there but little else attained. Beetles and other small grubs were occasionally mixed in with other sources of nourishment but this was always accompanied by a sour look upon faces and never eaten alone.

Willem had suffered from time to time, minor attacks of Porphyria Variegate coming to air, but never serious enough to see his basic health levels decline. At any time that an attack arrived out of the blue the men would give up most of their meal in order for Willem to go with a few extra days of nourishment, and it seemed to help. It was never questioned, but was a simple act of brotherly love. But was it simple, to give your life away for someone else to eat, an act of courage to best all acts.

Marinus was forever in recovery. His ribs had seemingly healed but there was plenty of pain in his left arm, something he often joked about: still having the ability to wipe his own backside.

"And what about you, Jan?" asked Pieter as Willem ate from a bark bowl to his right. "What are you contemplating?"

"Oh; nothing, really. I was just thinking about these shoes of mine. They're damn near the end of their life," and Jan looked down upon the big toes of both feet, showing through breaks in the leather, exposed to the torments of the cold. "I nearly burnt my feet the other night, soles bare to the flames of our fire."

"Wrap another blanket around your feet," suggested Seebaer. "You'll do even better if you keep dry."

A few of the men looked around; they didn't have spare blankets.

"I was thinking of getting some shoes made from one of those furs, like what you and Marinus have," said Jan to Seebaer.

"You can have the next one," said Ariaen, seeing that Jan had the biggest need.

"Thank you, Ariaen. I appreciate that."

"What other needs do we currently have?" asked Ariaen of all of them, "apart from food."

"We still need something for scurvy," said Wiebbe, thinking of Dirck Fret, the man so ready to avail himself to the aid of others that he had neglected the effects of what he had suffered: his bleeding from the lips being the first sign, his death being the last.

They all knew that Wiebbe was right. They needed to desperately find some form of nourishment other than meat and shellfish. Roots were needed, some form of edible fruit. But what did they know of this land other than what they had stumbled across by accident. What was edible and what was not?

"Dirck was a good man," voiced Marinus as he rubbed his arm, the pain showing upon his face, the joining of the two bones not being as perfect as it should. "I feel a little responsible for his death."

"Don't be," said Wiebbe. "He wouldn't have wanted you to think like that."

"He served me well," added Marinus.

"He served us all well," said Ariaen. "It wasn't your fault he died of scurvy. He must have been under its spell well before he arrived at Table Bay."

"He was transferred from another ship," said Cornelis. "He'd only be ashore one or two days, barely enough to fill up on fruit or cabbage."

"Ah, cabbage," said Wiebbe, changing the subject, pulling everyone from the misery of Dirck's death just days before, where scurvy had taken its toll on his body, killing him gradually over the past weeks where pain got the better of him. "That's what we need right now, something green."

"There's nothing here but scrub," said Seebaer. "What are we to do?"

Pieter looked at the others, "You all know what we need to do. The winter, so far, has brought little rain, the summer months will be even worse. Is it no surprise that the natives we've seen to date wore no clothing. We have no good food, and over the coming months, as we enter into next summer, we'll have no water to speak of. We have no way of surviving here without the help of the natives."

Again the same tune.

There was silence then and all dwelt upon the comments. They'd spoken a little on the natives several times over the past few days, in wake of Dirck's death.

"I think it's time we voted on the matter," said Ariaen. "All those in favour of making contact with the natives, raise your hand."

Some were slower than others, but all eventually had their arm held up high, a little pessimism seeping into Jan.

"But one thing must be said," announced Seebaer. "We must first wait until the end of August. If no ship has returned by then, then we should proceed."

"No," said Cornelis. "That's too late. We need to act now. I agree we should remain here, in this camp until, well, maybe even the beginning of summer, or when the water has run out, but contact must be made. Scurvy is treacherous to us all and Willem is also suffering and on a regular basis. We need help now."

Yes, the same tune, putting off a good endeavour.

"Good," said Ariaen. "So let's consider it. We'll remain here until summer or when the water runs dry, but contact must be made."

"And what are we going to barter?" asked Joannes. "Why would the natives of this land want to help us?"

"Well... we have nothing, really," answered Pieter. "Maybe some coins from the wreck."

"Let's not consider that, the sea's far too unpredictable," rushed Wiebbe. "We can't risk anyone getting killed over a few coins. They're not going to get us anywhere."

"We have nothing," concluded Ariaen. "All we can do is show good intention and hope for the best. I doubt for a minute they're aggressive otherwise we'd be dead already."

"He's right," defended Marinus. "Jan saw another one just a few days ago."

"Yes," admitted Jan, reminding all of the encounter, "He was quite far out and all he could do was stand there, watching me, clad in fur. I don't like them. That's the conclusion I've come to"

"A fur?" questioned Ariaen.

"Maybe I forgot to mention it," admitted Jan, "but yes, he had something on, something to keep him warm, I'm sure of it; but he was a fair distance away." He looked around the camp fire. "It was raining, he was standing there and then he walked off. He wasn't afraid, either, you could tell this by his leisurely walk. He just kept on walking into the landscape and disappeared."

"Clothing," repeated Wiebbe.

"They're not animals," said Ariaen, unconsciously scratching at the huge scar on his head where the bandage once rested, his wound having healed sufficiently for the cloth to be removed. "They must have lived on this land for many years. They know the way of the land. They know what is good to eat and what is not. We'll die if we stay here and do nothing. I'm growing tired of waiting."

"Let me take a party of men out into the east," volunteered Seebaer. "Let me do this for all of us."

Ariaen was silent for a moment and then nodded his head, "Very well. Take as much water as you can carry and eat well before you depart. How many days—?"

"Just a few," interrupted Seebaer. "No more than four."

"Very well," agreed Ariaen as he reached for his tobacco box and pipe. "I have enough for one more smoke, a large one to do us all. Let's finish what we have."

Seebaer, Cornelis and Jan all smiled.

Marinus then turned the question to Seebaer, "Who do you want to take with you?"

"Cornelis, Jan and Joannes."

Marinus then took the fur shoes from his feet and handed them to Jan, "Take these; I'll get the next ones that come along."

"Thank you, Marinus," came the most sincere gratitude Marinus had ever heard.

Marinus managed to get Jan's shoes on his feet without too much trouble and felt immediately the discomfort and cold due to the open toes being fed to the air, the leather worn so incredulously that holes larger than several coins were on display, almost half the front portion to each shoe missing. They would serve their purpose until such a time that something else could be gained and taken advantage of.

CHAPTER TWENTY-EIGHT

The group of four, under no charge except a comfortable leadership role being displayed by Seebaer, departed after having had enough to eat to satisfy the early beginnings of their journey, this being the first time in more than four weeks that the men had eaten more than their fair share and certainly more than Willem. They felt a little uncomfortable taking the source of the boy's good health away from him but they would probably not get another opportunity to eat again for several days.

They carried a receptacle each, differing in purpose and shape, which carried water, and although it was still winter and rain could be expected at any time their overall experience showed the land to be a dry place and very unforgiving. The fact that they were able to rely on a rock hole as a water source didn't distract their knowledge from the fact that summer would see them without such a valuable resource. Many times individuals had heard, or experienced directly, of the blistering heat of the region whilst sailing past on their way to Batavia, but none of that could experience them for the reality of what was to come as the sun commenced to grow higher in the sky as the months unfolded before them.

Between the four of them they also carried a blanket each, a little sail cloth, to be used as a shelter, and several long pieces of rope.

They hadn't travelled far beyond the extent of the third camp when they saw a familiar sight, a kangaroo hopping away followed shortly thereafter by two more, and within minutes an emu crossed their path. It was a common occurrence to them now, nothing out of the ordinary. They had even spoken of trying to catch an emu for food but all attempts to think of a beneficial way had evaded them.

More than three quarters of the day had fallen behind them before they encountered their first contact with the natives and that was only in the form of an old fireplace, a hearth which had been abandoned long ago. It was easy to see that a smaller animal than those they had seen during their time on land had been eaten, for several bones sat white and dry, having been cleaned well by ants and the weather.

There was a little consideration by them to employ the site as a camp but with just under half a day still remaining before nightfall and no water or food source having been encountered, it was decided to continue on a little longer before bedding down for the night beneath a blanket and sail cloth.

The solemn look upon each of their faces told the story of the hard slog onwards, even in winter the land took its toll upon them. Their food intake over the coming weeks had been scarcely enough to carry them forward in their effort to survive, but to exert themselves upon the current task was starting to look foolish, the very nature of their task sinking further and further from them as an appropriate means by which to secure longevity.

Now, just two hours short of the sun disappearing on the horizon, the day's trek had come to an end.

"I don't know if I can continue like this for much longer," said Joannes and at 37 years of age was starting to show the wear of anxiety and exertion upon his face, the only real non-smoker amongst the small group so much less affected by the stresses of the situation.

Seebaer stopped dead in his tracks, just behind Cornelis, who, being the youngest of the group, had pressed ahead.

"Cornelis; wait," stammered Seebaer. He turned to the other two behind him. "Let's camp here for the night. I can't take much more and we should try and find something to eat."

Cornelis said not a word and moved back a few dozen feet to join his comrades, who fell upon the hard floor of the sandplains, exhausted and nearly at a loss for words except for an unsavoury comment for the land upon which they had struggled to comprehend.

"Doesn't this place ever change?" asked Jan of the others.

"You came this way before, as did all of us," said Cornelis of Jan. "What did you see then?"

"Yes, the same as what we saw now," said Jan. "It's the same, no matter where you go. Sure, the scenery might change a little but for the most part it is dry and uninhabitable."

"Which is why it's important to make good with the natives," said Joannes.

"No good can come of the natives," said Jan.

"Then why are you here?" asked Joannes.

"Here or there, what does it matter?" replied Jan. "The inevitable will happen sooner or later. We'll all die on this damn land."

"Don't speak like that, Jan," insisted Seebaer. "There is always hope."

"Hope didn't help Harmen," continued Jan of his argument.

"Where there is God, there is hope," said Seebaer, but he didn't really believe it; he didn't really believe that any good could come from trying to befriend the natives, but he tried to agree with the others.

"Yes, well," said Jan with upturned eyes. "If ever there was a Garden of Eden, this is not it. God has nothing good in store for us."

"We're alive," said Seebaer.

"But for how long?" asked Jan.

'Why don't we try and find something to eat?" suggested Cornelis. "I'll take a look around whilst you set up camp."

"Very well," surrendered Jan.

Cornelis exchanged glances with Joannes and they both moved away from Seebaer and Jan. They would circle the area and find something for them all. They had about two hours of searching by Cornelis' calculation and should be able to scrounge something up... he was determined.

CHAPTER TWENTY-NINE

The dark of the sky had started to move quite rapidly around them, howling in the distance shaking both Seebaer and Jan awake. They'd fallen asleep shortly after the shelter had been erected.

"That's close," said Jan.

"Too close," agreed Seebaer as he looked around. "Where are Cornelis and Joannes?"

Jan looked around and fear gripped him. He knew that no good could come of the enterprise.

"Cornelis..! Joannes!" yelled Jan, several dozen birds in a nearby tree taking flight into the evening air, a band of orange spanning the horizon from north to south. "Cornelis..! Joannes!"

They both listened but nothing was heard, no reply, nothing but an overture of birds, insects and the howling of a dog.

"That damn beast isn't far," said Seebaer. "I saw one the other week, a great reddish-brown animal looking directly at me whilst I cooked upon the camp fire."

"Which fire?"

"The preparation camp. I think the smell of fresh meat must have drawn him in."

"Are they big?" asked Jan.

"Big enough," answered Seebaer. "It doesn't take much of a wolf to bring down a man. Cornelis..! Joannes!"

"Maybe they're lost."

Seebaer stood there silently and listened with his entire might, "They aren't answering. They must be out of range."

"What should we do?"

"We'll have to try and get some rest, take turns maintaining watch," Seebaer looked into Jan's eyes. "We'll get some firewood and see what we can do with the tinderbox Ariaen gave us."

"I only hope we live to be able to give it back to him."

"Don't talk like that, Jan. Nothing good comes of it."

Jan considered it for a moment, the way in which he always turned to the negative.

"A fire, Jan; that's our priority at the moment."

CHAPTER THIRTY

"Did you hear that?" asked Cornelis as he loaned his ear to the sound so far away.

"It's just a dog," said Joannes. "It's far too far away to worry about. I can hardly hear it. I'm more concerned about being lost."

"Impossible, Joannes," insisted Cornelis, "We can't get lost. All we need to do is to turn west and head towards the sea."

"That's over a day's walk and we don't have any water," pointed out Joannes. "Why did we leave the water behind? We only had to bring a little."

"Joannes, listen; even if we were in the middle of a hot summer's day, I'm sure that we would be able to make it back to the cliff if we had to, but we only have to go back as far as the others."

"I'm sure you're right, but even they seem so far away. So what shall we do?"

"We'll have to stay here the night and try and find our way back in the morning."

"Very well; as you wish."

"The tinderbox would be like gold at the moment," said Cornelis as he sat down upon the hard ground.

"You know something strange?" said Joannes. "I feel tired, so very tired, and yet I don't think I can sleep. The exhaustion I feel right now is the worst I've felt since we've been here."

"We'll just sit and talk awhile, listen to the land, see what it has to say," said Cornelis.

"Yes, I think..." and Joannes' jaw dropped sharply as he looked up and beyond where Cornelis was seated.

Cornelis had a look of bewilderment and froze there on the spot. He felt within him that he knew what it was that had drawn Joannes' attention. His eyes darted from left to right, looking upon more than one thing.

"There's someone behind me, isn't there, Joannes?"

"Yes," replied Joannes. "Please don't move quickly, for there are six natives standing behind you and each is carrying a spear."

"Looking for food," Cornelis said blankly, unable to think of anything else to say.

"Probably," answered Joannes, thinking nothing more than their immediate fate, "and it seems that they've found it."

CHAPTER THIRTY-ONE

The night had been long for both Jan and Seebaer who had taken turns to remain awake, concerned for the welfare of their comrades and of course their own. The fire remained reasonably well lit even though there seemed little need for it.

The two men tried effortlessly one more time to call their friends home and after another two hours of sitting and waiting, wandering around the camp fire and looking off into the distance, they decided to return to the others.

It was quite obvious to them both that the other two would quickly come to their senses and head towards the west, soon to find their way home; and that in itself was strange, to think of this as their home, nothing more than a campsite near the edge of a cliff.

The embers of the fire weren't doused and Jan and Seebaer gathered their things and prepared for the move back. The move was going to be harder than the day before as they now had more to carry, with the extra blankets, water and shelter.

The sheer effort in maintaining a reasonable pace was shattering to say the least, the exhaustion from the walk taking its toll on both the men, in particular Jan. Seebaer had removed a little of the encumbrance which his friend had to suffer and carried it for him as the last thing he wanted was for anything to be left behind, to allow anything to be swallowed up by the sandplains and lost forever. Their very livelihood depended on the comforts and warmth gained by the little things in life and all that they possessed was in some small way a tool by which survival was made all the easier to achieve.

The sun was hotter on this day than any of the days over the past few weeks and it seemed that they might be in for an early summer, or a very hot one, but as learned men go they did not know of the countries weather patterns, but a constant reminder of the weather was written all around them, a reminder from which they couldn't escape. The land around them seemed worthless beyond all contemplation, the ground unable to offer a single thing of use or worth. But what the untrained eye failed to see was a land of great offering, many gifts going unnoticed by the Dutch, much food and water being missed by them all. In so many ways the land they walked upon was filled to the brim with food and water, all it took was many years of hard living to uncover, and that was something they did not have.

Again the day grew long and commenced to draw to a close but not before the two men could hear the familiar sound of the sea breaking its back against the shoreline platform of where the wreck of the Zuytdorp had commenced to disappear, the ship no longer resembling anything but a reminder of the misery delivered them all.

They literally staggered in on the others, Ariaen and Pieter being the first on their feet to provide assistance, the crackling of the fire before them drowning out the approach of the weary men, their throats dry and lips cracking, not a sound coming from either of them.

Willem scrambled to give aid but was quickly ordered to throw some food upon the fire, a small bandicoot caught that afternoon along with another which they had already eaten, the skins already pinned at the third site and away from their main shelter. Marinus dragged out a water container for each of the men to drink from on seeing that the water containers swinging from the hung shoulders of Jan and Seebaer were truly empty.

"Where's Cornelis and Joannes?" asked Ariaen.

"They're gone," answered Seebaer through cracked lips, barely audible but understood.

"Let them sit and drink," urged Pieter, "they're thirsty."

"You're right," agreed Ariaen and saw to it that nothing further was asked of them until they were ready.

Several mouthfuls of water later and after a deep breath, Seebaer broke the news all were eager to hear, "They're lost."

"Both of them?" asked Marinus.

"Do you see them with us?" spat Jan in sarcasm.

"I'm sorry," said Marinus and sat back down.

"Forget it," said Wiebbe.

"Where did you lose them?" asked Ariaen as he helped Seebaer with a little more water, looking to Willem as he turned the meat upon the fire.

"Last night," answered Seebaer. "We'd been walking almost all day, much further than Jan and Harmen. We had several hours before nightfall and Cornelis took Joannes with him to search the immediate area for water and food. Me and Jan fell asleep and when we woke, just at dusk, we saw that the others hadn't returned. We called them but to no avail. That night we maintained a watch and by morning decided there was nothing for it but to return," said Seebaer, the look in his eye showing how he'd wished that he could have done more. "We had to return." He kicked out at the dirt. "This sodden place is like hell on earth. There's no place worse, I'm sure of it."

Pieter then broke the silence, "Do you think they're dead?" he asked no one in particular.

"Time will tell," said Ariaen soberly. "If we don't hear from them over the next few days then we'll have to assume the worst. As Seebaer has said, this place is unforgiving."

"Maybe it is just that; unforgiving," agreed Pieter, "but it can be tamed."

"No," said Seebaer, "it won't be us who is taming it, but 'it' will be taming us."

"Seebaer is right," surrendered Wiebbe, sucking his lips into his mouth and contemplating the facts. "We have to learn to live with the land, not the land with us."

"I thought that's what we were doing," said Jan, "trying to live with the land."

"No," said Wiebbe as he looked at Pieter. "We've been surviving on it, not melding with it. We have to become one with the land."

"What!" said Seebaer, "and become a savage?"

"Your so-called savages have lived on this land for as long as we've been sailing past it, and probably for a lot longer than that; maybe since Christ himself did walk the earth."

"No," disagreed Marinus. "Where are their houses, where are their accomplishments?"

"Maybe the land doesn't permit it," answered Pieter.

"I agree.... maybe it's for us to learn the ways of the land, by trying harder than we have before," said Wiebbe.

"I thought that's what we were trying to do, as civilized men, doing what needs to be done in order to survive," said Seebaer as he reflected upon the last few days and the exploration of the north. "We've been to the south, north and the east, and nothing has been found. Limited I agree, but still we endeavoured and made that asserted effort."

"It's not enough," said Wiebbe. "We have to do more. We have to make contact with the natives and we have to do it soon. When winter has gone and the last of the storms has passed this way the days will become hot and the ground crack from the heat. It will be like walking across the face of an anvil. Look around you; all of you. This land doesn't know anything but the harsh realities of life. I've seen other lands which have succumbed to the torments of heat upon heat, upon heat. I have seen other lands which have been spared no remorse, where the sun during the day was hot enough to melt the mind of a man in just a few hours. But I have never seen a land like this where the ground has been so savagely mistreated by the hand of God, where not a single flower can blossom nor a bee gathers nectar. We have to act. Summer will be upon us sooner than we think. We have to prepare ourselves for the worst by attempting to sojourn for a while in the best comfort we can scrounge."

"And what makes you think we're not here permanently, permanently incarcerated?" scoffed Seebaer. "To die right on this spot."

"Because I'll always maintain a little dignity and confidence; I'll always hold onto the hope within me," answered Wiebbe. "If I lose that, I lose everything."

CHAPTER THIRTY-TWO

18th July.

The weather remained rather moderate over the coming days, a little rain falling upon the coast but not enough to fill the gullies with running water. A few opportunities to catch food passed their way but it was rather a case of too little, as it always was, and there was no choice that they had in regards to what they could eat, there was no choice when it came to suckling on loins, leg or ribs; there was no tender choices to be held as a prize against the lips as the teeth ripped into cooked flesh, the face embracing all manner of delight; for all was bland here; and even though majestic feelings of grandeur enveloped them, for every morsel helped fill their guts, it all amounted to the same... food to get them from one day to the next.

Scurvy had remained a constant fear within the group in particular with the past death suffered amongst them, but little could be done other than for each, as an individual, to rip up the roots of any plant life that looked promising, to be devoured on the spot. Such morsels were never shared, always sheltered from prying eyes as they were devoured. Sharing was one thing, even with willem, but to leave oneself open to scurvy was not in the least looked upon as a nice way to die.

So greed had made its ugly presence early on in the days that followed after the shipwreck saw to their fate, but had quickly disappeared; and now, after many weeks, it had arrived again after a short absence. Some of the shipwrecked could feel the greed growing within them and others took what they found without giving it a second thought, yet some, like Pieter and Wiebbe, were quick to offer what they had to others, in particular Willem and Marinus.

Marinus was well on the mend and although he never complained about the pain in his arm and chest it was obviously present. Each time the man stood up, sat down, or moved abruptly, he could be heard to wince or be seen screwing up his face as his eyes closed tight. He was unable to throw a spear with full effect and even walking sometimes became a chore, the swinging motion of his arm taxing him over time and distance, though he never strayed too far from the camp fire.

Nevertheless, with the few unfortunate signs of greed and

individuality came signs of comradeship and sharing, many conversations being carried into the night, accompanied by the howling of dingoes in the distance. They had learnt to stay away from unfavourable subjects such as women and wives, relying more on the questions which plagued them from day to day, where the different aspects of survival could be gnawed upon until an answer was derived. But it was all more of the same whereby the answers were not altogether reliable. Willem had once suggested that they make shoes from the bark of a tree. The basic shape could be cut from a tree and the bark strapped to the foot by rope or cordage, but the rope underfoot was unwieldy, the bark work crack and fall apart, there was too little choice when it came to variety in regards to durability, and the list went on.

But what more was there to do? Survival was their ultimate destiny and so on the morning of the eighteenth day of July the site which had been their home for over forty days was abandoned once and for all.

Everything that could help them in the survival and quest was taken along with them. They would head to the north where it was known that ships from home would undeniably pass at one time or another, they in constant search of a better place in which to call their home; somewhere with a waterfall for bathing; some place thriving with meat and plenty of wood for which to corral their captives. They would do all they could to survive this land but the main boost to their decision in travelling north was to gain access to the native culture and their basic way of life, to fall upon their ways and techniques in gathering food and water. If a savage could inherit this land then there was no reason why an educated European could not do the same – but it was a shame that nature never bestowed favouritism to anyone other than those willing to adapt to the land itself and not vice versa.

CHAPTER THIRTY-THREE

Willem and Pieter stood in front of the tree at the third campsite and tied into place the arrow they had made. It consisted of a shaft with two shorter pieces of wood attached to one end and made to resemble a pointer.

"Do you think it will work, Pieter?" asked Willem.

"I don't know, Willem," said he in return. "In all honesty I don't think we'll ever see them again, but if Cornelis and Joannes do come back this way they're sure to check each of the campsites for materials they might be able to use. At least if they see this they'll know which way to go in order to find us, but we'd be stupid beyond all contemplation to go south."

Pieter helped with the final knot and the two moved back to the second campsite to find everyone ready to go, not a single thing left behind that would be of use to them in their forage for food, forage for survival.

Each and every one of them carried his own blanket or sail cloth; every second man had a container of some description for porting water, whether big or small, and the others carried one of the three knives or makeshift spears.

They stood around the burnt out fire, a slight glow coming from some of the hotter embers deep within the mound of charcoal.

"We should have made a note for Cornelis and Joannes from the charcoal," said Marinus thinking how terrible it would be to be lost in a world yet undiscovered and moulded by the hand of man.

"The arrow that Willem made is a good enough sign," said Pieter as he looked from Marinus to the boy. "If they come this way again then they will see it."

"I just wish we could have done more for them," continued Marinus as he reflected further on the realities of their predicament. "Maybe we should wait a little longer; just a few more days."

"No," said Ariaen. "Our decision is made and we need to stand by it. Nothing is going to come easy. There'll be many upsets that will confront us. We have to remain loyal to ourselves first. We can't keep holding onto false hope."

"You're right," agreed Marinus. "Let's go; let's get out of here."

The group commenced their journey, their eyes falling upon their home for the final time, a seemingly sad farewell to a place they had come to know and trust, and now they were leaving it behind to search for something more rewarding.

Ariaen led the way north followed shortly after by Pieter and Willem.

"Come on, Marinus," urged Wiebbe, "time to go."

Marinus tagged onto the line followed closely by Seebaer and Jan, who between them carried several poles for erecting a shelter should the need arise when they stopped each night, a temporary solution to aid in protection should it rain, until such a time that something more permanent could be found. Much rope was also taken along.

Wiebbe took up the rear of the single file, glancing one final time over the site which had many memories, most of which he'd look forward to forgetting, but nevertheless, he said his goodbye to the site which had seen them mature from victims of a shipwreck to men of the world, and there was still plenty of room for growing.

The group hadn't been gone long, less than five minutes in fact, when Marinus stopped in his tracks.

"What is it, Marinus?" asked Seebaer.

The others to his front also stopped and looked back to see what the matter was.

Marinus announced to everyone so that there was no mistake about what he was about to do, "I have to go back. We left no water."

"There's enough water in the rock hole," voiced Pieter from the front.

"No," said Marinus. That's almost gone," he looked to the ground and made his final decision. "I'm going back to leave my water at the third campsite. It'll make it easier to see the arrow."

"Marinus;" said Ariaen, "the animals will get at it."

"I'll hang it from a tree," insisted Marinus.

"You're wasting your time," said Jan, "and ours; and how are you to lift it with your arm like it is?"

Marinus was silent for a second before making a firm and final decision, "Don't wait for me," he said. "I'll catch up; I'll manage. All I have to do is follow the cliff; right?"

"That's right," said Wiebbe.

"Good; then you all go and I'll catch up soon."

"Are you sure?" asked Pieter.

"Yes; very sure."

"Take someone with you," suggested Pieter.

"I'll go," volunteered Willem.

"No," said Pieter. "You don't have the energy."

"No," assured Marinus. "I'll go alone; please. I need to do this for our friends."

A silent nod was all that was needed and Marinus headed off back towards the campsite to hang his water from the tree. He felt that it was the least he could do.

CHAPTER THIRTY-FIVE

Marinus stepped out upon the worn track which led up to the second campsite, and he was happy that he'd found his way so easily and without having to move nearer the cliff.

The slight pain he felt in his arm and chest was shrugged off as nothing more than a hindrance, as was his usual ploy. He turned to head towards the third campsite where just the day before they'd deposited the remains of some shellfish they'd managed to scrounge from the shoreline platform a little to the south. As he stepped out onto the nakedness of the site he was confronted by sheer surprise, four sets of gnarled teeth, viciousness he'd never seen or encountered before.

A deep throaty growl then surfaced from the first of the terrors which looked deep within his eye and then a second, and a third, then a fourth. Two of them commenced to encircle him, preventing him from escape, feeling within them that he was alone and susceptible to their whims.

Dingoes; massive and hungry for easy prey. They could sense the inabilities of Marinus, sense his fear; could smell the water that he carried, and above all his weakness. It wasn't their normal practise to attack something so large but they'd been known to take down large kangaroos and aboriginal women too frail to protect themselves, women left against their will to fend for themselves by a tribe unwilling to feed them in old age.

There was no sport in catching prey; it was simply a matter of survival, to take what you could get and when you could get it. Marinus was simply an easy target, frail, wounded, doused in fear, and a good source of meat and water.

The animals closed in upon him and then the attack came, from the rear, his calf bitten into.

CHAPTER THIRTY-SIX

The cry that filled the air was heinous to say the least, the worst death cry that the men had heard their entire lives. All they could do was stop, turn and stare, looking out in the direction from whence the cries came. And it soon fell silent.

"We should go back," urged Willem, "and help our friend."

"No!" said Jan. "It was his own foolish decision."

"It wasn't foolish to want to help a friend, no more foolish than it is for Willem to want to provide help to Marinus," said Ariaen. "But it's too late now. Marinus has met with a power greater than his own." said Jan.

"Those damn savages," spat Seebaer. "No good can come of them. They'll kill us all."

"He's right," said Seebaer. "The savages of this land can't be relied upon. We can't befriend them. They're uncharitable. They're swine; damn swines, each and every one of them."

"You see," said Jan. "They're cannibals, every last one of them."

"He's right," said Pieter. "Why kill Marinus for no good reason?"

"Maybe it wasn't the natives," advised Wiebbe. "Maybe it was a snake or something else."

"One of those dogs," suggested Ariaen.

"No. No, no, no; you're wrong," insisted Seebaer. "That's no dog that made him scream like that; no snake either. The savages were waiting for us to leave, watching our every move. They see us, they know where we are. We've seen them before, haven't we: some of us, have we not?"

"Yes, that's true," said Jan. "They've had plenty of time to show themselves. Why haven't they?"

"Maybe they're scared of us," said Ariaen.

"No; they're not scared. They've had plenty of time. No savage would wait as long as this before coming forward if his intentions were honourable."

"Then what do you suggest?" asked Ariaen of Seebaer and the others as he looked around, and the men moved into a tight ball during the preceding minute, to more easily access the situation and talk of war.

"Kill them," said Jan.

"Don't be stupid," spat Wiebbe. "We're too few."

"There is only one solution," insisted Ariaen. "We must continue north and hope for rescue."

"And if rescue doesn't come?" asked Seebaer.

"Then we find somewhere that will sustain us; find some savages that won't kill us," came the call for calm from Ariaen.

"I don't trust these people," said Seebaer. "I think it's time we had a new leader, someone more readily able to see to our needs."

Ariaen remained calm on hearing those words as did Pieter who stood beside him. Each and every one of them thought upon the call for an immediate election, the call for a change in leadership.

"Listen to me," said Ariaen, unforgiving, knowing the others around him better than he'd ever let be known. "If you wish for new leadership then you go off by yourself and find it. Pieter, Willem and Wiebbe are coming with me. What do you say, Jan? Are you with me or Seebaer?"

Jan could see the manipulation of the talk, as could Seebaer.

"Stop," said Seebaer holding up his palms in defeat, a funny little smirk upon his face. "I see where this is leading; do you take me for a fool? I'll stay with you, Ariaen. I'll not cause any further trouble, but remember this: we all have the right to voice our own opinions."

"So long as it's an opinion and not a confrontation for mutiny or war, then you are free to voice all you want. We need to survive... I suggest we continue on our way and do just that."

CHAPTER THIRTY-SEVEN

20th July.

The sun broke the horizon when an aboriginal fell upon the scene of Marinus ripped to shreds. All of the signs were there; it was a pack of dingoes.

He gazed around with his spear in hand and looked upon the tree, seeing an arrow made from wood, a curious device, its reason for being completely eluding him. And then it hit him hard. The white spirits had left a message that they were heading through the Malgana territory and towards the Yinggarda people. That's why the spirits - these people - had failed to make contact with them, they belonged elsewhere. But what of the other two spirits that had been found so recently?

Barega was his name, an aboriginal of the Malgana people, of the Wayle tribe. He was a tall fellow of handsome features, deep creases within his face displaying great character. He stood naked with a small shield and a spear, a small cloak of fur carried around his shoulder, a gift from the Nanda to the south, the people of that vicinity who had an interest in a marital corroboree in the near future.

Barega felt the urge bite into him, his new call to duty. He would have to provide this news to his elders for it was all of great interest. Many of his tribe and others around had heard of the white spirits that had fallen upon their land, making visit upon them from across the ocean. It was all new to him and very bewildering. Many times in the past were ships seen passing them by, out to sea and at full sail, and never in all that time did Barega or his people know anything about the strange site; but now they knew. The ships carried the spirits of the dead.

The Wayle tribe were currently camped several days walk away, after calculating stops for food and water. There was certainly no rush and Barega had all the time in the world but news on the spirits would have to be passed as soon as possible. If their intention was indeed to lay a visit upon those of the Yinggarda then the Malgana would have to make sure the way for them was kept clear. And then something more troubled him. How was it that a spirit of the dead could be killed by a pack of dingoes? If these visitors were indeed ancestors of the living then surely they'd not be able to perish as they would have once done at a time when they walked the earth.

Barega saw the obvious. Blood was everywhere, flesh and tendons bare to the world of the living.

This wasn't the spirit of the dead; how could it be?

The group of survivors continued reluctantly on their way to the north, pressing on into the misery that encased them.

It had become curiously clear that the natives of the land sought nothing more than to segregate them and have them killed one by one, a systematic elimination of the trespassers upon their land. Seebaer felt he could see more clearly than the others, that the cannibals were keeping them alive on purpose, and short of providing them with food and water, were treating them no different than they would cattle.

Seebaer could not restrain himself any longer, the episode of death two days before playing too much on his mind, "Stop; wait," said he from the rear.

"We need to keep walking," pressed Wiebbe.

"Stop, I say," repeated Seebaer. "Listen to me, all of you. Don't you see," he continued as the others gathered around. "They're killing us off, one by one; eating us at their leisure."

"That's ridiculous," urged Pieter. "Why would they do that?"

"Why would they walk naked in the glistering heat and freezing cold?" replied Seebaer. "I don't know their ways but it's clear to me now that they're intention is to eat us, one and all," he turned to Jan. "You heard Marinus scream; did you not?"

"Aye," said Jan, "The most terrible scream I've ever heard."

"Seebaer, you're ridiculous," said Wiebbe. "But presume you're correct about them, what would you have us do?"

"We must fight," he said, "stand and deliver... all that and more."

"Seebaer," said Pieter calmly. "We have rope, a shelter, blankets, a little water and three knives with a couple of makeshift spears. We are hungry, without the energy to work hard like men and have a boy... a young man to look after. How are we supposed to wage war against an enemy that is far stronger than we are, carry weapons which they are obviously experienced at using, and know the land like the back of their hand?"

"I don't know, but we must think of something."

"We're going to head north, Seebaer; all of us; I'm tired of repeating myself," said Ariaen. "There is safety in numbers. Stay if you wish. I still think you're wrong. I have no explanation for Marinus and don't intend to waste my time searching for one. Return to the old camp and you could end up like him. If you honestly believe that he was eaten by the natives then stay here and wait for them to come for you. As for me and the others, we continue north."

Seebaer was silent for a moment but quickly came to his senses, realising that his petty feud was useless, that Wiebbe, Pieter and Willem would not do anything to disrupt the friendship between them and Ariaen.

"Okay, I'll take my orders like a good soldier does," said Seebaer sarcastically.

"No one's pressing you to take orders, Seebaer, and no orders are being given. Decision rests with the best answer and the majority," said Ariaen, hoping to settle the argument by pointing out the obvious.

So they continued on their way with little further said until only a few short hours later, just before noon, when they came across what appeared to be a deep well dug into the ground, a poorly constructed hole in which to catch water.

The group fell upon it with excitement and quickly tied their empty water containers to pieces of rope, lowering each into the seemingly shallow well in order to get water from it; and they weren't disappointed.

It wasn't long before they were all full with water and sat in their exhausted state in a small semi-circle around the well, looking upon it with admiration even though it was not built of stone and cement.

"Where do you suppose this came from?" asked Wiebbe of Seebaer.

"You're trying to tell me that the natives aren't savages, that they possess ideas and abilities," said Seebaer.

"It's all there, right in front of you," said Wiebbe. "Take from it what you will. Any person able to live off a desert land like this one deserves more praise than can be afforded. Look around you, Seebaer. This place is of the devil's own making. To survive here you need guts and determination."

Seebaer stood up then, "I have to go for a walk... to relieve myself of this pain in my gut. Are you coming, Jan."

"Will Jan help the pain?" asked Wiebbe.

"He'll keep me company whilst I have my pants down around my ankles."

And without further ado the two walked off towards where the cliff lay in order to take time from the group and do as they needed to do.

Ariaen waited for the two men to disappear from view and were out of earshot, "Let them be," he said. "Don't encourage argument, please."

"I'm not like you, Ariaen," said Wiebbe. "I can't put up with the pessimism like you. You handle yourself very well and in all situations. I wish I was more like you. But I must say this, I—."

"Look," interrupted Wiebbe, "don't be startled; listen carefully. There... see."

The group of four looked up and saw six aboriginal men not more than eighty feet away.

They wore little adornment apart from four of them wearing what appeared to be small cloaks used to keep the cold at bay, blankets of fur from animals which the survivors didn't know were employed as blankets by night. Each of them also wore a waist belt and arm bands. Three of the men carried several small lizards which hung from their belts, kills that had been secured by the weapons they carried, which were numerous and diverse, including several spears and different types of boomerangs, bent sticks of which the survivors had never seen before. One of them carried a hatchet, a thick stick with a stone head attached quite securely with human hair made into rope.

The natives looked at each other and it was clear that one of them was talking to the others, their eyes fixed upon the survivors. Several nods of the head were then seen and one of the six stepped forward, followed shortly by the others. Once the distance between the two had been halved they stopped, the survivors having stood.

"Show no fear," said Adriane. "Smile and be friendly."

"Are these the spirits?" asked Kulan.

"I think so," answered Narrah. "But maybe they're men, like the others."

"What did they say?" asked Pieter, his question going unanswered, a simple 'shush' being emitted from Wiebbe.

The six natives fell silent and looked again upon the strange men until Kulan stepped forward, away from the others at his side and made his approach in peace, taking a small goanna from his belt in his right hand and offering it to them.

"Take this food; it's good," said Kulan. "The yellow fat of the goanna is a delicacy amongst my people."

"He's offering you something," said Pieter of the obvious.

"Quickly, take it or we'll be offending them."

Wiebbe took the food and smiled, bowing slightly, "Thank you."

Kulan stepped back and turned to the others, smiling, "You see; they're happy to receive it, just like the other two. They must know what it is."

"They look at it in such a strange way," said Nioka. "Show him that you killed it, that's it's a gift for him and his people."

It was unknown to the survivors that dance was a formality of communication in many ways. This was a corroboree and involved movement, often imitating animals and actions, hunters or bouts of conflict. All such movements told a story and many new ones were developed as new stories arose to be told, to be recorded for all time, the very history of the tribe being passed from one generation to the next. Most were accompanied by music but in respect of the current situation it was done without.

Kulan crouched low, knees bent and buttocks almost touching the ground, his spear taken a good grip of and poised in a throwing stance. Kulan moved around and then stood there silently before the men, a grimace of anger portrayed upon his face, the spear leveraged in Wiebbe's direction as though ready to kill him.

A knife suddenly appeared out of the blue, flying through the air with great precision and penetrating deep into the stomach of Kulan. The look upon the native's face was one of great shock and bewilderment as he looked up and saw Seebaer standing there behind the other four.

Narrah and the other natives, Nioka, Pindara, Daku and Woorin acted promptly and readied their spears as they pressed in on the survivors, voicing their anger at the suddenness of the attack, an unprovoked and unnecessary act of betrayal.

"No! Stop!" yelled Cornelis as he and Joannes came running up from the rear followed by another two aboriginals, Barwon and Kalti.

The stirred emotions of the other five were abated slightly but vengeance had filled their minds.

Ariaen, Wiebbe and Pieter could not believe their eyes, nor could Willem, the murder of the native, for no good reason, being delivered without second thought, Seebaer endangering their lives as though they meant nothing to him.

It was clear, all of it, that the men who had shipped from South Africa were about to meet their end unless reprisal was performed.

The presence of Cornelis and Joannes had proved beyond any doubt that the natives were friendly. They had given food and shown friendship. To now be struck down for the whims of a single man was simply senseless.

What was to become of them now?

Ariaen pulled the knife that he carried from his waist belt and within the blink of an eye rushed over to Seebaer and penetrated the point of his blade deep into him. The facial grimace of Seebaer was different from that of Kulan's; Seebaer's grimace was of horror and pain.

The commotion all around was full of emotion. The aboriginals had congregated around their fallen friend, looking up periodically at Ariaen and the dead Seebaer. And then Jan came to view, having crouched behind some bush to escape the horrors of being eaten alive. He had believed Seebaer to the fullest, understood what it was he'd been saying about these horrible natives. But he was wrong.

Cornelis and Joannes did well over the following minutes, comforting their new friends and showing they cared for the dead by embracing Kulan's fallen body, him being dead and void of life. It was this alone that settled the calamity of the situation, bringing the anger to a simmer, the simmer to a calm.

Wiebbe had pulled the bloodied knife from Seebaer as he fell dead and holding the blade had moved very slowly over to Narrah. He held the knife out and offered it to him.

"No!" yelled Jan from the rear. "What are you doing? Are you mad? You're insane; stupid beyond all comprehension." He turned and started to run, running towards the cliffs of the coast and on reaching the edge leaped into the air and fell to his death upon the shoreline platform below, secure in his own mind that he had escaped being eaten alive, that the pain of death he had delivered unto himself was far less than what would have been delivered by the savages he saw before him. But it was his mind that was corrupted, and only his. He failed to see what the others had seen, and had believed all that he had been told by Seebaer. Seebaer was his death, Seebaer and his own infliction, an affliction of the mind that could not be removed.

CHAPTER THIRTY-NINE

The afternoon had finally arrived, the sun seeking the horizon, and as the fire blazed in all its glory the men sat around it, not in their groups of white and black, but seated in equal terms, one survivor between two natives and one native between two whites: where possible.

There was plenty of food being cooked upon the fire as flames appeared here and there, and there was water in abundance. The aboriginals were pleasant and friendly, and seemingly content with the actions of Wiebbe, for he had inflicted justice upon one of his own in the face of the controversy, in similar fashion to how they saw justice delivered, but they usually maimed, rarely killed. Seebaer had done wrong by the Wayle and justice had been delivered.

"I still can't believe that you're alive," said Ariaen to Cornelis.

"Yes," Cornelis agreed, "hard to believe that we fell in with such good fortune. We've had plenty to eat since we were found by Barwon and Kalti," two aboriginal men looked to Cornelis when their names were mentioned.

"You know them by name, that's impressive," said Pieter.

"We've learnt quite a bit already. We haven't seen their main camp yet but I believe it won't be long now."

"How do you know?" asked Wiebbe.

"Do you see any women sitting around the fire?" asked Cornelis.

"What are they talking about?" asked Barwon.

"I don't know," said Kalti. He looked into Cornelis' eyes. "What are you talking about, Cornelis?"

"What did he say?" asked Wiebbe.

"It's beyond me," answered Cornelis. "He heard his name called."

"Ask him about the women," prodded Wiebbe.

"Where are the women," asked Cornelis and shaped the cup of a woman's breasts with his hands held at his chest."

"Ahhh," said Barwon, "He wants a woman."

"Then that confirms it all," said Kalti. "They're not spirits. Maybe we should get them a woman, each and every one of them."

"Including the small one?" asked Barwon, talking of Willem.

"Especially him," answered Kalti. "The time for marriage is near. We'll pass the word onto the Yinggarda as the agreement with the Nanda has already been struck."

"Maybe the Yinggarda won't want them," said Narrah. "Look at them. They look sick. We'll see what the Nanda can do for us."

"They're different," insisted Barwon. "Maybe we can learn from them. A man that can float on water in a craft so big and large must know something."

"Well," said Nioka. "They come from somewhere, a place that can't be seen."

"Are you sure they're not spirits?" asked Woorin. "They scare me."

"The elders will tell us, but meanwhile we must make the best of the situation and return when the sun rises once more."

Barwon looked into Cornelis' eyes, "Not far now and we can talk of women, when the sun crosses the sky and we have walked towards that direction," he said, indicating the north-east with his lips after making an arch through the air with his arm, "then we shall be home."

"One day away," said Cornelis, "I think."

CHAPTER FORTY

21st July.

They slept soundly that night and awoke the following morning to be provided more food, the natives sitting around the fire and talking of the day's journey, and after an hour of relaxed contemplation and feeding the group was hurried to be ready to move, ushered by their new found friends to stand.

Wiebbe and Pieter moved over to the poles and cloth that they used as a shelter but the natives shook their heads and tried with great effort to convey that the objects would only weigh them down.

"Leave it all here," said Joannes. "Bring the knives and the water containers, nothing more. We won't need them."

"You're right," said Ariaen. "We need to learn new ways of living."

Cornelis looked at Ariaen as he was pulling his hand away and saw in his eye that there was something he found hard to come to grips with; an abstract of his old life. "Do you have any tobacco left?" he asked, prodding a response.

"No," answered Ariaen. "We smoked the last, remember."

"I was hoping, that's all."

"Here," said Ariaen and pulled the empty tobacco box from his pocket, "see for yourself."

"I trust you," said Cornelis.

Ariaen simply smiled and threw the empty box into the fire, looking at it as it landed in the coals, where it would remain undisturbed for more than two hundred and seventy years, before being found by a white man in the future. He looked up then and saw that the last of the natives had almost disappeared from view.

"Come old friend," said Ariaen. "It's time to go. I don't wish to be lost."

"I don't think there's much chance of that happening," said Cornelis. You'd soon be found again," and Ariaen knew that he was referring to the tracking abilities of the natives they had befriended.

CHAPTER FORTY-ONE

The survivors had taken their first real step in cohabitation with the natives, the aboriginals of the land, and as time passed they commenced to learn of many new things.

Aboriginals lived together in tribes, made up exclusively of family members who formed a clan, each clan being responsible for ensuring the well-being of the land on which they dwelled. They lived with the land, not the land with them.

Tribes had many rules, many regulations, and this included the segregation of men and women into separate roles, tasks also divided according to age. Men hunted with spears and fished. They hunted animals such as kangaroos, wallabies, echidnas and possums, reptiles and birds. They used spears and boomerangs to hit, catch and kill, and could scale trees in order to get their food.

They hunted in groups and sometimes as individuals, and where there was an abundance of bellies to be filled the catch was shared equally amongst all. Boys coming of age often went with their father to learn how to hunt, to make and use tools and weapons. All children earned their place in their society. Values such as respecting elders and other social responsibilities were of great importance and older children also cared for the elderly too frail to tend themselves.

Women were also very important in the day-to-day survival of the clan, gathering the bulk of the food which was eaten on a daily basis, and they were also responsible for gathering medicine. Girls almost always went with their mothers to learn about bush food and bush medicine. Education of the younger children also came under the sway of the women and older siblings. Women also decided when girls would undergo rituals in preparation for marriage, they acted as midwives and story-tellers.

Each tribe had an Elder. He decided when to move camp and settled disputes. Elders were those considered to be wise in tribal knowledge and worldly matters. They decided when boys would be initiated and when girls would be married after having received their ritual.

It was all such an intricate network of rules and standards, but overall their way of life was rather simple and unhurried, very relaxing and maintained a pleasant mood for all as they abided by the laws laid down. It was now simply a time for the survivors of the

Zuytdorp to not just interact with the natives but to become a part of them.

But of all the most important attributes that the aboriginals had in play, the most important was the medicine man.

He was a powerful man, and was responsible for curing many physical ills, sometimes by massage and sometimes by sucking, removing the evil that caused the pain; sometimes he would administer natural medicines made from plants or roots. The emphasis on healing was on the spirit, not the body. Their belief that the spirit was the source of their illness empowered the medicine man to treat the sick. Sometimes however an individual was struck down by evil magic of another medicine man or powerful omen. The victim would usually become sick and die, not necessarily because the magic had worked well, but because the individual believed in the magic.

There were also Corroborees, each of which was of great importance to a tribe, it was their living history. There were two types of corroboree; the secretive, held during initiation ceremonies, and secular, which was a majority of what was held in full view of the survivors. The secretive was a gift to be awarded to an individual during his changing years from youth to adulthood, a change which saw many varieties of custom being performed and enacted.

It was common for a ceremony to be opened after five minutes of music and chants from instruments and throats. Beating a waddy against a shield, growing shouts, howling and didgeridoos; singers and dancers would join in, enacting a piece of historical past and of secular importance, and on special occasion these could go on for many hours, people having painted their bodies with natural earth pigments red and yellow ochres, white clay, and black charcoal. Bird down, plant down, flowers and seeds, many hues and shapes were employed during different ceremonies.

Once again, made clear to some, but not all, the survivors came to accept that they were being adopted. First the tribe would accept them and then the land would accept them. This was the accepted way of life. It was systematic. Tribal acceptance came before survival could be taught. There were many secrets that the land possessed and the aboriginals knew a vast majority of them, in particular the area in which they lived. Hunter-gatherers they were, and much ground was to be covered by the survivors in the years to fall before them, and with those years a vast knowledge of understanding would become so clear that it was as though standing in front of them all of the time. One thing of great importance was water and many wells, soaks, and rock holes existed upon the land, but only a few of the tribe knew them all. Along with their water sources came sacred ground, ground on which only a designated few were permitted to enter, one or two individuals of an entire tribe permitted access during specific rituals and ceremonies.

The survivors of the Zuytdorp had a lot to learn and at the present they were little more than observers. But as time passed more and more became clear to them all.

They hadn't yet been accepted to be a part of a 'sacred' corroboree but almost all other aspects of tribal life were showered upon them.

They were near the beginning of a new life and the only aspect of their survival was the barrier created by their language and of their morbid lives as single men. Each had a growing desire for a woman and Willem was also coming of age.

CHAPTER FORTY-TWO

21st November, 1712.

It had been four months since they'd come into contact with the Wayle tribe and the relationship was good; very good.

The campsite in which they now called home was split into family groups where each maintained its own fire. They came together during the evenings and made visits upon one another to prepare for a hunt or other activity which included excursions for the women into the vastness surrounding them to look for an assortment of food, be it seed, fruit, berries or small insects for making up what the hunters failed to kill.

It was now mid-afternoon and Ariaen approached the other five members of his 'clan', sitting down amongst them as Willem stoked the fire, Pieter and Cornelis shaped their spear points, and Joannes prepared for cooking: ever since the episode with the knife, where Kulan was killed by Seebaer, the instruments of death were cast aside as something evil. Such a valuable tool and it was discarded within the blink of an eye.

"Where's Wiebbe?" asked Ariaen.

"He was invited out for a short hunt by Pindara."

"Good," said Ariaen. "I have some news," and he smiled in Willem's direction.

"What is it?" he asked. "What are you looking at me like that for?"

"Firstly let me say that I've just been communicating with a man named Barega. I'm sure the tribe has been trying to tell us this for some time now but the point never got across. It appears that Marinus was killed by a dingo."

"I knew there was a perfect explanation," said Pieter.

"So why are you smiling?" asked Willem.

"Barega was organising a marital corroboree with the people to the south, the Nanda. It's a few days walk and all of the Malgana will attend."

"And..." insisted Willem.

"You're to be wedded, Willem, married off," smiled Ariaen.

"Married? But I'm not ready... not well," he pleaded.

"You're young, Willem," pointed out Ariaen. "It's the best thing for you; really. You have a long life to live and there's only one way to live a life on this land."

"But we might still be rescued," said Willem with a little confidence.

"Do you know what I believe, Willem?" said Pieter as he looked at the boy, a concerned look of worry caking his face. "Once you've spent several years here with these people you won't want to return home."

"Don't talk nonsense," said Joannes. "I wouldn't care if I was married to ten wives; I'd be the first one aboard if I saw a ship sail past."

"You'd have to live on the coast in order to see a ship, Joannes, and the coast doesn't provide all the necessities of life for the Malgana."

"But married," said Willem again. "Whose idea was it?"

"It must have been one of the elders, and if I had to make a guess I would assume Woorak. It's so hard to understand these people sometimes. Do you know, I was asking Daku how far it was to the marital corroboree and he said it was not far. 'No long,' he said, 'little, short,' and then he indicated to me that it would take twelve or fourteen days to get there."

"Yes, well... I'm picking up a little of the language but I'm finding it very hard," said Cornelis.

"Yes, you are," said Ariaen as he erupted in another smile.

"I don't like the look on your face either," said Cornelis.

"You are rather young, too," replied Ariaen.

"No, you can't," Cornelis stood up. "Not married, not to the Nanda. I don't mind the women, it's not that at all, but I'd prefer for us to stay together."

"Willem will wed and his wife will reside here, I'm sure that's the intention. And as for you, young friend, one of the young women right here has taken a fancy to you," said Ariaen.

"Not Kyeema, surely," said Cornelis.

"Afraid so," said Ariaen. "The women folk have seen you two at play. You should be more careful. Your manhood has revealed much to the women of this camp."

"And who here isn't man enough to have needs?" stated Cornelis. "I'm not the only one that's been corrupted by my needs as a man."

"I'm sure you're right," said Ariaen, "but if it comes from the elders then I don't think you're going to have much choice. It seems the decision has been made for you."

"How many days did you say till—?"
"Twelve to fourteen," interrupted Pieter.
"And we depart tomorrow," finished Ariaen.

The campsite had been packed and everyone was ready to move, only the essentials going with them.

This was the first time the survivors had moved camp with the natives and it was interesting to note that the camp itself was left intact with the grinding stones left upon the ground where they were used. Shelters were left as they were the night before, sheets of bark propped up with branches and the fire was simply smothered with sand and the hotter pieces of half burnt wood carried in other wooden containers to aid in starting the next camp fire when it came time to setting up a temporary site.

A small group of men lead the way; Narrah, Pindara, Kalti and Barega. Hunter-gatherers they were, always on the lookout for food, never turning down an opportunity to secure a meal for the tribe and as the day wore on the group found itself some distance from the others but would rejoin them later.

The days were long and hard for the survivors, still suffering from acclimatisation, their bodies still getting used to their surroundings. There was a noted difference between the two: the natives and the Europeans. The natives were largely thin and tall, with slender legs from the constant walking; they on the other hand were not built for long treks over rough terrain where the soles of their feet bore the brunt of the heat and vegetation. It would take an eternity to get one's feet used to the conditions.

They were travelling in a direction away from the setting sun and the further they went the more eastward they seemed to go. It wasn't for the survivors to question the direction, for the motive was well known, but the path they took seemed weirdly peculiar rather than straight forward.

After eleven day of walking they came upon a rock in the distance and Daku came up to Ariaen. The aboriginal pursed his lips and pointed with his mouth towards the object of rock silhouette against the clear skyline.

"Walga," said Daku, "Walga, Walga."

"What's that all about?" asked Wiebbe as they continued walking.

"I'm presuming that the rock formation up ahead is called Walga," announced Ariaen.

"Walga," said Daku again, confirming Ariaen's suspicions.

"That must be the ceremonial grounds," said Pieter.

"Maybe," agreed Ariaen, and then, "maybe not," and continued with the walk.

It didn't take long after that for all to realise that they were near the end of their long trek and some were growing anxious in regards to the ceremony that was to take place, but not Kyeema who smiled when she looked at Cornelis, and he too smiled back though deep down felt as though he should wait awhile before surrendering himself to a culture he wasn't sure was for him; but what choice did he have? His very survival depended upon it and he loved the idea of having children, regardless of the colour of their skin.

When they finally came upon the foot of the rock formation the women set about putting a camp together whilst some of the men took to a place where they knew an opening existed within the rock.

It didn't take long for the survivors to be introduced to the mouth of the cave and soon after several bark plates with a variety of colours were brought forth.

Ariaen and the others watched with great attentiveness as Woorin and Daku commenced to draw upon the wall of the cave entrance and what they drew shocked them to the very core.

These two men who had led them here were painting a picture, a piece of art, using charcoal and red ochre mixed with water along with other colours derived from plants that the women had gathered. It was a mural of sorts in dedication to these strange men from across the sea. They had been accepted by the Nanda and were now a part of their history. Right before them a sailing ship was being painted.

A tear welled in Ariaen's eyes and Willem asked him a question, "What are you crying for?"

"Because we have found our way, young Willem. We are now at peace with the land and with the people, never to return to Europe. We have a future here now. This is now our home."

Ariaen smiled at Woorin and Daku, they in turn smiled back, on this the happiest day of Ariaen's life.

Their history had now been recorded and they would never be forgotten. But this wasn't the end of their journey, for the corroboree was not very far away, and within time all of the survivors, all of them, were married in one of the most magnificent ceremonies the aboriginals had to offer.

PART TWO

Pride

AFGHAN
Camel Strings and the Australian Outback

CHAPTER ONE

Hergott Springs became known as Marree on 20th Dec, 1883, a town replacing the nearby settlement in name and commodity.

Its growth from its humble beginnings as a maintenance camp for the overland telegraph line could easily have been expected, and in particular for its growth in ethnic population; along with the nickname 'Little Asia'. Its populace of Afghan camel handlers was well known and could hardly be missed, raised from fledgling wings to portray a growing aspect of Australian society where sixty Afghan cameleers and their families maintained a thriving business... and sometimes it wasn't so thriving.

The cameleers would work for a quarter of what a white man would work, hence the white Australian falling cursed victim to the dark traders-of-the-desert, not to mention the fact that the white mans' bullocks and horses were no match for the single-humped camel, the dromedaries.

The cameleers weren't just from Afghanistan, even if collectively known as Afghans, but from a wide range of ethnic backgrounds; from Kashmir, Punjab, Baluchistan [Balochistan], Sind, Persia, Egypt and Turkey. Costs for cartage via camel were favourable to all. Camels ate the bush of the desert and needed little other supplement and could go so much longer without water when compared to a horse; and above all else, horses needed to be shod.

With the assent of the government to continue with the building of the railroad came an influx of activity to Marree; Marree was now an endowed part of the heritage towards the growing strides of a great nation and served well those settlements, homesteads and farmers, and whoever else might be in need of supplies and assistance, along the Birdsville, Strzelecki and Oodnadatta Tracks, not to mention the paths trodden hard by camel strings to other places upon the map such as Broken Hill, Alice Springs, Coolgardie and Innamincka. The entire area for hundreds of miles around was ruled by floods, prolonged droughts and sandstorms; all of which were certain upheavals for the settlers – the colonists who relied upon 'on-time' delivery of supplies and a method by which to get their merchandise to purchasers as quickly as possible.

There was a police station here which was manned by three men of uniform, a general store and a post office; somewhat of a formal arrangement in the process of being recognized as a dot on a map; but for the people that lived and worked out of this town in the middle of nowhere, it was a spectacle of judgement and life. One other aspect which concerns the people of any town, regardless of size, was the final resting place for those that had met with death, and it was the cemetery that showed likeness to prejudice and naivety, for it was split into three parts; Aboriginal, Afghan and white.

Marree was derived from an Aboriginal word meaning 'many possums', but how times change the face value of a place such as this, where possums may have once been in vast numbers: now in Marree, 1884, there exist over 1,500 camels and a mosque in which the cameleers could give praise during certain times of the day, a mosque surrounded by date palms and a system by which to draw from flowing water in order to carry out ablutions prior to prayer.

The bush, as was found around the town of Marree, was a hot place not to be reckoned with, an inhospitable place for many, if not most, with its seemingly natural infestation of flies and ants which were simply too numerous to count or waste time worrying about, pests of the world which doused every inch of land from here to Timbuktu, and in the scorching heat which was a replica of the days and weeks before, varying only slightly from one day to the next, anything from 40 to 52 degrees in the shade having to be put up with. It was the calling of the desert: hot by day and cold by night.

Christmas day was just concluded, not that there were any Christmas trees or decorations to be seen, and business for the inhabitants continued as always, where men, horses, camels and bullocks could be found in strings and pulling wagons of many sizes; and the telegraph line was planted, stretching its way north towards Darwin from Port Augusta, from August 1870 to July 1872.

CHAPTER TWO

Nak Kadir was 42 and looked long in the tooth, literally. His gums were well parted from the teeth and they neither glistened nor appeared to be looked after. Stained brown beyond belief, as with most cameleers, the mouth of teeth announcing their presence to the world, huge and almost bare to their roots. He wasn't smiling; his lips were seemingly held back from joining, as though an invisible barrier separated the upper lip from the lower, appearing more like a permanent grimace than anything else, scar tissue evident. He was set apart from all those that he knew, no other adorning the features which he displayed for the world to see, an uncontrollable fact about his character that he could have done well without.

He'd been standing at the gateway to Marree for some time, all morning in fact, awaiting the arrival of a particular person, a man of desperate measures that had left his home in the hills of Afghanistan to find his fortune in Australia, to ward off the countries sinful ways and to wrap himself around great reward and earning great praise from his family back home. Nak was awaiting the arrival of Abdul Hassan, a young man of just 23 years of age who had found himself with a wife and two children in this early stage of his life.

Nak surveyed the line up and down, a white turban upon his head needing a good clean, the robes that he wore more in tune to a robe that a rich man wore after dinner and prior to going to bed, clothing that was common but not altogether convenient in times when there was work to be done.

For the most part he didn't have a head for losing self-control, neither did he have a great amount of patience, and the time of day was starting to get the better of him. The train should have arrived some time ago and yet there was still nothing to be seen or heard. If the train was running late then surely a message would have been cast upon him via the telegraph line which hung over the town.

The Muslim men were quite exotic when compared to the Europeans, whether viewing them from Marree, further north, or further south. Anywhere upon the dry and barren surrounds of the very heart of Australia could be found an Afghan and a string of camels.

The Afghans were first brought into the country in vast number during the 1860s along with their camels; it was an introduction that was well suited to the desert terrain of the interior, much more so than the bullock or the horse, but this didn't detract from the fact that eighteen Afghans arrived in South Australia in 1838, a long and lengthy process then being suffered between the years before the trading of camels between nations really began.

Transportation between settlements and the like in the outback relied heavily upon the ability to deliver on time and with little sacrifice, considerations that could not be filled appropriately by the bullock or horse, let alone the men that served to drive them. The men of European cast were as unsuccessful as the animals which they worked and nowhere near as hardy and strong as the cameleers. The very determination within these exotic men was unbelievable and simply couldn't compare to anyone with white skin. Colonists were apt to fall jealous of those that served the settlements and interior, turbans wrapped around heads full of independence.

There existed little understanding of the Afghan in most places, in particular the settlements and homesteads so far from civilization. The further away you travelled from a major bustling city the more misunderstanding there was and quite often, more than not, they were feared for what so little was known about them.

Along the Birdsville Track, which lead to its namesake being changed from Diamantina Crossing to Birdsville, there were many small stations and homesteads such as Lake Harry Homestead, Mulka Homestead, Planet Downs, Alton Downs, and many others that spread far and wide, not to forget Pandie Pandie which was just over nine miles south of the Queensland border and nearer the destination of Nak and his crew than Birdsville itself. Birdsville was little more than a service centre for the pastoral properties that were sparsely fitted into the terrain like ore deposits spread across a barren landscape, but the Afghans were men all the same, more so than others, here in this country to serve the settlers, to carry on in business in order to make a living and in most cases to send money home to their families which were living hard lives. And the hatred for them grew in some places to the extreme where unnecessary actions were carried out upon them, simply because they were different. The Afghans were here to make their fortune, a fortune which eluded the vast majority for wages were trimmed in order to maintain a steady flow of employment; the colonists on the other hand, in particular those spreading their fledgling wings both far and wide, were in the race for pastoral land, a great land-grab in a harsh environment.

It was then that he heard it, saw the glimmer of hope reveal itself to him and the world. The train was inbound and the new man, Abdul Hassan, would be set upon his work without a shadow of a doubt. All men wishing to embark upon the lonely voyage to Australia in order to seek his fortune were considered a keen cameleer, and those that weren't would soon learn the ways of a camel handler as though born to it.

Nak then drew upon the common knowledge that he knew so well, that money in the pocket and work to be had was not always available... some more than the other and at other times hard to come by entirely.

Nak had received confirmation that a job was awaiting him and it was his great partner and friend, Shir Adji: 33 years old who was as ugly as a camel's backside - spoken politely, that was currently tending to the orchestrating of the supplies which they were to transport to a small homestead south of Birdsville.

Birdsville was a settlement of meagre worth, being fitted with three stores, a chemist, butchers shop, two hotels, a police station of almost dilapidated state and a blacksmith, the latter offering little to no advantage to cameleers for the camels didn't require shoes as did horses.

The small pastoral property south of Birdsville and Pandie Pandie also wished for their wool to be brought back to Marree and deposited upon the first available train to Port Augusta where the load would be picked up by a white man before continuing its journey on towards Adelaide: as for why they required such a vast range of extensive supplies for, as ordered, was bewildering: possibly expansion or simply to sell for a profit to others in the area: Nak was not there to question, but to make a profit himself via the delivery to them and then the delivery of wool to train.

Shir was a reliable man, as honest as the day was long, but far too desperate to find himself an Afghan wife, a matter which was to Nak's disappointment, for an arranged marriage was to unfold this night, the last night to be spent in Marree for quite some time, for the trek to Birdsville would commence on the morrow.

Nak needed Abdul as much as Shir in order to remain in good favour with those that he'd promised to provide assistance to, whether it be the arrival of supplies or the delivery of their wool and other merchandise to the railway terminal in Marree. One lost job could mean all the difference between survival and damnation, all the more prevalent with the threat of Faiz Mahomet hanging over his head, a forwarding agent and general carrier who employed many men and ran a profitable business from Marree. Faiz was a jemadar many years before, over five hundred men working beneath him on the Karachi wharves. He was well respected and seemingly favoured by Allah.

He pondered the life which was to befall Abdul as the train approached, thinking hard on what the young man had in store for himself, the dilapidated surrounds, the Ghantown that he had come to know and trust, where homes were built of the cheapest and most insufficient commodities that there was to offer and where corrugated iron roofs sheltered them from the rain during the onset of the rainy season. Even the mosque in which he attended was little different, but it's scanty look and appeal had no effect on the way in which they prayed, Muslims one and all.

The road beside the railway was busy, its hardened surface as good an indication as any to the traffic that travelled this way, countless hooves having contributed to the compacted ground, and the display of exuberance at present, from other men going about their daily business, did not distract Nak's frame of thought.

Nak looked at the railway track and then this road again, most briefly, as the train drew nearer, seeing another string of camels of Faiz Mahomet's entourage in business assets and interests going by, one cameleer to every ten camels, a little more than what Nak would like to undertake himself; it was normal practise for a single cameleer to handle up to eight camels and little more than that, but all depended, naturally enough, on the availability of good hands and the requirements for delivery.

There was much work in looking after a string of camels, much hard labour and foot slogging over beastly terrain, few luxuries and even fewer faces between post and settlement to ever be seen. It was a lonely life but one that was essential if Nak was to make a name for himself, to carve out a reasonably comfortable life for himself in his time of retirement from the endless days of tracking across the deserts along the same old land which he had traipsed before.

He brushed away more flies from his face, his skin dark brown and seemingly caked in dirt, though his skin was representative of many hours spent in the scorching Australian sun as it beat down without remorse.

CHAPTER THREE

As the train's brakes filled the air with their methodical screeching, the stresses of the joints, engine and moving parts screaming out to all around, heads could be seen looking out upon him from within the window frames, mostly men with hard faces, creases cut deep in their flesh indicating many hours of hard labour and for little reward.

The engine and a single carriage had passed him before the train slowed sufficiently, and then in the doorway of the last carriage he saw a man of lean build and relative height catching his eye, as each passed before the train came to a full stop.

The man was handsome and wore a turban upon his head, pantaloon trousers that were dark in colour and tucked into high boots, a white shirt with a few stains here and there, with the sleeves pulled down to the wrist. The smile upon the man's face would have been contagious and spread to Nak, if it hadn't been for the fact that Nak's grimace was a perpetual stain upon his character, neither wishing to be moved nor removable by force: many men had tried but so seldom was there a fight to attend that Nak couldn't remember the last time he'd been hit hard in the face; even here in Marree, where the main persons of the bush were segregated by colour and creed. Here in Marree they all lived in relative harmony, each and every one of them understanding his and her place that had been created from the sand and the vastness of space surrounding them: despite the fact that the cameleers had to put up with constant, ethnic abuses, for they swallowed their pride in more case than not.

The man stepped down from the carriage.

"Are you Abdul Hassan?" asked Nak.

"Yes," he answered with the smile still in place, "I'm Abdul."

"I'm Nak Kadir. Do you have many things with you?"

"No," answered Abdul, his smile dissipating slightly but still turned up at the corners. "I have nothing with me."

"Nothing at all?"

"No."

"Do you have a sleeping blanket?"

"No."

"Spare clothes?"

"No."

"An empty sack in which to carry things, perhaps?"

152

"I have nothing to carry," replied Abdul. "I'm burden free. I have nothing but the goodness within me. I'm a hard worker and ready to work for you as though you were my own father."

Nak put his hand out and they both shook in acknowledgement of the bond which was to develop between them.

"Come with me," said Nak. "I'll take you to see Shir Adji. He's been my friend for as long as I've been in Hergott."

Abdul thought he'd made a mistake for a moment, reflecting on what he'd learnt from the time he'd purchased a ticket at the office back in Port Augusta, and the short stopover at the stations between there and where he was now, in particular Farina which he remembered well. This place looked so... isolated.

"I see the flies are as friendly here as they are anywhere else," said Abdul, his smile replenished.

Nak looked at him as they walked, unsure whether or not the new man was being sarcastic of the place which was to become his home between jobs, or if he was sincerely unrelenting in his good manner which was part and parcel of who he was.

"You'll get used to them even if they drive you crazy."

"I've heard that work is good here," offered Abdul of an opportunity to provide further conversation.

"It's good so long as you work without rest, beat your rivals in competition, and don't mind working for little more than what is needed in order to survive."

"But better than Afghanistan," stated Abdul. "The office in which I subscribed said that both work and money was fruitful and ready for the picking."

"You have to know the ropes, Abdul, or you will be taken advantage of," answered Nak. "Don't worry; you're in good hands with me. We are a private enterprise and don't work for those that are keen to take our contracts of employment. You must stay with me, Abdul, and stay away from those willing to rip the shirt from your back. Stay away from men like Faiz Mahomet or you will soon drown in your own sorrows."

"I will, Nak. When is our first job?"

"We'll depart tomorrow morning for a homestead near Birdsville. Sometimes it's better to move by night, especially in this heat and during Ramadan, but we'll travel by day. There'll be plenty for you to see."

"So you are from Kandahar?"

"Yes," answered Abdul.

"Good," said Nak. "I am from Kabul and Shir is from Karachi.

"Did you leave Afghanistan before the British moved in, or after?"

"After," said Nak, his voice indicating a little unsteadiness. "I fought in action against the British for two years and came here to Australia just over four years ago."

"And now you serve them."

Nak stopped temporarily in his tracks, "I serve no one," said Nak, "except me and my ambition. I will not be a servant to the British but must seize my better judgement in order to live a free life in the years to come. Though we are all prisoners in some small way, Abdul. I have higher ambition than to serve the unworthy. It's not for us to be treated unkindly for the good work that we do, but we always go unrewarded, without recognition, and are looked upon as though we are peasants."

"I was a tribesman back home," said Abdul.

"A tribesman isn't a peasant and nor should he be treated as such. Almost everyone in Afghanistan is treated the same, but more, more than anywhere else that I have seen, position and money talk words stronger than justice."

"And what of your position here, Nak?"

"It used to be that I was forever looking over my shoulders, but I've now learnt to divide myself from my previous incursions upon the British."

"Australia is but part of the British Empire. It grows all around us," added Abdul. "There's no escaping it."

"No escaping it and no joining it. We are here to earn our own living. This country needs us for the services we can provide, for without such services it would shrivel and die. They think they use us but it is we who have learnt to use them; and we must improve upon that learning as best we can."

Abdul felt an inner urge then to remind Nak of something that he had divulged in a letter to the importers of camels and their handlers prior to travelling to Australia, "I served with General Robert's Camel Transport Corps. I was in the march of 1880 from Kabul to Kandahar."

"I know," was all Nak said. He had arranged for word on Abdul's arrival, or someone similar, to fall in favour with his needs, so that he could receive a good working hand – he had many friends in Port Augusta. Abdul had arrived with the shipment of 1884 when 259 camels and thirty-five camel handlers were brought into the country. Nak had always preferred to feel the satisfaction of doing as he needed to do. Recruiting Abdul was something he saw as fitting, avoiding the dregs that poured in and off of trains seeking employment. The demand for camel trade and services was high but work was hard to find, in particular now that more handlers were docked in Port Augusta and heading for Beltana.

"You served against the British and I served with them," Abdul continued.

"Why did you decide to answer my call for work?" asked Nak.

"It seemed the way to go; in particular where so many men and camels were bottle-necked into going no-place fast," answered Abdul, "and the man that grabbed my arm when I was lost and without work could talk fast and well. He persuaded me."

"Ah, yes... my old friend, Jehangir. He is a good man," and then Nak changed his tone. "Your escape from Afghanistan was no different than mine," said Nak. "We served those we needed to serve in order to find our place in life, but now... now we serve no one but ourselves. I sometimes regret my actions against my own when in Afghanistan but times were hard and I was pressed by my family's disposition, which I shan't talk about, to defend against the British and their incursions upon our country. But we must speak no more of this. War is a strange bedfellow. Besides anything else we are all Durranis and no different than Faiz Mahomet in a manner of speaking. Although he threatens our existence and job prospects we can still rely upon him if the need arises. You have no doubt heard that there is another in competition with him, Abdul Wade, a common and despicable Ghilzai. I'll spit upon his grave if I ever get the chance..." and Nak trailed off as he pondered the name of his new handler, for the Durranis were formerly known as the Abdulis.

"What of Shir?"

"He won't ask you of your dealings of war any more than he'll answer your questions about his dealings in it. For him the answer is as plain as the nose on your face."

"And that is?"

"That we have a new destiny and it is all the same to each of us, even though I am single, you are wed, and Shir is to be married."

"To be married?"

"Tonight," answered Nak, the grimace unchanging upon his face, the look in his eye reflecting the joy of the occasion, despite the bond between Shir and an Aboriginal being undesired.

"Is she an Afghan woman?"

"No," said Nak, "she is from here. She's an Aboriginal. A bride price has been paid and Shir will sleep little tonight. But tomorrow we must all be ready."

The concept of a bride price being paid was not formerly known by Aboriginals, but the failure in Afghan men to keep it disparate from their life in Australia had seen the Aboriginals take advantage. Afghan men had put into effect the idea of a 'bride price' being offered for their daughters very early on. No sooner had an Afghan man held in the power of his hand a daughter, whether she was from an Afghan woman or an Aboriginal, then he was requesting a bride price from any suitor able to pay: what goes around comes around.

"I assume that Shir is happy with the arrangements?"

"You will understand in time how lonely it gets here, so far away from home. You will be invited of course but currently we must provide you with the necessities of travelling with a camel string; getting you a blanket will do good to start for it can get very cold here by night, even in the hottest of summers; a good blanket is a comfort to sleep upon as well."

"Better than a woman," said Abdul as more of a statement than a question.

Nak laughed at the joke.

"Where are we going now?" asked Abdul.

"We'll go to where Shir is readying the supplies, counting and organising, confirming that we have enough camels ready for the task ahead."

"And if you don't have enough camels?" asked Abdul.

Nak turned to his new accomplice, "There are always enough camels in Hergott to purchase."

CHAPTER FOUR

They weren't long in the hot pre-noon sun when they fell upon the suspecting Shir, his hand held tight to a checklist of necessities, each item being scrutinized as it was being placed into a pile a little distance from the opened gates of the shed in which the stores were being acquisitioned. Not only were there stores for the homestead in which they were required to ferry but also the day to day costs of living, where bags, sacks and tins of flour, sugar, rice, vegetables, oatmeal, potatoes, tea, baking powder and many, many other requirements were painstakingly ticked off from his long list.

This was where the true semblance of Marree's exemplary service fit into the scheme of the culture of the times, a divine replica of society from Australian towns from all around, Afghan and white being treated no different than another, for the colour of their money was all the same, but nothing, not a single grain of rice, would be paid for in advance; everything would be paid for when the task was complete and Shir had returned with money bags jingling and purses padded to high heaven in notes worthy of praise, or with a banknote glued to his hand.

"Ah, so this must be Abdul," said Shir as he prepared to shake hands with the new handler by shifting the tools of his current task into his left hand, much activity being conducted around them, men ferrying supplies here and there, conducting business as was the everyday occurrence.

"Yes," said Abdul with a smile, a most familiar look falling upon his eye indicating his train of thought, as all others had done when first meeting Shir, that yes, yes indeed, Shir was as ugly as sin and Abdul would be hard pressed to find someone as ugly; but he was a good man. "I'm pleased to find my way here into the company of two fine men."

"The work is hard," said Shir, "but we find it rewarding, as I'm sure you know already."

Abdul was unsure what to say in return for he had already been warned that talk of war was a 'strange bedfellow' and the last thing he wished to do was to commence his acceptance into their ranks with barbs of tension which might quite easily damage their friendship to come.

"My time as a cameleer was as varied as was the degree of tasks set upon, but from what I have seen of Australia I am sure to be in for an education."

"Desert here, desert there;" said Shir, "It's much the same wherever you go, only the camels change... as do the handlers," and looked to Nak.

"Shir is referring to the colonists," said Nak in a voice quietened by circumstance and knowing, even if he was speaking a different language and largely ignored by the white folk standing around. "They are stupid, one and all. There isn't a single man amongst the Europeans that can do nearly as good a job as us. We might live in the same town... separated as we are, maybe, but nevertheless, we command over the very essence of all which is to do with being a cameleer... and a good one at that."

Nak looked around and saw that Shir had attended to his responsibility with great affection as usual, "You've nearly finished, Shir."

"I wanted to get the job completed before this afternoon," answered Shir. "I have a wedding to attend to, or did you forget?"

"How can I forget," replied Nak as he looked to Abdul and back again. "You've been reminding me every day for the past month." Nak looked again to Abdul. "Even in the middle of the desert, somewhere between here and Oodnadatta, all he can talk about is his wedding. I tell you this much, Shir; if I so much as hear a single whisper about your wedding after tonight I shall personally see to it that you sleep upon a nest of hornets, each and every night that we are gone from Marree."

"She will be sad to hear you say that," said Shir.

"Only if I say it in broken English," smiled Nak, referring to the point of fact that as an Aboriginal wife she understood nothing of Shir's language and extremely little of his place of birth.

"Nevertheless," defended Shir, "I shall promise right here and now that you'll hear nothing of my complaints nor bickering once we depart on the morrow: I promise."

"Don't make promises, Shir," said Nak. "You break your promises more often than you break wind."

Abdul burst out into a bout of laughter which caught many stares from all of those around, white, dark, black and brown, no matter what the colour of their skin they were all distracted by the laughter.

Abdul quickly took a grip of himself, "I'm sorry."

"Nothing to be sorry about," said Nak and looking at Abdul he added: "It's the beans that make him do it," and again Abdul burst out into laughter as his hands grabbed hold on his stomach to hold back the tearing pain of the joke.

"Come," said Shir, "help me finish with this lot, just a few minutes work remains and we can be off to prepare for tonight's sweet entertainment—."

"And the reception," cut in Nak.

"Ah, Nak," said Shir as he waved his finger in Nak's face. "You are tempting the good of our religion and faith by making such a remark. I would expect so much from a European, but not you, my friend."

"To have said nothing, would have been to allow a good opportunity to pass me by; besides, I am your friend."

"Come!" shouted Shir as he slapped Nak upon the shoulder, "you and Abdul help me finish and we can go home, to familiarize ourselves with one another prior to the wedding."

"Thank you, Shir," said Abdul.

"It's my pleasure," returned Shir with a slight bow.

CHAPTER FIVE

The custom in Afghanistan was for a bride price to be paid to the family of the daughter who was to be wed, a custom that dated back to times that all had forgotten. A father could stand proud in knowing that he had received a good payment for his daughter, the most beautiful receiving the largest payment – which goes beyond saying. To a man the spoils of marriage were just that and where permission could be sought from a wife, and money allowed for the upkeep of more than one, a man could have as many wives as he could muster; there was no such thing as greed and nor was there any accusation of a man being cruel by doing so. It was quite normal for an old man in his fifties or sixties, let alone older than that, to pay for the affections of a young girl, a fourteen to eighteen year old girl of little experience in life being married off to an old man with a dirty mind full of lust, relishing the thoughts of grappling with such young flesh, running his rough and aged fingers up the inside leg of a girl that had barely reached puberty. So seldom did a young girl suffering in such a way let it be known; they simply suffered in silence.

Marriages were arranged between families for reasons of stability, money, position and greed: causes of manipulation to favour the father of the girl, to increase the effects of his life even if just slightly, a family's position amidst their society being increased marginally or more.

As it happened the circumstances in Australia were not much different. There was little 'bride price' administered in the earlier days when the Afghan's first arrived in Australia, but as men had daughters and these were bid for by other Afghan men, so the custom came into its effect and stabilised itself as the custom it always was.

Men were always on the lookout for women with stable figures, being slightly plump but not overly fat and it was this reflection of eagerness in the eyes of an Afghan which originally dissuaded Aboriginal women to accept the hand of a cameleer, even though they had little choice in the matter, for it was all up to the parent of the girl to either accept or decline any reasonable offer. Aboriginal women saw the look given by Afghan men towards those with the plumpest of figures, this being their prerequisite; as well as a proof behind what many had been told in open talk between family members: that Afghans ate human flesh and enjoyed it.

The Afghans themselves didn't know this and their only concern was for their status in life to be seen, if not heard, and a thin woman was a mark of poverty which lead to disrespect and sour looks; it was simply a sign of low status and a common handler of camels was lowly enough, unless such position was that of a jemadar, looking over and caring for many men and camels.

It was only with the life suffered together in the small town of Marree that an understanding between Aboriginal women and Afghan men commenced to grow, for both were as lonely as the other and Aboriginal life was breaking down as European ideas spread across the country both far and wide. There was little use of the word 'clan' and belief in tribal ways was decaying by the day. This was a time when Aboriginal women and Afghan men saw eye to eye and understood with a clearer picture the customs and way of life that the other maintained or held in the past. The white Australians treated both much the same and it was in this that both races fell into stride and developed a meagre interest in one-another.

It was quite unlawful at the time for a couple to live together in sin; marriage was the requirement, but where such a ceremony could not be afforded, for one reason or another, a relationship could be maintained in secret and with little knowledge of such liaison taking place; but this was not without its risks.

Women were not permitted to pray in the mosque of Marree and no other place was established for their divine right as the sexes were not permitted to pray together. Separate quarters were required and to this note the men were afforded closer spiritual comfort than the women. Inside the mosque there was a permanent feature which was present in all buildings of a similar nature, where location and materials allowed, and where not, a temporary replica or representation was placed: this was none other than the mirab which faced towards Mecca, and the Koran was laid to rest here until read, wrapped and resting upon a stool. By general standards the Koran was treated as a National flag for it wasn't permitted to be placed to rest beneath any other book. Shir's wedding was therefore undertaken with special customs taking place.

In order to pay homage to the general law of the country which most had accepted as their second home, or their primary, two marriage ceremonies were the act of all communions into this sacred ritual of devotion and harmony, even though most were wed out of sheer loneliness or forced into the relationship by a pressing father.

The order of the day was to have the marriage recognised by law and in this both Shir and his wife, Arika, had attended to register their joining just yesterday. It was now time to formally recognise their joining in accordance with Afghan law by undertaking the Islamic ceremony.

CHAPTER SIX

Shir considered his wife and hoped she wasn't afraid. Her name in Aboriginal meant 'waterlily' and to him that was exactly what she was; his waterlily.

They were in separate rooms and prayers filled the air in Arabic, the ceremony led by the mullah of Marree, seeing to it that all custom was performed as required. Shir was dressed in nothing of particular flavour, ambition or excessiveness, nor was his wife; but he had a shalwar on – trousers that were wide at the top and narrow at the bottom, similar to pantaloons in appearance – and a turban of ivory-white, and Arika wore a dress of white with a veil, a cheap but acceptable offering to the ceremony.

Arika was comforted in her ordeal for she was lucky to have feelings for Shir as Shir had for her. Although she couldn't bestow unconditional love upon the man who was about to become her husband, she was able to commit herself to show that she felt the goodness of marriage fill her, the joy of heavenly bondage grip her loneliness and fill her with the joy of the occasion, she also had little choice but to accept Shir's religion and fulfil her daily life with the lifestyle and code of practise that every good Muslim followed. For anyone marrying an Afghan man the religion was not a by-product but a condition which simply had to be met and abided by, for there was no room, nor tolerance, for another religion.

The language, on the other hand, was something she would be fighting all her life but the words she shared with her husband would continue to be that of broken English, each knowing sufficient English to get them through the days.

There was also a huge feast to be attended, a celebration after the wedding to complete their transition from singles to a pair; she looked forward to that, to be showered with blessings and good fortune.

The dalak of Marree approached with a smile upon his face as though a line of boys had been prepared and made ready for their circumcision, each young man standing before him as eager as the other; but this was a wedding.

The dalak passed on his wishes with a bow and bestowed upon Shir a small amount of money which was his gift to him. The dalak was Zareen and he was a lowly man; not only was he the circumciser of boys but he was also the haircutter of the Ghantown. No one wished their daughter to be married to such a low caste man. The haircutter was in fact so lowly that there were only two others of less standing, and that was a thong and sieve maker, and a dancer.

"My best wishes to you and your new wife," said Zareen. "May Allah bestow upon you many favours."

"Thank you, Zareen," answered Shir, and although not having invited the man to the wedding ceremony as a main guest, he had insisted on his company for what the future might bring in the form of children and the fact that Zareen was a remarkable musician who played the flute well. It was uncanny how the feelings of despair and regret then hit Shir, for he felt that he had wronged the man that no one wished to seek when looking for a husband to take the hand of their daughter. Men looked for good payment for their daughters and lowly men had little, but Zareen... he had offered money to Shir, money which was scarce, and so Shir looked upon him differently that day.

Nak approached from the side as Zareen walked off with a smile, a facial expression that wouldn't be moved with a hundred lashes of a barbed wire stick. He stood beside him and his new wife and turned to look over the small gathering, tables full of food behind them, women in their veils and men in their turbans, all awaiting a continuance of the feast by pressing upon the tables and filling their plates.

"It is with great honour that I now ask you to make yourselves welcome here today by helping yourselves to this wonderful arrangement of refreshment," said Nak. "Shir thanks all of you for bringing what you have so that others may share in your wonderful presentations."

And without further ado the people moved slowly but surely with plates in hand to help themselves to all manner of food and drink, not a drop of alcohol in the house or an unkind word spoken on this day of great celebration.

Shir couldn't be happier as he looked upon his new bride, the Aboriginal woman who was remarkably beautiful for the life she had led. Living off the land in the desert, along the forages when creeks, rivers and streams flowed without restriction, under the scorching sun that beat down without remorse or the rain which beat down during the rainy season; none of its bleakness seemed to have been inherited by Arika, not a harsh days living showing upon her face. Most of all things that made Shir happy were the fact that she was also a plump little girl of just sixteen years of age, less than half his age; this alone was enough to make him very thankful and excited.

Arika was pleasantly comfortable in the surroundings of her new life and having spent a majority of it in Marree she was accustomed to the men and women of the Ghantown. Fear was present within her but at the moment it was at low tide and wouldn't surface until it was time to bring satisfaction to her husband. He hadn't pressed her for sexual favours during the time they had known one another and this she respected very much. The fact that Shir didn't force himself upon her offered feelings of security in thought that her father had made the right choice for her, and although Shir was an ugly man on the outside, he was a good man on the inside.

And this was the thought that remained with her when it was time to leave the feast room and all of those within it; the crowd dispersing after the ceremony had commenced to draw to a close. Shir's hand clenched hers for what was to come in this, their first night together.

Nak stood before the two with Abdul just to the rear of him, Abdul simply bowing with a smile, which was quickly returned.

"We're going to go now," said Nak. "I wish you both the very best, although your time together will be short, for tomorrow we depart and won't return for four weeks."

"Don't remind us," said Shir as he briefly looked upon his bride as she sat in silence to allow the men to speak. "Oh, I have several letters which I must give you, letters for the homestead when we arrive."

"Shir," said Nak with a lecture upon his voice. "You should not be thinking of work at this moment in time. I'll get the letters from you tomorrow when we load the camels."

"Very good," said Shir, and seemingly a little nervous opened his mouth to say something more. "What will you be doing tonight?"

"Nothing that should be concerning you, dear friend," answered Nak and departed without a further word.

Arika looked into her husband's eyes and spoke in English, her Afghan not ready to be attempted at such a time as this, "All nearly go home. We go too, soon. Is time for us."

"You are scared?"

"No," said Arika and then added something that she knew would excite her new husband, "wait no longer, look for good night with husband."

CHAPTER SEVEN

Nak was now compelled, more than ever before in his entire life, to seek the comfort of one that he'd kept secret from the others, thoughts of Shir and his new wife getting the better of him.

He knew of a prostitute not too far away, she was a Japanese woman of average looks who often slept with Nak as he wasn't afraid to pay a little extra. He was a single man and the temptations of the soul were simply too much to bear, even for him. He deserved, as anyone else, to feel the gratifying warmth of female flesh upon the palm of his hands, to be stroked and fondled as his desires screamed out in mounting frustration.

Why was it so easy to give in to the lures which manifested from within his manhood? It wasn't for Nak to answer, but simply to see the urge satisfied, the frustration quenched, for it was going to be a long time before he'd have the opportunity again.

She lived in a part of the Ghantown which was away from the remainder for she was considered unclean by many and never given the opportunity to make friends with those of respectable disposition, but what might be respectable in Marree was considered a dilapidated eyesore to those of the big city, and so she remained aloof of the Afghan Ghantown, the services she provided only tolerated in order to restrain the single man's anxieties.

Her real name was unknown by the community at large but not to the men that pressed visit upon her. She was known as Saki to most men but given pet names by some, and although she was shunned and kept at bay, neither recognized or provided the comforts of a community at large, she led a reasonably pleasant life, even though lonely for the most part. Her life was full of unpleasantness but criticism was largely ignored; those that paid and displayed the most discourtesy upon her were those that were new to the Ghantown.

Nak thought heavily upon the ambitions of Saki and understood, quite clearly, how misfortune played its part within the scheme of her chosen profession. She'd been married off to a much elderly man, a Chinese businessman whose interests in her quickly collapsed just weeks before his death, for he also had strong feelings for his cook. He had been a rough and bad man, kind to those that knew him best, but always slapping and punching his wife behind closed doors. For her there was nothing left in life but to make the best of what it had to offer, and to sleep with men for a wage was better than sleeping with an old man for little more than eyeful of fist. Left alone in a world she didn't understand, and without any real prospect of finding a husband, anyone to look after her, or a decent job to be made advantage of, she'd left Adelaide behind her to escape the racketeers.

Stuck in the outback with no money, except a few coins that might have been otherwise owed to the unscrupulous wielders of bad fortune, she soon found herself serving men the only way she knew how. And Nak thought about the opportunities that might be offered to him in the future, where a wife could be sourced from the Ghantown at any time in the years to come; but where would such a wife come from, in particular when considering his grimacing facial expression. Saki had more to offer Nak than even she knew.

Money; that's what was needed, and he'd quickly set himself up an account where savings could be hoarded away from prying eyes, for a future that would see him be the same as others he knew; a married man with children. Saki had come to mind; she always came to mind.

Unfortunately, it was entirely impossible for any of the Asian women to be married to an Afghan; it was simply unheard of. All Asian women refused to look upon the Afghan men as a possible husband-to-be, and as for most prostitutes of the time, Saki maintained little decorum and she disgusted all of those trying to better their lives, all around trying to live in harmony with everyone else, a life lead by religion and without fault, the characteristics of a well-manicured town being the esteemed ambition of most in a society fighting off prejudice by living together in such a confined space.

Prejudice was always present but in the outback towns it seemed to be tolerated more than elsewhere, for everyone's existence did depend upon cooperation, and cooperation was something Saki lived without.

Nak finally fell upon the out-of-the-way shack, a dry creek bed of little worth just behind and in good location to carry away great masses of water, and very quickly, at times that the weather turned bad – or fruitful depending on your frame of thought. There were a few date palms growing nearby that seemed to be thriving and the window shutters of the small building were closed with a single item of clothing hanging from a clothesline, a flag of familiarity which meant that Saki was home and ready to please.

Nak approached the shack and as he passed the clothesline he pulled the worn shirt from its position and placed it upon a barrel next to the front door. He knocked twice and waited: he didn't wait long.

Saki opened the door and smiled as the light of the moon cast itself upon her face, the shadow of the door moving across her, folds of her body disrupting the lay of the shadow upon her form, the outline of her breasts seen for what they were and her hips and slight plumpness coming to view.

She was a delight to look at, more beautiful to Nak than anyone else he'd ever laid eyes upon – which was easy to interpret from the point of view that very few women looked upon Nak with any respect or interest.

Respect: two issues; a single action. The action was sexual but the issues were of separate embodiments. Saki was looking for coins to pass her palm and Nak was after a night of lust.

"Good night," said Nak with a smile in the best English he could muster, for Saki knew less of Nak's language than she knew of the women who lived a little way down the dirt track and towards the main hub of life and activity in Marree.

"Yes," said Saki in reply. "Please, enter," and she opened the door and stood aside so that Nak could continue his night of excitement, entering the shack which was lit by a single lantern, several silks hanging from the walls, a rug of thick wool and a bed pushed aside in the corner, large and comfortable, Saki's place of work and confinement; there was little else in the shack other than a bench top and several wash basins – she did her cooking out of doors beneath an adjoining shelter.

"I go work, long time," said Nak.

Saki simply smiled at the information, the grimace upon Nak's face quite hideous, but Saki was used to such ugliness in her business and ignored what she saw with great compassion, great skill, and with much ease.

She moved over to where he stood, near the edge of the bed that he had come to play upon.

"I stay long time," said Nak as he pulled the colour of money from his pocket. Saki continued to smile and moved her hands skilfully over his body, feeling every slender curve offered by Nak's thin build.

Nak then returned the gestures of a formality he had come to know and enjoy, lifting his right hand to her breast and placing his left in behind the small of her back. He tenderly kissed her with much effort, the pain upon his lips evident with the strain. Saki took control then and did the kissing for them, rolling her lips and tongue over the coarse tissue of Nak's mouth and then removed herself from his mild embrace, taking several steps back from him. She pulled lightly upon the restraints of her thin gown and let it slip from her body, her nipples coming to full view and Nak's manhood became fully aware of its function in this ritual of his.

The stresses of his life were about to be lifted, he would soon be able to concentrate more healthily on the task before him, and without further ado they stepped towards one another and embraced.

CHAPTER EIGHT

The following morning was presented the usual ceremony of prayer and singing from the Muslims in the Ghantown as was customary and expected, the sounds of the mystic verses reaching the far voids of what was known as Marree and a town on the edge of civilization, though one would be hard-pressed to say it was on the edge of despair.

Shir had said good farewell to his plump wife by having his way with her for the fifth time in a single night and had seen to it that Abdul was provided good companionship by meeting him at his shack of residence, a single room building of corrugated iron that had been offered to him for the comfort of rest, shared with five others – the family of Goulam Bauz who was currently on a job to Oodnadatta.

"Good morning to you, Abdul," greeted Shir as he advanced on the new companion as he stood in front of the shack with a small bag of essentials in his hand, "for a good morning it is. I hope your night was comfortable."

"It was," answered Abdul. "Thank you for finding such good company for me. The home of Bauz was most obliging and friendly."

"As all are, here in Marree," said Shir as he closed the gap and Abdul fell in beside him for the walk to where the camels would be waiting. "You would be too put out to be asked to find anyone of sour nature. The community here would be no different than what you were used to back in your village in Afghanistan."

"I would say, in all matter of fact, that the company was better," said Abdul with a smile, falling into stride with his new friend as they walked towards several corrals, lines placed between posts where camels were tied and waited for their turn to be loaded and placed within a string.

Nak could be seen beside the enclosure as he waved to gain their attention and before they knew it they were together once more.

"You look refreshed," said Nak of Shir.

"Refreshed and tired," he answered. "You too, look... happy."

"I sought the company of an old friend last night," replied Nak, and although he never mentioned Saki by name, most of those that knew Nak the best understood his relationship with the prostitute that 'lived-down-the-road'.

"Then we are all in good fortune," added Abdul, unaware of Nak and his night of lust, "for I too had good company in the form of a small family."

"Yes," acknowledged Nak. "We have shared many favours, us two and Goulam. It would be hard to find a better man than he."

Abdul looked over towards the camels attached to the line between posts and asked, "Are those our camels?"

"Yes," answered Nak. "I tied them up early this morning so that they would be more easily and quickly taken to where the stores will be laid."

Abdul nodded, seeing for himself that many other camels stood unrestrained in the corral, awaiting their masters and a hard day's work.

Shir then handed Nak, the jemadar, two letters for the homestead in which they were to lay visit with supplies. It would be the last letters delivered by hand as a mail service had just been put into effect and commenced by Jack Hester, a service that would only grow as the demand for news and information flowed thick and strong between settlements and towns in the outback; the cameleers could only hope that the need for strong resilience in the form of camel strings didn't go the same way and fall to the whims of game-changers, bullocks or horses.

"I was handed this by the Postmaster late yesterday," said Shir.

Abdul was impressed and said, "It's good that word spreads and that people know one another here."

"The Europeans... or colonists: they are all the same... they have their differences of opinion and there is some division between us all," said Shir, "but they see fit to ensure that service is provided to those that reside in the settlements around, no matter how small or large. But believe me, if it was to a settlement owned by Muslims, there would be a different sense of urgency upon the Postmaster's willingness to provide assistance."

"But we will deliver the letters, regardless," added Nak. "Who knows, it could be for an order of more wool than we are expected to pick up, hence a larger reward in terms of wage when the task is complete."

"You never know," said Shir. He looked to Abdul, "There is always that, as Nak has advised. But let's talk on this more at a later time; we have camels to move and supplies to attend."

"Good," said Abdul. "I shan't forget this day; my first real work in this country."

"And it won't be your last," said Shir, "for there will be work where we continue to provide a great service, and we must work harder than anyone else in order to retain good customer satisfaction."

"When we do well for a settlement or homestead, we always receive further work," finished Nak, proud of his accomplishments as drawn from his stance as he pulled back his shoulders and shifted his head.

Abdul was rather proud to have a job, and with good people to accompany him on the long treks across Australia.

CHAPTER NINE

Abdul was in Australia, as all before him, on a three year contract, but where records fail the administration the imported will take advantage, and the news was soon provided to him, that he would end up staying till his heart was content or the hunger to return to Afghanistan got the better of him.

Abdul could only ponder the future which was yet to be cast for him, at this very minute in time, although inexperienced as he was with familiarity in regards to Australia, he considered one thing and one thing only. The comparison between the two countries, the hardships dealt to him day after day; all of it seemed to be one and the same. So what was it for him to hunger for Afghanistan?

He was a free man with no ties apart from the fact that he was married with two children, but others had abandoned their responsibility, so why not he? He wouldn't be the first to remain in Australia with family in Afghanistan. It was then that the pain of the thought hit his heart like a stab in the gut by a recently sharpened knife, long and broad, a cutting edge of teeth set to tear him apart from the inside out. He couldn't abandon his family, would never leave them to their own vices. If life in Australia could not afford him the option of importing his family so that they could stand by his side in this new life, no matter how long that life may be, then he would go back to them, dead or alive, on two feet or wrapped up in a blanket or cloth. Whatever the cost, Abdul considered his only alternative; to work his finger's to the bone and never complain, nor shirk a job. There was very little to him that meant more than his family. In some ways he felt as though he had deserted them but in reality he was doing what he knew was in the best interest for them all. The cards had been dealt him and now he needed to play the game.

The camel string was relatively easy to get moving, tying each by a long rope, neck to neck, an informality which wasn't the normal condition for handling camels prior to loading with stores and connecting nose pegs, but Nak was anxious to on the way, for it was a four week return trip to the homestead and back, taking the drastically close to the onset of a possible downpour of the likes none of them wished to experience more than they had to. Rain could be as treacherous as a sandstorm and the one thing Nak wished to avoid was any unnecessary delay, for the current consignment of wool from the homestead was required in Marree with such time restraints that the threesome would barely have time enough to scratch themselves more than once a day.

The initial process, as for the most part of what was to be carried out on the caravan, was nothing superiorly different or more difficult than what Abdul had known or experienced in the past, but routine played a big part in the process of preparing a string for the road as much as setting the camels down for the night after a long day's work.

CHAPTER TEN

The camels were tied in order of advance, from lead camel to the kitchen, the order of march in which the camels would find themselves once commenced upon their journey towards Birdsville, an order that they all knew and had come to be comfortable with. One of the camels came under the scrutiny of Abdul.

"You have a pregnant camel," he voiced.

"Yes," said Nak, none too concerned over the situation. "She'll give birth in a few days."

"It's not my place, but wouldn't she be better left behind?" asked Abdul.

"The camels are used to hard work, whether pregnant or not," answered Nak. "Besides, we can't afford to leave her behind and secondly the remainder of the string would miss her. Every camel here has its place. It's too upsetting to have one missing from its place in the line."

Little further was spoken other than a few words of affection and urging from the cameleers to their camels, Abdul commencing his introduction to the many names that flowed from Nak's and Shir's mouths. Each and every camel had a name and each was known at a glance. They were different sizes and of course, different colours. Dull greyish brown or yellowish brown where the hair grew the longest, and at shoulders and hump the colour changed in most concerns to brown. The hair at the mane also grew brown but the main coat was a slate grey, shades of black, chocolate, cream, and several of those in the caravan were white, a rare colour indeed. All had their characteristics, each was known for its abilities, likes and dislikes; they were family to both Shir and Nak.

Abdul was wondering about the situation with the saddles for the camels when the supplies came into view. He saw two Aboriginal boys hard at work setting saddles down into three lines, the centre line of saddles facing the opposite way to the other two. They were tidying up their task when the camels were led in and the string cut into three parts.

The twenty-four camels were now eight to a line and lead into position under guidance by the cameleers into their 'line of advance', the front and rear-most rank facing one direction and the centre most facing the opposite, Abdul following Nak's advice and the urging of one of the Aboriginal boys, whose teeth sparkled white through the darkened lips upon his face. The camels were soon positioned, each placed in front of the pack saddle which rested in place upon the dry ground.

"What are their names?" asked Abdul.

"That one there, closest to you; he's Amaroo," said Nak and as the name was mentioned he looked over and smiled briefly, "the other is Girra: it's the name given to a creek or a tree, but I don't know which."

"Amaroo is 'a beautiful place', a strange name for a boy," added Shir.

"They work hard and for very little," said Nak. "It's to their abilities that they serve us well by remembering how to lay the saddles down, each camel knowing his by smell."

"I've never seen a camel accept another's in good stead," said Shir as he commanded the camels under his control to sit, each lined up with his saddle. "Just there... that's it, Abdul." Some of the camels proceeded to sit without a word. "Some know their place well; it's only the lazy ones that need a whisper in the ear or a hit with a stick."

"A sting in the leg brings back memory rather fast," said Nak as his camels sat in place.

Abdul looked down the line to the eight under his control.

"Mine must be lazy, there are still six standing," observed Abdul.

"No, Abdul," said Shir. "They're testing you; that's all. Show them who's boss and they'll quickly learn."

With all twenty-four camels sitting in position the saddles were placed upon them with expert hands, the cameleers working marvellously fast, faster than any white man could do. One man stands to either side of a camel and quite purposely ensures that the pack saddle is secure before placing the load simultaneously, it being balanced upon the pack saddle with remarkable expertise.

Saddles were built with different interests in mind; firstly the packing of supplies upon a camel's back, and secondly, the comfort of the rider should a seat upon the animal be preferred to walking: or weight restraints permitted a rider to mount alongside the supplies.

A riding saddle was a simple creation of two forks, one in front and one behind the camels' hump. These were connected by a horizontal bar with an extension to the rear, the rider sitting upon a leather-covered seat with feet in stirrups. It was to many colonists' surprise to see that few Afghans allowed themselves the comfort of such a price position of being so high from the ground, most preferring to take their positions beside their strings where the control was more easily displaced and each was ready to react to any emergency that might unfold in their day's journey; and leather pouches and bags could easily be attached or simply flung over the camel's back.

Removing the pack saddles by night was one of many of the cameleers' duties, and painstakingly checking each individual camel was something that simply had to be performed before and after a day's labour. The loss of a single camel would have been too much to bear in regards to the cost in replacing it and the ability to continue with the load they had in transit – even though it was quite easy to shift the loads around between camels – was simply another task that required time, and time was more important to them than their own stomachs which would tremble with hunger during the long hours of daylight.

Pack saddles might need to be relined with jute, strong fibre from wool bales or wheat sacks, and in this, Nak preferred straw. It didn't occur too often but on occasion an un-muzzled camel of poor temperamental disposition might try drawing the stuffing on the saddle or stores before him, snatching what he could from the camel in line, not to mention bite at the rear-end of the camel in the string to his front. Where possible, Nak preferred to keep his animals free from bondage but always carried several muzzles for such an emergency.

The straw of the saddles was placed in through small slits and forced home by a wooden driver and mallet. With time the straw would turn to chaff due to movement and need to be replaced, a never-ending cycle of replenishment due to the creation of a bulge which created sores upon the camels' back. And here came the question of doubt which lingered on many minds; the option of travelling by night. Night offered a cooler trip and freed the cameleers of their duty to perform their prayers, but travelling by day was better in the long run as a good meal could be taken in by the Afghans at last light, in particular during times of fasting, and the camels allowed to feed once placed on short hobbles.

Saddle sores were to be avoided at all costs; the last thing needed was for a camel to become infested with a back sore that turned septic by becoming a fly-blown lesion that caused death. But their feet were also checked on a daily basis, ensuring that each was free from cuts and abrasions.

Yes indeed, Shir and Nak loved their camels as though they were family.

The loading of the camels came next, an arduous task to say the least. Much attention to detail was placed upon the loading, not only for the benefit of the camels but also the work to be endured during the last part of the day when the load was to be removed from the camels for the night.

Thongs and cordage were tied in such a way that they could be more easily removed in such quick fashion that the time was taken each morning to ensure that supplies were secured correctly.

The men's knees did most of the lifting but backs too were strained where straining should be avoided.

Loading was carried out prior to nose pegs being attached so that the animals could be more easily attended to with their loads starting from behind them and simply picked up, carried forward, and then tied into position. Nose pegs were then placed on.

The ability for a camel to be subjected to a bit in the mouth was non-existent and in respect to this the only other real alternative was for a nose peg of hardwood to be inserted. The sensitivity of the camels at the nose was such that a rude awakening would be jolted through each, via the use of the nose peg, when acting disruptively. Nose pegs permitted much easier control over the animal in strings than without and to pursue control by any other means was simply out of the question.

The nose peg was more cone-shaped than not and never made of heat-conducting metal, and was attached to a length of cordage long enough to be connected to the tail of the camel to its front with a sag between in order to reduce the strains upon the cordage during movement... such was life when a frightened camel jerked its head around, breaking the connection of the nose peg; but cameleers always sought to offer a reasonably pain-free existence, even if it meant that extra work was to be suffered, for they were seen on the odd occasion putting slow chase to a concerned camel with broken line prior to placing it back in file with the others of the string.

Of all the days before them this was the most time-consuming, for loading in the days to come would see to it that the camels would be in a more favourable position, one man required to stand either side of a camel with the load to be deposited upon the camel's back and secured into position with leather thongs and cordage.

The men worked their way down the three lines, fondling the camels affectionately as they preceded, Nak kissing the camels delicately, showing that he cared for them more than he cared for anyone else in the world... and then Saki came into mind, his exploits from the night before where he felt as though he were in heaven.

The last camel in line, which followed the other of his species so well, with little interest in mind, was the kitchen camel. He was much like the others, to simply step along in line, little to look forward to but the dreary hours of looking at nothing but the rear-end of the camel to his front.

The kitchen camel was so named as it was the camel with the mobile kitchen with gallons of water carried for 'specific needs'. It was upon the saddle, upon the hide, that this creature heard the consistent banging and clanging of any loose equipment, for his duty was to carry all manner of pot and pans, utensils for cooking and eating, food, camp oven and several tarpaulins which could quite easily be erected to hold back a miserable night of strong wind or heavy rain. But some fortune does shine down upon the seemingly least favoured for his load would diminish in weight whereas the others would have to continue each day with the knowledge that what was endured one day would be endured the next, and also that for no particular reason, he was the last to be loaded.

The three men attended their camels as expertly, if not more-so, than a soldier practising his drill movements on a drill square before heading off to war.

Abdul looked the lead camel in the face, the camel familiar with Nak more than he, for Nak was the jemadar and the camel knew it. His hare lip seemed more prominent than any of the others in the string, and Abdul grinned at a thought that crossed his mind. It was the story of Muhammad and how he kissed a camel upon the lips for escorting him through an enemy camp unheard; the upper lip parted, and a gift was bestowed upon it and all his descendants: from this day forth all camels would not only have hare lips but would move silently wherever it should wonder.

In a little under forty minutes the camels were all ready to go, loaded with all the requirements of the caravan and the needs of the homestead. Only one other addition was required and this was the weapon that Nak carried with him.

Nak looked up and down the rifle that he cradled in his hands. Al Halal meat was a part of everyday life here in Marree, for the Afghans and their religion, and for those that provided it. Although such meat was to be properly prepared for killing it wasn't unheard of for cameleers to carry out the preparations themselves when far from home and without a source of meat in which to sustain them during the long and hard hours of travelling to and from settlements. The hardest part of the transition from beast of burden to jerked meat was the actual jerking itself, for it was time consuming and took from the cameleer's valuable hours, a very good reason for a good supply of meat to be carried in the first place.

In most cases, in particular the smaller Ghantowns, it was the task of the butcher – who was also the mullah – to see to it that all animals were killed al Halal; all was carried out to the strict guidelines of the Koran. All meat was thus purified by the swift movement of a knife across the jugular whilst fully conscious and the mullah faced towards Mecca.

Animals killed in this way were left to bleed, the blood draining from the body and carrying with it any germs that might otherwise create any amount of intimidation and putrefy. With one's state of mind put at ease came the answer to a hungry belly.

The long strips of salted meat that Nak had made available to the three of them, meat of a goat which had been awaiting slaughter and drying, would be enough to supply them with protein until such a time that it ran out, it was therefore quite necessary for Nak to take along with him a rifle in which to kill a wild bullock or kangaroo. In this the hardest part of the task was not actually shooting the animal but to actually run up to it and slit its throat before the animal in question died, at the same time voicing the following prayer towards Mecca, 'Bismillah Wallahu Akbar', meaning that the sacrifice had been made to Allah and that permission was hence sought for the animal to be used for human consumption... if the animal died before this could be carried out then the animal was left to rot.

To this note and nagging thought Nak fondled the trigger and sights of the weapon he carried, ensuring all was clean, before placing it into its bag for possible use at a later date, fully loaded and ready to fire.

The packing and loading was now complete and with the lifting and strapping finished the two Aboriginal boys scarpered off to see what mischief they could find, their palms carrying a little money, their wage for the time spent helping the cameleers, help which was altogether needed but provided more for better relations between the two people, being both a different colour and of different religious belief as compared to those from other parts of the world or born unto Australia: they were unique.

Nak took his position at the head of the caravan, leading the string with little effort, for the lead camel knew his part in the scheme of things, leading the others into the wilderness which was to be their home for some time to come.

It wasn't long before the last of the Ghantown shacks fell behind them and the noises offered by the desert embossed themselves quite heavily upon the three men; the solace of the next two weeks only broken by them and them alone: and the twenty-four camels which they attended.

CHAPTER ELEVEN

The camels in their string were all from India, or of descendants that came from there. They were hard and fast, not a lazy bone amongst them, though some did bare reflection of that uncommon label. The heat of the Australian outback meant little to them, shrugged off like an annoying fly, over 104 degrees [40 degrees Celsius] on most days, and that was in the shade of the coolest tree, the weather being hottest in the early part of the afternoon.

There was no escaping it, no relief in sight, and all the string could do was to follow the lead camel who in all his glory held his head up high with his master to his right, the cameleer so familiar leading the way to their destiny where wages could be secured for the work that they performed.

The camel was so much better than a horse, in all respects and in particular in regards to height. Travelling through Spinifex country was not bad for a camel for he was so tall and carried his load out of reach of most of the lower branches of scrub where damage could be done to bags of all description.

A tell-tale sign of many hours' march through such terrain was the marks left by a caravan, the first three feet of a camel's leg being shred bare of all hair, the lower portions as black as night and as shiny as a new pair of boots. But their skin was as hard as nails and no harm came to them, whereas with a horse the skin would be torn to pieces. But without the Spinifex the Australian outback would be little less than another desert of the African north or savanna. The plant helped prevent erosion and provided a retreat for birds and other wildlife, not to mention that the Aboriginals used the plant as a resource by using it to the best of their abilities, to secure spear points to shaft and stone-sharpening tools to a woomera handle.

This was saltbush country edged with mulga where the sandhills undulated across the land for as far as the eye could see and the rabbit burrows that infested the ground were beyond belief.

Rabbit provided something different to eat, the white meat providing great satisfaction, so long as it was killed in the customary fashion required of a Muslim; which wasn't easy to procure as a single shot from the rifle usually meant the immediate death of the animal. There were also plenty of emu and kangaroo, but so seldom was one caught and eaten.

The mulga was a good meal for the camels but such animals can't live on mulga alone. The camel didn't carry water internally such as in reservoirs, although it did have the ability to reabsorb its own urine to a degree, but it was very efficient at extracting moisture from plant life such as mulga and paracelia. The hump, in contradiction to many voiced opinions, was in fact its fat storage and a camel which was fed poorly had a reduced hump when compared to those that maintained a healthy disposition. There were other aspects of the camels' disposition that came into play on the desert lands. Their pads were soft and enabled them to move much more easily across sand, to take short cuts between different parts of the worn track trodden hard by a million hoofs; their soles are hardy and take heat, cloven-hoofed and seemingly made for hard labour.

They had an uncanny sense of direction and memory, and would know where they were going if they had been there before. They could travel three miles an hour, eight to ten hours a day, with the cameleers singing traditional songs as they walked beside them, neither stopping for rest during the day nor for anything to eat, for lunch was too labour intensive and camels couldn't stand in one spot with a load upon their backs for very long.

The camels had great observation and they tended to look around all the time and if they saw something strange or out of place then they would stare at it for a long time as they walked towards and past the object of curiosity, and next time they came past this same place they would look in that direction expecting to see it again, no matter what it was, be it a dingo or other animal that has scared it in the past, or simply a small tent, torn clothing hanging from a limb, or bush or tree that stood out amongst the surrounds.

They were a most remarkable animal.

CHAPTER TWELVE

As they continued on into the wilderness the hours dropped off behind them, the sun peaking at noon, but not the built up of heat that still had room for further gains as the day wore on into the afternoon on this, their first day.

The figure of someone could be seen up ahead and the eyes of the lead camel fell on the object of his curiosity, a dark-brown to almost black camel of many years experience and named Chocolate for obvious reasons. It was a known fact that Nak had an almost pure black bull and that for more than anything else that the remainder of all of the camels within his string were yellowish brown and had dark manes; but certainly not all.

Nak loved this beast almost more than life itself, a working pet that was a companion on long treks across open plains of undulating nothingness. He looked up into the camel's eyes and saw that his attention was most assertively retained upon the dark mass that drew closer and closer as the caravan closed the gap upon the seated form of a man.

They came upon the Aboriginal who looked worse for wear and on passing him saw that he was a victim of his mother's cruelty, the three Afghans unable to refrain from looking upon his miserable state, the condition of his life forever affected by such horrendous actions against him that he would be forever shunned by those that came into close contact with him.

They'd heard of this man, both Shir and Nak, even though to Abdul he was nothing more than a sorrowful sack of flesh, seated their upon the side of the road with his palm held out flat, hoping it to be filled with food, the Aboriginal man being a shell of emptiness and emotionally scarred for life. But food he would not receive for the cameleers had only enough for themselves, and barely that, and if their journey was to falter by the way and be increased by so much as a day then they would find themselves without food, too.

His name had been forgotten but he was known as a wanderer, a man bound to the land for ever and a day, to walk the stretches of track and desert until his dying day. It seemed at first sight that he was smiling and happy to see someone... anyone of the real world; yet the reason he was seen to bare his teeth to the world was due to other matters which turned the eyes of many Europeans.

His mother had burnt his lips away when he was very young, a mother tired of his constant crying for food, and where a mother is bound by the viciousness of alcohol she always bears the brunt of its evil. What sort of mother would do such a thing to a loving child, a little one that clung to the one that had delivered him to the world?

A young child knows nothing of formality or the ways of the world until taught or experienced. How could a mother, no matter how deranged, lose all manner of semblance and pick up a red hot stick from the burning furnace of a fire and burn away the lips of the one she was supposed to care for?

But that was the way it was and as the string continued on its way the men could only look on with sadness and continue with the task at hand, and not so far up the track, out of sight of the one to their rear, another Aboriginal came into view. It was a half-caste, a person to be tormented all their life.

Pasted over the land, like freckles upon a face, was the 'yeller-feller', an encumbrance to society. Neither wanted by the Aboriginal community, nor the white folks alike, these half-castes were treated as nothing more than pests by all except their mother. Was it no wonder then that the strength in number of women begging for food began to be an encroachment upon all those that fell upon them during their task to supply farms and portage their merchandise back to a station where they could continue on to market.

These Aboriginal women were constantly selling themselves short, accepting a little coin or food so that a white man could partake of a little pleasure, to have his way with a woman, regardless of creed, nationality, colour of her skin, or standing in life, and then to throw her aside. Many men had been caught short by a woman showing up at his side with a baby in her arms, but none would shoulder the responsibility.

So it was that this old woman with a baby, abandoned to the world, to her own devices, caught the glances of Chocolate and the three men as per the previous Aboriginal they had recently passed. It was a shrewd awakening to Abdul, a presentation of a new world, the introduction to an Australia that wasn't advertised back at home before he'd decided to take the plunge and travel far from his family.

Abdul was here to make his fortune, to send money back to his family at home, and the real awakening of his future was now, more than ever, shrouded in doubt. He had seen very little in this land of fortune which was to appease him, make him rich, or do him the justice he believed he deserved. He had served in the army for the British Empire... wasn't Australia just that, an extension of that which he had served? He was owed more than this.

And as they continued on, none breaking their stride, several pots and pans came loose and clanged a metallic melody as the kitchen passed the mother and her baby, teasing her with what she would not receive.

CHAPTER THIRTEEN

The day continued rather quickly after the two scenes of Aboriginal neglect, the minds of the three men filled with questions and few answers, but Abdul's was in full swing, contemplating hard all that he had seen as the sun commenced to approach the edge of civilization, and a beautiful red and orange sky filled the horizon for as far as the eye could see.

In the midst of summer, as it was upon the land in which the camels had come to know as their second home, a place in which to make a fortune, it was as hot as the deserts of any other place on Earth, where camels were quickly trained to go without water for up to two weeks, three being possible, and when the opportunity arose to drink from a bucket, up to 20 gallons would be taken in, fuel that was the requirement for any creature that walked on two legs or four, or even wriggled upon the ground as a serpent does so well. So, to compare Australia with other desert regions of the world was realistically permitted.

The creek beds around were dry and cracking, bush, trees, and grasses yellow like straw and almost devoid of all nourishment, and apart from the morsels that could be extracted by a hungry camel, the string forever keeping an eye open for good opportunity, for they would be in hobbles soon enough and could make their way back to any place within reasonable distance, to eat at their pleasure and to have their fill.

It was best to place short hobbles upon the camels by night as opposed to the long hobble as this restriction within the camels' ability to move ensured that it didn't wander off too far by night, for the last thing the cameleers wished was to be displaced for hours on end searching for lost camels in the bush when time restraints were upon them and the sun was reaching over the horizon to get its first glimpse of the land before it. In this the two front legs were restrained and the camels never wandered more than a mile or two from the campsite, and when they did it was always together with the lead camel maintaining status over the others, and where one goes the others are sure to follow.

The men were always on the lookout for saltbush, spinifex and mulga during an advance from point of departure to destination, for the camel had a mind that put other animals to shame, its memory being of remarkable calibre. It was to this habitual practise of camels wandering off into the desert in search for food that each wore a brass bell around its neck attached to a bright coloured ribbon that might more readily stand out in the bleak contrast of the sandy dunes around, for it was very hard to see a camel over any great distance when the country was literally littered with spinifex, saltbush and mulga. For this reason above all others, Chocolate was an advantage, for he stood out more than the others and was usually first seen when sought.

CHAPTER FOURTEEN

And so to unloading, the threesome began their work, at a place where a little comfort could be received, the last remnants of drawn out shade disappearing into the night as darkness fell quite rapidly upon them.

There wasn't any great concern for the men to hurry, for the light of the moon would soon offer itself freely and the stars above the clear night sky would provide additional illumination.

The camels were brought in alongside the campsite and ordered to kneel, loads still upon them. Their forelegs folded beneath them and then front legs onto knees, back legs folded and then down onto hindquarters, and the loads were prepared for removal by Shir and Nak, starting from Chocolate and progressing to the rear as they loosened the thongs and cordage. As this was done, Abdul untied the nose peg from the camel being attended, to the camel to its rear, so that a loaded pack – where applicable – on the camel's back could be lifted by the men either side and then placed to the rear, front, or side. In this the cameleers were rehearsed well but each string had a different jemadar and each jemadar his mind set at a particular practise. It was most useful to place the loads, where light enough to be lifted, to the front of the camel that was carrying it, in this way the camel would seat itself before the load when loading was to take place early each morning, for each camel knew the smell of its own pack. In fact, Nak and Shir had a different practise for each caravan they attended.

For the most part it was a simple operation. With thongs and cordage pulled loose the loads were allowed to fall both left and right of the camel in question, the saddles then removed and placed at the head. Each load was secured to form a compact bundle of supplies which were easily manipulated, positioned and tied. As each saddle was placed before the camel the camel was allowed to stand, a hobble quickly placed upon its feet before being allowed to search for food; it wasn't possible to secure hobbles whilst a camel was seated on all fours.

The cameleers worked with remarkable speed, the essence of the task rehearsed in their heads prior to bringing the camel train to a halt, and after their work was done there was praying to be carried out and of course the meal which was to be eaten in the comparative darkness, for the sun was down and the moon was yet to show itself in its fullest splendour that it had to offer, but steadily it climbed its way into the heavens above.

CHAPTER FIFTEEN

Their camp was rudely prepared, prayer mats placed upon the ground beside one another and sticks for a campfire quickly prepared as the camels went about their task of finding food to eat, never straying too far from the lead camel, Chocolate. Tents were not prepared this night as the wind was low and no rain was expected, but sleeping blankets were drawn from the supply horse in front of the kitchen camel's load and laid upon the ground still rolled up tight to deter any likely intrusion of unwanted pests or reptiles.

It was a common misconception that Muslims should face the east when performing their daily prayers but there was a small point of fact that didn't elude Nak and Shir, who were quick to point out their knowledge to Abdul. Mecca was closest to Australia via the north-west and so this is the direction in which all prayers were cast.

Being on the road between homesteads and settlements was no excuse to refrain from prayer for the headman or jemadar of every group would carry a copy of the Koran and read from it as required at the times of the day identified as sacred to them all.

Their religion was everything to them and for the cameleers their faith was the 'five pillars of Islam'. Prayer was a crucial part of their daily life and separated them from the colonists, binding Muslims together as one, and where they should be in the middle of nowhere, be it alone or with others tied to the restraints of a string of camels, time would be taken to spread their prayer mats upon the ground, face towards Mecca, and conduct ablutions as laid down within their book of high esteem. As for the five pillars there were also five periods in the day in which prayer was to take place.

Ablutions were also an unnecessary waste of water and easily drew a barrage of discontent from the eye sockets of Christians and other men. It was custom for the water to be running and free of disease, to be clean of insects and larvae, the body parts to be washed prior to prayer being the face, hands, forearms and feet. But here in the desert where water was scarce another alternative was formed and so here they sat, all three men facing towards Mecca, each with a small cone-shaped pile of sand beside him, a symbolic representation of water which was so scarce and could not be afforded.

The pillars were more of a spiritual healing and way of life which included ones declaration of faith, five compulsory periods of daily prayer, the observance of Ramadan, the offering to charity of a portions of one's wealth, and pilgrimage to the holy land of Mecca during one's life; the five periods of prayer were as follows: at sunrise, noon, afternoon, sunset, and once at night: Salat-ul-Fajr, Salat-ul-Zuhr, Salat-ul-Ast, Salat-ul-Maghrib, and Salat-ul-Isha in respective order, time allotted each prayer and those periods being 10 minutes, 20, 15, 15, and 20.

Being on the road with camels made it wholly difficult to pray as required and so an acceptable alteration was made in accordance with the difficulties of prayer. Sunrise, noon, and sunset were maintained by some of those on the road, the afternoon and night time prayer being dropped, which meant in all reality that for those choosing to travel by day that the only interruption to the string was at noon, a 20 minute period of prayer being adhered to.

Camels could easily be halted and ordered into the sitting position whilst the cameleers absolved themselves for prayer but no time at all was wasted in the ritual. But camels couldn't stand for long with a load and sitting was essential during any rest stop.

Nak was jemadar and for that reason the decision was his to make. Nak refrained from stopping during the day as the heat of the midday sun was no comfort to those permitting their minds to wander whilst static, and secondly; all of his camels were considered as close friends.

CHAPTER SIXTEEN

The fire was small but was enough to light up the smiles on their faces as they sat with legs crossed and drank of the tea which they had prepared, looking up in wonder to the stars above, not a cloud in the sky.

The night ahead would be cold for them now, considering that there was no blanket aloft the earth, no cloud to trap the warmth, to keep the cold at bay, and before long they would have to draw their knees up to the comfort of their chests, bedding wrapped around them as tight as could be, but for the time being they were content to favour the friendship of one another along with many stories of past, present and future.

The brightness of the stars above was unbelievable, seemingly close enough to touch, more stars than most people would ever see in a lifetime, some winking as thou answering their prayers for peace and brotherly love, for their loved ones back home to be cared for, for sons and daughters to be tended to in a manner fitting a sultan.

And they reflected upon their vulnerability, in particular Shir and Nak, for they were 'old hands', contemplating their apparent loneliness; for they were even without the overland telegraph line which often accompanied them on their journeys to Oodnadatta, running silently above them, over their heads and dreary to look at. There was nothing worse than seeing countless posts being passed, one after the other for miles and miles on end. Such familiarities which brought reminders of civilization were not required when a vast land of sweeping plains, hills and creek lines, harboured the country in quiet solitude, delivering a peace to those that knew the land best. Maybe they were better off without the telegraph line overhead.

The bliss of the evening called for a delightful meal and in that Shir prepared them all something that would set them to heaven and back. Nak tended to the camels once more and saw that most had commenced to wander off some distance from the site where they had been relieved of their loads, and Abdul followed.

Although Abdul was the new man he didn't need to be shown how to handle a camel, Nak wanted to bestow upon him the way in which he and Shir did business and to this he could only pay undivided attention.

These camels were their life's blood and meant everything to them. Even Shir would choose to tend the camels over his new wife for he was a full-blooded cameleer and nothing in the universe could change that. But with duties aside and a full stomach to appease them all, the conversation continued.

Nak fidget slightly and before giving in to sleep decided upon a final story, and he told his story as they sat around the fire as it commenced to die, of a time before Shir and he had met and made a partnership between them. The story was simple and easy to remember for it was always easy to recall the viciousness of some Aboriginal people, succumbed to all matters of evil doing, inflicting the most heinous crime against their own simply because they didn't wish to partake of the celebration, turning down the opportunity to hold a newborn close to heart and with a smile upon the face.

There was an Aboriginal man. The Aboriginal man looked down within the eyes of the newly born girl, another mouth to feed, and of the wrong sex. A boy was wanted by the man, a boy to be moulded in likeness to himself: which is good enough reason in itself for him to be denied his wish for he was a cruel man and everyone knew it.

The disgust upon the man's face told the story within his head, told of his feelings, betrayed his very connection with the one that he should call daughter.

He picked her up by the feet and bashed her hard against a rock, caving her head in, splattering brains over the wife as she watched, tears filling her eyes like the water of a tap fills a bucket, the tears falling in one continuous stream, the hurt within her being heard far and wide. The sadness upon her face could not be denied the feelings of mounting sorrow within a bystander.

The man then took the body of the baby, thrashing loose of the mother's clutching, the mother wanting to hold the dead child one more time, wishing to hold the murdered flesh and bone that was hers and hers alone.

The husband scolded her and kicked out hard before disappearing out of sight and into a creek line where he built a fire and threw the body into it. And here is where the manner of his evil made its final play, for the fire didn't hold and died like the child, and many dingoes came in to tear the lifeless body apart.

How did the cameleer know this, how could he be sure? It was the story told by a friend, a man who had stumbled upon the scene of the feeding when looking for firewood, and the story of the man having bashed the baby's head in by bashing her against a rock was delivered to his ears by a friend of the mother, a witness to the tragedy who was searching for food.

Abdul wasn't sure of the accuracy of the story but couldn't see why he would be lied to. He had seen little in respect to Aboriginal life and even though what he had seen wasn't pleasant it was all too much to think of these people as unforgiving murders; yet it had happened.

With the final story told and minds in a spin over what had been passed between them, it was time for sleep. And with sleep the dreams of the future and past lay visit upon them all, and in their own different way. Shir dreamt of his wife, Nak of his military duties in Afghanistan, and Abdul dreamed that he had wings of gold and flew over the Mungerannie Gap without a care in the world.

CHAPTER SEVENTEEN

They slept heavily that night.

When morning broke it was met by three men, all three having woken and stowing away their blankets, each in midst stride of his duties, be that packing away the camp, gathering the camels, or simply checking the stores to ensure none were damaged and that all seams on the sacks were intact and not torn.

The sounds still penetrated all around them but they were of a different language, coming from right across the desert and just during sunrise – the break of day. This was around the hour of morning when most are rubbing their eyes for forgiveness, and the last hour before the blazing sun once again beats down upon the earth without remorse. It is a time when birds, insects and frogs in their multitudes voice their presence to the world, ever more so before a storm fills the air and releases a deluge upon the earth.

Other sounds can also be heard from far away, including storms that bypass the area a hundred miles away or more. It is a time of great solitude where the men are kept busy, where time is of the essence and there isn't a minute to spare.

Breakfast, of all things, is a hurried affair for there is much work ahead of them before the string is ready to continue with the move northwards.

CHAPTER EIGHTEEN

The camels are relatively easy to find, the bells around their necks giving them away fairly easily.

They were within a half mile of the campsite when Shir fell upon Chocolate; the camels had quite obviously had a good night's sleep and had partaken of a good sized meal prior to slumber and another on waking with the morning sun. Shir could see it even from a distance that they were one and all, well-nourished and ready for work.

The camels were brought in, each following the lead of Chocolate, like good soldiers following their leader's orders as laid down.

Abdul confided in Shir for he didn't wish to look the fool in front of the jemadar.

"I feel the social isolation upon my shoulders and the effect it is having on my mind; it's almost too much to bear."

"Try not to worry on it too much," said Shir after a few seconds, walking along with Chocolate next to him, the bell sounding as each step is taken, all but two camels following close behind, for two camels were currently still at the campsite and content with remaining there for the duration of the night, both pregnant, one much closer to birth than the other.

"I suffered, too," continued Shir. "And I know Nak has suffered. He doesn't speak much of the infliction he has but the expression upon his face is not his friend."

"I feel so lonely," said Abdul with true conviction, the sorrow of his voice coming to air, the remark on Nak's grimace hardly being heard.

"You will get used to the conditions and the lack of community whilst attending the caravan, and when in Marree you will find that the support offered by everyone around is enough to help you progress from one day to the next. But believe me; you won't be spending too much time in Marree. From the day you arrived into our arms, as employee and friend, you said farewell to the rudiments of civilization. We support one another now, for all time."

"I miss my wife... my family," said Abdul.

"I understand, as I'm sure they do," said Shir. "We must all do what we have to do in order to survive. It is unfortunate that your sacrifice is more than what most must suffer in order to get ahead in life. But take my advice: think less on this, your predicament, than you do. You won't survive if you keep thinking about it."

"What else is there to think about when on the road for days on end, if not of our predicament?"

"That is the hardest question to answer for everyone is different; we each have a different mind. I cannot answer your question, Abdul."

"Then I shall find the answer for myself."

"And maybe that's the answer," said Shir as they made final approach towards the campsite to see Nak standing there and watching them as they drew closer. "Set your mind free of the shackles that inhibit it and cast your thoughts far and wide, but also... consider everything that is around you, look at every detail, take in all there is to learn. I can't tell you any more than that, I'm afraid."

"Thank you, Shir."

CHAPTER NINETEEN

The loading of the string was a basic reverse of the unloading of the camels.

Each camel knew its place by smell and sat behind the pack saddle that was to be placed upon it, and as the stores were already placed into bundles, strapped and bound together tightly, they were more easily tied into position upon the backs of the animals.

Shir reached for his soldered canteen of iron that sat to one side of the camel near the rear of the string, a reservoir of drinking water that sat snugly against the girth of the camel.

He took a handsome mouthful of water before returning its plug.

The string was now ready and with bells and hobbles removed, and nose pegs attached, the camels were given the order to stand.

Each and every one of them stood on hind legs first and once straight the front legs opened at the knees, forequarters raising a little, pushing forward onto one front leg at first and then the next.

Nak looked around and saw that the campsite was indeed cleaned of all necessity and that the string behind him was ready to move off with Shir and Abdul in position. This was their second day of many, another eight to ten hours of walking ahead of them; a long stretch of time to contemplate.

So they stepped off, one foot in front of the other, setting themselves upon their journey of a day's march, taking the seconds, minutes, and hours in their stride, the accompaniment of flies ignored as much as the heat of the sun and miles upon miles that mounted behind them.

Nak knew several short routes that the string could take, cutting the trip short by up to several miles a day, making an effort to keep from the main track used by horses and bullocks, for most of the white men of the outback, when on duty and making money from carting supplies here and there, were not very friendly and were prone to slinging abuse, rocks, and generally causing havoc: but in all fairness the extent of abuse was usually kept to a minimum.

At one particular part of the move to the north a segment of track was favoured above all others as it provided better means for which to save time on the road, and it was here that Nak saw a familiar sight coming towards him as the camel train continued.

Chocolate looked up ahead and voiced his opinion. It seemed that he well knew the silhouette of the man and wagon to his front, even at such a distance as confronted him. The sight, however, confused him a little, for the last time he saw the man and wagon they were on another part of the track, and that was a long time ago.

Nak gave warning to the others behind, "Missionary!"

Abdul looked from front to rear and saw that Shir had heard, for he gave a little wave.

Abdul had no idea what was meant by the call but took it to be a warning. The only thing he knew of missionaries was their unsavoury voicing of opinion when it came to God and the son which he delivered unto the world.

Brother Ernest Jacob could be seen up ahead and approaching their slow and tedious move towards the north, the gap between them closing. He had a bullock team under his control and was happy to walk beside them as the Afghans walked beside their camels; it seemed, therefore, that Brother Ernest took as much liking to his bullocks as the cameleers did their camels.

Nak made mention of the Brother as he approached, calling out to Abdul that he was of the Christian religion and a very good man who could be found on the road almost every day of the year, walking his team to and from Port Augusta, supplying the mission at Killalpinanna as required by their service to God. But the endless journey across the desert was now a thing of the past for Jacob, for the train at Marree meant that Brother Ernest had far less distance to travel.

Killalpinanna Mission was first decided upon when the missionaries first arrived upon the land on 31st January, 1867, some three and a half months after first setting out from Langmeil.

Nak considered the move he must make in order to allow plenty of room between the two parties, and although in his familiarity with the bullocks he knew them to offer little aggression or upset towards the camels in general, he still wished there to be a healthy gap between them as they passed each other on the track.

Killalpinanna was not too far ahead, just 25 miles south of Cooper Creek. The out-stations, Kopperamanna and Etadunna, were incorporated into the establishment of the Bethesda Mission, a lot of time and energy being spent on the erection of a post office, church, school, four houses, two store rooms and a dormitory for both boys and girls, and on top of this there was the police station which, after being relocated to Kopperamanna, provided the essential law and order required by the isolated region.

By this time the missionary was passing Nak and a friendly nod was exchanged between the two, Brother Ernest familiar with Nak's grimace and Nak, too, well-adjusted to the man's sermons as he passed, even if beyond understanding.

"May God be with you, brothers. Let him build an altar within you all, a church for which to heal your souls of the savagery enlisted by your beliefs."

Nak understood little of what the man had said as usual, mainly due to his accent, and replied the only way he knew: "Allah be with you."

The name Allah struck Brother Ernest hard but he hid it, as usual, behind a soft and mellow smile.

Two friends, or bitter enemies, showing each other that civilized people could live in harmony; if only for a brief moment. And within minutes the bullock team and their master was gone.

CHAPTER TWENTY

The days continued to fall behind them until they came upon Cooper Creek.

The crossing was endowed with a 3.5 mile expanse of floodplain, dreary to say the least, but to be compared so pessimistically with the other aspects of the Birdsville Track was beyond contemplation for the entire length was sodden with that tedious plodding along, one foot after the next; but the first call of duty was to cross the flowing waters of the Cooper.

The line of trees on either side of the Cooper were quite prominent and made for a good home to the fishes, birds and amphibian life that remained close by the life sustaining waters. Shadows cast upon the reflective surface of the creek gave it a life of its own, dancing shades of colour flickering upon the surface as the waters passed by at a slow and leisurely pace.

The camels would, without a doubt, have smelt the water from when before they woke for the day's walking and the only considerations in deterring the camels in having tried to advance upon the creek was the restriction offered by hobbles, the fact that they'd only recently (several days before) been provided ample water at Marree, and that they knew they would be passing this way as was the normal procedure on this route. But one thing other than all else was known by the camels before they even stepped foot upon the cool approach to the water's edge and that was the fact that the cameleers were not going to stop for a drink.

Nak knew that if the camels were to be provided time to water that the training of years past would be going to waste. Camels were hard workers but got lazy when men got lazy. The Europeans suffered most of all by camels that couldn't go three days without water, simply because they were provided every ample opportunity to fill up when given the chance.

The camels' water intake allowed them to go longer distances without the need to replenish themselves. Where the strings were trained to go without water for greater stints of time, they did so; the camels were quite capable of going up to ten days or more without water.

It was a sad fact that camels tended to by white colonists were spoiled, for the better use of the word, by being allowed water at any given opportunity, in particular where exploration of the interior was the call to duty of the men that lead them. No one knew where the water holes were and when the next one was to be encountered, but even in reflection of this the whites would see fit to allow the camels water whenever possible. Due to this reason the camels tended to go fewer days before being stressed with the calls for water intake being heard.

A camel would take in anywhere between 16 and 20 gallons at a single sitting and if anything less was drawn then it was a good sign that the camel was being spoiled and not worked to its fullest ability.

Such poor water discipline was dangerous in the case that a waterhole or soak, which was expected to have water in it, turned out to be dry as a bone and in essence prolonged the camels' period between drinks.

A handler, being Afghan or other, needed to weigh his options and knowledge of the land, in particular to take heed to Aboriginal warnings; but the Afghan cameleers stood supreme over all that dominated over the 'ships of the desert'.

During a move towards a settlement where the map was laid at one's fingertips, water was a resource known about, so why endanger the loss of good training and ability?

"We don't stop," yelled Nak over his shoulder as he half turned towards Abdul and continued walking. "The camels will drink if we stop for too long but the need is not present; we also have plenty for our cooking needs."

"It looks like a good place to stop and pray," voiced Abdul.

"We shouldn't change our daily routine," replied Nak. "We must think of the camels; always the camels and then ourselves. Without the camels we have nothing. Allah knows that we are loyal to Him and His beliefs."

"Water is for the weak," added Shir from behind, "and we are not weak."

Camels were a most remarkable animal and there is one solitary thing that stands out most about them... when standing beside a horse they are like giants.

A good camel can be eight to nine feet tall to the height of its hump where the middle of a horse's back will only come to a man's head or chest. This aspect of the camel rarely provided their handlers with better visual options during a supply run because all cameleers walked beside their camels, never upon them, but where space was available and a river needed to be crossed, any white man given the opportunity to ride upon the back of a camel could see the advantages immediately upon entering a river.

The waters of a river would literally soak all that a horse carried upon its back, which included the legs and waist of the rider, whereas riding upon a camel offered greater potential for avoiding getting wet in the same circumstance, for the soles of one's feet would barely be touched by any moisture at all.

Another aspect of great worth was the camels' ability to portage supplies, not just to pull but to literally carry upon its back. A very strong and sturdy camel could carry up to 960 pounds in weight, much more being possible but not desirable, in particular over long distances (600 pounds being a modest benchmark), which was vastly more than a bullock or horse; and even then further weight could be added once the animal was stood on all fours, but rarely was the beast of burden subjection to such pains. Such an advantage proved priceless during river crossings at times when white explorers crossed the land from South to North or East to West.

Pulling a wagon was uncommon amongst the Afghans but others trying to attract a good wage from settlements and mines would see the labour of bullocks used to less effect than a team of camels; in effect the cameleers proved time and time again their superiority in regards to delivering supplies and merchandise, in good keeping with restriction to times, and able to handle the animals with the care and respect that was necessary in order to draw fullest capability from them. And here, once again, a wagon, unless built with height in mind, was subjected to getting quite wet.

There was one other important factor that was praised with great ovation and that was that a camel string could do in two weeks what a bullock team might do in a little over a month: the comparison was simply too daunting to even consider the use of bullocks, but yet there existed the urge to employ them.

Nak and the others continued on alongside their string, neither worried about getting their feet wet nor replenishing their water bags or iron canteens, although Abdul couldn't resist the opportunity to reach into the water with his cupped palm and draw a little of the freshness from that which was offered.

The water cascaded down his chin and neck but also the inside of his throat, the cool and loving freshness like luxury he couldn't believe. It was like being in heaven, and even without the seventy-two virgins permitted each man, the water would have been enough.

Within minutes the string was across the creek and the camels were brought to a quick and temporary stop.

"Check the nose pegs, Abdul," advised Nak. "Sometimes they get broken by the camels in the water."

"Mine are all okay," advised Abdul.

"Mine too," said Shir.

"Good," and without second thought or reflection, Nak turned again to face the north and ordered the camels on.

CHAPTER TWENTY-ONE

Not far ahead was the Natterannie Sandhills, yellow ridges of its descriptive name filling the scene to their front, a wedge-tailed eagle then caught Abdul's eye, who looked up at the outstretched wings of fortitude as the animal glided high above, seeking a meal in which to feed itself or its young; even though it was a little late in the year for fledglings. The bird was huge, black and long, a diamond-shaped tail with a band of tawny brown across its wings and a chestnut nape.

This was eagle country as far as Abdul knew from his little experience of the country, but he did know that the eagle circling up above was attracted to steep hills, gorges and peaks, and no sooner did he see the bird, and it vanished without a trace, falling out of sight behind a hill not so far away.

Abdul felt like asking a question of Nak, about the wildlife, about his experiences in Australia, but quickly felt the better of it for they would have plenty of time at night when seated around a campfire and drinking tea with their main meal or a little damper. Talking now would do little but dry the mouth more than it was already and expend valuable energy over no better defence than to help keep himself occupied.

It was a wonder in itself, the minds of Nak and Shir. Many hours a day, many days a week, many weeks in a year; year in and year out. What was to occupy a man's mind during such extended lengths of time where there was nothing to do but plod alongside a string of camels, knowing full well that at the end of the day you had to suffer the same burden the following morning and the morning after that.

But Abdul also considered the alternative, living in Afghanistan and doing little else than he was doing right now, where boredom of a simple task could quite literally rattle one's mind into thinking he was insane, even if partly so.

Australia was better than Afghanistan, but only just. The fortune he was to make was a long time coming and the reality of the life he was leading, right here and now, was that there was no fortune to be made, unless your name was Faiz Mahomet of the Durranis or Abdul Wade of the Ghilzai.

He considered, too, the man he had come into contact with; Jehangir, Nak's friend in Port Augusta. He somehow felt as though in debt to the man for Abdul knew deep down, even with so little time in country, that falling into employment with Nak and Shir was nothing less than a blessing. He had good company, a stomach full of food, and a job which offered consistency in pay, so long as they maintained good relations with all they came into contact with.

Abdul pitied the unemployed, those in long lines back at Port Augusta, where men would sell themselves for practically nothing. It was a shame, a disgusting shame, that the men of Afghanistan should be so poorly that they needed to grovel upon the soil of the earth in order to sustain their miserable lives. For some the trip to Australia was a living hell; but there would always be the fortunate few.

A man made his life from what was to be had on offer, and should never take what was on offer to make a life, for such life would often be unrewarding. There was always more fruit on the tree to pick, all you needed to do was to move a few branches; that's what Abdul had done, had carved his own future from stumbling across an offer that couldn't be refused, but only after turning down many other opportunities. He had paved his own path, the way to his own future, and he was currently happy for it, and before he knew it the caravan was pulling up for the night, to take to prayer, and something to eat for both man and beast.

CHAPTER TWENTY-TWO

North of Mulka, they continued on, and it wasn't long before they fell within distance of Mungerannie Gap.

Mungerannie, as most other establishments, be they a small town or simple homestead, was bypassed for convenience more than anything else.

Nak knew other tracks that could be employed in order to avoid any unpleasantness and that would provide the eye with much more pleasantness than the cold stare of a white colonist.

It wasn't only the Afghans themselves that disgusted many of the white men of this country but the camels too, for most understood that their husbands and sons were going without work because of the camel: but was it the camels themselves or the wages that the Afghan managed to procure from the errands run for settlements and thriving businesses that disgusted them the most?

A majority of the white mans' failures in the outback were not only his inability to maintain a real and proper timescale in respect to the task at hand but more so his greed and hidden ambitions which lead to his depression.

It was shameful to admit that even of those that they aided in regards to carrying wool back to Marree, that a good percentage, in particular the wives – for some ungodly reason – would stare them down, and if a look could kill then they'd all drop dead in an instant: so similar it was to the glance shot at an Aboriginal searching for food or shelter.

It was here that a history lesson was dispelled upon Abdul for this was the place where the Sturt's Stony, Tirari, Simpson and the Strzelecki Deserts met in the quiet solitude of the dry air, any disturbance brought on by sound usually coming from the many types of birds that could be found during the wet season when more than 140 bird species would gather around and bring into the world the next generation of birdlife.

But there was another grand scene that awaited them, for the Mungerannie Gap was closing fast.

It was a sight to appease even the most selfish of eyes, for the beauty of the emptiness came alive on all portions of the ground that they approached, passed, and shrunk into nothingness behind them.

The hills around were a master artist's imagination come to life.

Their minds, however, were soon brought back to the reality of life and for the remainder of the journey north further expanses of floodplain could be expected, undulating plains where stones get underfoot and in some places there appears to be nothing around for miles on end but wide open nothingness.

Here, more than anywhere else, the camels feet would have to be looked after and attended to. And they continued on and past Clifton Hill, now eight days into their journey with six to go – or five nights for the optimistic of mind.

CHAPTER TWENTY-THREE

Just before dark, as the sun commenced to disappear for the night and the air had already cooled dramatically, Nak saw a dingo up ahead, head high and sniffing the air, up to no good and mischief which could easily be calculated; no man needed to be a graduate of a prestigious school to know that a dingo seen at dusk was a recipe for disaster, whether it be a small inconvenience or the meandering mind of something more.

"We have a dingo up front, and we're not far from camping for the night," said Nak to the others.

"Will you shoot it?" asked Abdul.

"Not just yet, but keep your eye open for him when we camp. I don't want to upset the camels by pulling up just now, not being so close to removing the nose pegs."

"What was that?" asked Shir of Abdul.

"Nak says there's a dingo up ahead. Keep your eye open for it in case it comes snooping around camp."

"I see," replied Shir. "Maybe you should tell Nak that we have something more. Slate is ready to give birth soon; she's been grumbling for about ten minutes now."

Nak heard Shir's reply, the wind from behind making it easier for him to hear than Shir.

Nak pulled the string over to the side of the track leaving a little space for any caravan that might come their way at night, for some Afghans preferred to move by night and avoid the heat of the day.

"We camp here," was all that Nak needed to say, for he was the jemadar and his word was gospel: he gave the orders and read the sermons from the Koran when in the outback running supplies to settlements; he needed little more than to voice his opinion and an order could be deciphered for the betterment of what was said.

Nak could see that the dingo had retreated a little but was still stuck nearer the track than not and so Nak turned to where his rifle lay hidden at rest, tied with thongs to the side of Chocolate.

He undid the ties and prepared the rifle for firing, bringing it into the shoulder after seeing that the string of camels was seated upon the earth and took aim down the sights set for the distance required.

Nak wasn't an accomplished shot and often missed targets that were no larger than a dingo, and so seldom it was that the need arose for the rifle to be fired at all, for the idea of the rifle was to wound an animal in order for it to be killed Al Halal in accordance with their belief.

It was quite understandable that Nak didn't wish to kill for the sake of killing, nor wound an animal that might crawl out into the wilderness to die in agony, but with a calf on the way and the delivery imminent he wasn't about to take any chances, for the price of a camel was substantial enough to provide a more than suitable windfall and provide good reason for celebration.

The other two men stood by their camels that sat waiting to be seen to, ready to be unloaded of their packs and kitchen, Slate slow in reaction to the orders of command and showing great signs of discomfort in the face of what lay ahead over the next few hours. There was no telling how long it would be before the camel gave birth but the walking would have helped bring the delivery along.

Nak aimed the rifle as best he could and with the dingo standing side on and looking directly at him he pulled the trigger instead of squeezing and missed completely the opportunity to hit the pest.

The dingo just stood there as though completely unaware that he'd been shot at, never before having experienced the sound of a bullet from a rifle; in fact, the only movement the dingo made was a sideways glance at the sound made by the bullet as it sped through the air.

Shir laughed and the camels jumped.

"Good shot, Nak," said Shir. "Maybe you should try using your sights next time."

Nak turned to the remark in kind gesture and met the smile with a little wit of his own, "If you bend over, Shir, I won't miss," and turned again to see the dingo standing his ground. "Watch this."

The trigger this time was squeezed gently, the sights having been re-adjusted, and after Nak had opened his eyes from the firing of the mechanism he saw before him a dingo sprawled on the ground. He put the rifle away and stepped off to the carcass.

"Abdul," said Shir, "help me with the camels whilst Nak drags the body away from the campsite."

CHAPTER TWENTY-FOUR

That night, soon after their prayers had been given in praise of their belief and their tea had been drunk, Slate gave birth. It was of similar colour to its mother and nothing out of the ordinary. The other camels had been set loose on their short hobbles but Slate remained nearer the campfire to tend to her newborn.

The calf sucked upon Slate's udder which was no bigger than a goat's in comparison to overall size.

"Shir," said Nak. "She's your camel. You get a bag made and ready and I'll get some food for Slate. Slate can also be prepared to carry the kitchen; she'll do best at the rear and the further we go the lighter the load will be for her. Abdul, come with me and keep me company."

Abdul saw this as an invitation worth merit, for Nak didn't ask Abdul to 'help me' but rather to 'keep me company'.

Not a further word was said as Abdul stood to follow Nak and Shir set upon getting a bag ready for the calf.

The calf would be spared the anguish of the hard walk ahead – the newborn was needed alive, not dead. It was customary in these times, when a calf was bestowed upon a string upon the road, that the calf should be tied up neatly in a sitting position with its head protruding from the bag and placed upon the mother's back. Shir knew from experience that the mother would look back during the onset of the continuing move northwards, checking that the calf was still upon its back from time to time, giving it a lick if possible and if not then a simple stare of attraction, its head bobbing up and down as the stare was returned.

Slate would continue on knowing full well that the calf was being looked after with her milk, all seven pints of milk from her bladder going to the hungry mouth of the youngster.

The calf would remain in such a position upon her back until they returned to Marree where it would be tended to in good fashion until the next job was ready, and if the job in question required Slate's attendance then the calf would once again be bundled up and taken along.

After weaning the calf could tend to itself and even accompany the mother, attached to another line other than the nose pegs associated with the string until three years old. At three it would be considered old enough to break in formerly and at eight years old enough to be considered as mature.

Nak and Abdul didn't need to take more than a few steps before they came across some food for Slate, spinifex being presented them for easy picking, and they commenced to cut the tussock grass into hand so that Slate could be fed a good quota in order for her strength to be maintained.

Camels ate much of what was found in the Australia bush; Mulga, fifteen to twenty feet of grey foliage with seeds in pods; spinifex (tufts of grass); weeping mulga which was larger than normal mulga bush and rather pretty to look at with silvery leaves, branches weeping as though a willow and usually in reach of a camel's outstretched neck, but out of reach of cattle. There was saltbush which thrived in salty soil and was a good stock fodder, white powder covering its blue-grey leaves... a rather shrubby plant. Herbage like the Sturts Desert Pea was a favourite of the camels where they ate the whole bush including the roots by pulling it out of ground and shaking it free of soil, its seeds dormant during dry times: it was a low trailing plant with hairy grey-green stems and leaves.

There was certainly no paying for fodder, for the outback was like an open market, free for all that could stomach that which was provided free of charge. In a matter of fact the only thing that they really refused point-blank was the eucalyptus.

A camel would grab a branch in its jaws, not its teeth, and pull down, stripping away the foliage of the mulga in particular. There was a small gap between the back and front teeth which made it easier for a camel to take what it wanted and bulls had a small tusk in this gap; thorns were hardly an issue for the camel.

"You've been working hard, Abdul," praised Nak. "How do you find it, here on the Birdsville Track?"

"It's like much of the rest of the country from what I have seen."

"Ah, yes; it doesn't change much in these parts, but the seasons bring enough to provide your mind with a different outlook. Sometimes you can't move because the land is flooded for miles around and at others there will be no rain for many months on end."

"You have experienced this?"

"Yes, Abdul," replied Nak. "I have been here for four very long years."

"And you have yet to make your fortune?"

"Money is hard to come by in Australia. It's hard work being a cameleer. In order for us to keep a job running year in and year we must keep our prices low, too low to make a fortune. Life here is only as comfortable as you make it. It also favours the man who keeps many friends."

"Friends like Jehangir," stated Abdul.

"Yes; that's it, exactly," agreed Nak. "Friends will help you, always. Jehangir was out to look for a young man as yourself, to help me with the camels I have."

"You and Shir must have been working hard these past years with so many camels between the two of you."

"No, no, no, no; not at all," said Nak. "We had another to help us but he met with an unfortunate... accident."

"Is it permitted to tell of this?"

Nak stopped what he was doing and stood up to confront Abdul with the answer.

"He was shot; I was going to tell you," said Nak to an astonished Abdul and Abdul looked over towards Shir who looked over towards them as the words left Nak's mouth. "Shot dead I tell you. That's no lie."

"And why would you lie to me?"

"Listen to me, Abdul," said Nak as he grasped Abdul's arm. "There are very few that you can trust in this country, other than those that read from the Koran. Everywhere you turn you will be met by those wishing to see you dead. Why do you think it is that we stray from the worn tracks, keeping clear of places like Mulka?"

"Tell me," said Abdul.

They moved over to where Slate was lying and placed some food before her, before they too, took a seat upon the desert floor with Shir joining them, an empty sack in his hands being turned into a bag for the calf.

"The rifle I carry is not just for food. It's also for self-defence."

"Have you ever needed it?" asked Abdul.

"Never; not yet," said Nak. "But our friend, the one you replaced, his name was Muschky. He was a very good man, like yourself, with the ambition of becoming a great man, a great cameleer. Do you know that he had this idea in his head that he could become a businessman and recruit many men for the biggest of jobs, working hand in hand with the miners of all description? He wanted nothing more than to meld with those of this country, to help them as best he could. He never had a sour word to say about anyone. But one day, last year and before spring fell upon us, we were on this very track and heading for home. We were near Mulka when a shot was fired and Muschky dropped dead; shot in the head."

"That's no accident," said Abdul. "That's murder. What happened next?"

"Nothing happened, Abdul. I think the shot was meant to scare us but the bullet ricochet off the supplies we were carrying and hit poor Muschky in the head."

"You didn't catch the murderer?"

"No," said Nak in disappointment. "We had little chance. He rode off quickly and had several accomplices with him."

"So why do you tell me this now?"

"When I killed the dingo I was reminded of poor Muschky," said Nak, Shir simply listening intently the whole time, Abdul taking in the story as it was told. "I'm not very good with the rifle and not very good at killing."

"But you were fighting against the British at one time," reminded Abdul. "That must account for something."

"I fear the day that someone finds out about my betrayals; not my betrayals against my country, as you have done, but my betrayal to Australia."

"My betrayal?" said Abdul. "I'm offended by that."

"Abdul, you are our friend and friends speak openly. I mean nothing by what I say. I know you believe you were just, in fighting alongside the British as I am confident in my quest against them, but now things are different. I have a life here and can't go back. If I am found out then that will be my undoing."

"What are you saying?"

"I wish you to carry the rifle, Abdul. You have the right to refuse but I would like to see it in your hands."

"No, that won't happen. Maybe I fought with the British in the past but now I have a family to look after and send money to. You should not hold any of this against me."

"I hold nothing against you, Abdul, but in defence of any action you might take against a colonist... it would be easier to prove self-defence. I can't prove this, nor can I jeopardise my safety."

"What of my safety?"

"Abdul, I feel I have offended you enough," said Nak. "I am your friend, you must believe me. I needed you to understand my position here, the predicament that could rise from the ashes of last year. You now know the story, you know where I keep the rifle, and you are clear in your mind of your position in this society and ability to prove self-defence."

Shir then spoke for the first time, "It's for you to know everything, Abdul. We don't wish to hide a thing."

"And what of you, Shir?" asked Abdul. "Why don't you take the rifle and kill in self-defence?"

"Because I am a wanted man," replied Shir. "I killed a white man before leaving Afghanistan. I am wanted as a spy by the British." A sad look fell upon Shir for he was revealing something that should not be revealed.

"I should not be telling you this," continued Shir. "No one knows this except Nak, and Nak is a very good friend of mine, better than a brother," and Nak smiled, even in the uncomfortable situation that had arisen. "We could both be treated poorly by judge and jury, myself risking the most. Ah, I see in your eye the questions you have, Abdul, but only one question I will answer. No; that's the answer... you don't deserve to be surrendered to judge and jury any more than us, but it is simply our willingness to go against a conviction that could see us both dead. I will risk it all for a single shot at that infidel that killed poor Muschky, but I might falter in the kill, I might have second thoughts, and any delay in pulling the trigger could easily reap an unpleasant affect upon any of one of us. I didn't receive any great joy from killing the man in Afghanistan; that is the truth."

Abdul was silent for a while as many thoughts went through his head.

"Do you think that killing would be easier for me?" asked Abdul

"In self-defence... maybe," said Nak.

"What you have revealed to me tonight could be dangerous for you both," said Abdul. "Why should you believe that I will look after your secret?"

"For one thing," said Nak, "if you didn't then you wouldn't have asked the question and risked putting yourself in jeopardy, even though there is none."

"Your secrets are safe with me," said Abdul. "But I won't carry the rifle."

"That's fair," said Nak. "I'm happy you know the truth."

"Yes, I now know," said Abdul. "I shall sleep now. Good night."

"Good night, Abdul," said Nak.

"Good night," said Shir.

As the three fell asleep the only noise from the camp came from Slate, who was fast asleep herself and snoring as camels do.

CHAPTER TWENTY-FIVE

The following days were met by cheerful praise by Nak and Shir who both felt much weight being lifted from their shoulders, but in the same token they also saw the uneasiness within Abdul, a look which dissipated as the days fell behind them.

It was good that the truth was finally revealed, that there were no more secrets to be spoken of between them, and it was good that such had been revealed so far from home, and when so far was to be travelled before reaching the homestead to the north.

The many hours to be endured over the next few days would be filled with thoughts, in particular where Abdul was concerned. He had so much in his head that at one stage he felt quite faint but picked himself up from the depression by taking a good drink of water and by looking around him at the countryside. He was simply amazed by how time had passed since the morning sun had struck the earth and rose clear of the horizon, each day was as seemingly quick as the last.

Before Abdul knew it the darkness of night was almost upon them, on this their last night before reaching the homestead.

The string was permitted to halt for the night as the sun commenced to say it's goodnight to the world and as the orange expanse of beautiful hue stretched across the horizon like a blanket or shawl the camels were painstakingly attended to.

Cicadas as usual, forever in their midst, continued to press their evening joyful song for all to hear, males calling for a mate. It's the heat of the late evening that brings them to life, crying for water and mateship, seeking company as any other creature of the world. Their song is majestic and a delight to hear, a sound so soothing that it helps the men sleep rather than impose many hours and sleeplessness. It's like how a mother's breast can dim the noise of a baby's crying; it had a calming effect, and there was no mystery in that.

But the desert as a whole was a mystery to most, appealing to a majority, and sheer bliss to all by night, for when the sun has said its goodnight the story of the desert commences to unfold, where things unseen are released of the burden of the day's heat where the bright light and searing temperatures of the day do nothing to herald the creatures presence, creatures of the night that come out to play and sing their songs of praise to the world around.

CHAPTER TWENTY-SIX

The world around Abdul was being revealed; little, by little, by little. The more he saw the more was shared, and this night was no different than any other.

It was important for Abdul to know the whereabouts of nearby towns and settlements, even places where hermits were lodged temporarily in their search for gold, and the police station not so far away was of little exception.

The Diamantina Police Station, put in place not far from the Birdsville Track and just 15 miles south of the Queensland border, was in operation in 1884, a station spoken of and accepted as being established, even before it arrived upon the scene and commenced its role in supporting the wider community. It wasn't much of a dwelling, in poorer condition than the Ghantowns dilapidated shacks of corrugated iron, where corrugated iron could be sought, but was nevertheless duly sanctioned with keeping the peace within the area, collect tax and prevent the selling of alcohol where unlawfully sold. The general location of the police station was provided to Abdul who was advised to seek aid from it should he ever need it.

"Furthermore," said Nak, "is the fact that I'd heard in the air that there might be the need for the station to be supplied with rations, and several times a year at that."

"A good job if it's available," said Shir.

"What will you do about it?" asked Abdul.

"I will consider a friend of a friend," replied Nak. "I know a man in Marree that might be able to sway a contract or two."

"I hope so," said Shir. "Once we get the wool back to Marree from the homestead, we'll be without a job, and we'll be at the homestead tomorrow."

"Unless Ahmad Mohammed comes up with something by the time we have returned," said Nak as he looked at Abdul. "He's quite gifted, in many ways, and can feel the needs of the many and sometimes the few. It's the bigger picture that he sees."

"Who is his?" asked Abdul.

"He works for a man who knows both Abdul Wade and Faiz Mahomet, and for a small the price to be paid for this knowledge – knowledge that is derived from a young women coming of her maturity – this man will release all sorts of valuable information;

valuable to us, not necessarily valuable to another," answered Nak as he took a drink of his hot tea.

"It's amazing," said Abdul, "the power that a woman has," and he thought of his wife back at home.

"And Shir can attest to that," said Nak with a smile.

"Ah, yes," agreed Shir, "to think that I am now married."

"Ha, ah," said Nak. "I see it in your eyes. You'd forgotten all about her, hadn't you? Thinking more and more about that pesky camel of yours: Slate and her calf."

"To surmise that I feel more for a camel than I do my own wife is utterly absurd," defended Shir.

"I don't believe a word of it," said Nak and turning to Abdul asked, "do you?"

Abdul stammered, "I, ah... well; to be honest I think Shir has been rather taken in by the delivery of his calf."

"I'm utterly disgusted by you both for thinking so unkindly of my attraction to Slate... my willingness to—."

"Ah, ha; there you have it," said Nak cheerfully, happy that he was right all along. "You feel more for your damn camels then you do your wife; and that proves it."

"Maybe so," admitted Shir, "but a camel can't do the things that a wife can do."

"That depends on the cameleer that you ask," said Nak as he burst out laughing, followed shortly by Abdul and Shir.

CHAPTER TWENTY-SEVEN

All three men awoke on the morning of the fourteenth day in tune with those that preceded it, before the sun rose above the horizon and together.

The duties commenced post-haste with Shir preparing the morning meal – conducted shortly after sunrise, their ablutions and prayer – whilst Abdul and Nak stepped out into the countryside in search of the camels that had strayed as usual; all that is, except Slate and the new born calf.

As a dingo had been shot most recently the urge within Nak pestered his subconscious, that he should carry his rifle in case of need, but experience had shown him that this wouldn't be necessary and so he left it behind, wrapped and secured back at camp.

The two men hadn't gone far when the bells from several animals gave them away and they were quickly advanced upon, their silhouettes standing out above the spinifex, the sighting of which might have been missed by the untrained eye for the camel blended in quite well with the surroundings.

Abdul approached one of the bulls of the string and could see the excitement starting to build within him for he was blowing his bladder out, a signal that he wished to mate. The stench of the camel was hardly noticed by Abdul as he tended to it, a big black patch of tar-like-ink sweating from pores at the back of its head, most prolific when bulls were in season; they would take every opportunity to rub it off against anything they could, hoping to draw the attentions of a female.

"A bull is blowing hard," said Abdul to Nak.

Nak was half bent over, looking at the feet of a camel he had a hold of, "Which one?"

"I think it's Joy."

Nak looked up and over to where Abdul was standing, "Yes; that's Joy alright. You'll have to keep him away from the folks at the homestead; they'll not appreciate the smell. The last thing I need is to upset negotiations: I'm trying to ensure next year's contract remains intact and these people get upset rather easily. The man's name is Alfred and his wife is crazy."

"Crazy is a funny name for a woman, is it not?" asked Abdul.

"No; I mean she's simply crazy; her name is Marge, but you must call her Mrs Stapleton, if at all."

Abdul remained perplexed for a moment as he continued with his work, having seen that Nak was going about his business.

The camels were gathered reasonably quickly, just ninety minutes this morning; compared to some days that was a sheer blessing.

Nak reflected upon the ease of the gathering and recalled one time that the camels came in by themselves just as he was about to look for them, led by Chocolate – there was no explanation for it.

"Let's get back now and be off," said Nak. "With any luck we'll be at the homestead well before noon."

CHAPTER TWENTY-EIGHT

When the homestead came into view the first thing Abdul saw was a reflection of pure picturesque beauty. There was a wooden house and a shed for storage; another for shearing; each with a roof of corrugated iron. A small windmill stood turning slowly as it pumped water from the ground and a dry creek bed sat not too far away.

It was easy to see that the high ground upon which the homestead was erected was chosen well and alleviated all concerns of flooding; that is, for the couple that lived here, not for the sheep which lay in abundance across the expanse of undulating ground, trees of mulga spotted all over.

There were several eucalyptuses near the dry creek bed and ghost gums, too, seemingly lining the lower ground and positioned to take advantage of the water which was offered by the creek during times of rain. It was all too familiar to Nak and Shir, but Abdul was taken in by the savoury solitude of the area.

Abdul could see the farmer – or 'pastoralist' as some preferred to be called – standing to the front of the house and rubbing his hands clean of dirt, a symbolic gesture if any that he was friendly and about to offer his hand in exchange of introduction, but the hand-shaking never came, just a simple nod between Nak and the colonist being shared.

Abdul remained with the string for the time being as Nak stepped towards the tall man in trousers and shirt, the hard work of living off the land evident upon the fabric, stains blemishing what his wife could never clean. He removed his hat temporarily and wiped his brow before returning it upon his head, looking Nak up and down quite briefly before staring at the turban upon Nak's head.

An exchange of words was taking place which Abdul couldn't quite hear and even if he could he doubted that he'd understand any of it. English was hard to learn and only years upon years of working with the white men of the land around would provide any advantage.

Nak used simple words as was his way in order to defuse the pressure of a long-winded sentence from anyone white, for the last thing he wished was to show too much confidence in understanding and then be bombarded with sentence upon sentence of words he simply couldn't piece together.

"So," said Nak, "wool ready, where?"

"Look," said Alfred, the look upon his face showing that he was impatient and couldn't tolerate the lack of English understanding, but nevertheless had a head for business and didn't wish to jeopardise the good relationship he currently shared with the Afghans. "You see, over there beside the house. You take and put on camel after unload."

"Where unload?" asked Nak.

"Over there, in the shed," said Alfred as he pointed over to the dark interior of his storage area. "The same place as last time you were here." But to Alfred these Afghans all looked the same.

Nak could hear the frustration but failed to understand it, for he was simply being polite by ensuring the supplies were unloaded in a convenient spot, for the rainy season would be upon them soon enough and the last thing Nak wished was to unload the supplies upon the ground and then to find that he was required to place them off the ground.

"You lucky," said Nak, forgetting himself and offering conversation where he shouldn't. "No vermin."

"No what?" asked Alfred with a curious look upon his face.

"No rat; you no rat."

"Ah;" replied Alfred. "Yes, plenty rat. There are rats right across this damn country. What do you think; we don't have rats up here?" Alfred was forgetting himself, and the words flowed from his tongue for a bit.

"Unload on ground, yes?"

"No!" replied Alfred in a huff. "Same as last time..! off ground, up; away from wet."

"Okay, I work now," said Nak as he turned away to attend his duty.

As a grower of wool could easily testify, the essence in making a living from conducting such a business was in the actual return of wages for a hard years work and no grower was going to constantly be dealt bouts of depression and stress by having to deal with teamsters and the bullocks, where delay upon delay was the normal outcome, when a good string of camels could do the work under the strong and delicate hands of an experienced cameleer.

Although the camel industry had expanded quite vigorously and it was sometimes hard to find a good job, where a constant flow of work could be taken advantage of, once you were able to prove your loyalty and be on schedule, a job was as good as sealed for the longevity of the unwritten contract which could easily dwarf the decades as they fell behind you. In this, Nak and the others were quite fortunate.

The homestead in which they now attending was enough to provide them with a good wage for their part in the transition of wool from sheep's back to storehouse, and in matter of fact, it was this particular homestead that had seen to it that Nak's current future was set rather comfortably for the beginning of each year to come, but would have to be looked after with delicate hands.

The camels fidget slightly and it was easy to see that they wished to be watered, but unloading was to come first. Chocolate could be seen, discontent written on his face as he chewed his green cud, hidden within thick lips, awaiting any opportunity to spit, with 30lbs of pressure, half a gallon of filth upon the man's face... it was written in his eyes.

As the cameleers set about sitting the animals and unloading each from the front to the rear, refraining from setting hobbles as the camels were to be watered, not fed. Alfred pulled a thick chain near his tank to allow the water to fill the troughs with their quarry so that each and every camel could be filled.

As the men talked and worked they could see Albert's wife approach one particular package that was wrapped in red cloth.

She turned briefly to see that her only child of three was safely hitched by a single lashing of rope to the post of the home they had come to know, for the last thing she wanted was for a camel to trample upon her pride and joy.

Shir watched as she tended to the article and Alfred carried on his business with Nak most temporarily, for Nak was too busy with what he had to attend to worry about anything else, in particular the farmer's idle chatter, pointing over to the wool on occasion and doing well in his efforts to signify the cargo to be transported by caravan to Marree. Nak wasn't a stupid man and could see without a doubt that that was where the wool was, breaking the invisible borders of the shed in which it was stored, piles and piles of the merchandise ready to be taken away.

Shir continued to watch the woman that hadn't seen him as yet and she unwrapped the article without any thought on the matter, being stupid and half-witted or simply rude and out to cause bitter mayhem.

The sight that was revealed to Shir was unforgettable. There before his very eyes, thirty feet away, was a stack of bacon slivers for the family of three.

Bacon; anything for that matter to do with a pig, was unclean both physically and spiritually. Pigs slopped on the faeces of other animals and such contamination could easily transfer from pig to human.

The Koran forbade the eating of pig, the mullah prohibited the transport of pig and its by-products, and even the eating of a can's contents, where the can was offered unlabelled, was shunned for what it might really be.

"Nak; NAK!" shouted Shir with great terror within his eyes, a display so wrought with horror that Marge Stapleton initially thought that something was wrong with her child.

"What is it!" answered a panic-stricken Nak.

"There, the woman," pointed Shir with wide open eyes and a pointing finger. "Bacon... we've been transporting bacon."

Nak stomped over to Alfred with the grimace upon his mouth twisted out of fashion for his persona, "What this!"

The farmer saw immediately what was the matter and put his hands up in defence, knowing full well that he needed his wool to market on this string or be damned, knowing full well that he couldn't afford another to transport his wool.

"Wait!" said Alfred as he stepped back. "Sorry; me sorry."

"You damn man," cursed Nak. "You very bad."

"No, look... you watch," and with great fury in his face, his lips tight and full of energy, creases forming upon the skin around his eyes and cheeks, Alfred stepped briskly over to his wife and slapped her so hard across the face that she fell to the ground along with the slivers of bacon: It was hard enough to farm wool, and so grateful Alfred was that he held a tract of land upon a small basin which allowed for a reasonable pasture to supply many hungry mouths: such an uncanny site it was.

The woman burst out sobbing, holding the red mark upon her cheek, rubbing her hand delicately where it hurt the most, reaching for the bacon as it lay upon the ground. Alfred kicked it out of reach, "You stupid bitch!"

Alfred looked back to Nak and the others who were quite shocked by the ordeal and had most temporarily forgotten about the bacon laying there upon the ground. Alfred quickly moved over to the cameleers and all could see the sorrow in his eyes as he displayed great apology for what had happened.

"My wife is so ridiculously stupid; I didn't know of the bacon," said Alfred. "It's finished with now, yes?"

"No," said Nak, sorry for what had been done. "No more work. You do own wool, we go home."

"No, wait," pleaded Alfred, forgetful to whom he was speaking with, his English gone haywire. "I didn't know about the bacon, I swear it. If I'd know about it I would have stopped it in Marree. This should never have happened, you must understand," Alfred could feel the contract falling from his grasp; he needed the money from the wool more than the cameleers needed their wages.

Alfred calmed down a little, "I pay more, little extra," said he. "Pay for five more days on road, you get extra money, pay at post office in Marree," Alfred put his hands up to hold back any interruption. "Look, I get letter and give you. You give post office and he pay much; you understand? You give letter to John Arthur O'Brien."

Nak nodded as he looked around at the others, each glum-faced and not sure as to what they should do.

"No more bacon," said Alfred, "never any more; all finished; never see again."

"Okay," said Nak. "We do... job, for you. We water camels and load wool; we go Marree."

"Oh, thank you, thank you," said Alfred, showing his true face, the anxiousness of his need and the assurance offered, the urgency in which he needed aid. The cameleers now knew that they were in a better position to barter if they wished to do so.

"Ask for more money," said Shir in his native tongue. "Take from him what means the most."

"No," said Nak. "I won't become one of them. We do job, is okay," said Nak. "Bacon finished."

"Yes, yes; thank you," said Alfred and for the first time he shook hands with Nak, showing his gratitude for what the cameleers were about to do for him.

With sudden forgetfulness having fallen from Nak's mind he turned one final time to Alfred and procured two letters from within his pocket, and with a forced smile he handed them to the farmer. Alfred opened each and briefly read them before giving a final farewell, much appreciative of the letters which required no reply.

CHAPTER TWENTY-NINE

With the camel string watered, loaded, and ready to move by mid-afternoon, the cameleers decided on making way for a waterhole that was known to be situated just off the main track of Birdsville. The homestead had provided water for the camels but it wasn't enough. Maybe it was a part of the farmers mean streak to see the cameleers put out, but this consideration was soon waived for Alfred required the wool back at Marree as soon as practically possible and could not afford to delay them.

The string was made to stand and the march back to Marree commenced, each camel carrying four to five large bales of wool. They would remain loaded for the short stop at the watering hole and continue a little further so that they could keep away from the main flux of mosquitoes that were prone to inhabit such places.

The waterhole was a delight to see and something that the camels took good advantage of, neither entering into the water nor rolling in it, simply standing upon the edge and drinking politely as did the men – it was more of a billabong than anything else, but was not part of an anabranch.

A water fowl was then seen as it took off into thicker scrub, away from the intrusion upon his haven, water lilies and hyacinth catching the men's eyes, a wonderful sight if ever-one was seen; it put the picturesque homestead to shame. Abdul hadn't seen anything like it for many years and Nak cherished the moment for the never ending bleakness of the desert put much strain upon his shoulders; Shir saw the true nature of the waterhole and what it had to offer... more than just water.

The waterhole was far from dry and there would be little semblance of anything so sublime on their return journey; this they knew from experience. So it was for them to take the time now to water the camels and finish with the contract for another year, each man feeling some regret over the episode with the bacon and the debacle that was suffered.

A little further on and their camp was erected, sleep sought with more silence than normal dominating the scene. The camels were left on short hobbles as usual but this night they seemed to remain close to the campsite, the rest at the homestead and their intake of water holding back the pangs of hunger.

It was just before the blankets were put to good use that Abdul went over to a large piece of wood upon the ground, to be used on the campfire. It was unfortunate indeed that he should be bitten by the scorpion, the small creature of the Australian bush being interrupted by this intruder from a foreign land. The upturning of the wood had disturbed the solitude and therefore a welled amount of fear for the unknown burst its banks from within the arachnid.

It lashed out at the little finger of his left hand that was so close... too close for comfort, the smell of the flesh easily detected but unknown. Such an unknown danger with the ability to upturn a home was an invader which required killing and so the scorpion plunged his stinger into the finger of Abdul who retracted himself from the predicament in such shock that he missed the opportunity to see what it was that had bitten him.

He cradled his left hand into chest and slowly revealed the damage to himself, moving his right hand away and then looking down upon the redness of the sting.

Abdul was lucky in a way for he was strong and young; too old and or frail could have meant a prolonged death with much agony when in the outback and without aid, but death was so seldom seen that it was rarely, if ever, raised as a concern, but Abdul wasn't free from the encumbrance incurred just yet.

The pain was throbbing and grew from bad to worse very quickly and the fear that welled up within Abdul was too much for his mind to decipher, hence his panic overflowed and he went running to Shir and Nak, stricken with pandemonium.

"SHIR! NAK!" he screamed as he approached the campfire, the two men standing up from upon the ground, initially lost in bliss, enjoying their tea and looking up to the sky as the stars revealed themselves for the world to see once more. Now they were nothing less than very worried.

Abdul saw the silhouettes of the two men and his panic subsided slightly.

"Nak! Look; I've been bitten," scrambled Abdul, of an explanation for what had happened. "Over there, by the wood, where the ground... it was under it and... look at my hand."

Slowly, Abdul pulled his affected finger from the security of his clench.

"Move closer to the fire, Abdul," said Nak with a slight sense of urgency, fearing that it might be a snake bite.

"Strange it is," said Shir, "but not a snake bite."

"No?" said Abdul.

"No," concurred Nak. "It's a scorpion sting. Look, you can see that it lacks the puncture marks of a fang... the redness is clear and no venom upon the surface of the wound."

"Are you sure?" asked Abdul. "How do you know? How can you be so sure?"

"I've seen bites before, Abdul," explained Nak. "Plenty of men have been bitten and then died by the viciousness offered from a snake. You have to be careful not to step on them during the day. But this is night; you see; past dusk too late for snakes to be out in the closing cold."

"But it hurts so much," confided Abdul with the pain of the bite scribed upon his face, his eyes seeking compassion without his knowing it.

"There's not much that can be done, I'm afraid," said Nak. "This pain will be with you for some time now, but I've never seen a man die from such a wound."

"No?" asked Abdul for some clarification, wishing to be assured of his safety, looking for the word 'not dead' to be ushered to him.

"No," said Nak, "never have I seen anyone killed by such a thing. You'll have to suffer the pain, I'm afraid, and that's not a nice thing to have to say."

"Will the pain last long?" asked Abdul.

"Maybe tomorrow you'll feel better," said Nak.

"Or the day after that," advised Shir, trying to ease Abdul's concerns, but only managing to escalate the idea that there was much pain to be suffered over the coming days.

"I won't sleep well like this," said Abdul. "I don't wish to shy from my responsibilities."

"You can try and look after the kitchen; if you can, Abdul," advised Nak. "Both, Shir and I, we will take care of everything else, even laying your prayer mat out when it is time. Only do what you think you can do and never shy from requesting help."

"You must promise, Abdul," said Shir. "Say you will give warning to us when you are troubled by the work you do."

"I shall," said Abdul and he smiled with the comfort of the thought that he was going to be okay after all.

The men soon found themselves bedded down for the night with the fire between them stoked and piled sufficiently, the camels going about their business, whether that be feeding or sleeping, though mostly sleeping. As for Abdul, he suffered much that first night but the worst was to come, for the pain only increased over the coming days and would not go away.

CHAPTER THIRTY

The next day revealed much unpleasantness, in particular for Abdul; the gathering of the camels also took longer than usual, and was an occurrence that Nak just couldn't figure out; normally they were much easier to gather but today several more hours was spent conducting what was considered to be the normal routine.

Abdul had managed to put the kitchen away before Nak and Shir returned, but had refrained from placing it upon Slate. Slate had been doing well as the kitchen camel and didn't seem to mind being shuffled in the order of march by being placed to the rear of the string.

Abdul stood up gingerly so as not to knock his hand, his finger held against his chest, being in much pain, protecting it as best he could. The putting away of the kitchen had been a choir for him but with the extra hours spent in gathering the camels Abdul seemed to have had more than enough time to carry out his duty.

"I was becoming worried," said Abdul to Shir and Nak as they led Chocolate in with the other camels close behind. "What kept you?"

"The camels were dispersed over a wider area this morning and growling more than normal," said Shir. "Not many were eating... they seemed to be looking for something."

"Maybe they were looking for each other," said Abdul.

"You'd be surprised how silly that is, Abdul," said Nak. "The camels can hear the difference in the bells around their necks. They know, believe me; Chocolate wouldn't be hard to find. When a camel wants something bad enough, he'll get it."

Abdul smiled and turned to his handy work, seemingly proud of what he had accomplished, having carried out his task in more pain than Shir and Abdul could ever realise.

"Good," said Nak. "We'll sit the camels and get them loaded; time is running out and the day is growing old."

They smiled again and Abdul's expression painted a severe warning for the others to see, his face lighting up, the eyes within his head opening wide as though he had suddenly seen a ghastly image.

"What is it, Abdul?" asked Nak as he turned towards the direction in which Abdul was looking and there before him, upon the horizon and approaching fast, was nothing less than a foreboding sight which needed no deciphering.

From north to south, across the entire expanse of the sky came a darkened mass of billowing red sand. It was a sandstorm of the likes Shir and Nak had never seen in their entire lives and they had little more than seven minutes to react before it was upon them.

Sandstorms were not that frequent but were dreaded by all that suffered them, for what they delivered was anything from much lost time to several days of misery.

The large dark cloud of sand that approached from the horizon just kept rolling towards them, great billows of surging force that seemed to literally roll over the ground towards them, mushrooming balls powering on and quite unstoppable.

The sheer terror for all those that witnessed a sandstorm was nothing compared to what was now approaching the three of them.

A sandstorm could last for such short periods or blow for hours on end, it was impossible to tell as it bore down upon them.

"Quickly, Shir, get the shelter from the pack saddle, put it up over there next to the mulga tree," ordered Nak. "Abdul, get the water and some biscuits from the kitchen, we don't have much time; quickly now."

The men rushed to their tasks and Abdul aided Shir after seeing to it that the calf was untied from the sack near its mother, giving it free reign to wander off as it needed to. Shir looked over and saw what Nak had done as he unrolled the shelter, a tarpaulin more than anything else, the most expensive commodity they could afford, the next best thing to a tent, but its size was only enough to protect them during times of inclement weather, not large enough to sit in as though one might wish to sit beneath a spacious tent and cook a meal whilst the night passed them by. No; it was nothing like that; it was nothing short of a very large blanket made of coarse material, used to shelter them from the rain.

"Nak!" jolted Shir for the jemadar's attention. "Tie the calf to Slate, keep them together."

Abdul froze for a split second and then did as Shir had requested, placing a cord between mother and sibling, nose pegs set aside. It was then that Abdul reflected upon Shir's request. There would be no need to tie the calf to the mother unless the storm was to last for more than a day. Was there something in Shir's foresight of what was to come? Nevertheless, Nak was extremely grateful that the camels were not yet loaded.

With the camels quickly forgotten and the shelter briskly erected, it representing nothing more than a small collapsed tent, the centre tied fast to a branch of the mulga and the sides pegged down as best could be achieved, the men took their biscuits and water to the dark interior of the new home, crawling under the shelter on the side facing away from the approaching storm.

Shir looked up again to Abdul, further advice to flood from his mouth, "The Koran! We need it."

Abdul was the jemadar and knew precisely where it was stored and how best to retrieve it with the minimum of fuss, so without further ado he crawled back outside as the edge of the storm hit him with full force whilst the other two felt the impact of the storm hit them, too, the sides of the shelter pushing against them and conforming to their body shapes in rough fashion as they sat there, the canvas sheeting held upon their bodies by the force of the wind which wasn't about to relent.

For Nak, who had experienced less savage storms of this nature, the experience was terrible. It was as though a blanket had been cast upon the world, it turning from day into night, the cloud of black engulfing him and everything else for miles around, vision denied as a means for which to sense direction, Nak relying on his common sense and basic wind direction to calculate his position and that of the camels, of which all were laying still with their heads away from the grains of sand that pelted their hindquarters

If the camels were moving it would have been a different story, in particular if the wind was less savage and lasted for a short time, for the camels would continue on their way, following one another as each is connected like the cars of a train, the lead camel and cameleer leaning into the task and continuing the move forward, the cameleer unable to see but the feet feeling the way. The camels were a little better off, for camels would simply close their nostrils and breathe through the slit formed where the nostrils met, hair filtering sand from the air as they breathed. The camel's eyes were also fifty percent opaque and so in a less severe storm were able to negotiate their way reasonably well.

But the severity of this particular storm was obvious from the onset and Nak experienced its savagery first hand as he fondled his way from camel to camel, looking for Chocolate and his sacred Koran, the book which meant so much to him and his comrade. He could feel the stinging of the grains of sand as they lashed out upon his body and in return all he could do was to try and keep his head low and in full gear, making sure not to lapse in concentration, not for a single second.

The noise was also quite deafening and seemed to get worse as the storm wore on, whether it was because it was in fact getting worse or because his ears were being deafened by the delivery of the screeching wind as it lashed out its evil upon him.

He felt around each camel's body, leg and neck, seeking out the one he needed, his fingertips doing the hard work for his eyes, the lids of which were beginning to waver. The pressure of his eyes being held shut against the pelting sand and other debris was commencing to take its toll, and before long Nak was starting to feel the pressure of quitting what he had started until he fell with great relief upon the lead camel and the compartment which held the leather bound book of his.

The book was secure between his fingers and now was the time for him to return to his comrades.

He was now more than ever forced to remain upon the ground crawling, making his way back to the tent foot by foot, hoping with his entire might that he was going the right way, the single and most important of all the factors that offered themselves to him being that the direction of the wind was known and computed.

It was then, as he began to question his progress back to the others, that he considered whether or not the wind may have changed direction on him, even slightly. If it had then he'd never find his way back to the shelter.

All he could do was press ever on, trying to keep a mental track of the distance he was covering as he searched the tent out.

He screamed at the top of his lungs for Shir and Abdul to hear him but they heard nothing but the impact of the sound from the storm, the ferocity of the wind almost pushing them over from their seated position within the discomfort of their little hide.

Abdul tried to say something to Shir but he could hardly see or hear his friend; Abdul couldn't even hear himself. He pulled his left hand in for protection and with his left reached for Shir's ear.

Abdul cupped his good hand into a concave shape and yelled into the ear of his friend, "Do you think something has happened to Nak?"

Shir reached for Abdul's ear and yelled back, "No, but even if something is wrong, there is nothing we can do but leave the shelter and crawl around until we find him. If he is lost then he will never be found."

CHAPTER THIRTY-ONE

Time was taking its toll upon Nak for he'd been in the storm for almost an hour. The thrashing that it gave his body was simply too much to believe for bruising had commenced to accumulate all over him, debris a big factor in what he considered to be the worst storm he'd ever had to face.

He fumbled on in the darkness, his Koran held tight in hand. Of all the things that could go wrong, to lose the Koran would be the worst. He felt for his friends then, the unselfish thoughts that accompanies one when death is considered. He was happy that the Koran was in his grasp for it meant he was with his belief in time of death, and his belief was with him, but his friends would be without it.

He collapsed then upon the ground and the grains of the storm pillared around him, commencing to bury him partially with the landscape of undulating nakedness. He then reflected again upon Shir and Abdul. What need would they have of the Koran? They were alive, not dead; he would be dead, not them. Buried alive! Would anyone find him? Would his final burial place be discovered before he was fed upon by the creatures of the outback, by the winged scroungers that soared through the air far above the surface of the land? The ants, too, would have their way with him, eating every scrap of flesh upon his body until there was nothing left but bone. And what of his secret love for the prostitute of the Ghantown? He would never again be able to lie with Saki.

How he would miss her and the comfort of her soft voice, the warmth of her flesh against his in the heat of a passionate night.

No! He wouldn't allow this to happen, he would do all he could to ensure he survived this ordeal. He had to think positively. Even if he had to remain outside in the storm for its duration he would only go without food for a short time; even water intake wasn't that important, for several hours without water would be fine: he could survive that, surely.

But what if the storm lasted longer? How long could it last? He was beginning to feel thirsty already.

NO! He shook the thoughts out of his mind. He would continue to try and find his friends, if it was the last thing he did, and if he was to grow too tired to continue he would simply find the best shelter possible, like a tree trunk or rock, and curl up into a ball and ride the storm out.

He had a lot to decide upon, but for the moment he had to try and find his friends.

CHAPTER THIRTY-TWO

Abdul and Shir shared a little of their concerns for their friend, Nak, but in due process figured that he would survive the ordeal, for the storm couldn't last forever. As for them, they had biscuits and water to share and these commodities alone would be enough to keep them occupied.

The thoughts of home now grew within each man, each in his own way, more than ever before. It was like a complicated saga of endless emotions, a roller coaster of fear, apprehension, sadness, and many, many memories of happier times.

The shelter they had erected was certainly not spacious, by any degree. The slashing of the wind against them saw that every inch of space, other than the portion behind them where the interior was protected from the wind, was seemingly sucked from existence.

The two men had moved closer, their backs against the coarse material which sheltered them, a little area to their front made for no other purpose than to deliver them both a feeling of control over the surroundings. Here they lay their biscuits and water, in easy reach. They couldn't see very well at all, it was practically pitch black and they had quickly decided that fire was out of the question.

Every now and again they would share a little conversation but for the most part they remained tight lipped. Their thoughts were on family and home, and Nak. They had no idea how he was coping on the outside or whether or not he'd managed to find shelter. It was hoped that he'd curled up beside a camel or two and remained in the protection of the large animals, but they both knew that he would have tried, heaven and earth, to get back to them with the Koran that he had sought.

In a way it was their own faults that had delivered them this scenario, where two men were without the third, simply because of their need for the Koran. And so they blamed 'it' for the situation and quickly saw the error of their ways, for such a sacred thing should not be accused of delivering such evil upon them.

Neither Shir nor Abdul had requested the Koran be retrieved by Nak, it was Nak's idea to retrieve it, but Shir did bring the object of their obsession into view, it was he, Shir, that had put the idea into Nak's head, had said that they 'needed' it when in fact all that they needed was one another. Shir had dangled the carrot in front of Nak and he had taken the task of retrieving the Koran as being his and his alone.

So Shir sat in silence as best he could and thought about the man that was leader of their treks into the outback and beyond, the jemadar that was seemingly without fault, and was one of the best men that walked the face of the earth. It was only his grimace, the facial expression upon his face and couldn't be moved, that allowed people who didn't know him to think differently of him.

It was of very poor character that anyone should think badly of Nak simply because he looked different than most, in the same way that people perceived Shir, for he was quite ugly, very unpleasant to look at, but had a heart of gold and could never be faulted for who he was and what he represented. Shir was a free man and lived with a free spirit, but followed his belief to the ends of the earth.

Shir was a religious man and it was here in the midst of the storm that he felt the urge to pray to himself for hours on end in order to keep himself occupied, to give him hope.

CHAPTER THIRTY-THREE

Before Shir and Abdul, beyond their sight, the day had fallen behind them and the dark of the night was being delivered unto the earth. If it wasn't for the fact that the storm was still thrashing solidly against them and their shelter then they would have known about it, they would have known the time of day.

Their biscuits were gone and so was half their water, having been drunk out of sheer boredom, not out of necessity, and it was for this reason that Shir felt the urge to pass water and needed to depart the luxury of the tent for a short time.

Shir cupped his hands around Abdul's ear as Abdul put a biscuit into his mouth and shared with him what it was he wished to do and Abdul was fluxed with sudden realisation that if he'd wanted to relieve his bowels of the previous days meals he'd consumed he'd be in true difficulty.

Shir departed the tent, crawling upon all fours, and Abdul finished his biscuit before deciding that he wanted no more. It would be difficult enough to pass water, let alone anything else, and with that still in his mind he decided to try and get some true rest by lying upon the ground... after Shir had returned and they had the opportunity to pray.

Abdul touched his finger then and the sheer pain of the gentle touch rode up his entire arm. The pain was getting worse, certainly not better, and he was worried for what might lay ahead for him and the scorpion bite. He'd been bitten the night before and the full cycle of a day had passed him by. He could feel the tiredness within him, tiredness which comes with the passing of many hours. He knew the day was over, even if he couldn't see anything of real value from within the shelter that he sat. Twenty-four hours with increasing pain: he would see what the morning brought.

Shir came back into the shelter having relieved himself, a majority of which had ended up running down the inside of his leg. He refrained from saying anything to Abdul for it mattered little, and so they gave praise where they sat and laid down as best they could to get some sleep.

And so, rolled up close to each other, the material of the shelter covering them both, flapping hard against their bodies, they eventually fell asleep.

Abdul woke with a great fright falling over him and as he woke he felt a suffocation crushing him. The pain in his finger suddenly shot through the roof as he jolted awake and he tried sitting up, but his efforts gave little reward.

The stirring of his body against Shir also woke him and together they did all they could to sit up again, the weight of the sand upon the skin of the shelter that covered them making it extremely difficult to move.

The panic within Abdul was slower to subside than with Shir, not because of the pain within his finger, but due to a dream he was having, a nightmare that tore at his fears.

Shir fondled around until he found Abdul sitting there beside him and searched for his ear.

"What happened?"

"I had a bad dream," answered Abdul. "Is Nak back? Have you seen him?"

"He hasn't come in."

"My finger is very bad," said Abdul at the top of his lungs. "I fear the worst. I've never had pain like this before."

"We'll have to have a look at it once the storm clears, but at the moment there's not much we can do."

"What time do you think it is?"

"I have no idea," said Shir in reply. "Maybe I should have a look outside, see if the sand has given way to clear sky."

"The wind is still blowing hard."

"It's worth a try," insisted Shir. "I don't like the idea of sitting here for another day if the outside world is clear and we can see what we are doing. We have to find Nak."

"He would have found his way back in here," said Abdul.

"Not if something has gone wrong," advised Shir as he crawled out into the sandstorm that had continued in its ferocity.

Within seconds Shir had returned.

"It's no use," said Shir. "It's as dark as before."

"What time of night or day do you think it is?" asked Abdul

"I'm still tired so maybe it's night; I also feel a little chill."

"I'm tired too but the pain is worse."

They continued in their friendly way, the need for each other's company so very important and required. They needed to support each other, now, more than ever.

"I think I need to do something about my finger," said Abdul.

"What, exactly?" asked Shir.

"I think it needs to be removed."

Shir fell silent for a few seconds before deciding that there was nothing further to do or say. Both men were silent and they considered the predicament that they were in. They had very little water and no biscuits. He would lie back down again, until the build-up of sand upon him woke him or Abdul once more.

CHAPTER THIRTY-FIVE

The two men slept on and off for what seemed to be an eternity, sitting up to push the sand from upon them every now and again, this effort alone draining them of all energy.

Abdul had never before, in his entire life, ever had so much time to contemplate his life. He considered the errors of his way, the friends he had treated poorly and those he had treated well.

Friends were friends, and all were of different character. He thought of those that were weak and those that were strong, how each characteristic brought on different meanings in each, how they differed in their perceptions of life and death.

In reality, one was no different than another. They were all friends; they simply had a different perspective on life. Why would he treat one more favourably than the next?

He would, from this day forward, treat each and everyone the same.

Shir, too, was exposed to many thoughts, some which bothered him and others which instilled great confidence within him.

Shir concentrated more on his past, the way his life had unfolded to lead to this day. He had a father and a mother in Afghanistan, both of whom were dead and buried; but nevertheless he reflected upon them and his country.

Had he done the right thing in his fight against the British, his actions as a spy? He had killed a white man and now he regretted it. The long day before Shir now paved his train of thought and within the span of a few short hours he had courageously confided unto himself a promise to never kill another man for the remainder of his life.

And as the contemplations of life continued for them both, the outside world continued in its day to day rituals, where the sun rose and then fell again; day turning into night.

CHAPTER THIRTY-SIX

It was quite some time later, Abdul not sure exactly how long, but long enough it seemed for him to get enough sleep before the entire world that encased him came tumbling down, the large branch of the mulga to which the shelter they had erected was attached, broke away and smothered both him and Shir.

The panic within each of them in those few seconds was overwhelming. One moment they were able to quite comfortably breathe and get some rest and then suddenly they were woken and being crushed by the weight of the sand upon the makeshift tent.

Both men fought to get out from the mess of the fallen tent and scrambled as best they could for the outside world, losing one another in the process, moving blindly into the storm which hadn't yet appeared to settle.

Abdul could feel the searing pain of his entire arm, now nothing more than an appendage that he couldn't move. He moved around and found the base of the mulga and sat there, covering his face as best he could with the clothing he wore, cradling his arm against the force of the wind to no avail.

Where was Shir, where was his new friend, the one he had come to learn so much about over the past few days. And that's when it hit him hardest. The reality of the situation was that they had been suffering like this for quite some time and his arm was nothing less than testimony of the amount of time that had passed since the storm arrived.

Abdul sat in his misery and looked up, thinking he'd heard something but not quite sure. And there it was, the shadow of a hunched figure running towards him against the wind, and then the shadow disappeared.

The figure of Shir then collapsed beside him and clarity came once more to the area, a little light to shed some visual aid to the dilemma they were in.

They snuggled together, Shir doing all he could to help Abdul protect his arm, for Shir was not a selfish man; none of them were.

The minutes ticked by and slowly, but surely, the wind dropped away and the sands settled, the surroundings becoming clearer and more easily seen.

All of the spinifex in the area was covered in sand which even now

246

became unsettled and fell upon the ground like tiny dry waterfalls of grain. The sun came out from hiding, away to the west as night commenced to grow. There would be around three hours of light left before night visited them once more; three days of darkness they had suffered and yet there was more to come.

Shir was the first upon his feet as he stood and looked towards the tail of the storm as it moved away and seemed to die. With abruptness he turned to look for the string of camels; what he was confronted by was shocking to say the least but he had expected it.

The wool and pack saddles were strung everywhere, some having moved up to twenty feet during the storm and the camels could not be seen, none that is except Slate and the calf. They were nothing more than two piles of sand, one large and one small, in the same place they had been left, two carcasses ready to be filtered by the food chain to the pores of the earth: in a few days there would be little left of them.

Shir tried with his entire might to listen for the bells of the camels, to try his best in locating them... how far had they gone, were any still alive?

Suddenly Shir turned and saw Abdul sitting there with tiredness in his eyes and the pain of the arm written upon his face. His friend, Nak, was nowhere to be seen.

"Nak!" yelled Shir as he moved over towards Abdul. "Nak! Where are you?"

With a great surge of joy erupting from within him he heard the reply, music to his ears, from about two hundred feet away.

"Here!" cried Nak. "I'm over here."

Shir looked over towards where the sound was coming and he could see Nak's outline emerge from the desert with a single camel following; it was Chocolate. Nak had found himself a little shelter, and although not the best it had served him well, for Chocolate was a true companion.

Shir smiled as the bell around Chocolate's neck swung into action and by the time Nak was just metres from his friend a few other camels could be seen to come out of the desert landscape to join them.

They sat around the fire and looked one another in the eye, each thankful for what they had been given; this second chance, for it seemed as though death had visited them all but had decided not to cast his vicious spell.

The fire was lit in plenty of time to prepare something good to eat for they all had big appetites, in particular after so many days, and water went down rather fast. They discussed several issues which confronted them, one of which was the camels, for without them they had nothing.

"It's almost dark," said Abdul. "I think it's time to do something about my finger."

"What can we do?" asked Nak. "There is nothing."

"I need to amputate it," said Abdul.

Nak looked from Abdul to Shir and then back again, "Are you mad? Maybe the storm has affected you," said Nak.

"He's right," said Shir. "Something needs to be done."

Nak saw the reality of it all within Abdul's eyes but didn't wish to respond.

"It has to be done, Nak," pleaded Abdul. "I can't move my arm, the pain is unbearable, and I fear that death will be the result if something isn't done soon."

"What is cutting your finger off going to do?" asked Nak, disturbed by the talk.

"It will take away the source of the pain," said Abdul.

"The source of your pain is your arm," said Nak, not too bluntly, "shall we amputate that?"

"I hope not, Nak, but if it must be done, then it must be done," replied Abdul.

"He's right," concurred Shir. "He should take off the finger. I have shared much with Abdul whilst in the tent and I recall, quite distinctly, that a man of Afghanistan, near my village in fact, took off his finger under similar circumstances."

"Yes," said Abdul. "I, too, have heard—."

"We have 'all heard'," interrupted Nak. "That story is very old and has been told many times. Much has been forgotten in its translation and passing from one to another. You can never rely on fables."

"Nak," pleaded Abdul, "look at me; look into my eyes."

Nak did as he was asked and felt the hurt within him, that his new friend had to disfigure himself. Nak had lived with disfigurement for some years now, with the grimace of his mouth the way in which it was. He always received unkind stares from onlookers. But at least Abdul's disfigurement was small and could easily go unnoticed.

"Okay," said Nak. "I'll do it. I'm the jemadar, it'll be my responsibility."

"Thank you, Nak," said Abdul and without further ado the preparations were carried out before the sun disappeared completely, for Abdul feared he wouldn't see the light of day if the injury got any worse.

Shears... clippers for the cutting of hair whilst on the road... instruments employed for many reasons, cast in rust stains but oiled well and looked after, for such pieces of equipment were quite expensive.

"These will do," said Nak to Abdul and Shir as he held up the shears that were to do the job of cutting away Abdul's finger. "It'll work as good as a knife... they're very sharp."

Nak sat down beside the other two men, a small rock in front of Abdul.

"I'll not use them as I would normally, Abdul," explained Nak. "I'll simply hold the blade over your finger and then hit down hard with another rock upon it," Nak looked him in the eyes again. "It will hurt, Abdul."

"It can't hurt me any more than I hurt already," said Abdul with seeming difficulty. "I can't take much more. Please; be swift."

Nak looked to Shir as he placed the blade over the finger and prepared the rock for its delivery upon the shears, "Look away, Abdul, so you don't flinch. Are you ready with the bandage, Shir?"

"Yes, I am—" commenced Shir as he held it up in display, and before he could finish the sentence, and without any further notice or warning, Nak smashed the back of the blade and Abdul's finger came away without any trouble.

Abdul had been taken by surprise, as was Shir, and Nak was amazed by the small amount of pain that Abdul displayed as the finger came away from his hand. Nak could only think that the amount of pain Abdul suffered was so great that the amputation was nothing more than a tickle, either that or the paralysis was so bad that the pain somehow failed to register with him.

Shir moved hurriedly with the bandage as blood seeped from the wound and secured it in place quite masterfully after a brief pause to allow the wound to cleanse itself of any poison.

Abdul looked upon the place where his finger had been and then to where it lay upon the ground before Nak picked it up and threw it into the spinifex.

"That's it, there's nothing left we can do for you, Abdul," said Nak. "The rest is not up to us. If the paralysis in the arm does not go away and the pain gets any worse then I don't know what we can do."

"My arm will have to come off," said Abdul.

"That will be for some other to decide, not for me; nor you, Abdul," said Nak. "Only a doctor or nurse practising in such things can decide upon the fate of your arm. Our job now is to see you, and the load, delivered to Marree. If your arm doesn't improve then we'll try and find help in one of the other settlements close at hand."

"But your load," said Abdul. "It'll be late getting to Marree."

"Better late than never," said Nak. "Besides, we're already behind schedule and will have missed the train. The shipment will be sent in the next available train."

"Will Stapleton be settled with that?"

"Maybe not, but he knows as well as anyone else that you can't rule the weather conditions; besides, he knows that the wool will be delivered, even if a little late; he'll just have to suffer the inconvenience of getting paid a little less for his wool. He'd not have done any better with bullocks or horses; he knows that as well and we do."

"You are right, or course," agreed Abdul. "I think I'll get some sleep now."

"Yes," said Nak, "you do that. Good night."

Shir woke to the sound of a bell, the night very still and the stars out in all their glory.

"What are you doing, Nak?" asked Shir.

"I took Chocolate's bell from him when I tied him up. I thought that ringing it during the night might bring some of the camels home."

"Home," scoffed Shir. "A funny place this is to call home."

"You know what I mean."

"Yes," said Shir, "I know. So what do you intend to do, sit up all night and ring that bell?"

"I'll sleep," said Nak. "As I wake during the night I'll ring the bell and sleep some more."

"I'll help, too," said Shir. "It'll help if the camels return by their own accord."

"Thank you, Shir."

Shir smiled and Nak lay down to go back to sleep and as he drifted into a dream, Shir stood up and looked to the heavens.

The stars were out in all their glory and although the moon was of little help the brilliance of the stars were enough to provide that required amount of light for a search to be conducted.

Shir considered that he was currently the strongest. Although the shelter of the tent wasn't great it was enough to provide shelter from the worst of the storm, whereas, Nak was exposed to its full ferocity. He also considered Abdul and the lack of sleep he had suffered due to the pain in his arm. If Abdul could be afforded sleep then he should be left to slumber.

Shir left the bell where it was because he didn't wish to confuse any of the camels by ringing it and then shifting his position; he'd simply move out into the wilderness and search them out as best he could, using the fire as a guide in the night, for it would be able to be seen from quite a distance.

As luck would have it, Shir came upon the first of the camels within a few minutes; it was heading back to the camp. He took hold of it and led it the remainder of the distance before tying it up, the camel being as weary as the men from the ordeal suffered in the face of the storm.

It stood to good reason that most of the camels would be awake and feeding as they wouldn't have had much opportunity during the weathering of the sandstorm. The natural fodder from around would be enough to provide the camels with a little moisture and a good fill, ready for all the days' work that was to fall upon them all, be they ready or not for a hard day's labour.

Within the first thirty minutes of Shir's expedition to search for the camels he had found almost half of them, and as the tiredness of his efforts commenced to build upon his wearied form he turned back towards the campfire to get some rest. As he walked he fell upon a carcass, a camel dead and decaying, open wounds quite clear; he'd been taken advantage of by some of the wildlife in the area, be it dingo after an easy meal or some bird of prey.

The flesh seemed to move and it was then that he realised that the flesh was alive with maggots.

Shir turned away from the vision of hopelessness and continued to the camp.

CHAPTER FORTY

Abdul rose the next morning to find the sun making its approach upon them all, with Shir cooking a meal upon the open fire and Nak standing up near the edge of their small camp and looking out over the desert surroundings for any visual sign of further movement, camels that might be returning.

"Good morning, Nak; Shir," greeted Abdul.

"And you too, good friend," said Shir with a smile.

Nak turned upon hearing the voice, his grimace set fast upon his face, no smile evident but softness within his voice indicating his pleasure at seeing Abdul rise.

"How is your arm this morning?" asked Nak.

Abdul moved it around in display, "I think it's getting better. A little walking will do it well, some circulation to get the blood flowing."

"Probably true," said Nak, "but you shouldn't over do it."

"But the wool," said Abdul. "It must get back to Marree."

"We're late as it is, like I said," said Nak. "Any further delay will not alter the price at the depot. Our friend at the homestead was to be paid for delivery by deadline, not lateness in delivery."

"Do you think further contracts will be lost?" asked Abdul.

"No," said Nak, "but he'll try his best to alter the price he pays us for transportation and we'll have to consider accepting it in order to keep the job."

Abdul saw the camels sitting upon the area where the packs had been re-laid in position, "How many camels are missing?" he asked.

"We're missing ten camels," answered Shir, "and three of those have been found dead. I think there's a fourth out there," and he pointed into the distance, in the direction to which the sandstorm had been carried, out into the east. Scavengers could be seen flying around.

"That leaves just fourteen camels," said Abdul without need.

Nak turned on Shir, "They're good camels. They'll carry the load, even if we have to make the days shorter."

"Well... shall we start?" asked Abdul.

Nak stepped towards him then, "After breakfast," said Nak. "We'll commence after breakfast. Just six hours on the road is all we'll do today. This will aid the camels and you, too, Abdul."

254

Abdul was happy that he'd been considered well by Nak, his arm still a little painful, but the camels were also given much consideration: Abdul was not much more than an equal... or so it seemed, and this dwelled upon his mind: man and camel; one and the same.

CHAPTER FORTY-ONE

They hadn't been on the road more than an hour when they came upon a sorrowful sight, a small Aboriginal community on the move and in search of food.

The Aboriginal way of life seemed to be in turmoil and growing worse, ever since the Europeans had commenced their colonisation of Australia, and the expansion into the desert regions of its centre was commencing to take its toll.

Times were changing for the Aboriginal and for the better, but it was the people themselves that stood in their own way for improvement to be gained in their everyday life.

If there was one thing that Abdul had learnt it was that the Chinese, Italians, Japanese, other men and women from many lands, as well as the Afghans, had poured into Australia and were doing reasonably well under the circumstances of the times. Sure, many lived in poverty, but for those that chose to work hard and make a living from their opportunities, all praise must go. But there seemed to be one thing that made the difference between success and failure amongst the Aboriginals, whether it was true or false, and that was the availability of alcohol.

Abdul had heard many times of drunken Aboriginals falling over the land that they claimed as their own, even though their Dreaming proved that man did not own the land but was simply a part of it, the land owning man more than the other way around.

There were five men, four women, and six children of between four and nine years of age, each with something in their hand or upon their shoulder; vessels for the portage of water or for the digging of roots; bags or bed rolls and other utensils.

Several swags came into view and this was followed by the powerful stench of each. The swags were nothing more than rolled up blankets and within the roll of each were things such as tea, dried bread, and cooked kangaroo (the head and shoulders cooked in ashes with the skin still attached, where the juices of the flesh seeped into the blanket). The Aboriginals, too, were unwashed and simply wreaked of odour so powerful that even the camels had a hard time keeping a steady head as they continued on past.

The women were quick to offer their hands for food, asking in broken English for a handout.

"No," said Nak as he passed. "No food; is all gone."

Next in line came Abdul, who also shook his head and displayed an uncomfortable disposition with regards to offering nothing, for like his friend, Nak, he hated to see people of this country go without; but there was nothing for it but to continue on.

He shook his head as he looked down upon the sad faces of the children, two of which also held out their hands, hands that bore the brunt of their way of life. The palms of their hands were nothing more than large scars where several fingers had been fused together, their hands burnt by accident as they wandered around camp and fell into open campfires. It was also quite common to see little children of Aboriginal background stumbling around as they walked, having stepped onto a campfire that had been doused with sand but still very hot, parents of the young ones not doing enough to care for the children in their life. Abdul could only wonder what it must be like to be one of them: out of work, without food or money, drunk and seemingly uncaring, treating children as little more than labourers.

Shir was last to pass the small group and as he did so the cries for something, even small, were pleaded for and reached his ears.

Shir reached into his own pocket and threw one of the women some dried meat, not considering for a moment that the Aboriginals may well have had more than he with the kangaroo head in the swag, for a majority of his own food had been lost to the desert, having broken open and being lost in the wind, sacks of flour disappearing without a trace.

Nak looked behind and saw Shir giving what was his own. Shir met his glance. No words were necessary, Shir knew full well that what he gave was his, that he wouldn't get any more to replace his handout and that tonight he would have less to eat than the other two; but he also saw the reflection of understanding and felt that Nak, too, wished to give.

There was no doubt about it; Nak was the stronger of the two and it was fitting that he should be a jemadar.

CHAPTER FORTY-TWO

By late afternoon the misery of the past week came to call upon the memories of each man differently, so vivid they were, and no surprise really considering that it had been only a few days since the worst had occurred.

The episode with the bacon at the homestead shone light on the subject of ridicule and poor understanding, where the Europeans and colonists – no matter what they were called or referred to as – simply ignored the trivial aspirations and aspects of Muslim life: what was so common to them was a thing of disgust and mockery to those of Christian belief. In fact, the white men of Australia appeared to accept more, the other religions commuting around, and even respect them a little, though not so influential as that of the Christian belief where men like Brother Ernest Jacob set out with the pure intention of delivering sermons to the Aboriginals of the country. But did the Aboriginal ever endeavour to impose his own beliefs of Dreaming upon the invaders of this great land? To Shir it was simply too much to live with at times. Why should it be for him to openly accept all other nationalities and their ways if not a single one of them was to accept him? What was it exactly that disgusted the white men so much in regards to his beliefs?

The work was hard; always so hard, and sometimes even intolerable. Insurmountable pain must be suffered by some, as it was with Abdul and the scorpion bite, amputation, and feelings of incompetence due to issues with missed family, and his personal responsibilities. Such responsibilities were a great weight which simply couldn't be lifted from within, and it was only due to the pain of his arm that he received a little reprieve from his thoughts on family and home.

But of all the problems that were suffered by all three men it was Nak who suffered the most. It wasn't his lack of companionship, for he had the bought love of Saki; it wasn't the grimace upon his face, for he had the friendship of the community at large which accepted him with open arms; but it was the inability to deliver the wool on time to the Marree station.

It was certainly no fault of his own that the sandstorm had been suffered by them, but it was his reputation amongst those that didn't accept him which mattered. He felt obliged to be on time with delivery for this, he felt, was the only way to secure good relations between the Muslims and the others.

The loss of ten camels, and a calf, was going to have a great effect upon his abilities to perform his duties but he was confident that he would find a way. He had the reputation of good quality and spirit; good understanding of the way life was in Marree and other towns and settlements similar to it. He knew plenty of men from whom he could squeeze a deal in good favour without damaging his natural ability to remain friends. So what was it that was getting into the mind of Nak? It was everything as a whole, the entire weight of mounting misfortune and poor treatment. It was his life in general, not a single episode or emotion but everything combined. He was like a well-built dam that could handle the insurmountable weight of crushing abnormality, but his banks were on the edge of bursting. He was at the end of his tether and he wasn't sure he could take much more before he collapsed into a ball and surrendered himself to death. But for Nak, death would never be an option; he could never surrender. He didn't surrender to the British back in Afghanistan and he wasn't about to admit defeat here, in Australia. He would defeat and conquer before permitting himself to decay and rot.

So it was these three men, each carved from granite of different solidity, that the future was about to deliver the heinous acts of religious and racial hatred upon them.

By the time they reached Mulka they were still three days behind schedule and the camels were growing weary of the weight being carried day in and day out, many miles per day being suffered over the stretching hours that fell behind them.

CHAPTER FORTY-THREE

Each camel was carrying five bales of wool, some carrying six, and the three cameleers trod ever on, proud of their accomplishments in the face of misfortune but disappointed in what they knew the future would deliver them in regards to the cost of replenishing stock. A few smaller jobs would be okay to accept but this was a growing country that wasn't prone to quit in its efforts to succeed: And unknown to the cameleers, they were being watched; watched by five pairs of young eyes, and from some distance away.

It had been delivered to the ears of those that watched that the camel string was coming their way and they wished very much to meet it with their frustration of the camel industry and what it had taken from their fathers and families in general.

The five young white men, barely of age to drink or partake of gambling, had lived in Mulka for as long as they could remember, having been brought up on the harshness of the land which was their home and place of great joy.

Each one of them loved the soil beneath their feet, even though they condemned it to hell on many, many occasions, for the flies, dust, ants, snakes, lack of water during summer, and lack of dry land during some wet seasons, were just a few aspects of misfortune they loved to complain about. Each was a comparatively able bodied stockman and had a future which could be well suited to them and a wife. A proud life could easily be scored from what they knew about the land and the industries open to them. As general farmers go they were no different than any other, but they did have the mentality of derangement which is brought on by animals in a pack.

The five young men were tying up their horses in the low ground not far from where the camel train was to pass, a creek that flowed well with water during the wet season and offered much in respect to water for stock at a time when the water tanks were dry and watering holes were little more than dry pans of scorched earth for the weeks before the weather turned from dry to wet.

The young men were known to one another by their nicknames and rarely, if at all, ever used their Christian names. They were Scotty, Snake, Bullock, Horse and Fly; Scotty for Scott, Snake for he was thin, Bullock as he was large, Horse for his appendage, and Fly as he was tiny in stature and seemed to literally fly through the air when

260

riding upon a horse at full gallop.

Scotty pulled a can from the saddle bag upon his horse and held it up for his friend Fly to see, a red label wrapped around it. It was a can of bully beef, an invention of a man from the Booyoolee Station and adopted into the Australian psyche, chunks of beef drowned in gravy, a staple that could not be lived without.

"What do you say to some bully, Fly?" asked Scotty.

"Shut your mouth, you fool," scolded Horse. "Those damn freaks'll hear ya."

"Calm down, Horse," said Bullock as he pushed himself up from his position upon the edge of the creek, relieving his vision of the camel train. "They're still a ways off yet."

"I'm gonna clobber me one of those fellers damn good," said Fly.

"You and what army?" said Snake jokingly, pushing into the side of him with his shoulder, a smile upon his face.

Fly looked around a little perplexed by the meaning; for that's what they were there for, to act as they'd said they would, to fulfil their act of revenge upon the men and their stinking camels.

"Shut up, Snake," defended Scotty, "leave him alone."

"You don't have to defend me," said Fly, puffing out his chest. "I might be the youngest but I can lick those men as good as anyone."

"You won't need to," said Bullock, the eldest, "because I got me-self something hidden away," and with that said he drew out a rifle from hiding, from deep within his bed-roll.

"Where the hell ya get that?" asked Horse with a little panic in his voice.

"It's me dad's rifle," replied Bullock.

"You're not gonna use it, are ya?" asked Horse.

"Why the hell wouldn't I?" said Bullock. "What the hell do ya think I bought it for if not to scare those buggers off our land once and for all?"

"Scare them," protested Fly. "We should shoot the bastards!"

"No, no, no," interrupted Scotty. "You don't want that, Fly. We don't need any trouble with the law."

"What law?" said Snake and he too took a rifle from his bed-roll.

"What the.... What the hell you two doing?" stumbled Scotty

"Look," said Snake. "If you don't want in then go home; but I'm staying. I've had enough of these bastards, once and for all."

"They're just men," said Horse. "Scotty's right, we shouldn't be shooting them. The law'll get us all."

"Look," said Bullock. "The closest police is in Marree. We're not gonna get caught; not unless someone here tells on us; turns us in, maybe."

"Don't look at me, Bullock," pleaded Scotty. "I do what you think is best, but I don't like it."

"It's what they deserve," said Fly.

"I would've thought you had enough sense not to be so... power hungry," said Scotty.

"Hey; he's with us," said Snake, "aren't ya, Fly?"

"Sure am," answered Fly as he looked at Scotty. "Ah, come on, Scotty. Them fellahs have been taking our fathers' work for ages. It's gotta stop."

"He's right, Scotty," said Bullock. "The lines gotta be drawn, once and for all."

"Come on, Scotty," urged Fly.

"What do you think, Horse?" asked Scotty.

"I don't know."

"Ah, come on," said Bullock.

"I don't think we should," said Horse. "It aint right."

"You're either with us or against us," said Snake with a mean look in his eye. "If you're not with us then get on ya horse and go."

Horse looked around to everyone in turn, "I'll go," and mounted his horse.

"You'll go south," insisted Bullock. I don't want them stinking camel herders to know we're here."

"I got ya, Bullock. You don't need to tell me anything," replied Horse. "You should change your mind, Scotty, before it's too late."

"Shut your mouth, Horse!" said Snake

With that said Horse turned away from Scotty and leapt upon his horse before heading away from the scene, Scotty looking to the ground and then to Bullock.

"You're either in or out," said Bullock. "What's it going to be?"

Bullock had made up his mind. His father had told him all, spared no insult, regardless of how small.

Bullock had grown tired of the thievery, the Afghans taking the work from them all, the Afghans conducting the work at a cheaper rate and handling their camels to conduct the tasks with seemingly great ease and without infliction. Regardless of the fact that the

Afghans were answering the call from settlers, mines and explorers, the young and old men of the Australian bush could simply not come to terms with the loss of employment.

There was no word of forgiveness from the white man, no word of thanks. The Afghans had insulted the colonists... they didn't drink alcohol, failed to consume the luxuries and amenities offered by the white man, and above all, spent very little of what they earned; and when money was spent it was mostly in stores run by other Afghan men or hawkers of a similar caste.

"I'm in," said Scotty after a little silence.

"That's great, Scotty," said Fly with a smile, "fantastic," but Scotty simply frowned as Snake turned to edge his way towards the lip of the creek line, to see for himself how the cameleers had progressed.

CHAPTER FORTY-FOUR

Bullock shuffled up and lay beside Scotty.

And what was about to unfold was but the tip of the iceberg and only the beginning in regards to the dissatisfaction to be displayed by colonists for the contracts between the cameleers and pastoralists, for the hatred against these great men was about to get worse.

Bullock had failed to realise that it was in the 1860s that many camels and their handlers were imported into the country to aid in the widening of Australian occupied territory, discovering more and more, far and wide. It was all an exercise of the great awakening where the laying of the telegraph from Port Augusta to Darwin was but pittance to the actual advantages to be won from the land over the decades to come.

But regardless of Bullock's knowledge on history, regardless of how much he actually knew about these men, the Afghans had to be put into their place and shown once and for all who was boss.

But there was something else that infuriated the boys even more than words could express and it was a story that had been passed onto them from their fathers, a story which could not be tolerated.

Bullock told Scotty, as he laid there, the story.

This Afghan that they saw before them, as advised by a friend when they were seen bypassing Mulka far and wide, was a villain.

Their eyes looked upon the jemadar and his string through branches and over spinifex. He was surely the one; he looked the same, even from that distance... that grin, the way in which his mouth was present upon his face without a move, steadfast in a grimace of never-ending hatred for whomever he met.

It was said that he and several others had been spotted at one time, somewhere along this very track, drinking water from a small waterhole during a time when water was scarcer than any other. But that wasn't the crime, oh no. The crime was the fact that it was time for prayer and the Afghans, with little concern for others that might pass that way, took their shoes and socks off to wash their feet – to wash in the only water for miles around. This act simply could not be tolerated.

"That's one of many stories I know," said Bullock. "It has to be stopped. I can't take any more."

Scotty looked into his friend's eyes, not really knowing him at all.

264

"Do you think he deserves to die?" asked Scotty.

"I do," said Bullock, "for all he's done, for all his grievances against us."

Snake appeared beside them, "Come on; you ready or what? Get back here so we can spread out proper."

The four congregated in the low ground behind the bush and prepared themselves as best they could, Snake and Bullock taking position so as to be closest to the string when it passed them by.

CHAPTER FORTY-FIVE

Four men, as seen through their own eyes; four boys as seen through those of their parents. They had settled into wait and watched the caravan of 14 camels and three cameleers draw ever closer.

Bullock thought it strange that so many cameleers should be required to accompany so few camels and surmised that they were 'three' simply to provide one-another company during the long treks across the country. He couldn't help but briefly consider the work that they did, the time they sacrificed in order to bring a little luxury to the lives of settlers. It was all for nothing, for the ideas were quickly syphoned through what intellect he had and put to waste like common garbage, and his eyes fell to the barrel of his rifle.

He'd never killed a man before but the hatred within him was sure to put him to ease, just for a moment, long enough to pull the trigger and see a man die.

Snake was of dissimilar view and only thought of how badly these cameleers had been towards him and those of the past, of all he knew of their callous ways to deny his family the ability to earn good money and put food on the table.

For Snake the killing would come easily and his only wish was that the cameleers were riding upon a camel so that when the shots were fired the dead would have further to fall, toppled from their high stations upon their pets.

Questions rose within Scotty, he wondered about the effects of the rifles. He'd seen rabbits and dingoes killed sure enough, but never a man. Did a man bleed the same as a rabbit? Did a man squirm upon the ground in the same dying fashion; or did he yelp like a wounded dog? But last of all he considered what they were about to do and couldn't help but have second thoughts, wondering whether two rifles would be enough. He picked up a couple of large rocks to appease his need for security.

Fly had a smile upon his face as he looked out upon the approaching string but quickly lost all feeling of excitement when he looked over and towards Bullock, the menacing look in his friend's eyes leaving no doubt at all as to what was about to be delivered.

The cameleers had no names to the young men but their features were enough to distinguish one from another.

Nak was to the front as usual, leading Chocolate ever closer to the torment that was about to befall them all, with Shir at the rear and Abdul to the centre as usual. Nak was thinking of the love he held for Saki and the need to hold her in his arms, as well as the string which he would have to increase in number as soon as the opportunity presented itself. It was all possible that Faiz Mahomet would provide him with a few animals to help in the bad times ahead.

Shir considered his wife, for he missed her immensely, the Aboriginal woman that was different from the rest. There was simply no way that you could compare her to the others that were seen during his treks across the desert. He could see Arika smiling down upon him from within the comfort of their bed, their eyes locked in unison before making good the opportunity to make love once more.

As for Abdul, he was by far different than the other two. It wasn't from lack of experience or work ethic when it came down to operating strings out of Marree but simply that he was married to a wife who was still in Afghanistan and had children. For him there was no other place on earth but his home... and he had left it to make his fortune.

CHAPTER FORTY-SIX

Nak frowned upon the behaviour he was now witnessing, Chocolate becoming unsettled and looking off into the bush upon the highest portion of high ground to their left, a small lip of extended ground that fell into a dry creek bed.

Nak thought that a snake might be nearby and scoured the area with his eyes, looking rather intently for any sign of reptilian life within the spinifex around.

"What is it?" asked Abdul.

"I'm not sure," replied Nak. "Chocolate senses something... I'm not sure."

Nak pulled down hard upon the harness of Chocolate and at that moment the unmistakable sound of a rifle shot pierced the air.

"My god!" yelled Abdul as he took to the ground, forgetting his finger for the moment but brought quickly back to reality as he fell with all his weight upon it, releasing his hold on the camel.

Nak too, was quick to find comfort in security and within a matter of several seconds; and by the time the second shot rang out he had his own rifle pulled from hiding.

"Shir," yelled Nak, seeing Abdul laying flat upon the ground, but unsure of Shir's safety. "Shir; are you okay?"

There was no answer and so Abdul chanced a look in his direction, seeing the prostrate form of his friend lying upon the ground.

The four Australian boys then broke from hiding and raced down towards the three cameleers, unsure whether or not any of them had been hit fatally with the firing of their rifles. Bullock took a brief look towards Snake, who having fired a little slow for his liking, was making up for his poor showing by being the first of them to reach the string of fourteen camels.

Snake's eye fell upon Shir as he lashed out with a knife and cut in one smooth action the string attached from nose peg to camel. The kitchen camel simply pulled away in the build-up of panic from rifle shot to screaming assailants. All along the line camels reared their heads, some pegs breaking loose from camels and others requiring a little aid from a sharp knife.

Snake looked down again upon Shir and saw blood oozing from his back, lying there flat, dead as an autumn leaf, the colour of death spreading across the cameleer's back.

Abdul quickly stood as Scotty and Fly swooped past him, one to either side and slashing at all manner of throng and leash, the camels bucking and pulling, groaning and racing away into the desert around them, all unrestricted by hobble.

Abdul hadn't yet seen Shir lying there with blood seeking from the exit wound upon his back, nor the seated form of Snake as the boy collapsed beside the dead man, a great surge of sorrow having burst the banks within him. Snake had killed a man, the first and last he wished to kill, and even then he found a momentary loss as to why it was so important to have killed this man, the cameleer with no name.

Fly grabbed hold of a camel, that quick as a flash bit him upon the hand. Fly pulled the hand back with the pain and fright of the bite but was quick to take revenge on the seemingly pathetic beast by thrusting his knife into the animal's neck.

Abdul hit the boy hard in the side of the leg, the pain of the hit destabilizing Fly who then fell upon the ground. Abdul rallied all his strength and pulled himself upon the fallen and for only the second time in his entire life lashed out with a closed fist.

Fly pulled his arms up to cover his face as he lay there until rescued from harm by his friend Scotty, who braced himself for the worse and tackled Abdul from the rear. With the pain of his amputated finger forgotten, Abdul needed to now contend with a surging fury of pain in the lower part of his back and he crumpled into a ball, screaming out for the world to hear.

Fly was upon his feet in seconds and prepared to escape with Scotty close behind.

Bullock, meanwhile, having forgotten to reload his rifle after the initial shot being fired, lashed out with the butt of his weapon which connected squarely upon the jaw of Nak. Nak fell heavily as Bullock went to work upon the camels' restraints, not noticing that Nak was quick to recover and pulled the rifle to him.

Nak got the weapon ready for firing and brought it into his shoulder but Bullock had since taken off between two camels and was currently unobserved. Fly fell within Nak's field of view and as the boy stood, Nak fired a single shot whereby the boy fell down dead in an instant, his mouth open to the world as his last breath ever was inhaled.

"NO!" yelled Scotty who went to his aid, tripped by Abdul and ended up with his face buried in the ground, his nose breaking in place upon his left cheek.

Snake shook the reality of the dead man beside him from his mind and looked out and over towards where the third rifle shot was heard. He saw his friend, Fly, fall hard upon the ground and knew, right then and there, that Fly was dead.

CHAPTER FORTY-SEVEN

Horse heard the first of the rifle shots in the distance far behind him and realising that the attack had commenced couldn't help thinking that he should have done more in preventing the massacre of the three cameleers.

Suddenly, on hearing the second shot, he pulled upon the reins of his horse that came to a dead stop, neither fidgeting nor having a care in the world as Horse considered what should be done.

The third shot rang out and Horse turned the head of the beast he was riding and headed off back towards where his friends had been left to their own vices of evil doing.

Horse was overcome with different emotions and wasn't entirely sure which emotion should be adhered to and which should be discarded. The fighting within himself was little more than the question of good over bad. He understood full well that the idea of Bullocks, which he so easily implanted within the others, was to cause as much disarray as possible, scattering the camels to the four winds. The death of the cameleers was simply a bonus, as far as Bullock was concerned, and whether one died or all, it mattered little to him.

Horse knew of their plan to escape to the south, hence creating a little confusion before heading back into Mulka at a later date, and before any suspicion as to their involvement could be readily formulated. If he continued in the direction he was heading in he was sure to come into contact with them.

He wasn't entirely sure why he was returning but he felt as though something had gone wrong. It was the third shot... it somehow sounded different than the others. From so far away from the action he was sure that he could hear a difference between the third and the first two shots being fired.

He was trotting at a reasonable speed when he'd reached the point just half way between where he was and the site that Bullock had chosen for delivering his mayhem. He could make out a little noise not so very far ahead when he realised what it was.

"Bullock," said Horse, "is that you?"

Bullock lifted his head from behind some brush followed by the head of Snake.

Horse dismounted and walked over to where they were crouched, himself crouching as he approached in fear of being seen by any prying eyes. He could see that both were filled with grief, Snake more than Bullock.

Horse knelt down beside the other two.

"Where's Fly and Scotty?" he asked

The silence that followed was clear, but clarity askew.

"Were they caught?" asked Horse.

Bullock looked him in the eye, "Scotty was captured."

"And Fly?"

"He's dead," said Snake flatly but decisively.

"We don't know that for sure," said Bullock with his rifle in hand.

"I saw him," said Snake, "before I got away," and looked to Horse.

"Where's your rifle?" asked Horse.

"He left it behind," said Bullock. "Now they have two—."

Snake punched Bullock in the face before being set upon by Horse.

"That's enough; no more!" insisted Horse as he got between the pair. "I'm more concerned about Fly and Scotty."

"It's no good," insisted Snake. "Fly is dead; I know it. When I heard the third shot fired I looked up and saw Fly fall. Scotty fell down after but I think he's okay."

"So what happened to your rifle?" asked Horse.

"I guess I dropped it."

"Dropped it!" repeated Bullock sarcastically.

"Enough," stabbed Horse. "We gotta think now. We can't just leave Scotty there with those men."

"I don't think I can do any more," said Snake. "I feel sick inside," and the look upon his face was sincere.

"You should have thought about that earlier," said Horse. "But now it's too late and we have to help."

"I still got my rifle," said Bullock.

"I don't know," said Horse. "They have two, we have one."

"We'll shoot first and ask later."

"This isn't funny, Bullock," spat Snake.

"No one said it was," said Bullock. "We have to go in armed, we have no choice now."

"You're right," said Horse. "I don't think we have a choice."

Snake looked up dismayed and sad, feeling the horrors of his deed growing within him, "I killed one of them."

"Don't feel guilty, Snake," said Bullock. "They got one of us, too.

I think we should finish this and get back to Mulka."

"He's right," agreed Horse, looking into Snake's eyes. "We have to save Scotty. Where are your horses?"

"We don't have them."

"Then we'll have to get them back, too," concluded Horse needlessly.

Shir had been laid in a blanket and placed in the shade of one of the trees aligning the dry creek bed, a swarm of flies trying their luck at gaining entry to the dead man in order to lay their eggs.

"The flies I hate the worse," said Nak. "Forever on our backs and in our eyes and ears; and now poor Shir is dead and they want some of him."

"What shall we do now?" asked Abdul of the jemadar.

Nak looked over to where the dead boy, Fly, was laying, infested with flies, Nak having done nothing to prevent the onslaught from taking place for he felt that the boy deserved all he received.

"Let the maggots have their feast upon his rotting carcass," said Nak and then he looked to the other, tied to the base of a tree and in easy vision of his dead friend. "What name you?"

Scotty didn't answer at first; he had a broken nose and it was bruised and bloody, he also had two black eyes where he'd been hit uncontrollably by Nak earlier on.

Nak stood up and hurried over to him, but before he could lash out with a kick to the boy's body he screamed out and curled into a ball as best he could, "SCOTTY!" The kick didn't come and Scotty returned to his original position, shaking from his ordeal. "My name is Scotty."

"You friend coward, run quick, much far away now," said Nak as he tried to break the boy. "Horse now mine, you nothing. I get pretty good money of horse."

"I don't think he cares," pointed out Abdul who fell silent briefly and then asked the question upon his mind. "What are we to do now?"

"We'll have to tell the police, and hand the boy into the authorities," answered Nak. "I don't see any other alternative. I don't exactly trust the police but what choice do we have. We can't let the boy go because he'll tell lies and we could end up being convicted of murder, but with the boy in custody, along with the horses, I think we can fairly well sell our story of self-defence."

"Don't you think we should cover the boy's body before the maggots eat too much? The police won't take kindly to us leaving him to be eaten like this. His parents will take unkindly—"

"I don't care, Abdul," interrupted Nak. "The people here can think what they like. I'm sick to death of them all. Even those we serve have condemned our beliefs by smuggling bacon upon the loads we carry. None of them can be trusted."

"When will we leave?"

"Tomorrow morning," said Nak. "We'll take the few camels we have along with the horses. The horses can be used to carry the dead; the prisoner we'll make walk for a while but let him ride later, when he's tired... I want to get to Marree as quickly as possible."

"What about the other camels; the lost?"

"They'll have to stay lost. We have to move quickly. Maybe we can come back for them later."

"In that case, wouldn't it be best to leave the wool here; there's hardly enough to worry about?"

"You're right," said Nak. "I'll consider it tonight."

"You realise that the other boys might come back, and from my recollection they still have a rifle."

"We have two," said Nak and then thought of the wool. "We won't get far now, anyway. We have just three camels with us and four horses. We have no stores to speak of except a little water; my Koran is gone along with our prayer mats. We have nothing left. Help me, Abdul. We'll secure the camels in the creek bed beside the horses. Scotty can stay where he is for the night and suffer the cold. Get a fire going.

"And the others?"

"We'll maintain watch, just like when in the army. We can set up a small watching post and watch for the others, and I wish good visuals to be maintained with the rising of the sun. If they approach the fire then they must be shot; we can't afford to be caught unaware."

"They have the advantage," said Abdul knowingly.

"Yes, but we have a prisoner and two rifles."

"You know... I'm not afraid to die, just concerned for my family back at home," said Abdul. "They'll never know what happened to me. I just think it's more kind for them to know what I did here and that I just didn't abandon them."

"Your wife loves you, Abdul. She'll not think unkindly."

"And what about you, Nak? Are you afraid to die?"

"There is life after death, dear friend. I will be thirty-two years old for eternity and have seventy-two virgins to appease my every need. What more could a man ask from heaven?" and he thought then of

Saki.

"It's good for you," said Abdul, endeavouring to make a joke. "You are forty-two at present and so get a good deal if you die; I'm only twenty-three at present, so gain nine years."

"And you are married," said Nak. "That will have an effect on your ability to enjoy seventy-two virgins."

Abdul smiled, "You're right," he said, "It's too many for me. Maybe I'll give you some of mine."

"My dear friend, Abdul, even seventy-two virgins is too good to wish for, any more and I'll die a second death."

CHAPTER FORTY-NINE

Snake led the way with Bullock close behind with Horse leading his horse on foot.

The advance was suddenly brought to a temporary close as Snake put up a hand to halt those behind, seeing something to his front that wasn't particularly of any great surprise.

"What is it? What do you see?" asked Bullock.

"Another camel."

Bullock lifted his rifle into his shoulder and looked down the sights on seeing the animal, his head held low and teeth raking at the spinifex that it had found.

Horse approached from behind and slammed his palm down upon the barrel of the rifle, knocking the sight picture from Bullock's grasp, unsettling his friend who was hiding his nervousness of the entire situation from the other two, "Don't be foolish; idiot."

"Damn; that hurt," said Bullock as he looked at Horse. "I've got a good mind to smash your face in."

"Why don't you?"

"Because it's what the cameleers want," intruded Snake. "They'd love for you to give our position away."

"No shooting, Bullock," said Horse.

"I got a better idea," said Snake and headed off slowly towards the camel after taking an axe handle from Horse's gear.

"What are you doing?" asked Horse.

"Do you want these camels to fester the land you call home?" questioned Snake and the as he turned to his task whispered, "you damn fool."

Snake approached the camel as the other two watched on, the sun slowly disappearing below the horizon with the camel eating what he'd found, food for the taking, now at his disposal.

He crept ever closer, more slowly as he closed the gap, to the impatience of the other two. The camel appeared to ignore Snake's presence as he moved around to the rear and moved ever closer. He moved his hands around the axe handle and took a good grip. Once satisfied and close enough he swung hard and low, the camel's leg breaking instantly.

The noise that erupted from within the camel was so loud and disgustingly horrific that Horse covered his eyes beneath is palms and

Bullock simply watched on open-mouthed as Snake moved up to the camel laying upon the ground in great agony and proceeded to smash its head in until the head of the axe handle was so covered in membranes and blood that it was hardly recognizable.

Bullock approached Snake, "Come on, Snake, that's enough," he pleaded. "It's dead now; give it a rest will ya."

Snake stopped pounded down upon the carcass, "I'm sick of these bloody animals. Good for nothing is what they are, taking what work is available away from me and me dad."

"It's not just you," said Horse as he drew alongside, looking down upon the blood and the brain of the camel. "We all suffer."

"And now it's time they suffered," said Snake. "We'll wait till it gets dark; they'll have to light a fire sooner or later: won't they?"

"I'd sure hope so," said Horse, "otherwise poor old Scotty's going to have a terrible night."

"Well, let's see if we can't help him out a little," said Snake. "Come on, let's get out of here; this camel stinks."

CHAPTER FIFTY

The sky above was a brilliant dark blue, a darkness never forgotten, and a peaceful reminder that man was a small part of a larger picture. Abdul didn't know much about the heavens, other than what he'd read in the Koran, but knew enough to find his way around at night.

He was sitting next to a large bush and facing towards where the campfire burnt low and bright, the brightness evaporating into the night and extinguishing itself, the edge between light and dark fairly distinct.

The cold of the night was starting to take effect upon him but he had a warm blanket wrapped around his thin form, the flesh of his hands the only thing not protected as they held on tightly to the rifle in his lap.

Abdul was content to sit where he was for half the night; to await the boys he knew would return sooner or later. He had both rifles with him, both with a round of ammunition up the spout and ready to fire.

Nak rolled over in his sleep and the boy, Scotty, was stretched out from the tree, his feet seeking as much warmth as possible. He'd had a gag placed over his mouth prior to the cameleers preparing for the night so that the boy wouldn't be able to alert his friends of the predicament when they came calling, for a second bed roll had been placed out beside the fire to look as though it contained another person; and in fact it did. The dead man, Shir, was placed beside the fire to trick the other boys into believing that both men were asleep.

Abdul cocked his head a little having heard something off in the distance. He couldn't be sure but he was sure that he'd heard a stick being trodden underfoot. He strained his ears, leaning his head a little to the side in order to gain better hearing. A horse could be heard far, far away and this was followed by the sighting of a silhouette, a single figure.

Someone was approaching and with much stealth, crouched a little to help hide his presence from view.

Abdul looked over towards where Scotty was lying and knew immediately that he had fallen asleep, otherwise he'd be thrashing about to alert the one that was near.

Another two figures then appeared out of nowhere and the first beams of light from the fire revealed the front figure. He wasn't carrying a rifle and so one of the others held that. They were a little too close for comfort. If Nak was to stir or jump up once the shooting had commenced then he was in great risk of being shot himself.

Abdul decided then and there to do what he must do. He had sworn unto himself to treat everyone the same, not to do unto one that he did not expect to have done to him. And so this was the reality of his promise to himself, for there was a rifle amongst the three and although it had not been revealed just yet, it was still there and very dangerous.

Abdul lifted his rifle and without a shadow of a doubt crossing his mind, and with the fury of the death of Shir behind him, squeezed the trigger of the rifle as he had been taught back in Afghanistan.

The loud firing of the rifle was enough to wake the devil, not to mention Scotty and Nak.

The shot was a success and Snake fell down hard, wounded heavily in the stomach, a wound from which he would not recover. A heavy gasp for air erupted from within him.

Nak sprang to his feet at the same time that Bullock panicked and fired his rifle, having not taken good aim like his counterpart, the shot flying not so far from its proposed point of aim and hit Abdul in the right shoulder.

The pain was instantaneous but remarkably held at bay, for the reality of the situation was overpowering to say the least.

Abdul had the second rifle in is hand with swift ease and steadiness. He pulled the trigger this time, anxious to get the shot off, and with as much luck as can be afforded him the shot hit Bullock square in the head, killing him instantly. Bullock's body fell like a sack of spuds upon the ground, not a sound coming from him other than the thud as he fell.

Horse raced over to where Bullock had fallen, his mind clear and decisive, understanding fully the predicament he and his friends were in. He picked the rifle up and searched quickly for the ammunition that Bullock carried.

The scene was alive with men and boys moving around, gasps of pain and grunts of effort being heard, but not a single word, sentence or phrase was uttered in those few seconds that had led to the growing misery that surrounded them all.

Nak was now upon his feet and raced towards Horse only to be confronted by Snake who unselfishly kicked out with much pain being suffered in his gut, the sheer effort enough to tax him hard of all his energy.

The bleeding of Snake was largely internal and the pain just then surfaced like a volcano bursting its banks: not only was the larva now spouting from the top but it was forcing great pressure on his inside. Snake gasped for air just then, drawing on every effort to take another breath, but no breath came. Snake died, the last fragments of thought rushing through his mind being those of his family at home. He could see the face of his mother gently fade from memory as his mind went blank once and for all.

Nak fell hard upon the ground, a blade of spinifex forced into his eye. The shock of the fall and the pain of the spinifex that had penetrated the eye was enough to keep Nak occupied whilst Horse quickly found some ammunition and loaded the rifle. He brought the stock into his shoulder and shot at comparatively point-blank range the body mass of Nak.

Nak's stirring fell silent. The range from firer-to-target had seen to Nak's death as surely as the penetration of the spinifex had seen to the pain within his eye.

Abdul saw all of this but couldn't tell who was alive, who was dead, or who was down and out of the fight. It was now that the pain in his arm commenced to build slightly. He fumbled around for what he had placed beside his knee and reloaded the first rifle. He brought the weapon up into his shoulder as best he could with the injury he'd sustained and awaited his next opportunity, to fire the weapon at the strongest target, for it was better to deal with a wounded enemy opposed to a live one.

Horse threw the rifle to the ground at that moment, spurred on by several emotional traits. He could see Scotty over by the tree as he kicked and rolled upon the ground, trying to draw his friend's attention, but the largest of Horse's weaknesses was the fact that he'd just shot a man for no other reason than that surrounding his prejudice.

Horse was in a flurry, unsure what he should do and whether or not he should do it, and before he realised what was happening he found himself kneeling beside Scotty with a knife in his hand and cutting away at his bonds.

Abdul couldn't believe the stupidity of the boy and how he'd simply raced up to his friend. Such comradeship was hard to find in men. These whites were not much different than he, but he would not have killed for the sake of killing. He, Abdul, would not have shot at defenceless cameleers as they made their way from town to town to try and earn a little money for their hungry children. And so, without further thought, he squeezed the trigger and killed the one that Horse was trying to save. Abdul shot Scotty, the wounded, to let the healthy live, to give the one with courage that last opportunity to save himself in the face of his honour and courage.

Horse heard the shot fired and in the light of the campfire saw the blood erupt from Scotty's head. Horse knew then and there that he was up against men who had dealt with weapons before, and had killed in their past. Horse didn't wish to be a statistic and was quickly brought back to reality.

"You go," shouted Abdul. "You go long way, no come back. You got horse, you take and go home. Me forget quick. Me not care. You live, me live; we both live. You know what meaning is?"

"Yes," replied Horse. "I know what you mean."

Horse looked down into the closed eyes of his friend. Of the five he was the only one left alive. "You've killed four of my friends. That'll be hard to live with."

"Alive is good, dead is bad," lectured Abdul. "You go and me go. We both go."

"Yes," said Horse as he stood, sheathing his knife. "We both go." Horse turned and commenced to move away. He stumbled to a stop. "Thank you," he said and continued on his way.

"Okay," said Abdul. "You do thing, one more. You make horse speak, me know you gone."

"Yes; yes, okay," said Horse, understanding full well that Abdul wished to ensure that he, Horse, was actually out of range and not to return for vengeance. "But I'll be back tomorrow, to get my friends. If you are still here then I'll not make any promises."

Abdul nodded but it wasn't seen as Horse disappeared into the desert.

CHAPTER FIFTY-ONE

Abdul was on foot now and staggering a little as he made his way south. He'd patched his wound up as best he could but wished to be on his way and in the company of his new friends at Marree.

He'd left the bodies of the whites behind but his friends were with him. Nak and Shir were strapped to two of the camels in the string and the third carried nothing but the last of the water that he had. The thought of riding upon the camel hadn't even entered his mind; such was the decay of his normality. His thinking was askew and thoughts mostly of home. This was his first real job and might well be his last.

As he continued towards Marree, the camels knowing the way as much as he, he considered the two corpses that he carried.

Nak was a good jemadar and little was known about his personal life. He never spoke much on his feelings of love and loneliness. Shir on the other hand couldn't shut up when it came to speaking of his wife and the love he felt for her; it was enough to make him ill with home-sickness.

Nak Kadir was from Kabul, single and aged forty-two. Shir Adji was from Karachi, married to Arika; Shir was thirty-three and his wife just sixteen. He would remember them, remember them always.

The blistering heat of the day continued to build as he made progress. His water was gone and he had no food. With little experience of survival in this new country, and with the weight of keeping clear of any settlers, Europeans, colonists, and the like – although they were all the same when it came down to it – he was starting to feel extremely weary.

He looked down upon the ground as he walked, unable to see his shadow for the sun was high in the sky. He'd had no sleep the night before and had suffered badly over the past week or more. There was so much that he'd been exposed to that he wasn't sure if it was all reality or simply a dream.

He continued on for several more hours and before long he tripped upon a small rock that was half buried in the track, the loss of blood from his shoulder wound having taken its toll upon him. He fell silently and quickly upon the ground and darkness came once more.

The jolting of the wagon woke Abdul up and as he stirred a familiar voice echoed in his ear.

"Ah, praise the good lord that you have risen," said Brother Ernest. "You've been in and out of your daze for a few days now. How do you feel?"

Abdul understood enough of what was said but still had a lot of blurriness to contend with. He rubbed at his eyes and was suddenly reminded of the pain in his shoulder.

"Ah; I fixed that as best I could," said Ernest who had moved from walking beside his beasts of burden to having taken a seat upon the wagon to more readily view Abdul. "I stopped the bleeding, but it took some time."

"Where we go?" asked Abdul.

"I found you beside the track, unconscious. I was on my way to Killalpinanna but have decided to turn about and take you to Marree. It's the least I can do for a religious man, even if it goes against the grain."

"Where friend?"

"What friend? Ah; you mean the others? I don't know. You know; I thought it was strange that they should leave you alone like that. Did one of them shoot you?"

"No. You no see friends? They dead."

"Are they dead? I don't know," said Ernest slightly confused.

"No, no. Not meaning. Friend is dead; you find; you see them and camels?" asked Abdul sparingly and with a little difficulty.

Ernest handed Abdul a water canteen, "Here, have a drink," he offered. "No, I didn't see anyone. No camels, no friends. Just you; and lucky I came across you when I did otherwise you'd be dead."

Abdul thought on the matter and came to the only conclusion possible at present. Nak and Shir were strapped to the camels. The camels must have taken off into the desert after he'd collapsed. They were lost forever upon the backs of the camels that carried them.

"We shouldn't be long into Marree," said Ernest. "You'll have to report this to the police."

Abdul considered what was said. This was a problem which just wouldn't go away easily. Without the bodies of Nak and Shir he had little to tell the police. Other than a few people that had seen him the day before their departure to the homestead, and the two Aboriginal boys, whose names now escaped him, no one really knew of him. The circumstances of his being shot could not really be confirmed or proved. The white boy, on the other hand, he could say what he wished and would be believed.

Maybe it was time to let sleeping ghosts lie and say nothing of what had happened. Maybe he should try and return to Afghanistan whilst he had the chance.

"No," said Abdul

"No!" said Ernest. "Well, it's not my place to force it upon you, after all you were found alone. It seems to me that justice should be delivered to those that left you there to die."

"I forgive, and forget," but Abdul wasn't so sure that he could ever forget the ordeal he'd suffered.

"I'll take you to the Ghantown then," offered Ernest. "Would you like that? I have to do something, I can't just simply, 'not' help a man in need."

Abdul smiled then and looked up at the man known as Brother Ernest Jacob.

"You good friend," said Abdul. "You good man this place. Me never forget."

Ernest simply smiled and turned his eyes again upon the track to his front as he continued on across the wilderness.

Abdul considered his final option. He'd return home to his family in Afghanistan. Life in Australia was simply too hard.

And with reflection upon his wife and children at home overpowering the thoughts of Nak and Shir, he smiled a heavenly smile and thanked God for his being allowed to survive; for what would he do with seventy-two virgins?

PART THREE

Honour

TOM OF TWOFOLD BAY

IMPORTANT NOTE

Some of the evidence and general information concerning Typee and Jackson, during cross-examination, appears misconstrued and vastly different, as do other aspects of this work. I have put forward the history of the bay as interpreted and recorded by the interview of witnesses by others.

This is a work of Historical-Fiction and should not be used as a source on which to base the history of Eden. Whaling events over the years have been pruned and extended to bring to light the charismatic behaviour of the interaction between man and killer whale as best as possible; I apologise if I have dealt an injustice to the truth by doing so.

This is the story of the killer whales of Eden.

FAST FISH

A harpoon entering the body of a whale did not kill it; it was meant only as a means by which to secure the line and maintain a measure of control over the whale whilst lancing took place and the animal then killed; this might take some time and some number of lances. It was therefore not surprising to see that a rule was employed by which means a crew could announce quite categorically that 'it' owned the right to the whale in which its harpoon was attached; it went something like this: where the harpoon shall remain in the fish so struck, and a line or boat shall be attached thereto and continue in the power of the striker or headsman, such whale shall be deemed a fast fish, and although struck by any secondary or subsequent harpoon shall be the property of the first striker or headsman only.

COMMON BOAT LAYOUT

Nine metres long and pointed at both ends with a sag in the middle, wide in breadth around where the centre thwart lay, each differing slightly but built objectively the same, depending on the maker. There was planking across the first 1.5 metres of the stern where the loggerhead could be found, a short post where line was checked, it being drenched in water from buckets during hectic times when whales took off with the line attached, the friction of which was quite easily capable of seeing the loggerhead burst into flames. Tubs which contained the line (fed through the loggerhead) were found between the middle and aft thwarts, depending on the headsman, 200 fathoms of line (manila rope) to each. The line was fed through the loggerhead and continued on through a niche in the bow, under an iron bar and then back over it to the harpoon, where it was attached securely. A typical boat would have anywhere from 5-8 oarsmen, the number most favoured being that which allowed for an equal number of oarsmen to be positioned either side of the boat once the battle against a whale was commenced, a number derived upon by the headsman.

From the bow the following positions were normally filled: harpooner, bow-oarsman, midship-oarsman, tub-oarsman, after-oarsman, headsman (at the stern); each seated upon his own thwart. The headsman was responsible for exchanging places with the harpooner once the delivery of a lance had been secured within the beast, the harpooner responsible for securing 'fast fish'. The headsman, once having exchanged places with the harpooner, would then deliver as many lances as was required to fulfil his duty. The harpooner now controlled the sweep (steering oar) with great precision, it being 6.7-8.2 metres in length.

THE FAMILY TREE

Parent:	Offspring:	3rd Gen
Stranger [F]	-Tom [M]	
-Hooky [M]		
Typee [M]		
Humpy [F]	-Walker [M]	
Cooper [M]	-Young Ben [M]	
Big Ben [F]	-Albert [F]	-Charlie Adgery [M]
Jackson [M]	-Brierly [M]	
Sharkey [F]	-Skinner [M]	
Jimmy [M]	-Kinscher [F]	
Big Jack [F]	-Little Jack [M]	

PROLOGUE
GENERAL INFORMATION

Killer whales; the orca; they are black and white dolphins, mammals of the sea, warm-blooded creatures which are at the top of the food chain for the territory that they hold within their power, man being their only predator. Their upper and dorsal surface is black and their lower [ventral surface and the face (left and right sides)] are white with a saddle patch upon their backs just behind the dorsal. They have a light coloured underbelly that blends with the light of the surface, and prey from above are confused by the killer's darker upside. Camouflage has hence played an important role. A head-on-attack from a killer, whether speedily or more relaxed, can easily be confused as nothing more than shifting shadows, for the blazes upon their head - in contrast to dark upper and light under - can betray the mental deciphering of a hunter on the approach, a salmon falling easy victim, moving too late to avoid the menacing jaws as the killer closes its mouth over another meal.

Their dorsal fins literally tower above the surface of the sea, standing 1.8 metres tall in the case of an adult, where the male displays the most easily viewed of its signatures, and the female displays a shorter and more crescent shaped dorsal: similar to younger killers. It rekindles the melody of 'ebony and ivory' for it is black with patches of white upon its body, to break up its shape and threatening presence, so that other mammals and fish of the sea are drawn into a sense of false security when one swims near. It also has distinctive pigmentation behind the dorsal, a patch noteworthy for its aid in identifying one member from the next.

The tail flukes have no skeletal support but are more fibrous, the propulsion obtained from powerful movements of the tail stock (or caudal peduncle). Their eyes are suited to both sea and air, killer whales lifting their heads out of the water to spy on their surrounds, to take in the beauty of the scenery around, and in the case of Twofold Bay, to look at those figures of flesh and bone that stand tall in little boats with harpoon and lances in hand. Yes indeed, sight plays a major role in the killer's day to day life, it seemingly being as good above the waves as it is below, but sound is a more important quality, for sound is its tool of manipulation and strategy whereby food is placed before them like dinner upon a plate.

Of all the mammals of the sea they are the most travelled, the most widely distributed across the waters of the earth, the only significant winner in regards to travel being man, and although widely versed with the oceans of the world it tends to stay clear of the mid-Pacific, mid-Atlantic and mid-Indian Oceans, for no other discernible reason other than the fact that it endeavours, through all its daily rituals, to preserve energy and feast on flesh, whether it be the tongue of a baleen or the rump of a porpoise. Due to such reasons it is understandable that the highest concentration of killer whales can be found along the latitudes of both hemispheres where the temperature is more suitable for energy preservation and close to the coastlines where fertility in life plays a large role in sustaining a leisurely and measurable existence.

With its mouth of teeth, torpedo-shaped body and sheer size, it can outplay, out manoeuvre, chase down and intercept even the noblest of other species of dolphin. The killer is extremely intelligent with a brain that dwarfs a man's. The killer's brain is three times the size of a man's, but size does not indicate a superior intelligence but more of an ability to undertake daily chores. But most of all the brain can decipher incoming sounds and piece together an intelligible communicative idea or action.

The killer can be classified into three main groups, each group depicting their general displays of behaviour and feeding. Killers live in a matriarchal society whereby there is a strong bond between mothers, daughters, and granddaughters. This is the strength of any structured group comprising any number of animals, be it 'resident', 'transient', or 'offshore'.

In regards to the 'resident', the dispersal of individuals from the group does not occur; not whilst the mother is alive in any case. Groups are very large groups, pods of several dozen related killers, feeding exclusively on fish. Made up of a mother, and her sons and daughters of 3-10 killers, each contributes to the group of several dozen animals per pod (as a whole) via its matrilineal binding, up to several hundred individual animals becoming evident in its community. Matrilineal groups within a pod are created on equal terms where the size of any given pod is stretched to the limit, command and structure forming break-away groups of the same, or similar, matriarch society, known as sub-pods. Vocal strategies within a sub-pod are used extensively and remain throughout their lives, such a repertoire of dialect being shared to a degree by other sub-pods within the pod and/or drawn from the pod in question.

Sub-pods can be looked upon as a 'constant' in a killer's society and remain steadfast for the entire life of the matriarch at least, and a killer will not usually defect from one sub-pod to another sub-pod, but smaller extensions of such a pod/sub-pods can be created from the larger. Pods also contained killers that shared, unequivocally, their complex mannerism of social and vocal range of communication, including their specific and unique language – call it accent or basic understanding of a different dialect.

The 'transient' are less social than 'resident' and travel in smaller groups of six or less, mainly feeding on sea lions, seals, porpoises and sea mammals. The 'offshore' usually constitutes a large group of thirty to sixty animals and they prefer open waters and feed mainly on fish, including salmon. Predatory habits are therefore harnessed in respect to each group and are a good reason why other sources of food are not exploited.

Taste for food is as variable as the variety, although many areas where killer whales have grown accustomed, do tend to spend a vast majority of their life feeding upon distinctive forms of prey. The world is a large surface area which provides many staples, some coastlines offering sea lions, seals, porpoises and dolphins; others may tend to feast on the fruits which are offered seasonally, such as salmon and other small fish like herring, even squid and seabirds. The Arctic offers penguins, humpbacks and seals, as does the Antarctic, not to mention more tropical areas where dugongs, turtles and manatees make a great meal. Where whales are concerned, in particular their migratory range and location, it isn't hard to understand how pods of killer whales can follow and maintain a full belly of humpback flesh along any of the world's coastlines which extend up from the Antarctic, one such migration route taking whales along the east coast of Australia and bypassing Twofold Bay, and in some cases with the intention for a short frolic within the deep bay. For an orca to maintain a reasonable source of energy it must consume around four percent of its body weight per day in the search for food, or starve and go by the way of death's door.

To secure food it must act with constant stealth until such a time that an order is given to move in for the kill, for this reason above all else the killer spends around 95 percent of its life under the waves and out of view, stalking its prey like the predator it is, using its physical and mental attributes as best it can to suffocate the source of its temptation in order to fill its quota for the day. But lack of food isn't the only killer of the orca for man also plays his hand in its demise. The cruel and efficient whaling programmes pursued in the past have seen to it that many of those that choose to feed off baleen whales have had their dinner plates cleaned for them and by the decreasing numbers of baleen whale available comes the inability to feed as required, hence a drop in the population of the killer which is continuing at an alarming rate – this also includes the sperm whale population which was decimated in years past.

When food becomes scarce the killer will draw energy sources from its high-calorie reserves of blubber, its huge bulk serving as a means to survive. Where weeks without food can turn into months the killer is able to hold back death, but age, whether young or old, can alter the survival rate of a killer more readily than it would one in mid-life.

Young seals or sea lions are preferred over adults, adults rarely being attacked, for adults are dangerous and can cause great injury to the killers. The killers purposely beach themselves upon the land, the pebbled beach, to take a pup in its teeth, pups that consider the shoreline safe, and being out of harm's way. Killers have mastered this skill which is called 'stranding' and teach it to their young, sometimes in slow motion, and although only a few females participate in securing meals this way all females and juveniles appear to do it, not so much for play, but to harness the skill. Juveniles may strand themselves and adults come to the rescue by stranding themselves alongside, helping them back into the water – some things are not necessarily taught by the mother and it is here that other adults teach the young the skills they need in life to survive. Others may act as decoy, thrashing the water to distract the pups. The killer acts with lightning speed, its dorsal cutting through the water's surface, parallel to the beach and suddenly turns inwards upon the unsuspecting prey. The body is almost entirely out of water when it snatches onto a pup. From here the killer can thrust forward its attack to further beach itself and gain victory if the pup is too far out of reach or simply falls back with its mouth full or empty. It will shake its victim mercilessly in order to disorientate or kill. Killers will take their prey so that the pod can be fed equally, the calves coming first.

The calves might even play with the meal, like an adult, harnessing its techniques on the killing of its prey; in its capture, in its demise. Lessons must be learnt and maintained by young and old.

Another method which delivers results is in the case where a seal might hide on the bottom of the sea, in a cave or rock crevice. Two killers will take turns in surfacing and taking a breath, always one maintaining its watch upon the rock crevice, so that once the seal runs out of breath and tries to escape there will be one killer at least to secure the meal.

They can hold their breath for several minutes in a dive of 400 metres or more, where evolution has provided it with unique abilities in its consumption of oxygen. It is able to exchange gasses more readily, each breath being manipulated in different ways to cater for different dives, being shallow or deep. Its rib cage can collapse under pressure from water, surplus air collecting beneath the blowhole in nasal passages, and even more complex to this it is able to store oxygen reserves in its bodily fluid and muscle tissue as well as in the red blood cells. Its heart beat can be slowed, in particular where a deep dive is concerned. Oxygenated blood is also diverted from other muscle and tissue, like the brain and the heart. Most amazingly they can reabsorb, with no effort at all, blood nitrogen, thereby it can avoid the bends which is so common to man, avoiding the formation of nitrogen bubbles in the blood.

Breathing, in particular with respect to smaller groups and any term-based scenario, or where such is deemed appropriate due to depth of dives and the importance of a hunt, can be carried out collectively and for the good of the pod. When many killers are seen to surface at the same time, or within a very short space of time, this is not sheer coincidence but a manipulation which is conducted by all involved in a particular act which deems such to be employed.

When a calf enters its watery world for the first time it gulps in air to satisfy its need to survive, as any living creature will do, and shortly after this the mother and the calf's breathing becomes synchronized and will remain so for much of their lives, their breathing aligned for the benefit of them and the group, the mother becoming somewhat of a conductor of an orchestra whereby the remainder of the pod will take its breathing from her, for the needs of one and all, for the social binding, for the maintenance of life and their constant forage for food.

Generations of hunting tactics are taught to the young, they are shown first-hand how to combine their abilities and this is reflected in their success. Crucial skills are passed down from one generation to the next, both individual and social, all for the securing of food. They acquire the ability to hunt fish on their own at six months and speedily learn vocalizations, echolocation techniques, social protocol and hunting strategies. Calves mimic lessons demonstrated with great patience from mothers and grandmothers.

They usually place great distance between pods and travel in the same direction and when they encounter food they will noisily leap and splash in the water to signify the find or simply send a vocalized message, though use of sonar is questionable due to alerting prey of their presence, in particular dolphins and other mammals.

They devour creatures great and small, fish and whales; whatever they can get their teeth into.

A message is received from another pod, a school of fish close by. Three pods move in and slowly force the school towards the surface. The school is compacted smaller and smaller. They then vocalize their movements in the coordinated attack, flash their white markings to disorientate the herring that immediately panic and set themselves up as a meal. The killers slap the water with their flukes, stunning the herring and take a mouthful or two of their prey. The killers then take turns so that each has an equal share. An orca beneath flashes his white underbelly and the herring continue in their panic, remaining near the surface where they are needed, with no escape, and can be easily taken into the mouth. A burst of fluke-bashing is then commanded by the matriarch and the stunned herring are devoured quickly as they float unconsciously. Other orcas continue to keep the herring massed together, corralled and ready for feeding. Another killer gets its fill and retreats, another comes in to feed. Once all have fed and had their fill the killers turn and depart, leaving the remaining herring to disperse into deeper water; bodies that remain afloat, be they full or half devoured, are picked up by birds of prey as they swoop down and take what's left of the pickings.

Others find larger morsels more rewarding. A blue whale, being 18 metres in length, is surrounded by a deployed pod. Killers swim either side and below to prevent the whale from making a move towards deep water. They move in closer and at high speed, allowing their presence to be known, maintaining the fear factor, those either side creating white water as they continue alongside the blue whale. Some move to the front to slow the prey, some behind to prevent it turning tail and trying to escape. They disturb the whale's rhythm of breath. They snap their mouths open and closed, gnashing to terrify their prey. The chase continues for 32 kilometres and the blue whale becomes tired. The killers move in one at a time and take great hunks of flesh from the whale, but he swims on. The attack continues for five hours and the killers, either tired or having had their fill, discontinue with the chase, the blue whale continuing on, a great gaping mass of white blubber showing through where it's dorsal once existed, it having been ripped to shreds. Death is just hours away and the blue whale is now a beacon for sharks everywhere, sharks that keep away from the killers, for the killer looks upon the shark as nothing more than a plaything.

Orcas are one of the few animal species to have distinct cultures, and hunting strategies of one orca community are usually unique to that community. Their cultural behaviours are learned behaviours and not instinctive behaviour. When an individual initiates a new behaviour, others will copy it and youngsters will be taught it by adults. In the case of the seal hunting orcas of Argentina, orcas practice beaching and rescuing themselves and pass the skills on to their offspring in preparation for catching seal pups on the beaches of the seal colonies.

For thousands of years, before man recorded such events, killer whales did hunt all manner of baleen whales in every ocean on this planet, and only once in all that time has it been witnessed, and recorded for the prosperity of understanding and knowledge, that they cooperated with humans in their hunt for whales, in one place and one place only. A family which went by the surname Davidson did make a living by the help given in exchange for aid, where the killer whale taxed the human hunt in accordance with their needs: fresh meat, the flesh of the baleen, the unmistakable diet of a particular pod of killers so fondly referred to as friends and co-conspirators, and took place at a place known as Twofold Bay on the East Coast of Australia. And it is here that an extraordinary story unfolds of an unwritten contract between man and beast, one of nature's most powerful and intelligent, one that is misunderstood and labelled unkindly. This story of the killer is not meant to specifically qualify anything in particular, nor to superimpose one quality or behaviour over another; it is to reflect upon individual characters, both man and beast, and the reasons for their cooperation in order for us to grasp a better understanding of the overall picture, and in order to do this we must see the combined story of both humans and killers alike.

CHAPTER ONE
1862

From a distance the dorsal of the killers could be seen to perforate the surface of the sea, cutting effortlessly through the gentle rolling waves, each of the mammals beneath fully aware of all around them as their flippers helped to guide them through the water which encased them.

They surface from time to time, more often than not at around the same time, in particular where a mother with a calf is concerned.

The spouting of water, as air is ejected from the blowhole, looks like that of a great cloud of mist exploding from within, and the water dissipates in the air as it gets carried away by the fresh breeze coming up from the south, and they prepare for another dive by sucking in more oxygen.

It is a wonder in itself to see these mushrooming clouds erupt from the killers, unlike the other cloud known by man where devastation rocks the world and kills people in their thousands, an unforeseen tragedy which has yet been delivered to the world in mass. There is a calm about it, something surreal, where one can become lost in his dreams, forget his place in the world, sitting back and watching the event unfurl. But an even bigger event is about to take place far from land, in the tropics and close to Hawaii where the pristine waters are very soon to be visited; but only for a short time.

The matriarch knows of better places in the world, other bays and inlets that she has visited in the past, even for one as young as her.

Her name is Stranger and she is rather young at just fourteen years, although she had reached sexual maturity at eleven years of age. She was currently surrounded by members of her pod, other killer whales that had joined her in her adolescence, seeing for themselves that she had great vision and purpose, knew of things that they did not. Stranger had been accepted as their matriarch without argument, setting themselves up beside her so that they could learn to act as one. Even now in the few short years that they had been together their dialect had transposed itself as different from others, a uniqueness unfolding with their traits as a unit. She had fallen pregnant when falling in with a large pod of 'offshore' killers but had soon decided to leave, her mate remaining with his mother and grandmother: for the good of the community as a whole.

There was Typee, and at twenty-three years of age was the oldest of the pod. He had a mate, a killer whose dorsal was completely bent over; her name was Humpy. Humpy was seventeen and she had partnered with Typee several years before, Typee having left his previous pod due to his mother's death. They were of breeding age but had yet shown little reward for their prowess in love-making.

There was also another pair, a male by the name of Cooper and a female by the name of Big Ben. Both were eleven years of age and had coupled many years before, being very dependent on one another and practically inseparable, even when called upon during times of hunting. It was their spirit as a couple, their overwhelming desire to be as one, which had forced them to separate from their larger pod of the Antarctic.

So here they were, a small pod of five that had swollen from one; Stranger was about to give birth and the exploding of their population was just around the corner, for Stranger's abilities in the hunt would become legendary amongst all that they came into contact with, many male and female alike soon to give up their post in their pod to join with hers.

Little communication was shared between the members of the pod as they continued slowly on their way, patrolling the waters far from the main coast, just off Hawaii, communication which is even less used when nearing selected feeding locations, for prey could be almost anywhere, and even though a new mouth was about to be born the killers were always alert for an easy meal.

Searching constantly was their only reward but communication between killers is a natural part of life and so takes place during parts of the day or night that are more appropriate, using dialect which becomes modified over the years to correspond with a particular pod, regional variations that are perfected and used methodically without thought; it is that which they now suppress.

Being a very social animal, in particular where without a family representative – namely a pod of siblings, brethren, mother and father – they have been known, world-wide, to seek out the company of humans. In this alone we find it hard to believe that creatures of the deep feel as though they have a connection, of any description, with the human race, but they do. They feel the effects of loneliness and embarrassment, as men do, and they experience fear as well, but yet this is far from their minds for a birth is taking place, Tom being delivered unto the world, and it is now that vocalization can be heard as sound echoes out across the ocean.

The mother's abdomen is swollen with a foetus that has been gestating for seventeen months, it's wriggling and squirming within being felt more easily as the days pass Stranger by.

The mother swims around displaying a little discomfort, her restless commotion drawing little concern, and she rises to the surface for breath, remaining there, just below the waves, for the moment is near. She can feel the soft breeze upon her skin, feel the warmth shine down upon her on this marvellous day. Her first born is about to make its way into the world.

She swims about and then suddenly pauses for the birth has commenced. Her flukes and head are lifted up, her back arched; she gives birth whilst amidst the pod, all other killers close by and surrounding her, protecting her in her time of need, watching with bated breath for the first birth of this new pod.

It is normal for the flukes to be seen first, rarely the head, and the calf emerges after a reasonably short period of delivery, contractions having been suffered in a delivery which rewards the mother with a healthy birth. Her thrashing about, which is necessary on some occasions, has provided the reward, the somersaults and barrel rolls aiding in the birth.

The calf is pushed out, Tom jettison delicately away from the mother as Stranger gently accelerates forward and the calf, amidst the red mist of blood from the torn umbilicus, swims immediately - if not clumsily - to the surface just above, to suck in its first breath.

Tom is born; the calf's triangle dorsal fin droops, its fore flippers are rigid, and its flukes unfurl and thrashes in the watery world in which it has been born.

Tom is free at last, to swim and splash about, to breathe in the air above the surface of the sea.

He is lifted into the air on several occasions and much rubbing of skin on skin takes place, for all are overjoyed to see him born unto the world. A little percussive activity now takes place though Tom is not hurt in any way. He will maintain a very close connection with his mother for the first year of his life and even after this, as he grows further into maturity, will always remain a member of her pod and have close ties with other members too. But for the first year he remains solely in the care of his mother, sheltered by her body, protected by her flippers, provided sanction by the pod.

Stranger is exhausted, but such exhaustion is dependent on the type of delivery, easy or hard. Tom had joined with his mother and both are happy, the ordeal forgotten and far behind them now.

So now they are swimming side by side and commence to breathe in a similar pattern in order to stay close, and the calf out of danger. They have much to be thankful for. But Stranger is a little concerned for there is safety in numbers. More killers in the pod would be welcome however. A matriarch with great hunting ability and strategies to share was worth her weight in gold.

Stranger knew a place not so very far away; a place where hunting whales was a common occurrence. She had seen the pod in action and had even shared in the sport herself. The pod was small but Stranger also knew of another. There were several animals she knew she could influence quite readily.

She would rely on Typee's aid, for he was majestic and quick, good at hunting, good at killing, grand at reading the thoughts of others. He was too much of a commandeering sort to be made the leader of a sub-pod but he had abilities which she could milk. She then reflected upon Typee's mate, Humpy.

Humpy was a vicious type, not afraid to lead a charge, not afraid to take a risk when needed. Stranger would use her as a sub-pod contender when the time was ripe, allowing Humpy to remain close by her side. Yes indeed, Stranger would have Humpy as an ally, this would keep Typee close and others even closer, for those intimidated by Typee would be subjected to Stranger's calling.

But there was plenty of time to reflect on tactics, for now she was simply content to see Tom now swimming behind her right flipper, searching for the retractable abdominal nipples and he soon began to suckle for the very first time and then routinely. Touch is sensitive and sometimes commanding, where a calf requests feeding from its mother. Nudges, nibbles, and fore-flipper caresses, a bond grows between the two. An orca might even rake its teeth on another's back, cavort and wrestle, but never fight. After some time at feeding, Tom precariously takes up a position behind the dorsal fin to swim effortlessly along in the slipstream created, but soon returns to the protected side for more milk.

Tom is 2.5 metres long and weighs 200kg, a grand specimen.

CHAPTER TWO

In the early Days and beyond, it was well known across the face of the whale fishing industry (apart from the few) that seafaring vessels which frequented the oceans on a regular basis, and for great stints of time, in some cases as long as four years, were more easily controlled by commandeering different nationalities to work upon the ships, and in the case of Australian vessels it was seen that aboriginals and South Sea Islanders were the best breed for manning the vessels, a lesson learnt quickly by the Davidsons and their interactions with the Yuin.

A steep hill reaches for the sky at Snug Cove and here can be seen the town of Eden, upon a saddle in the high ground. It looks down and over the bay, its harbour, where a magnificent blue attracts the eye and sandy beaches of honeycomb break the line between sea and forest surrounds.

The lookout (Boyd's tower on South Head) was severely damaged by lightning in the 1860's and never repaired, but still put to good use; it could be seen for kilometres out to sea and served whalers well on more than one occasion.

It was back then, in May of 1863, that George Davidson was born in Eden; Alexander's grandson. This was his world now, where the true semblance of a bay whaling station could be seen for what it was, where two weatherboard homes could be seen situated upon the banks near the bay and an open shelter procured from wood sat waiting for whale blubber to be delivered. Beneath the shelter is the brickwork of the try-works, large iron vats and large tanks for the storing of oil. A windlass would see to it that a carcass was heave-to by way of a large rope, the carcass hauled up and deblubbered. By the time George was crawling on hand and knees he had become familiar with the boat house where the shelter sized at 4.6 x 12.2 metres secured the boats employed in their whaling ventures. The boats are shallow and nine metres long, sturdy and ready for rowing, prepared for launch at a moment's notice, only vacant the crew to power them through the turbulence of the sea.

Set upon his way, Alexander Walker Davidson (who was initially Boyd's carpenter), a Presbyterian who believed in treating everyone fairly, including the indigenous crews he hired and paid with a full wage, built a home from the wreck of the Lawrence Frost, along with a boatshed and workshop. The whaling station try-works consisted of iron pots in a shed with a long ramp, and changed little for the entire time that the bay whaling operation remained intact. He had a capstan to haul the quantities of blubber into position for extracting the oil, where 9-inch strips of fat were ripped from the flesh beneath, and when the job was done, all that was left was a carcass of red lying in pools of blood. The Davidson cottages and whaling station was positioned on the Kiah River, across from the town of Eden, on the other side of the bay and away from the mainstream bustle of country life.

Many different crews were stationed at Twofold Bay at one time or another, including the Walker Brothers, the Barclays, Rixons, Whelans, Newlands and Powers; but of all the men and boats that were cast into the sea in an effort to kill a whale it was the Davidsons that had secured the majority of assistance offered by the killers, for the killers disliked the explosive harpoons that some crews employed when hunting baleen, modern technology which held little interest for the Davidsons. This favouritism seemed to infuriate the other crews even more, to such a degree that more artillery came into play, which saw to it that the killers assisted the Davidsons only, their green boats rather easy to identify, not to mention the silhouettes, faces, and characteristics, of those that they had come to know so well; the green colour was in fact based on the traditional Scottish Davidson tartan which was of the same colour.

Davidson and his small band of five boats had secured an ally for all time. The Davidsons eventually won the assistance of the killer, all others being ignored by the black and white Wolves of the Sea. This saw great favour shine upon the Davidson's for more than one reason, though mainly for the decline in the numbers of right whales passing along the coast in tune with the culmination of the hunting of the sperm whale, a decline in numbers which had commenced in Tasmania around 1841.

With learning being a two-way street, and Alexander open to all that the indigenous crews offered, Alexander came to understand and put into practise the Law of the Tongue, whereby, for the aid in catching the baleen, the killers were permitted to sup on the tongue and lips of all that was caught, and it is here that we shall mention that dorsal fin and body markings were soon recognized as familiar faces and allowed the bay whalers to easily identify with the individual killers on a name-basis, names which were derived from the Yuin deceased. Particular animals that were given attention over the years were, Tom, Hookey, Humpy, Jackson, Cooper, Charlie, Typee, Stranger, Kinscher, Montague, Old Ben, Young Ben, Sharkey, Jimmy, Brierly, Youngster, Walker, Skinner, Big Jack, and Little Jack, many others remaining anonymous (to the tune of around fifty killers spread over three pods, each pod, in some cases, again split into sub-pods) as no records have enlightened me further. It was truly amazing how the killers would cooperate, not just with one another, but also the Davidsons. In a concert of manipulation, and well-tuned and orchestrated manoeuvres, the pods would attend their different tasks like a military juggernaut going through its paces, with one pod positioning itself out to sea to prevent escape and drive the whale in towards the coast, another to cut off any escape to the front of the whales migratory route, and the third to hone in the attack which in some cases could take all day, and on most occasions far less time lost than what would normally be expected if there was no aid to be offered by the skilful throwing of harpoon and lance from the bay whalers upon their little boats. The baleen had no way of escape, even unable to dive, for killers would surround their prey on all sides as well as below, and could even be seen throwing themselves upon the baleen's back in an attempt to smother its blowhole in order to restrict its breathing when he came to the surface.

Each year the killer whales moved from their Antarctic station to the coast of East Australia, moving with the weather, following the fresh breeze of winter as it approached the coast and the streamlined move of baleen as they swam to warmer seas. The move into warmer waters during the winter months was not something that could be considered as common amongst other pods, for many remained stationed where food was in plenty, but the killers of Twofold Bay had learnt to help themselves during hard times. Here they lay, just off the coast, in wait for their prey as they made for the breeding grounds, rarely far from shore, for the migratory routes of the baleen brought the great whales up from the south and along the coastline, past Leatherjacket Bay and then to Twofold Bay. It was at Leatherjacket that the killers initially sprung their ambush in an attack of several phases, one of which was to dispatch one or more of their own towards Twofold Bay where, unbeknown to them, a lookout was positioned at Boyd's tower on South Head, atop the lighthouse that Boyd had abandoned so long ago: not to be confused with the lighthouse above Snug Cove.

The prowling killer, on the loose, searching for his prey; there he was. The sperm whale fed on octopus, the dolphin upon fish, but the black and white of their close relation fed upon them. They fed upon the grampus, seals where available, and whales for their tender choices of lip and tongue. But in most cases the killer whale was after the humpback and lacked much interest in the fin whale and blue for the present, for both were faster in the water, certainly too fast for the rowing power of the men of Eden, unless aided by a pull on the ropes attached to a boat.

This was the pod's way of life, the chosen path. Some pods chose to remain in the colder climates, a minority preferred the warmer, but all chose to occupy very large areas and wander with purpose from one region to the next, whether they did so in order to change their diet or not was up to the animals in question. If a particular fish is found to be less unavailable due to its own cycle of life and death then there is good reason for diet change or change of scenery, and preference is always given to survival, in particular the survival of the young.

So it was here that the killers had congregated, seen by few darting eyes from the coast, watching as the identities of those beneath their dorsal glide effortlessly through the water, Tom with his mark and Hookey with his, distinguishing one from the other as the pod makes its way to the grounds which are to become home for the winter months ahead.

Initially the pods are split, one more than a kilometre out to sea, another at twice that, and a third at three, set upon an angle in order to channel their prey towards the shore and upheaval, where the crews of Davidson's boats awaited with glee. And then, finally, a cow and her unborn calf make an appearance, heading northward for warmer waters and into the trap.

On seeing the spurts of a whale the lookout would take to his horse and ride at a great pace the six kilometres to the Kiah Inlet only to find that his time had been wasted, for Tom the killer, in more cases than not, had swam to the mouth of the Kiah River, where the Davidsons were housed in two isolated buildings, each constructed for life and leisure.

From within the bay, Tom commenced upon alerting the men

ashore of the approaching quarry by flop-tailing until such a time that the whalers made their way into the waters of the bay aboard their boats to the waiting escort. The flop-tailing was for the Davidsons alone, and none other, a visitation seen nowhere else in the world. Tom alone, or the small sub-pod of 2-3 killers of which had been detached, would then lead the boats out to where the baleen was growing weary and distressed, being led as though by leash: more so by sight than by following the glowing bioluminescent trails which would light up the ocean on nights where the moon was not to be seen. It was to become fate, therefore, that Tom would become the most recognisable of all the killers, for his regular contact with them saw to it that their trusting relationship did grow, regardless of his sometimes annoying and playful nature.

And at some time later, from the dreary night, comes the calls of the fight.

The harpoon is thrown and sticks fast. HOORAH! bellows out for all to hear, for the whale has been stuck well, the unborn calf moving inside her, the mother's fear for her young making itself present upon the minds of the killers, and the killers like what they register and feel, for the fear within the humpback will be her own undoing. STERN ALL! then becomes clear and the boat is dragged, all oars pulled in unison with great strength, pulled back in order to aid in the slowing of the leviathan, and escape from threat is seemingly thwarted as the whale turns abruptly and the water surges in greats masses, the boat bobbing about upon the waves of the sea and the turbulence of the fight. The boat was built for the stresses of the fight, pointed at both ends for easy momentum forward and aft, made of good cedar and built to last, but nothing can handle the thrashing flukes of a whale gone mad.

In the unforeseen misfortune of a capsized boat the killers would also assist with the charged duty of ensuring their safety by swimming around the boat's crew and protecting them from the sharks drawn haphazardly to the commotion of the fight against the whale and the men's struggle to stay afloat in rough seas. Tom was truly a member of the family and trusted heavily. Such damage to boats was seen often, caused by the baleen in their effort to survive, and it was here that the Davidsons did well, for the maintenance of the boats and equipment was kept in-house, Alexander's son, John, helping with carpentry skills that put most to shame, and aid was also sought in regards to manning boats in the form of the Davidson cousins, the Greig family.

CHAPTER THREE

George Davidson in 1877, now fourteen years old, was soon to commence upon his own whaling journey through the decades by picking up the struggle against the sea at the same time that sperm whaling was considered by many as a thing of the past, for the drain upon their schools – or pods – had proven fatal for the industry which saw them slaughtered to near extinction. He wasn't tall in stature but was to become respected amongst his peers and others far away, to be placed within the annals of history, to be toasted as a most remarkable man. But now, as a boy turning into a man, his strengths were both hard and easy to see and all he could do was dream of what was soon to be a reality.

He had a spring in his step, walked with arms swinging as though without a care in the world, confident but certainly never cocky or juvenile. He bore a distinctive arch upon his nose and his eyes were a clear blue; most remarkable and hypnotising, though in a friendly way. He wished to be a whaler, like his father, and his wish was about to become true.

He stood upon a hill and watched as the men battled against a leviathan of the sea, gaining ground on the whale; it would be his turn soon. George was utterly astounded, to a great degree, on how the killers felt the prolonged urge, or requirement, or need, to lay visit upon Twofold Bay, every year, one after the next, not missing a single season; but still, they returned, like a gathering of children to their place of birth. Even with the exceptional hearing of the whales within their environment it did come to pass that the occasional humpback was missed by the pod of killers; but it wasn't so much as missed but more to the point that the pod was making a decision on the best form of attack and which whale to take down first. Scenarios had to be measured and food secured, so the pod would always make a preference in favour of themselves. But from the crew's point of perspective the situation was more widely varied and it was the humans who had failed to see a particular whale and not the other way around. The Davidson's would hit the surface of the water to alert the whales to the presence of a humpback and their current position, the killers turning in unison to accept the ultimatum, for it would save them much time in bringing down a whale with the help of the harpoon and lance, regardless of their strategic position.

Tom could see, feel and hear the other killers around him, those of the pod in which he belonged, the pod belonging to Humpy.

Humpy commanded over the pod with extreme precision, courtesy and steadfast will, leading by example and displaying a great understanding of those within her pod and of those that were about to be eaten, but before the formalities of the hunt could take place they were to be joined once more with the matriarch (Stranger) and the others.

A ceremony was about to take place, one that occurred from time to time when one of the pods of related killers joined back together after a degree of absence, having gone their separate ways in forage and exploration.

The two pods were lined abreast, opposite each other, facing one another once more and preparing to be joined again as one. Slowly but surely both groups approached one another, drawing closer, closer the gap. They were now twenty metres apart and they came to a stop, sounding their calls delicately, looking upon one another over the space between them. Then, after half a minute of ceremonial action the two groups swam towards each other and submerged, to surface shortly after, mingling again as one entity, a single pod. They were now ready for the hunt, changing their diet to match their tactics, for the lead up to this day saw the killers in their smaller group's source other prey of smaller girth.

Now the pods of strengthened unity moved towards Twofold Bay for they had heard the movement of a whale close by and they were soon to find themselves in the fight for food. The baleen puts up a grand resistance, stubborn and most worthy of being called a whale-so-grand.

From time to time the killers of the pod would free themselves from their watery surrounds and propel themselves upon the back of the whale, to cover its blowhole and prevent it from breathing, aiding the efforts to drown the beast so that a meal could be secured. The whale would usually try to then sound (dive) but its efforts to do so would be warded off by killers beneath.

Another animal suddenly shoots itself out of the water in order to block the blowhole, a gasp for air in the build-up of fear denied the pregnant humpback. It is as though the whale is under protective custody, flanked by killers. Others further out to sea now act upon the calls, some heading to the front of the chase to slow the escape down and others to help with the capture, a concerted effort by all, and none will go without a meal, the youngest being fed first, regardless of their actions within the act of the kill.

The stress within the humpback mounts quickly but doesn't peak; it just keeps on growing, the whale's thoughts falling upon the unborn calf that she carries, the calf that she has been carrying for eleven months and two weeks - on the verge of giving birth. It is so obvious, even to this humpback of little experience, that there will be no solace from the predicament she is in. She had departed the waters of the Antarctic some time ago, to make way for the traditional breeding grounds further north, following the coastline as close as she dared, for she was alone and without company; as this is the way that most travelled.

The humpback's concern now was for the safety of her unborn, and although she soon realised that she would no longer voice her songlike choruses to the world around her, or even behold the loving sweetness of weaning her young over the next eleven to twelve months, she had to try.

A killer made another strike upon her frail body of twelve metres, one that had been supporting her and the unborn, another chunk of blubber being taken from her flank, the pain searing via shooting pains through her body, triggering receptacles within her, further thrashing of her body hence erupting from within.

What had she done to deserve such torment before death and was her unborn still alive or dead? She shook the thought from her mind, to seek the only option open... complete and utter survival. She wished to feed again upon the capelin, herring, mackerel, and sand lance, to feel the wonder of feeding, to purposely draw in as much water as possible, and then close her mouth once more, forcing the water out through plates leaving the meal behind. If she didn't fight now then there would be no tomorrow, never again would she feel the thrashing of fish against her 380 baleen plates, the comb-like plates covered in a series of olive-black bristles, never again to feel the warmth of a full stomach. But now... now she could see death on the horizon, but still she fought on heroically, the fight for survival taking control over her every movement.

And it is now that the bay whalers make their first appearance, to aid in the killing of the whale, to help provide sustenance to the pods, and they don't disappoint, being very quick with decision and action, even if late and after much effort and energy on behalf of the killers has been depleted.

The harpooner exchanges places with the headsman as quickly as possible, the headsman positioning himself and readying a lance for the killing to begin, the lengthy hours that lay ahead, the cold of the night to be endured, the thirst, the rapture, the torn muscle and sore throats. And with the concerted efforts of gigantic proportion the killing of a whale could take quite some time but the strain of the fight being more equally shared between human and orca.

Tom would quite often be seen to jostle with the rope fastened to a harpoon, enjoying himself more than ever, hanging onto the harpoon line for anything up to thirty minutes, being dragged along by the force of the humpback as it made its way through the surging sea walls which grew and then subsided, being dragged along like a dead weight, the surges of white water turning over upon the surface of the sea; he did this by biting upon the rope and holding it in his mouth or simply placing it beneath one of his flippers. Tom was not a mature animal, to say the least, but his efforts in the catch would still be rewarded with an equal share of lips and tongue.

The battle continues well into the night, lances thrown with great effort, to be placed between the ribs of the whale being targeted, to penetrate deep and cause that very inflicting and deadly wound; and the incorrect placement of a lance would see the effort wasted, for little damage may be done, or the lance might simply fall out and sink to the floor of the sea, equipment lost forever, never to be retrieved. The moon then shows itself and then, with sudden realisation, the men stand up and cheer aloud for blood comes rushing from the blowhole of the humpback, the best sign ever to indicate that the kill is almost secured, and with the rushing of red into the air around them the whale commences with its death flurry, the piercing red pain of one or more wounds growing in torment. The end is so very near and the humpback knows without a doubt that she will never get to share the next two years of bonding with her unborn. And then the end is met.

The joy of the win is exuberating to say the least, man and beast receiving great joy from what they have achieved, their combined effort rewarding both parties.

The men commence about the task of attaching an anchor to the carcass as fresh as it is, the killer whales moving in for their prize.

The killers force open the humpback's mouth as the men continue their work, orca forcing their way into where the tongue sits ready, ready to be devoured. Calves are fed first and then all those that remain take turns, none taking more than they should: all is shared equally. By the time the first of the killers have fed, the others have moved in from far out to sea, where the flanks were protected, preventing escape, for the humpback had to be kept as close to shore as possible – inside the bay itself would have been most welcome.

The tongue is completely gone, eaten away, nothing left remaining, and the lips are munched on, ripped apart, taking into the killers' jaws. It is also around this time that the anchor has been well secured and the crew has turned to make headway for home, to return the following day to claim the carcass, when the gases of putrefaction has seen to it that the body resurfaces, usually in twenty-four hours; sometimes sooner, sometimes a little later.

The killers continue with their feeding, taking the last of the lips into their mouths, finishing up with the last of what they wish and now undertake the last act of their silent agreement. The killers grab the humpback's head, flukes and flippers, and take it down into the depths, to be left near the ocean floor, away from the worst of the swelling sea and turbulence, for it to rest in peace before it is time to be exhumed.

Yeah; that's what George saw, without a mistake, looking out over the bay, having watched the scene unfold and end the way it had; it was breathtaking, and many more days similar to this one were to unfold before his very eyes, before he himself was made ready upon the boat and became a whaler.

CHAPTER FOUR

Two boats spearheaded towards the open sea, heading towards the entrance of the bay, both boats competing for the prize that they had to have, for without the oil from the whale their children would go hungry; but the years did not favour too many partnerships competing for the same whale, and competition within Twofold Bay soon subsided over time until there were just a few other hindrances in the way of the Davidsons' vision to be the only whalers in the bay.

Each boat surged forward, shoulders rolling, oars in hands, and five oars apiece; but the harpooner of Davidson's crew was already contemplating the desertion of his position, to take his post with his thigh placed in the concave of his thwart, to ready with a harpoon. The, most sudden-like, there was a great spout of water erupting from the surface of the bay, where a right whale had surfaced most temporarily, the water foaming for an instant and the being disrupted by the gigantic lifting of the flukes, the ever dangerous tail then quickly disappearing back into the sea, diving once more after having replenished its breath. A split second later and the unmistakable dorsal of Tom erupted from the water as his entire body lifted out and seemed to freeze, for just a second, in mid-air; it was like a holy man witnessing a true vision of Mother Mary.

Jackson was alongside Tom and now headed to his port side, endeavouring to cut off the right whale's dive, but little good it would do either, for the harbour was restriction enough, but Jackson was also aware of a possible retreat gained from beneath the waves, where the harpoon and lances of those upon the boat could not see or reach.

George could be seen, his silhouette upon a hill, overlooking the cliff where he stood, watching as the two crews sweated it out, thrashing at the sea with all their strength, trying with all their power to be the first within distance of the whale, to hurtle a harpoon against the great mass that had temporarily disappeared from view. It was George's dad, John Davidson, his jet-black beard upon his face. It was his boat against another, a boat manned by Bob Love, the competition between each extremely fierce, as could be told by the screwed up looks upon their faces, and where every muscle tore at the oars. This was the fight of champions, where the rule of the 'fast fish' is what mattered the most.

The sea was choppy and breeze non-restricting, the freshness doing little to upset the situation, but the work was hard enough. And as the oars continued to beat at the sea from within the security of the row-locks, the Davidson crew stroked ahead, making more ground than Love, making that extra assertive effort to make the grade.

John looked behind him to realise the headway they had gained on the opposition, seeing the sun as it commenced to set behind the bulk of Mount Imlay, a second of mesmerised freedom settling upon his soul, for this was his home, where waves of gentle surf plunged upon the rocks at the foot of the cliffs, where the swells of undulating sea moved within the bay as though caressing the earth beneath, and then towards the mouth of the Kiah River, where long waves of white water broke along Whale Spit, an elongated portion of beach that sheltered, to some degree, the river beyond. Some debris from the 'Lawrence Frost' could still be seen sticking out of the spit, from which the two cottages above were made, buildings painted in white and used for the enterprise of whaling.

The fight beneath the waves continued, the killers trying with all their effort to prevent the right whale from getting past them and on out to sea, but even if such a move was possible and the manoeuvre successful, the whale would still have to contend with the other pod further out, those awaiting the call to join in on the feeding of lip and tongue. Their patience was their virtue.

Tom then abandoned his manoeuvre and raced to the surface, for the whale was changing direction as surely as they had thought, and whilst the other killers, both Jackson and Humpy made the effort to impede on the right whale's progress, Tom broke the surface and half turned, crashing down upon his flank and turning to face the crew of the green boat. He looked upon them momentarily, trying to gain their attention, and John, the headsman, saw what was to play before his very eyes. He had seen Tom do this before but could not clarify what it was that was passing between them both. Tom seemed to look at him directly in the eyes, communicating his dire need.

Tom then turned into the choppy waves and sped off, leading the boat to where the whale was to surface when next requiring a breath of air. Tom was showing them the way, and John saw all the cards fall into place, the connection between Tom's antics of the past and the commotion being performed before him this minute. They were being escorted from the front, shown the way as any usher would do, and Tom wished nothing more than to assist as best he could in the demise of the right whale.

The dark flesh of Sam stood out, easily seen by Tom. He knew then that the harpoon would fly soon enough. Sam placed the end of his oar into a socket opposite the thole-pins. The harpoon was then picked up and position sought. He barely had time to place the weapon upon his right shoulder, a grasp taken upon the shaft of iron, when Tom veered to the right and the whale surfaced briefly between the killer and the crew, but it was long enough.

Sam hurtled the harpoon forward and down, into the fatty layer and penetrating deep beneath the dorsal. The whale lunged forward with a suddenness expected, water splashing over the crew as they pulled back on the oars, the manila secure to the harpoon, the line tight but able to run freely through the loggerhead if required. All oars were now quickly peaked, pulled from the water in hurried unison, secured into position and out of harm's way, well clear of the surface of the sea which could snap an oar instantly or see to it that one was delivered with great wretchedness against the body of flesh and bone of the man that held it, crippling a crew member beyond expectation.

The right whale thrashed mightily and dived, the boat surging forward under great duress, John manipulating the sweep in a manner of grasp and control that was hard to match, watching the right whale and the surge of the sea as carefully as one could, considering all possibilities, watching for that dreaded moment when the whale might quite easily turn tail and surface from beneath the boat, or simply capsize it by turning swiftly and with great thundering power.

Tom looked back again, seeing the harpoon stuck fast and considered for a brief moment the other crew, Bob Love and his effort to stay put, continuing on in the hope that the harpoon might break clear of the right whale or that another might surface for him to call his own.

John now stood as Sam drew closer, the two exchanging posts, Sam taking up the sweep and John moving to the front of the boat, to prepare the lances for action, to get ready with the actual killing of the whale.

Tom now acted accordingly and dove beneath the surface where Humpy and Jackson continued to harass the right whale, preventing him from diving and heading out to sea. He then turned and headed to the surface, surging out of the water and upon the whale's back, trying with all his might to cover the blowhole of the right whale, to prevent it from breathing properly, to hurry up the arrival of death.

The first lance was then thrown, it penetrating deep and between the ribs, exactly where it was aimed, and the right whale began moving around in circles, taking the boat and its crew with him, John throwing another lance which also hit its mark and within minutes a spout of red erupted from the blowhole after an extraordinarily short dive.

The whale was dead but the deal was not complete. John saw, as the others did, that Tom and the others were moving in on the fourteen metre long carcass. With quickness delivered they set about tying an anchor to the right whale and a buoy too, and then set it adrift, to sink to the ocean floor, where the killers could have their feed and the gasses would form within the whales gut, to float again in a days' time, to be collected and drawn into the try works for deblubbering after the killers had fed upon the lips and the tongue.

The call was made and the pod out to sea came thundering in, another to the north of the migratory route also making for the site of the kill, where each and every one of them would get their just reward, none more than another, all equally shared between them, for there was more to come in the following days and weeks, with or without the help of the Davidson's, though the help was a benefit to the killers for their energy reserves would not be depleted.

Stranger watched with anticipation over the feeding, ensuring that none of those under her sway took more than their fair share, but greed wasn't something strived for in killer whales, wasn't even a contemplation of mind. These mammals were one and the same, of the same pod, of the same line. They owed one another more than any man could realise, for each one acted in accordance with the will of the others. Sure, they were individuals, each could think for his or her self, but their pod was their religion; was their faith; was everything to them.

Humpy was looked upon as a strong leader, and Stranger knew her well, but she also looked to her young, both Tom and Hooky.

Hooky was a male, as per Tom, and only four years younger; again born of a father that she would never see again. Stranger, the matriarch of all before her preferred it this way, preferred to partner with fathers that would have little sway in the years that were to fall before them, for Twofold Bay was unique to her and all those that followed.

And so; Typee, Humpy, Cooper, Big Ben, Tom, Hooky and Jackson, all favourites of their matriarch, all known to the men aboard the green boats, had their way with the whale before swimming off towards Leatherjacket Bay for some hard-earned rest, and the other thirty members of their small community followed.

CHAPTER FIVE

George's task at the beginning of his long and rewarding career – rewarded by the love of what he did, not the monetary reward – was to assist his Uncle Jim upon the lookout of square shape and footing, which had been leased by his father... in fact, all the land from South Head to the Kiah River had been leased by him, and this gave him the desired advantages over his competitors. Not only did he have the best post for which to look for whale signs, but also the killers to help with the catch of a prized casket of oil.

Boyd's Tower was still a very fitting building, even with the damage of the storm so many years before, and the visual graces of the sea from South to North was an ally of strategic importance for it meant that the Davidson crews could be launched before all others, and in the case where whale sign was missed, there was the comfort in knowing that Tom would be flop-tailing to his heart's content, drawing their attention to the fact that whale was coming. Jim quite often found himself straddled upon his horse, racing towards the Kiah, raising the alarm of an approaching whale, the sound of the hooves, in particular in the still of night, providing further advance of the news to come, news which was acted upon immediately, even before Uncle Jim had the opportunity to unhorse himself.

On this particular morning, George was to accompany his father in the boats, all three being launched and making their way across the smooth surface which reflected the clear skies high above, moving out towards the mouth of the bay in order to commence with their morning patrol, to search for whale sign, to hope that their efforts would be rewarded by a quick catch and an early lunch – which rarely ever eventuated.

They worked the oars hard and moved out towards the shelter at South Head where a large rock, the colour of red, acted as a wharf, where, very close by a cave of substantial size which provided them with adequate cover from inclement weather. Stores for the cave and the lookout were displaced and the crews on the move once more, making the most of the opportunity to be in the right place, at the right time.

As they stroked the sea and moved out of the heads they could see the spouts of several killers nearer to Leatherjacket Bay. They seemed relaxed and complacent, neither thrashing about, flop-tailing, nor making a general nuisance of themselves as was so common with Tom. Further behind there was another, the waterspout jettison from within its hide whilst surfacing was in progress, the force pushing with it much water, the warmth of the killers interior providing sufficient temperature that when the blow came it was with much mist, the water condensed to form a cloud of spray that mystified any experiencing the sight for the first time.

They were at work, listening intently on the movement of the sea, trying to catch that ever elusive signal that a whale might be approaching or moving a little further out to sea. And that was the real concern. The pods were positioned in good fashion, three pods of equal strength at different intervals from the coast, to act as a curtain for any approaching prey, but if a whale was to be moving further out than expected the killers would have to make their move and try with all their effort to force their prey in towards the killing ground where the men would be ready with harpoons and lances; although in all reality the effort and wasted energy did not always give good cause for a chase to be undertaken and the lessons of years past proved that another whale would end up closer to shore... sooner or later.

Tom saw the patrol of three boats and summed up the action, realising that the men were doing as he was doing, patrolling the ground and waiting for their opportunity to strike, in unison if possible. He now turned around and moved stealthily towards the others of his pod, each conserving their energy for when the need arose, waiting patiently and with a skill that had been perfectly engineered over centuries of evolution. It was then that a signal was received from several kilometres out to sea, that a small whale was bypassing the mouth of Twofold Bay, a minke whale with unborn calf, a small whale which the killers favoured over others but for the moment didn't really provide sufficiently for three pods of gnarled teeth to feed upon. The killers' jaws opened and closed several times in quick succession, noisily clapping the jaws together in mounting aggression and to press the fear of the impending doom to be driven deep within the minke's mind. With their mouths closed tight they now shifted into higher gear, the teeth of the upper jaw fit snugly into the gaps provided by the teeth of the lower, so the fitting of one into the other resembled the cogs of a wheel.

The signal was their call to duty and unbeknown to the men in the boats the killers took off beneath the surface of the sea to begin the chase, to pester and provoke, to bring the whale down by all means possible so that sustenance could be gained. The minke would be fairly easy to catch but not really worth the small effort, for it would do little in helping hold back the tide of hunger in all the hungry mouths looking forward to a good meal. But the facts of the case were mounted as normal and no single food source shrugged off as dreary. He would provide a little sustenance and wouldn't tax them too much, and hopefully there might be more than one to come, but regardless of the situation which was currently unavailable to Tom and the pod, the minke was now fully aware of the killers presence, for the signal had been sent, the alarm bells were ringing, and the getaway had commenced.

The normal procedure for a the killers of Eden to undertake when hunting a minke was to see it stranded in the shallows and then consumed of all it had to offer, and although the same size as the killers, was certainly unable to outrun it and was entirely out of its class when being run down; in particular where a large pack of hungry mouths were looking for a quick fix.

The minke swam through the sea, the beak and pointed shape of his head gliding through the water, nine metres in length and powering along at great speed, but not fast enough. Her body was streamlined, fins pointed at the tips, and flukes broad and concave along the notched rear margin. It dove then, arching the tail stock high but the flukes remained beneath the waves, the commencement of a deep dive being commenced. The effort was keenly cut off by two killers and the minke was forced to surface, surrendering itself to further torment as mouths tore great chunks out of her flank, all eager to kill her. The rush of red billowed out and merged with the sea, a large cloud expanding out, growing bigger and bigger. Several sharks in the vicinity could hear the calling, the dinner bell ringing, but fear stopped them from approaching too close, for even the great white shark feared the hungry and gluttonous killer.

The three pods gave chase and made ground upon the minke in remarkably quick fashion and soon had her surrounded, the bulge in her undeniable, easily seen for what it was. The unborn calf would also provide great nourishment for the killers who in their ultimate wisdom would take more than the lips and tongue, for although the minke wasn't scrawny, it was simply not enough. Each knew without doubt that the preference would be for a larger baleen to tempt their desire but the minke was not something that went by the way. Many of those in the pods at the present quite preferred the flesh of smaller whales and dolphins, porpoises and fish, and good reward was infectious, in particular where men from boats could freely assist in their downfall.

The minke was a krill feeder, harmless and often alone and today she was to see her end, the end of her life and the unborn calf, the one in her womb that she had not yet got to know, the unborn to which treasured her thoughts of future commitments to come.

Tom got to the site of the killing at the same time that the others had had their way with the minke, enough left to feed on but the delicacy gone and forgotten. Share for the sake of sharing, for the needs of the group, for the desire to remain in community spirit and be unselfish as always; but first in, best dish; the unwritten law that ferried from pod to pod, a rehearsed consequence of life which transpired over all else.

Tom tore at what little remained along with the others of his flock, those of his pod that had been the furthest from the find and patrolling their ground as good killers should. The situation was shrugged off and normal patrol duty assumed immediately, the pods returning to their station post haste, silence once again restored and the tranquillity of the sea took hold. As for the crews of the green boats; they would receive no joy from the kill.

CHAPTER SIX

A great anxiousness fell over them all, heart throbs pushing the excitement of the word to the culmination as one would expect, and then it came again; RUSHO!

George burst through the door and exclaimed through sheer exhilarated enthusiasm for the crew to man the boats, for a whale had been seen, and no sooner were hands on boats then Tom could be seen flop-tailing to the front the Kiah River Bar where the calm surface of the bay lapped pleasurably upon its sands. Even now, as men threw themselves upon the thwarts, grabbing at their oars and thrusting them into the water via the thole pins, jackets were pushed aside and boots forced on by the few that hadn't time to respond to the words that flew through the air of this bright day, the afternoon air fresh with several clouds racing across the sky.

All indications were that it could become a long night affair if the sun was to fall from view. A quick kill was required; if the whale was not secured by nightfall the air would become as uncomfortable as a hindered sea on any stormy day, for wind-chill was always a factor, hence making a short night long and a long night longer.

Tom, having seen the rush of men to boats, assured of their fast action and soon-to-be presence, turned tail, his flukes thrashing at the surface as he sounded for a little depth, picking up immediately on the situation with the right whale, sending signals through the water.

Tom was no different than any other killer and had normal hearing as well as echolocation. Orcas possessed the ability to see, with quite remarkable vision, both above and below the surface of the sea. Aerial scanning was referred to as 'spy hops' and was where killer whales lifted their heads out of the water to see, but where light quickly dissipates in respect to depth the killer had no alternative but to employ another means of hearing and sight.

Tom was some distance from the fight at the present and could hear without much trouble the thrashing flippers, flukes, and bodies in the water, but a clearer picture of the scene was an advantage to Tom as he sped off wearily towards the right whale.

Echolocation engulfed the area, penetrating all that was literally aimed for, the picture being painted in strong transcendent colours, echolocation being the sensitive sensory system based on sound. It was ten times more accurate than the best sonar in submarines, echoes generated by short pulses of sound directed out to sea to their front. Pulses were emitted via staccato styles, high-frequency sounds that lasted but for a few milliseconds, produced in the nasal passage and deeper, below the blow hole, directed to his front, passing through fatty tissue which acted as a lens (known as 'melon' – its bulging forehead).

He continued focussing the sound in the direction that the killer required as he swam effortlessly through the water. Many segments of the emitted sounds were refracted back, the segments painting a picture as sound returned through the thin bony walls of Tom's lower jaw and was transmitted along the jaws length to acoustic conduits before reaching the sensory organs of the middle ear on either side of the skull near the base of the brain. This was an ultrasound in effect where a clear picture of what rests ahead could be formed and acted upon instantly. The returning sound, travelling at four times greater speed than that through the air, provided detailed information on texture, size, shape, distance, and composition.

Tom zoomed in then on the object and bombarded it with further scrutiny, gathering further information, much more precise than before, and above the surface the race continued unabated.

As immediately as the men met the first of the waves, the heat of the work commenced to mount, a blanket of false-security against what could well be a night of mounting displeasure.

Three boats mused to pull in unison at first, in file, though slightly askew, each beckoned by their headsman to be the first in range for a harpoon to be thrown, colourful language filling the air, being carried haphazardly across the bay and to the few that watched from the banks, those watching from afar taking little heed as to the words of encouragement as though water off a duck's back, for the language was a part of bay whaling as was lancing or deblubbering. And the voiced encouragement continued and the erupted into a symphony of chorused bellows, for one of their competitors could be seen launching two boats, oars striking the water with as much unrestrained and unchecked jubilance as John Davidson's crews had performed: it was Whelan.

Spray lifted from the bows as muscles taunt and pressed for a little extra speed, surmounting efforts of gigantean proportion being reflected on all faces as teeth were exposed to the world and grimaces painted deep lines of passive aggression upon their faces. This was a race for survival, for the promise of wages, for the security of their families. Each and every one that manned an oar put in an effort that dwarfed all else and the headsman's efforts at the stern pertained no less, each one full of character and measured agility, with men controlling their sweeps and looking forward, providing direction and instilling confidence, encouragement, and threats of sackings if they were not the first to net the 'fast fish'.

The pod of killers today only numbered three, others stationed further out, for there was another whale which had bypassed their trap. Nevertheless the tactics of the day for the pod of three didn't vary from their normal procedures.

Tom returned to reform the threesome, acting upon their instincts and harrying throws, wrestling with great torment the right whale as it was slowly turned towards the mouth of the bay, and towards the boats that drew closer and closer with every passing second, oars thrashing at the surface of the sea, boats surging forward towards their victory or demise.

The killers had turned the right whale and it commenced to head for the boats, strung out as they were. The gap between the three warring parties now closed at a tremendous rate and the right whale sounded one more time, disappearing most temporarily from the surface for one of the three killers positioned itself haphazardly beneath the leviathan, preventing it from diving deeper, restricting its movement as though by leash, forcing it to surface before its time.

The disruption in the contour of the bay's surface drew the immediate attention of those in Whelan's front contender, the uplift of water created by the whale as it surfaced bringing a little more than surprise to dawn upon their faces, and as the back of the whale broke the seal between water and air, the bow of Whelan's boat was lifted with no effort whatsoever upon the crest of their passion's bulk.

Oars were lifted out of the water, still in their thole pins, riding high for the briefest of seconds, and not milliseconds before men began to consider jumping from the peril of an unstable and contemptuous predicament the boat slid harmlessly back into the chop of the waves and the oars were once again handled accordingly.

Tom took an instinctive second to peruse the situation above, lifting his eyes out of the water to look upon the position of the crews and their boats of glorious empowerment. A green boat was close to Whelan's, so close in fact that the harpooner stood ready, weapon of trade upon his shoulder, thigh braced against the thwart and ready to fling with great accuracy his iron. It left his hand and fell towards the right whale but there was insufficient power behind the throw, a somewhat underestimate by Pigeon, the last throw he would ever make, for the loss of the whale meant his immediate termination from employment, sufficient evidence being accumulated over the past weeks to indicate that Pigeon had been paid-off by Whelan himself: the throw had been... thrown

But the task at hand was still afloat, harried continuously by the killers, and as the jaw of John Davidson dropped in disbelief the man of Whelan's second boat, known by all as Bedford, tossed his harpoon with great victory, a mass of energy, precision, and testimony to his ability, securing itself hard.

The 'fast fish' had been achieved by Whelan and the lancing began, Davidson's boats moving aside and waiting to see if the harpoon were to fall from grace, but it was not to eventuate.

There was no escaping the trap, even with the gigantean effort of the right whale as it sprang for the mouth of the bay and the wide-open sea, pulling the boat in tow, attached quite securely by harpoon and manila rope, never to abscond from its delivery upon the ramps of the try-works with the windlass working to its fullest potential.

John saw the dilemma as it was and fell upon the only conclusion; the battle had been lost due to the unfettered conviction of one of his own men, a soon-to-be figure on the unemployment line or working for his opposition, but the opposition would not last, for the end was being delivered to them this very minute.

Davidson and his three crews could not believe their eyes as the whale gave up its fight for life, sooner than expected and pelted well by the two boats that were positioned one on either side. If it hadn't been for the help provided by the killers, then the kill would have been enduring to say the least. And now, in the cold victory that had been won, Whelan was towing the carcass in towards his workshop, to be deblubbered then and there, towed under the power of two boats, delivery assured. And as the boats tugged on their oars the three killers came in for their reward, trying with great effort to get close enough for them to sup on the lips and the tongue.

Some of Whelan's men picked up a tool-of-the-trade that had been stowed aboard, razor-sharp boat spades, square in shape and very sharp, normally used for deblubbering. They were striking at the killers, keeping them at bay, holding back their attempts to take their reward, denying them their means to survive.

Tom surfaced and looked the men in the eyes, one at a time and summed them up. He took note of the boats and remembered them well. Davidson's boats were green and never shied from providing the reward for their combined victory over a whale, but these others... who were they? What were they playing at? They would be remembered and never forgotten, and never again would another be given the opportunities of the hunt which only the killers could provide... unequivocal assistance... never again would another boat be provided as much as a wink of recognition or assistance.

CHAPTER SEVEN

The sun had not even commenced to light the day when two of the killers commenced flop-tailing in front of the Kiah Inlet, throwing themselves out of the slightly choppy waters to crash upon the rolling waves, the wind strong and cold but not as bad as some mornings the men had come to know.

Weather was an important factor in the industry, in particular where the crews were concerned. A hard south-west wind was cold and its after-effect was that it brought the sea up: choppy in the bay and out by the mouth of Twofold Bay, and further out the swells and disturbance upon the sea would be in full effect. Factors: a mind full of what-ifs. The weather may worsen, for the wind could change direction as opposed to dropping off and push the bad weather closer into shore. But at present all was fine.

RUSHO!

And the chase was on.

George was fourteen, full of vigour and extremely keen: 1877.

Arms found their way into jackets as the figures dashed about, dark upon the backdrop of the ground around them, running as fast as they could towards the boats, dashing out of the bunkhouse like greyhounds on the loose and after a hare, having no time to waste. The night revealed further information, enlightenment as to the source of the killers reason for attracting the bay whalers, for the unmistakable sound of a humpback could be heard in the distance, somewhere just inside the mouth of the bay, where many more killers were present and attempting with all their might to keep the whale from heading out to sea, trying to force it further into the bay where it would be stuck between a rock and a hard place, between killers of sea and land, where mammals and their flippers, and the hands of men, could come together and contemplate great celebration on the killing of another humpback. The killers could taste the tongue as they moved into position, and the headsman was considering the tonnage of oil that might be obtained from the fish in the bay.

The men wasted no time at all in closing the gap between themselves and the fray, battling the resistance offered by the sea as they powered along, muscles burning at the effort which each man poured into the task. And the dark of the night was temporarily forgotten as they pushed on towards the noise in the distance, knowing full well that the killers had a large humper to contend with.

The light of the bunkhouse and the cottage now far behind them gradually grew smaller and smaller. There was no light of the moon to aid them for it was a cloudy night above, and yet reflections from the sun shining bright upon the crust of the earth, from somewhere far over the horizon, shed a little light upon their world along the horizon's rim, or possibly a reflection from the clouds, the stars above adding nothing of worth, but all bay whalers know of one thing that could be counted on when stalking a whale at night, in particular where the killers were concerned, and that was the clear presence of the phosphorescent trails that cut tracks upon the sea, a navigational aid which paved the way to where the whale was waiting, killers harrying as they did so well.

George sat up in front of the forward-most thwart and did what he could with providing direction, though the headsman, his father, needed little prompting as the trails left by the killers were easy to follow. Two of the great whales then moved back to see what was wrong with the boat, to see if there was something amiss, for the killers felt as though the men in their tubs were not performing their tasks in an adequate fashion.

Tom pushed against the lead boat, shoving it sideways, endeavouring to point out that he could aid the boat if only they were to think about the situation. If a harpoon had been thrown then there would be a rope, a rope which could be pulled by Tom to aid the boat in gaining speed and much time. With the absence of the rope there was little Tom could do, and wrestling with the progress of the boat was doing little to invoke the imagination of those rowing.

Tom took off then, a few curses from the men aboard rising into the air, voices that bellowed out for kilometres, to die upon the wind which commenced to grow in its ferocity, the cold night air now stinging at the men's faces for the spray of the ocean, coming up from the rolling waves and the bow of the boat, cold which made itself known to the rowers, each and every one feeling the chill commence to grow, even in the heat of the moment where muscles stun at the work they performed.

The headsman ordered for silence for the last thing he wished was for any competitor to hear them chasing down another whale. They had lost one just the day before and another would just not do. They were heading towards Middle Head now, past Snug Cove and Eden, where the sleeping town winked once or twice, a lantern being lit from somewhere upon the shore.

Tom and two others were moving just below the surface, the bulges of sea moving with them, the tops of their backs and a little of their flukes seen from time to time due to the most temporary appearance of the moon. They were pestering the whale to no avail.

The night was dark and spy-hopping was no guarantee of good visual contact with either the men on the boats or with the whale as it surfaced, blowing out and breathing in more air. The killers decided on another action, to force the whale deeper, to see it use its air once and for all, to deplete it emphatically of its facility and drown it then and there. This was the thought that ran through the killers, the tactic they would employ, and deprive the men above of the ability to anchor the carcass. If the weather failed to improve, and got any worse, the carcass could well drift out to sea before they had the opportunity to bring it ashore. But Tom knew as well as the others that they needed the man power, they needed the strength offered by harpoon and lance in order to stress the whale beyond recovery, to siphon the humpback of its will to live and increase the opportunity to kill it by any means, for there was no such thing as a fair go when speaking of dining upon a fine meal.

The whale was held tight, forced to enter further into the bay where it would meet with death, its efforts constantly parried by the killers remorseless strides to heighten the dilemma of the humpback's predicament, savouring the moment when they would gain the upper hand and a mouthful of lip and tongue, the delicacy that they loved so much.

Still fresh of mind and of the ability to perform manoeuvres well, the humpback shifted gear and away from the lurching, snapping jaws of a killer, another chunk of blubber torn from his bulk.

The whale raced for the surface and broke it fast, great volumes of spray pelted here and there, the rowers of a nearby boat smothered from head to foot in cold and dampening hell, the cold of the sea penetrating fast to the bone, stinging at their flesh, numbing the feeling in their hands, toes, and face. But the quality of any bay whaler, as with George, young of heart and confident of mind, having been brought up with the knowledge instilled by his father of many years' experience, saw greatness in opportunities provided, and George lifted the harpoon above his head in both hands. He thrust down hard at just the right time, where the phosphorus sign of presence pointed to the whale's position both loud and clear, the point of the harpoon penetrating deep, securing itself well within the beast that swam the seven seas.

The 'fast fish' had been secured and Alex Greig's boat, with Fred at the forward thwart with harpoon at the ready, was called to inaction, for the last thing they wanted was for two harpoons to be stuck fast to a single fish, in particular at night when the weather was not sound and it was all the more difficult to keep the boats apart and from smashing each other to smithereens.

Fred Wilson moved to the rear and changed places immediately with the headsman, John's own boat conducted the same manoeuvre, George moving to the rear and changing places with his father, the lancing of the whale to commence immediately... as soon as it surfaced once again.

The whale had reared its barnacled head at the initial stinging of the harpoon, brought to the reality of the situation as the end commenced to become clear, that he, a humpback of little threat to anyone or anything, other than what could be taken in his mouth and digested within its gut, was being chased down from beneath and above the waves. He was meek, meant no harm, and wished only to move on towards the breeding grounds, to find himself a mate for the season of joy, to pass on his genes at one of the many social gatherings of his species, a gathering place as per many that could be found in this world. He sounded immediately on feeling the sting of the harpoon enter his body, diving as deep as he possibly could, the manila rope of the boat dragging out behind him, the rope looped around the loggerhead for ease in control and manipulation, manipulation which did not come easily, although with the help of the pack of killers the men had less to concern themselves with; except the unenviable.

The temperament of a harpooned whale was rather unpredictable, easily pressed into thrashing about in a manner that could not be read by forecast of experience. A harpooned whale was a dangerous animal, as dangerous as they come, the flukes of the animal quite capable of cutting a boat in two.

The ploy of the killers had changed once the harpoon was embedded within the blubber of the whale, for this meant that lances were to follow. The call went around for the pod to change tactics, the need to press the humpback deeper no longer fitting; they now placed all emphasis on keeping the whale as close to the surface as possible.

Tom then leapt from the water, his entire body lifting out of the sea, and he came down hard upon the back of the humpback, sliding upon its blowhole, restricting as best as possible his breathing even for just a few seconds, to impede upon the whale the ability to breathe right, think straight, and act with precision upon the predicament he was in. He was growing tired, tired of the chase, tired of the restrictions imposed upon his abilities, tired from the stress, strain, and overpowering fear.

The whale was forced to remain surfaced, killers either side and one below, the boats now closing in, dragging the line of manila in through the loggerhead, bringing the catch home.

George gave the order to turn towards the whale as he picked up a lance and readied himself against the thigh-crunching thwart, steadying himself before unleashing his fury, and as the gap was closed between them both he hurled the lance with great precision into the flank of the whale and between the ribs. It penetrated deep and the whale curled in pain, his head lifting out of the water, spray covering the crew once more in salt water as the particles of moisture drifted quickly away in the wind, to mingle again with the rolling waves, where white crests broke against the unsettled surface.

The humpback endeavoured to sound one more time and his flukes lifting out of the water, Alex Greig's boat coming dangerously close to being hammered hard, the downward pressure of the tail's movement creating such a disturbance upon the sea that the boat was pushed rearward, unsettling those on board.

A warning broke the air for all hands to peak their oars, to ready themselves for the fate none looked forward to, preparing themselves to be delivered into the sea with the fury of the whale and the hunger of the killers. No one knew if the killer whales would take the time to chomp on one of them, whether or not they had a taste for man-flesh. None had found the thought a comfort and in particular, none of the men wished to find out.

The tremendous crash came quick and loud but failed to hit anything of concern, and the battle continued to be waged with a further two lances breaching the outer skin of the humpback and the 'red flag' flew high, and a deafening noise erupted from deep within the whale, a noise so penetrating that it had to be heard to be believed.

When finally the victory was won, the carcass afloat and being mauled by the killers, the whale's mouth being forced open and its tongue eaten hurriedly along with the lips, the crews sat back in exhaustion and looked upon the feeding killers. It was now that George gave the order for a lantern to be lit per each boat, to aid them in their ambition, to provide that little something in order to acquire their desire and need, to assist them in attaching an anchor and for positions within the boats to be changed with ease and control.

The job was done, the fight lasting fifty minutes. The work to anchor the carcass took a little under forty-five minutes and no sooner had they finished and the sun decided right then and there to show itself. George's eyes fell upon the biggest humpback he'd ever seen in the bay, dead or alive; it was 15.9 metres long and quite literally dwarfed the boat he was in. This day amongst many others would be remembered by him as the turning point that moulded his life forever, though sculptured in his youth to follow the footsteps of his father from a very early age.

The glamorous side of things had come and gone, the adventure was finished with and the hard work was yet to be done; and this by no means should insist that killing a whale was easy, for that would be laughed upon by more than those accommodated with the process of bringing-home-the-bacon.

The site of the slaying was to be visited once more by the men in their green boats, twenty-four hours after the carcass had been carried by the killers to its watery grave, even if only a temporary place of rest, carried there by Tom and his entourage, the flippers, flukes, and mouth held tight in their mouths, the whale hence dragged down deep in order for the killers to finish with their feeding upon the delicacies so often sought, in particular during the winter months on the East Coast of Australia, and deep upon their minds were other interests that existed farther south towards Leatherjacket Bay, simple contemplations of mind.

The carcass would remain beneath the waves until it had filled with sufficient gases to force a resurface, for to drag a whale in directly after a kill was more cumbersome, far harder to conduct when considering how tired and drained of strength the men all were: unless reasonably close to home.

The anchor was retrieved and the rower's arms bent to the work, the whale being turned in over the bar and to the mouth of the Kiah

River, high tide allowing them easier access than if brought in under more severe conditions such as low tide and or bad weather, bringing the prize home and delivering it to the try-works, where capstan and boiling pots awaited its heavenly duty. Boat spades were picked up by the men that had gathered, sharpened points as sharp as could possibly be, the blubber cut into squares with great effort and much sweat, shirt sleeves wiping constantly at the brow and eyes, wiping the salt of the flesh away to reform again.

Seagulls filled the air, brought together by that ringing of the dinner bell, to congregate for their opportunity to come, swooping in and pestering the work detail, making a right nuisance of themselves as they always did, squawking that piercing squawk which sounded more and more like the words formed on a drunkards lips, 'mine, mine, mine'. The stench was wretched, beyond belief, uncannily offending and most assuredly the worst George had experienced, but to the seagulls it was the perfume of the gods.

The entire process was hard and consuming. First the sheets of blubber were cut from the whale and then turned up the ramp to have further work undertaken upon the blubber, each large portion being cut into strips that were 38cm x 13cm x 13cm deep (as deep as the blubber, most dependent on the size and species of the whale). The strips were cast into a vat; soon after they were minced into smaller portions and boiled within the try-pots. A man then has the duty to skim the surface with a perforated utensil and watch with much attention the boiling take place, ensuring that all went well and that the oil that had been rendered flowed into smaller pots where it was later stored into caskets.

CHAPTER EIGHT

It was a sad time for all. It was 1890, just three short years after George had taken to the boats that Typee and Humpy, birds of a feather, decided to leave the pod. They were to leave behind them a great friend... many great friends in fact, but Stranger was their closest; she was their matriarch, their friend, the pod's strength when times were bad.

It was always the way when breeding season came around; some would leave and others would show, but for the majority of the pod the members always remained the same. Members of their close-knit community were seldom changed by more than a half dozen new saddle patches each year; quite often less. But love would have its way and times change for the worst and the better.

Typee and Humpy would be missed dearly; Typee for his exuberance and will to win over any whale, and Humpy for her ability to lead attacks where she would rip chunks of blubber and flesh from lips, flippers and flanks. Her dorsal, the flag of her back, bent completely over and easily recognised by all in the pod, would be sorely missed by all.

The pod gathered around the couple at a place slightly north of the icy coast of the South Pole, resting as they did between attacks on seals and other creatures of the sea, taking the opportunity to rest a little before their return to Twofold Bay.

Typee and Humpy looked upon the members of their fraternity, their clan, their identity. They stared a deep and longing stare, a submissive look upon their peers that indicated their feelings of remorse, sorrow and apology. Maybe they would one day return but for the time being they wished to endeavour isolation for the well-being of their future, to set upon new routines, new feeding habits, new environments for which to bring up their young.

Typee was strong in conviction and was set upon starting a new pod and so with the goodbyes given the pair of killers turned tail and swam away from those that they had come to know so well.

It had been some time now that Typee and Humpy had taken to the ocean on a voyage of discovery and growth when the appearance of another turned the heads of all in the pod.

Stranger was the first to approach the killer whale and had to glance twice before seeing that it was indeed a new saddle patch, but the comparison to Typee was absolutely astounding.

The pod gathered around to introduce themselves as they do with a little vocalisation, skin rubbing and general nosing around. Jackson, the new killer, was quick to accept the offer of dominance handed him, quick looks and broken stares indicating his place in the pod, but nevertheless they were all more than willing to accept him.

It wasn't known where Jackson had come from but he wasn't overly thin so was able to look after himself. He was a stray from somewhere, possibly discarded by another matriarch for disobedient behaviour, or possibly a transient looking for another harbour, one that might offer him better opportunity; he may even have lost a loved one and felt a strong urge to leave the pod of which he was a member. Regardless of his circumstances he fit in well and by the time a return to Twofold Bay was called upon, Jackson, a male of eleven years, saw a resemblance in one of the younger females. She was Sharkey, just two years of age and far from sexual maturity.

At first the attraction wasn't sexual or inappropriate, not at all; it was simply that Sharkey had the appearance and mannerisms of one that Jackson had known in his life; but the years would unfold and both killers would one day couple, parenting two young of their own, but that was many years away and still nothing more than vapours of mist on a dark horizon.

Jackson fit into place quite neatly and he was accepted rather quickly into the pod. Maybe it was his familiar look, the fact that he resembled Typee that he was taken in with little fuss... or maybe it was his pleasant nature.

CHAPTER NINE

George lances his first humpback, a small animal which provided ample pleasure and confidence; the crew under the eighteen year old headsman seeing the man unfold within, aspiration forming like the callous upon a workings man's hand, but the kill was followed immediately by many weeks of frustration as the presence of killers and whales were both equally vacant from the bay.

George and his crew, along with John and his, were sheltered at South Head at the wharf of rock, settled within the cave of substantial size and awaiting the call to action. The weather was fine and it was far easier to put out the boats from the cave, there beneath the shelter of South Head, than to put out from the Kiah Inlet: which provided their opposition with the opportunity to move in on a whale as fast as they when one decided to show.

The men had just polished off lunch and were at rest with mugs of tea tantalizing their senses when a sudden call came from atop the cliff, a whale sighted and followed closely by no less than 6 killer whales.

It was a right whale of large proportions and currently the only fins able to be identified were those belonging to Tom and Hooky. By the time the two boats were cast from the rocky wharf the whale had been well and truly pressured into the mouth of Twofold Bay, Tom and Hooky leaving the mustered whale behind with the remainder of the pod streamlining along on both sides, rear and beneath, keeping the front clear, a the path to its demise being cast like the script of a movie.

The two killers recognised for the markings set about swimming around the boats for a short period, as though assessing the situation for what it was worth, John's boat pulling away quite substantially from George's.

Kind and straight forward insults were pressed upon the crews by their respective headsman, verbal assaults of friendly coercion saw to it that know-how, self-confidence, and aptitude came boiling to the surface, each man taking control and seeing to it that the oars were employed to their fullest ability, the crews' potential at its peak. The culmination of the combined effort saw the two boats speed off towards their target and the killers that hampered it. It was then that Tom and Hooky, seeing all was faring well, departed the boats and joined the others of their pod in the continuing subjection of their prey.

The right whale was heading straight for John's boat when he ordered for the harpooner to take position, which Alex did with little ado, picking up the metal rod of power and readying himself in position, bracing himself against the thwart and eyeing the whale with suspicion, sizing up and confirming an action within his mind.

George quickly acted upon the situation to his front and moved to the starboard, shifting his position and approach in order to head off what might be a good target, in particular if it surfaced after going beneath his father's boat; but it wasn't to be. The right whale came up quickly, bolstered by the efforts of the killers beneath to bring him up, availing himself as a target to the harpooner, providing him with a clear and steady shot. Alex let loose with power in his arm, the harpoon racing through the air to its target, but the moving target was still far out and the shot only embedded itself just in below the dorsal, a throw that stuck but did not penetrate.

The fish was fast but not overly secure. It could easily, and quite readily, release itself of its encumbrance, to try and flee the scene that had now proved to be a dangerous place, the slight sting bringing coalesced thoughts to mingle within his mind.

Sam Haddigaddi obeyed the order slung in his direction, the friendly suggestion which needn't be called but was made nevertheless. He stood with his harpoon at the ready, to take a shot himself at the back of the right whale, to see if he could do better than Alex, a throw which he had made many times in the past, such experience that had made him a legend of the bay and an asset for the Davidson's, his skill and unwavering commitment given more than praise over the years that had passed. He hurled it then as the monster passed them by, hounded by the killers as they took chunks from his sides, another beyond and one further down, the containment holding firm, the whale having nowhere to move. And as the harpoon was hurled towards the right whale the oars were dug into the sea, reversing the shift of the boat, putting a halt to its speedy delivery upon the beast's back.

The line was secure and the loggerhead attended to, water too was poured over it as the line ran out and wood became too hot and worrisome. The headsman now changed places with the harpooner, as had already been done on John's boat, two ropes now connected to the whale, two boats now in tow.

John was closer to the whale than George, George being several boat lengths behind his father, both being towed along and unable to do anything about it, the killers doing all they could to muster the great whale, one of the biggest that any of them had seen for quite some time.

The whale had experienced quite enough and was soon heading out to sea, the boats in tow, the killers doing all they could to prevent it from diving more than a few metres, snapping at its heals, biting at its flanks, throwing themselves occasionally upon its back to prevent it breathing properly, but the whale just kept on keeping on, heading further and further from the neck of the bay, out towards the horizon in the east where the sun had already deserted, the last fragrant of light disappearing over the crest of the range around the bay in the west, where their homes beckoned for the men to return, where the warmth of fires and a hot meal could be presented to quench their growing hunger. There was not much for it but to sit back and wait for the whale to tire, for the killers to drag him down, both boats in tow.

The work over the coming time, as the kilometres grew behind them, wasn't hard. Their oars had been peaked and they were being dragged along by the whale. The surf created upon the bows of both boats curled upwards and sprouted out, white crests which commenced to turn phosphorescent as the day became night. It crept upon them rather quickly, not a single star to be seen in the sky, no moon to aid them; the only factor that was currently providing them with any degree of optimism was the fact that the weather, in general, had not turned against them, for although the wind was fresh it was not overall cold and nor was there any rain, drizzle, or water being splashed over them by gigantic flukes.

Jackets were placed on, more or less at the same time, some a little too small for the wearers, as the men, when first clambering aboard the boats to give chase upon the whale, hadn't taken to quibbling about which boat they were attending. So long as all oars were manned, that was the concern, but now, as the cold commenced to penetrate their bones some of them began to wish that they had their own personal gear to wrap around them, to encase their bodies like a little nut within its shell. This was the case in many circumstances of a hunt, where men found themselves pouring over an oar that was not accustomed to their grip, the portion of an oar which had seen many years of handling worn down by the press of flesh against the grain. It was a little different for harpooners and headsman for they had a command and structure to heed, harpooners hard to come by and employed specifically for the task set them, and headsman... say no more, for a boat was worthless without a leader and someone to hurl the lances – two lancers to a single boat was absurdly useless.

The sign of the whale's intermittent exchange between water haven and surface was made clearer by the phosphorus display before them, the rope in the water also making its mark. The whale was making no sign of giving up, surrendering far from its mind. The killers had no way of knowing that they had bitten off more than they could chew when the whale seemed to place himself upon their menu for the day, waltzing comfortably into the bay, being headed off by two boats, two harpoons, and several lances. But the whale had persisted and had turned the power of the play. The land behind them was getting further and further away, and before time they were twelve kilometres out to sea, and their momentum into the darkness didn't waver for a second.

George held his arms tight around him when John's voice broke the noise of the boats being dragged through the water, advising with just anxiousness that the ropes had somehow crossed over and that George needed to cut the line. A sudden upheaval then delivered itself to the air, a thunderous crash which could be none other than one thing and one thing only; the other boat, that of John's, had been hit hard and smashed to pieces. The wrangling of the wreckage reached their ears and Sam leapt to action and with a tomahawk in his hand delivered a blow to the secure line, releasing the boat's connection with the prize that had showered them with its unbelievable courage and fortitude.

The members of the other crew had been cast into the sea, the great whale having turned back on the boat and smashing it hard with its flukes as it sounded and then rose from beneath them, killing Peter Lia immediately, the mass of fluke falling upon him with no warning, the continuing momentum of the downward force splitting the boat into two pieces whereupon it sank.

The mass of wood and lances, tug of manila and thwarts, keg of water and rations; all drift helplessly to the sea floor or floated upon it, including the blond Norwegian who would be remembered always for his happy contemptuous persona and his singing in the try-works where hard labour was always met with a cheerful smile.

The work was now cut out for them and they had to act quickly. The water temperature was cold and too long in the sea would lead to no lack of problems. Cries for help appeared from out of nowhere, the black surrounds enveloping all, a little phosphorus providing assistance into where someone was splashing, treading water, or swimming precariously towards the only boat afloat, the only item of worth that the surviving eleven men had between them and Twofold Bay.

A few of the killers then separated from the remainder of the pod to undertake a different task, a task which went unnoticed by those in the water or at safe harbour in their little green boat.

Under the command of Cooper, Big Ben and Tom took positions around the scene to protect and serve. It was clear to the killers that they were far out to sea and that sharks would be in the vicinity. The last thing Stranger or any of the others wished was for their allies to be picked off by hungry mouths which in turn would diminish their ability to maintain energy levels as they currently experienced as an unmistakable advantage in their survival.

One by one the men were drawn out of the water, drenched completely, utterly and miserably cold, the chill of the sea having sapped them completely of all energy, depriving them of everything except their spirit to live and the thoughts they had for their friend Peter.

And the ring around the boat afloat was maintained during the ordeal and once all of the men were secured the killing was continued, a return to the excitement of the fray pitting all the killer whales to frenzy.

The gunwale of the boat was just centimetres from the surface of the sea, so dangerously close to being sunk by a surge of water. The only thing that saved the day was the fact that the sea was as calm now as it was when the sun disappeared over the horizon, taking with it their ability to see. Nothing at all could be seen. Individuals had been plucked from the sea, guided by voice and phosphorus. One by one they were pulled from the chill of the water, taken into safety, their friends pleased to see them alive.

Positions within the boat were quickly taken up, each and every one taking turns at the oars, those that were dry assuring their comrades that they would draw enough water to have them safely ashore soon enough and those drenched to the bone remained at the ready for a turn at the oars in order to warm themselves as best they could, to hold the cold at bay.

Instinct now took command and the coast was made for: land which could not be seen, not a light upon the shores of the bay evident whatsoever.

After many hours of stroking the oars upon the watery grave they came upon the sound of surf hitting the coastline and not long after they sighted their first real break... Jim was on South Head with a lantern in his hand, waiting as patiently as he possibly could for their return, and then they drew into the bay, eleven men in bad shape, some worse off than others.

None would forget this day, the worst day that any of them could remember. Peter Lia was lost; a boat was lost; a whale had made clear its intention and had either made it safely away from the killers with harpoons still attached, or been eaten as the men pulled the boat ashore; either way they were not going back to find out. In memory of their loss an inscription was cast into the stone of Boyd's Tower, dated September 28th, 1881; to Peter Lia, who was killed by a whale.

CHAPTER TEN

Tom and the others had broken off their quest to catch the fin whale, a hazardous fight with so few killers available, for something had caught their attention; they were coming up from the rear of the grand steamer, the SS Ly-ee-Moon as it made its way towards Sydney.

She was a steamer of great prestige and held in high esteem, for when she was built she was one of the fastest at seventeen knots and furnished with only the best that money could buy, initially built as a paddle steamer in 1859, a ship which measured eighty-six metres long and 8.2 wide, powered by a coal fed steam engine which turned the huge wheels. She was originally rigged with three masts and fitted with sail and could make good speed where weather permitted, but times changed and within twenty years (1878) was returned to service after being modified by the removal of a mast and turned into a schooner-rigged vessel.

There were few lights on board and all seemed quiet, the ship plodding along at a leisurely pace and all on board completely unaware as to what lay ahead.

She'd departed Melbourne on Saturday 29th May with fifty-five passengers and a crew of forty-one. Captain Webber had left control of the vessel in the care of the Third Officer, James Fotheringhame, at 8:30 pm, a man soon to be considered of great worth, to be handed much respect over the years due to his efforts in rescuing survivors. They were approaching Green Cape with the lighthouse of three years and were to fall within sight of them soon enough. The lighthouse was twenty-nine metres high, forty-four metres above sea level, and sat upon the crest of the land and able to be seen at distances of up to forty kilometres.

The killers of Cooper's pod escorted the ship and it made its way over the gentle rollers, white surf thrown up from the bow, the sound of the sea wasted upon the night so young; Green Cape was soon to appear as a dark projection upon the horizon before growing larger and more eye-catching in the window and Fotheringhame fought better of his abilities and considered his position before making a hasty decision, for the captain had retired most definitely and wasn't to be disturbed until passing Green Cape which sat at less than twenty-six kilometres south of Twofold Bay. Unbeknown to Fotheringhame the captain was snug within his cabin, suckling on a bottle, getting rather drunk: what was Fotheringham to do; was there protruding rock, was there a reef, shallow waters? Where did such exist, to what extent?

Tom could see as he spy hopped a little, how a man departed the bridge and made his way down towards the rear of the ship, throwing waste into the sea from the stern, unaware of the killers as they swam without a care in the world. It was at this point that Fotheringhame made the hasty decision to call upon the services of the captain, for him to be called to duty, but the captain flatly refused to attend the bridge.

Time and time again, Fotheringhame saw to it that he pestered the captain as he believed was his duty until the constant calls for him to return to the bridge got the better of him and he attended with a huff and eyes full of scorn, filled with alcohol and not giving a damn for Fotheringhame's urgent need.

It was now 9:28pm and the captain's return quickly saw to it that a little soberness entered his otherwise blunted views and from there upon the bridge could plainly see the rocks of Green Cape growing through the windows of the bridge and ordered engines to be reversed, but he was too late and the ship hit rocks: a minutes absence from the bridge by both men had seen to their undoing. Tom and the others could not foresee the danger as it pressed ever forward, unlike the captain with his years of mounted experience, and within two minutes the SS Ly-ee-Moon broke in two, the stern upon the reef and the bow floating precariously towards the rocky shore.

The dangerous predicament was an accident out of all proportion, the rocks at the base of Green Cape most dangerous and offering nothing at all in regards to cushioning the blows of flesh upon them; but the fight for survival commenced in a rush where adrenalin took place over clear thinking.

The lighthouse workers heard the commotion, the grinding of the ship, the thrashing of it against the rocks, Daniel Whelan and George Walters coming to the assistance of those in dire need. They were alerted well to the unforgivable sea, where wood was superficial when compared against the jagged edges of rock and cliff.

Tom and the others of the pod in which he was a member moved in, but not too close, for even with their skill and experience of the sea, the rocks proved to be treacherous and unyielding.

The foremast upon the bow fell and landed upon rock where

seamen and others started to crawl to safety, a fishing line was then thrown to the ship on which was attached a rope. With the rope tied fast the first of the passengers, Herbert Lumsdaine, made for the safety of the shore with the help of the lighthouse workers, swinging beneath the rope as it swayed; Andrew Bergland, a passenger, along with Fotheringhame, also made it to safety along with a further 10 people including Ola Thorpe, the boatswain, and the captain, who was last to leave the ship, the only duty he performed admirably this night. Amongst the survivors was Mrs Flora Hannah MacKillop, an elderly lady, mother of the Mother Superior of St Joseph's Provident Institution; mother to Mary MacKillop.

Tom took to the scene, trying to rescue some that were clinging near the rocks, but they fear for their lives, not knowing what Tom is or what he is trying to attempt – their salvation. He swims in as close as he possibly dares and then away again, giving up on the hopeless situation, as he is thrust against a formation of large rock, a large piece of his jaw and several teeth being knocked out, a scar for life that would tell his tale of courage for ever and a day. He retreats having secured no victory, for it was too treacherous, even for him.

It is then that further screaming continues unabated and for the remainder of the night twenty persons can be heard crying out for help, all aboard the stern which is washed further out to sea.

The killers move in under the directions of Tom, and although he is not the leader of the pod, what he has to say is most important. A rescue attempt must be staged, in similarity to what they would do for those within the green boats of Twofold Bay... the Davidson's and their crew. He could recall quite clearly how the man, Peter Lia, was killed by the flukes of the whale gone mad and how the body sank lifelessly towards the bottom of the sea after remaining afloat for the briefest of moments, the visual picture clear in his mind.

Again the killers attempted to move in and help those aboard, trying with all their effort to grasp the people's attention, to help them to safety where possible, to provide protection from the hungry mouths of the sea, to do justice where justice could be served. The Davidson's had served them well over the years and in return they should do the same, for the society of humans was as much a part of their pod as they were to theirs. Like brothers and sisters they were intelligent and emotional, showed semblance in many respects, but still they feared the worst... the people did not jump to salvation but allowed themselves to be dragged under the waves, fighting off the killers where one strayed too close.

And so many lives were lost unnecessarily, seventy-one to be exact, three of which were very young children; and the killers swam off as the sun rose above the horizon, swimming towards Leatherjacket Bay, to head off a whale that they had heard swimming in the waters the night before, and although the monster fish was too large for them alone there was the distinct possibility that other members of their community would happen along sooner rather than later, for the pods were to congregate for further fishing near Twofold Bay, to assist in the killing of whales as the season fell upon them over the coming weeks. A surprise was also awaiting them.

Humpy had returned to the pod she had known so well, returned with her son, Walker, who was barely one year old.

It seemed strange that she should return alone, but it was not possible for Humpy to portray the tragedy that unfolded during a clash with a humpback whale and calf. Typee had taken a fluke directly in the side which was enough to split him open, an uncommon and freak occurrence. He died some time after... Humpy had no real choice but to return to the Eden pod, leaving behind her fond memories and the estranged community of other killers that had pegged her at the bottom of the chain, treating her with defiance rather than showing gratitude for her skilled and athletic hunting ability.

Humpy's years away from home were a reflection of her mind she cared little to remember. Other than the fact that Typee would never be seen again, the years away from Stranger was a time she didn't wish to recall. Walker was also accepted and looked after as any other young mouth; as a true member of the family that evolved around him.

CHAPTER ELEVEN

By the 1890s, George Davidson, or Fearless George as he was known, took over the family business, relying on ingenuity to survive from year to year where vegetable gardens, chicken runs, fishing and livestock were a part of everyday life, in particular during the off season. But where winter was waited upon so the rewards were set, and when the reward was close to shore there was fighting to be done.

When the fighting had been done and a victory secured the crew would tie an anchor and buoy to the dead mass which sank quite quickly, it was then that the killers took great joy in feeding on the baleen by eating the tongue and lips only, as was usual. In around twenty-four hours, give or take, enough gas would build up in the dead whale to such a degree that the prize would float to the surface; it was now that the bay whalers would row out and tow back the reward for their patience and collaboration, back to the try-works on the banks of the Kiah River, fresh from the rigours of the catch the day before.

The relationship between the two species continued to evolve and whenever a killer became tangled in ropes a rescue attempt would be set into motion, a just reward for the great advantage that the killers had offered in the past and by seemingly protecting the crews from wayward flukes, preventing the green whaleboats from being smashed and torn apart. Serious accidents were numerous, but rarely fatal. But of all the things that had evolved there was one that will always be remembered, and that was the incident of the painter.

Several killers had ventured into the bay, to give warning to the men ashore, that a humpback was within reasonable distance and ready for the taking. Two other pods were taking all the normal precautions except the distance between the pods was drastically reduced. It was a big fish and required extra hands to impede on its efforts to get far out to sea where the ability to dive could strip the killers of all advantage, placing great stress upon their combined effort, to force a victory over those that pressed home the attack.

Tom lead the way and all three commenced flop-tailing, jumping from the water and then hitting it hard, the unmistakable calling travelling far and wide, a beacon to hold fast the interests of a whaling man, to call him to duty, to express without any doubt that there was a whale to be had but it would not wait all day or night. And from the dark depths of the whalers cabin, where men lay asleep, dreams filling the few that had not partaken of any alcohol (or less than the norm), came that call which shred the anxiousness from men stricken with the fear of going an entire season without as much as seeing a single whale.

RUSHO!

Unmistaken in its sound and shrill; unmistaken in its command and call to duty; unmistaken in the offerings ahead if they were to be successful in securing another kill.

There had been a heavy night of the spirits for some, only a handful of men available, and capable, of filling the positions within a single boat, a boat which George took under his command, giving the words as appropriate to extricate more power, for each occupant to heave his arms to the task at hand, to hit the sea hard with each stroke and pull with all their might the oars under their charge.

George looked carefully towards the heavens above, as a student would study his books before compiling his work, looking to the hours which lay ahead, to understand the situation as it was now and as it would be in several hours from now. As it stood there was a half moon and a sparse cloud covering was making its way across the sky, a westerly breeze blowing strong, but the sea appeared quite calm. By all appearances they were in for an easy night where the sea was concerned; but what of the whale?

Rising from the darkness the rowers then heard the familiar sound of a humpback whale in the midst of its dilemma, it being hounded by the pods a little further out to sea, and the killers could clearly hear the presence of the beats, the oars pounding the sea.

Tom remained at the stern of the boat, having gained the men's attention and leading the way, phosphorus showing the direction to follow when the light from the moon took to hiding behind the occasional cloud, the bond with their friends of the sea instilling great confidence and satisfaction.

Tom came then to the side of the boat, understanding as he did that time was of the essence and in this case, more so, for there was only one boat to do the task of which would normally go to two or three, hard work ahead which required great masses of stamina. He sideswiped the boat gently from beneath, oars pushed aside, which drew the obvious attention of the whalers as they rowed, dark eyes falling upon the mass, to where the dorsal stretched out from the sea and towards the sky, a fin which was enormous and struck them all with a little fear: it showed itself as possessing empowerment and stability.

Queries were passed around between breaths as the boat pressed ever forward, questions on the aggressive behaviour and the possibility that the boat could be pushed over, and they all in the sea and thrashing to stay afloat. They were trying to row the boat and were being hampered, their progress affected drastically. And the then one of the seated declared a solution, Tom Earl allowing a little chuckle to escape his lips as he suggested that they throw him a rope, the painter at the bow.

George looked inquisitively upon the suggestion and saw that Tom was growing anxious, seemingly annoyed at their progress, and beneath the waves, as Tom sped along, he feared the humpback would make its escape and the youngest of the pod would not survive the winter, for they were all hungry but currently preferred to remain at Twofold Bay, for the aid provided them by the men and their sticks of iron did much in keeping at bay the dissension within their group, where mothers were concerned for their young; but one good whale could change all of that and provide them with enough sustenance to carry them on until the next kill.

The killer hit the flank again, oars in danger of being lost, and George gave the command for the harpooner to throw the painter in the water, to see what Tom would do with the rope, to see for himself if this killer whale was up to no good or trying emphatically to provide them with assistance.

The quizzical look upon the harpooner's face drew a collection of eyeballs, each clicking into position as the fell upon the dark man, the oar lifted most temporarily from the water and the painter reached for, thrown into the sea with very little effort, and the oar put into motion one more time.

Jaws dropped instantaneously and the forward motion of the boat slowed dramatically as Tom opened his mouth and allowed the rope to fall into place before the bellowing voice of the headsman brought them back to reality. Tom was pulling them through the water, aiding them as best he could, the first time ever that a killer whale, or any mammal for that matter, had allowed himself to aid a human upon the undulated waters of the planet earth.

This was a scene to remember, one for the books, an incident that would never be forgotten by those experiencing it, and the two killers that were with Tom looked upon the manner of his action and tried with all their effort to understand it, for there was no immediate reason why Tom would be doing such a thing, for this was no time for play, this was no time for fun; there was work to be done, and a lot of it. And then it hit them, the boat was making good headway now, better than before, the men rowing as hard as before, with true conviction encompassing them all and Tom was assisting them with an ingenious method that was simply absurd; but yet it worked. But how was it achieved, what had Tom done to procure the rope?

Whistles, clicks and calls filled the ocean around. The expanse around was a-buzz with the noise of echolocation clicks, both isolated and in trains, the nasal passages beneath their blowholes created upheaval amongst the killers. The pods combined repertoire of calls was quite large in number, around twenty-three employed by Tom and his immediate family, both immediate and secondary, some sounds made at times of chasing down a whale, others for directing signals and commands to particularly pods; other signals and signs were used extensively for reaping harvest and reward; as well as this there was a call that distinguished one killer from another, a name that identified a particular individual where distance was an issue.

The sonic signatures of the acoustic communication consisted of pitch, loudness, harmonic structure, tone, urgency, mood, and action; all aided in understanding and enabled the killers to perform tasks that complimented their every movement. Sometimes they employed singular clicks as opposed to click trains and this depended largely on the type of prey they were hunting. Marine mammals would pick up quite easily on the clicks of the killers, but fish could not. Passive listening was simply an extension of their ability to sound commands and requests. Calls to indicate strategies, prey species, and pod members; that's all that was needed, that's all there was.

The very effort and commotion of the fight to keep the whale at bay was doubled in all its constituted values, the boat nearing its final approach, the whale, too, trying with one last gigantic effort to get away from the pods, turning upon the mouths baring teeth with herculean effort surfacing its raging scorn, strength erupting like a volcano from its sinew as energy was eaten up at an alarming rate in order to secure an escape. But escape would be hard to win for a humpback could only muster twelve kilometres an hour, where the killer could do up to thirty kilometres an hour – but rarely travelled more than 160km a day.

Tom dropped the rope, to be ignored for the time, the importance of the game growing clear to their front, the escort of three killers joining in the final fray where the humpback came towards the boat.

The harpooner got ready in an instant, seeing the large mass of black coming full steam from the front, the gap closing fast between the two. The headsman grasped the steering oar with both hands and pulled it into his chest as he leant back, the boat moving to the side and the whale coming up parallel. The harpooner stood then, cloud moving in front of the moon most temporarily, and then with the sudden realization that a clear target was available the harpooner struck out hard with the iron in his hand.

The harpooner, with more luck than could be afforded the situation, released a good throw that penetrated deep and stuck well; the 'fast fish' was made. The whole issue of fight and slander, their 'repertoire', it had worked to a means and their purses could feel the colour of money before the try-pots could smell the blubber of the carcass just won.

The humpback reared its slim head, though broad and rounded when seen from the top, a rounded protuberance beneath the tip of the lower jaw, fleshy knobs of barnacle covering most of its head, spouting clear from its blowhole, the water vapours void of that reddish tinge so often sought, which flew two metres into the air in bushy contrast, thrashing from side to side and its back commencing to arch, the flukes coming up towards the surface in preparation to dive, a small dorsal fin two-thirds down its back: a nubbin of little consequence. He was black with white around the throat and belly; the flippers too were white underneath but darker on top.

Water fell upon them from beneath the crushing flukes, a convex shaped surge of surf that disassociated itself from the molecules of the sea, a separate entity with one concern and one concern only, to drench those within the boat, to soak the wearers of jacket and shirt to the very core.

Gasps of shock erupted from their mouths as the cold of the water hit home, the stabbing of the ocean's dousing driving home the horrors of the sea at its mildest, and lucky they all were that the boat did not go under and stillness came over the sea, for the whale and the killers had disappeared from sight. Several men surrendered their oars and quickly emptied the boat of what water could be baled from the bottom before once again returning to their duty.

The surface then erupted once more and the body masses of all involved surfaced again; the harpooner then changed positions with the headsman, lancing to commence immediately. All of a sudden silence fell over them again and for a brief second or two there was nothing but the cloud in the sky, the moon and its light, and the sea and its stabbing cold.

By the time George had taken to the stern the fighting amongst the two species of whale had culminated with great chunks of blubber being torn from the humpback, but the fight below the surface was far from being won. The humpback was heading further out to sea, making for an escape from the smaller-than-usual pod. Again they surfaced and the oars were pulled back in bursts of fury.

In many cases, if not all, the killers would rally together when their prey had been trapped within the bay or it was evident that the whale in question was securing a victory by escaping into open water. This was such a scenario and as the predicament became more than clear the killers swarmed in from all sides in a frantic effort to kill the whale once and for all.

As the green boat continued to maintain its visual connection with the fight, the harpoon still secure, the killers did all they could to hamper the escape. Killers were throwing themselves upon the blowhole, others were snatching on tight to the lips in order to prevent the humpback from sounding, and others continued to rip chunks from its bulk and take bites from the fins. In another effort to throw the assault into affray, the humpback sounded and turned, the line between boat and harpoon falling slack, and the order for the men to counter the turning beast was shrieked out loud for all to hear but it came too late. The movement of the rope and boat had caught George's leg and into the calm sea he toppled, the stabbing cold knocking the wind out of him like never before. Sam and Albert sprang to life and commenced to cut the line free, for the humpback had returned to the stern and was heading further out to sea, pulling them away from where George had gone under.

For what seemed an eternity the headsman was being dragged beneath the surface of the sea, alongside the boat in tow, but seconds later he shook himself free and released himself of the weight of his shoes and jacket, working himself quickly to the surface where the light of the moon brought great relief, but for a short second only, for the boat was more than four football fields away by the time the line could be cut and the men able to return to rescue their captain.

The solace of the sea in those few minutes shook the very foundations of George as he tread water in order to stay afloat... sharks! Cowards they were, one and all, scared to life of the killer whales but would come running to the party as though gathering to the sound of a dinner bell, drawn by the action of the fight and torments of the whale, to sup themselves upon the carcass once the killers had had their way with the humpback, ready to devour what they could of the meal before it was wasted to the sea grave far below. And where could one find more sharks than out in deep water, far from the encumbrance of the shore, where trouble was brewed from their gatherings and misdemeanours of the sea.

George could feel their presence, he was sure of it, as sure of that feeling as anything else in his life to date. And then it came upon his ears, the swirling of the sea, the disturbance of the surface, the sound which pushed dread and surmounting fear into his fragile shell, for he could be no more at risk than as he was at present; by himself and far out from shore, no boat by his side and no knife to ward off an intruder of the dark passages of the waters about him.

His eyes popped from his skull as the view of the fin came to surface, heading towards him on a slight angle, the unmistakable mast of a shark on the prowl. But what was this? More fin rose above the surface of the sea, far too much for it to be a shark, and the knob atop the fin... it was Tom. But this didn't release the dread and terror from Fearless George for the killers were more menacing than the sharks. If a shark feared the killer then the killer was the most feared of all. No shark ever interfered with the joys of a killer whale as it played and fed upon its victims. This killer whale before him, Tom the killer whale whom he had come to know so well from the safety of his green boat, was about to snack on him, take him within his jaws and crunch him like a peanut beneath the heel of a foot.

Many times had George seen a killer take on a shark and win; many times – more than any man could imagine – had he seen them take on a whale that was so enormous by comparison that it was beyond all belief; imagine what it could do to him. And Tom looked upon the form of the man, seeing George close up and personal, seeing the man bobbing there, up and down, a salmon ready for the taking. George stared back, watching the beast as it closed the gap even more and swam around him, George turning on the spot, not daring to take his eyes from the killer he had come to know so well. He tried to console himself then, that the killer known as Tom would not trouble him, that he would be left alone... he didn't wish to be toyed with, thrashed about like a plaything before being drawn into the throat of a killer whale.

The minutes ticked by and the boat from which George had been thrown came out of the darkness and the moon above released itself from behind the clouds in the sky.

Tom was still circling and George saw friendship in his eye. The boat drew alongside and pulled George to safety, wrapping him in a blanket as quickly as they could. George maintained the visual on Tom and Tom nodded his head as though in a friendly gesture before turning into the task ahead and returning to fight the whale with the remainder of his pod.

The experience was unbelievable; this great monster of the sea was as friendly as a lap cat. Tom meant George no harm; he had in fact surrendered himself to the protection of George until such a time that he could be rescued by the others. Tom was indeed a good friend and if it wasn't for him, George would have been taken by a shark; of this he was sure.

Tom had returned to his pod under Cooper, looking briefly upon Big Ben, Jackson, Jimmy and Albert. Cooper easily recalled how they had protected the men before by encircling them in a protective case of flesh, but Tom had taken it to the next level. It seemed nothing more than stupidity to get so close to the men when danger was looming and all was tense. They could easily be seen as a threat and had seen men act against them before. Tom could easily have been mistaken for a danger and skewered well by the lance of a man upon the green boat, put in his place once and for all.

Tom couldn't understand the unfamiliarity for they had all experienced nothing more than great salvation from the men. The men served them well by providing food, allowing them 'first rights' to lip and tongue, giving them sustenance as an offering or reward just as the Yuin had done for Stranger in years past.

Tom had laid the last of the questions upon the foundation of understanding. The men and the killers now seemed to have a better understanding of one another. The bond between them was now secured as strong as it could ever be and it would never break.

CHAPTER TWELVE

The following year, 1901, only nineteen killer whales returned: Humpy, Stranger, Cooper, Big Ben, Tom, Hooky, Jackson, Sharkey, Jimmy, Big Jack, Walker, Young Ben, Albert, Brierly, Youngster, Skinner, Kinscher, Charlie Adgery, and Little Jack. The group were split amongst three main pods, Stranger (as matriarch), Hooky and Cooper being sub-pod leaders.

The humpback population would receive a reprieve this year for they were still numerous in number and although easy picking for such a fine pod, all knew that there is safety in numbers. And there was an obscure clue to the dwindling numbers of the killers, and it had nothing to do, whatsoever, with a food shortage. The Norwegian whalers were in Australian waters and shooting, quite openly, killer whales as they swam harmlessly about, and this was clarified by the numerous reports of Norwegians boasting, quite recklessly, of their poor behaviour upon the sea. They were concerned that the killers would eat the whales that the whalers caught, hence taking money from their pockets. It was a demoralising dilemma to see that the traits of human ignorance had the effect that it did; even the Yuin people were moving away from Eden and with it a great pool of hard workers which would be sorely missed.

The Davidson's use of oared boats, as opposed to motor boats, continued to favour them in regards to their friendship with the killers, the pod returning year after year. It wasn't so much as a requirement to survive, for now after so many years of collaboration and showing of affection (which was completely dissimilar to human touches and strokes) they simply wished to cooperate with the crews of the green boats for the pleasure of the chase, the thrill of the kill, the satisfaction of being so sacredly formed with a human that walked the surface of the earth instead of swimming within its waters. But during the final stages of the Davidson's enterprise, where bay whaling was starting to die out due mainly to the cost of effort and falling value of oil, the crews were drawn to a friend named J.R.Logan who would quite happily tow their rowboats out to sea, to deliver them within reach of a corralled baleen, by use of his yacht the 'White Heather'.

The use of silent and effective hand-thrown harpoon and lance were still employed, for the cooperation of the pod was needed now more than ever before, and if it should be said then let it be said now, that the whales felt more affection for the crews than the crews did for them until such a time that mournful memory of the past would come back to haunt the dreams of all those that hunted with the killer whales for around 90 years: which occurred at the time of Tom's passing and was still far, far away.

CHAPTER THIRTEEN

The passing of a relative and friend is poorly accepted, none more-so than the death of George's father, where memories of the great man came flooding back over the pursuing days and nights, where dreams were filled with the laughter and fighting spirit of the one called Dad. It was 1903 and John Davidson was dead.

It is the bond between father and son, a bond which can be thicker than that between a mother and her siblings, but a bond that is so seldom celebrated. Whaling was a tough business and a tough business builds tough character, a character which often hides the pains of death and fails to reflect the love that one feels. But George wasn't afraid to show his feelings, in particular amongst his family... but the job of hunting must continue and so the reflections of a special bond is held back for personal rumination and the green boats of Twofold Bay once again become the apparatus for which to deliver their prowess.

George looked over the men in the boat as they rammed the bow into the little surf that sprang up before them, breaking upon the sleekness of their tool-of-the-trade. He lapsed most temporarily upon his father and then saw the characters of those to the front of him leap out of their skins. Another boat could be heard as it too entered the water with a thud.

The men before him, stroking the sea with their oars as only they knew how, their backs facing him as he steered from the stern, were men of adventure, men of the sea, men one-and-all. Most were becoming old men, not just in years but also through the tally of years, where mounting hard-yakka piled on the age in double helpings, two serves for one. Charlie, Archer (George's brother) and Boyd (not to be confused with the opposition) were rather long in the tooth but for the most part George could not be more satisfied with those that manned the boats: Sam, Bert, Peter and Albert Thomas, Harry, Bobbo, Dan, and of course, Alex Greig.

And from the corner of his eye he caught glimpses of shadow, noises from afar reached his ear, his senses heightened and he perused the shore and bay around him, looking intently for those of the competition... Boyd and Glover. Both were as keen as he to see a 'fast fish' secured, each had crews with ambition and the power to press upon an oar more fatigue than could possibly flow through their own pores, for there was more strength in character, persistence, and ambition than there was in the strength of muscles, sinew, and tissue.

Glover could be seen from the flank, but slightly back and behind George and his two boats. The competition was lacking this morning but that didn't allow for anyone to slacken off; not for a second. Anything could happen... an oar might snap, a man could be thrown – or fall – into the water, or the whale could simply change tactics and come up at the bow of Glover's boat, giving him the opportunity of a lifetime. If there was one thing that had been learnt, it was that the killers and their prey were unpredictable, even with the killer's cooperation.

The men continued to lean into the work, their backs breaking as they asserted their efforts, their muscles tearing from lean to pulp in order to grow in power and strength. This was a regimen of instilled action, a commandeering action learnt over many years where it was impossible to know how many days or weeks would elapse between each opportunity for the men to show their grit and fortitude; but still their solid builds, each hardened like steel, dealt out all that could be given.

With sudden realisation and the clarity of the chase racing back to their minds in flashes of black and splashes of sea upon them and their boats, the humpback burst from the horrors of the sea and lifted almost entirely out of the water, only the flukes remaining attached as though by some sacred umbilical that provided sanctuary and peace of mind. It came crashing upon the sea then, a killer erupting from below the surface of the sea, throwing himself upon the back of the baleen, and the horror struck faces of the men in the green boats followed the action of the chase as it unfolded before their very eyes.

Orders to the rowers were issued in calmness and with ease, in loud bellows that were surely heard over the theatre of war, of that which was unfolding around them. But some of the men were haphazardly slow and several oars bore the brunt of the whale gone crazy, where thrashing of body and fluke, as she passed them by under full steam of the chase.

Sam Haddigaddi poised for less than a millisecond before thrusting his harpoon with all the power that he could muster and the iron rod of death departed his calloused hand as the oars snapped like toothpicks, Sam thinking briefly that he had somehow broken an arm with the power of the throw.

The squelch of the point entering the whale went unnoticed by all around, all but the whale that bore the brunt of the throw; for him the noise went raking across him and cascaded down his back, deafening to say the least. Every throw was the same, no matter what the species of whale. Every whale in every ocean of the world heard and felt the same, the heart-wrenching threat of Death calling for death. The agony of knowing was the worst as the whale continued to fight the fight which could not be won. The sinking of the great leviathan was swamped at that instant, drowned in the torment that man had aided the death blows of the killers of the sea. What had he done to man to deserve such foul treatment?

But fight he did and it continued with a spurting of energy, a coalesced force of supernatural energy that burst from all its pores and with the curtain drawing to a close the whale raced towards the face of the cliff that overhung the sea. It then turned with one final attempt of escape, melee being entered, killers in the fray and the boats of men close behind. It was no good; the channel to freedom was open to the humpback. He turned again towards the cliff and sped off with the powerful thrashing of its flukes, the killers feeling within them that now was the time to finish the whale once and for all.

With all suddenness the humpback disappeared under the water and the green boat turned as though upon a merry-go-round. The whale began to surface with the boat upon its back, the men jostling for a hold upon the fragile shell that surrounded them. The head of the whale began to surface and the boat too. George jumped to his feet without second thought and leapt forward, landing upon the whales back. Within seconds flat he pushed hard upon the stern of the boat with the power invested within his legs and the boat began to swing to sea; he leapt again, this time back towards the boat, clinging to the safety of his beloved and scrambled to victory. The looks upon the men spoke more than words and for the briefest of moments the entire world sang out loud that the name Fearless George had true meaning. The chase then continued.

The demise of their situation finally bit hard when the humpback refused to fall victim of the whims of both killers and man. A last ditch effort was made once more. The instinct to survive was strong within the humpback and it was up to the killers to bring the final demise to fall upon the mass of blubber at it tried to escape the snapping jaws of those around him, and with one last ditch effort the killers forced, undeniably, the humpback upon the rocks near South Head where the last breaths of life were confused in rapid action, panic and torment having taken its toll. The whale was dead.

It was a sad state of affairs for both man and beast who had secured the victory, for the carcass was going nowhere; out of reach of the killer's mouths and in difficult surroundings for the securing of blubber. There was no need to anchor and buoy the carcass, no wait for the gases to have its effect upon the mass of flesh and bone, for the easy access to the blubber – the usual means by which they secured their pay – had not been denied them all. But what God gives with one hand he takes with the other and in respect to this the dilemma is surely realised, for the whale was going nowhere, literally... they would not even be able to tow it into harbour and then the try-works. The mass would have to be deblubbered where it lay, upon the rocks of the shore, from beneath the cliff where the afternoon sunshine never struck, where blasts from a westerly wind lashed out relentlessly. It was here, amongst the rocks and the surf, where the waves thrashed out upon the legs of the men, their stability drowned like the sorrows of a drunkard on a bar-room stall. It was here, amongst the dangers of the sea and coast that the men had to suffer their burden and do all they could to muster the appropriate will to conquer all fear and work their fingers to the bone.

The men, on occasion, looked out and over the sea, where the swells from further out began to crest higher and higher, where the weather began to turn sour and fill itself with scorn. They all knew well that they had several hours of work ahead but they did not know how long it would be before the heavens opened up upon them and the current crashing of waves upon the rocky outcrop of their demoralising station grew in ferocity and lashed out in anger. It was as though there was a god that lived amongst the waves, a titan of gigantic power and skill, Poseidon by name and by justice, for they had taken a creature from the sea, forced it ashore from its garden of Eden, to slash at its body, to cut away its life in chunks and strips, for it to be melted down within pots before being stored in barrels and readied for market. And Alex Greig thanked God that he wasn't Greek.

And far out from shore the killers congregated and swam around in circles, annoyed to the hilt that a meal of sustenance had been denied them. The men weren't to blame; they knew this; and neither was it the fault of the sea. It was the damn whale, having beached itself upon rocks, rocks that cut easily into the thick skin of any animal of the sea, the rocks buttresses and sharp edges cutting relentlessly, sawing at the flesh as the sea rolled the embodied mass up and down, a slab of meat upon a butcher's chopping board and being hacked at mercilessly.

The killers gave to spy-hopping and watched the men work their skill at securing the catch as best they could. Tools had been ferried from the try-works and the carving had begun, the upper-side worked on feverishly, the under-side a bloody mess where oil from the blubber caked the rocks. There was much urgency in their quest and Tom could see quite easily how the men's attention was drawn to the sea on occasion; not to look at them but to maintain a watching eye upon the storm as it commenced to wander in; and with the storm came another opportunity, for a call was then received further out, a whale was bypassing their position, a sperm whale with calf further out to sea, an uncommon occurrence which grew in popularity, the offering of fresh veal crossing their path less and less as the years rolled by. This 'was' to be blamed on man for his relentless pursuit had seen to it that the sperm whale was becoming less common in the waters of the world to such a degree that it was seldom seen. But the calf; that would have to be taken, for joy of taste; for the joy of the chase.

The signal came again, the calf being of reasonable size. The pack of killers would do well to swim the extra distance, and although the sperm and her calf were on a course which led them away from the pack, they were sure to catch up in no time at all, to be able to return to Twofold Bay by morning's first light... if the killing went well.

One last signal then came from where the sperm lay, to cease with all further communication, to continue the hunt in silence. The whale and her calf had been drawn to the vocalisation of the killer whales but they did not know that they meant to commence a chase for the purpose of feeding. To the whale there was no real concern, for the killers were so far away, yet she would maintain an open ear to the goings on, to ensure the purpose of her and the calf remained solid, that their quest to warmer waters for feeding purposes could be secured. The Hawaii Islands were a long way off but she knew the waters well, knew of great abundances of food at this time of year.

With their attention turned again to the path ahead, they continued unabated.

The shadows of the noise around them, the movement of the sea and other creatures of the ocean, all gave to the accumulative effect which helped to masquerade their move. The killers were on the hunt, dangerous and hungry, meaning to deliver their combined skills, to sink their teeth into the best blubber around, to rip at the calf in manipulative action before setting their sights upon the female of the species. It wouldn't be easy for the female would hinder their moves, give her all to secure the survival of her young, but try as she might, the killers would win their prize and get their fill.

By the time Tom and the others were feeding upon the calf the men upon the rocks had completed their task, had set their oars into the waters and not before time, for the weather commenced to grow in its ferocity once more, mounting waves of surging white crashing with great intent upon the place where the humpback's remains were washed into the sea for the smaller fish to have their way, for crab to take their share, for seagulls to make their move. But the move should be delayed shortly until after the storm, and by then it might be too late, so the creatures moved in immediately and made the most of the little time they had.

CHAPTER FOURTEEN

The proprieties of bay whaling were appalling in 1904, and from one year to the next the ambitions of many men were dashed by the infrequent appearance of whales, whether they be minke or fin. It costs money, and plenty of it, to run a bunkhouse full of men, several boats and a household with a wife and siblings. It is true that idleness breeds discontent but where Twofold Bay and the community were concerned, in particular those that required candles or lamps to aid in the consumption of their after-dark activities, discontent wasn't accompanied by the inappropriate, mismanaged husbandry of fellowship and personal discipline, but more so for need's sake alone.

Although drink was permitted it wasn't something easily afforded, but gambling was an inbred vacuum which sucked the pockets dry. What one man wins one week he loses in another, but pay was seldom offered until the oil and bone were sold. So when the time comes for the call to be made, rousing itself from the roll of the tongue, men jump into their boats and shroud themselves in the comfort of warmth as they scamper for the thwarts and oars of their beloved, and they do this with such urgency it is as though the entire town is on fire and they are the only firemen for kilometres around.

Not only were they in competition with others of similar mind, like Glover and Boyd, but were also in a timely chase against the second hand of a clock, for every breath was a milestone and a humpback could quite often break free of his capture, heading out to sea with the killers in tow, and a lost whale was lost pay.

These men were not on a contract, were not promised good wages for the nil-return of blubber, but were only paid with what the headsman could suckle from the sellers of his merchandise. In most cases this was quite substantial, even though prices rose and fell like the waves of the sea, but mostly rewarding for the work conducted. Such businesses did provide good wages and on a regular basis, but when times were hard and money scarce the opportunity to pay on time was not always possible. Even so the men would not abandon their captain, and besides, the wages he paid the islanders, whites, half-castes and full-blooded aborigines, was the same all round: there was no racism here.

And so the men sit at table, playing cards and hunched over a cup of tea when all of a sudden the call comes from aloft a horse, the beast breathing heavy and being ridden like a champ, sprinting down towards where the men are housed....

RUSHO! RUSHO!

The men jumped to action as though nothing else mattered – and at that moment, nothing did. The killers now made a showing as cobbles were shaken loose from the ground below the feet of men as they thundered down to the boats, the fresh morning air doused with the mist of action. Individuals clambered aboard their boat with quickened ease, oars picked up and thrust into position, the water of the bay quickly stroked in order to propel them ever forward and towards the prize which at this stage remained unclear. And then the spouting caught the eye of George, most definitely a humpback— no, two... two great beasts of the sea being forced into the bay by the hound dogs of the sea; the wolves of the water, the encumbrance of the baleen, and devils of the murky surrounds. They were the evil at the backs of angels, the shackles of torment, and above all, the dorsal of death.

Corralled now the two humpbacks were forced towards the boats that sped towards the battle of wills and the will of man is as strong, if not stronger, than a killer whale, for man would will himself to death in order to feed his family, where a killer whale would only stress itself to the limits of its energy, and where a battle is not won in good time and all strength is wasted away, the killers will fall back to try their luck on something more easily won.

Harpoons and lances were struck and stuck, the two whales secured within an hour of fighting, two boats with their sidekicks against two humpbacks of medium size. They were both good kills, secured within good time, and the relief that fell from the men's faces was apparent to even a blind man for their purses now had something to look forward to, even if for only a short time; about a thousand quids worth.

The drought had been watered, the show was on the road, and everyone thought how lucky they were with the good fortune of two such quick kills. And without second thought the humpbacks were anchored and buoyed, the killers taking their reward as they always did and the men made for shore. They would return on the morrow to bring home the bacon, but something was brewing, something further out and unfortunate, for the reason that the humpbacks had made for the coast, to be so easily captured, was that they wished to avoid the storm fast approaching from the south-east.

That night the winds blew, the men's slumber being shaken from them like a strong wind wakes the deeply embedded roots of a gigantic tree. For three days the weather grew in ferocity against them and their fears grew. The gases within the whales would have had their way with the carcasses after the first day, each floating to the surface, ready for harvest, but no move could be made upon them in this weather. The water around Whale Spit Beach was like a kettle on the boil, far too dangerous for little boats and men so fragile. It was a wonder in itself how such fortitude in men and their tools could be so easily swayed by the power of the sea, but that's the way it was, and will always be.

But on the fourth day it could be accepted no more and the boats forced themselves into the ferocity of the sea, the coast scoured both up and down for any sign of the whales they had left just four days before. They had broken from the anchors, were lost to the sea, would more than likely be afloat somewhere, but so far unattainable. Worst of all were the faces of the men. They had gone without wages for so long now. The thought that the drought at the commencement of the season was over, was optimistic to say the least. It was now that they had to be faced with the reality of the situation.

George walked in on the men as they sat in their gloom around the table of the kitchen, drinking tea and pondering on their next call to action. The headsman posed the trouble to them all, posted them well with the few choices open to them. But the men refused to hear of it, refused to admit defeat and rallied to their captain's side, to remain loyal. They would stay on and continue, sure in their minds that their fate was not written and that the tide would change soon enough, that the opportunity to deblubber more whales would be just around the corner. And it was indeed just like that for they had caught themselves two whales just a few days later and there was more to follow, all told there were nine in as few as three weeks: their wages had been secured.

CHAPTER FIFTEEN

The conditioning of both species had sprung to life more than simple feelings, gestures, smiles and jumps for joy. There was camaraderie amongst them, for they each served the other, although from the killers point of view the humans were nothing more than pawns for which should be used to the best of their ability. But the understanding was there also and all the killers knew well that the duties performed by both parties amalgamated to cooperation.

They weren't competing for food but were in fact escalating their abilities by relying upon the energy and prowess of the other species. But there was always room for improvement, and yes, room for amazement.

The simple fact that both man and killer were working together was amazing enough but to the men of the boats it was all part of the day and working roll; the killers too, thought nothing more of the collaboration being anything other than manipulation tethered to a secular importance... the harvesting of their sustenance.

People and animals do all they can to secure a living, whether one receives money as reward or a meal for its effort, it is all one and the same. It is therefore of utmost importance to seek any opportunity which will reap the bigger harvest and in the shortest amount of time. This was something that Tom knew well and had put into practice many times in the past, but the time had arrived for a new weapon to be brought into view.

The flop-tailing had called the boats to duty as any other night. One boat was faster than the other which was a disappointment to the killers within the bay, for the more boats available meant a quicker kill and increased energy savings.

George's crew flashed ahead of Alex Grieg's boat, both separated by poor vision and a good football field of misery. But where the misery was a little longer suffered by Alex, it was short lived for George, for a right whale showed itself by spouting high and wide, moon beams glistening off the skin of the monster as it surfaces amongst the churning of the waters around it, the killers, every one, biting at the fish with all their might and thrashing about in the sea.

Arthur Ashby took his position with pride and hurled his harpoon with all the power he could muster. It stuck; the fast fish was secure. It then turned tail and commenced to head back out to sea, away from the two boats now behind it.

With the whale secured and the rope let out, the whale was in a prime position to pull George and his crew further away from shore then they would have liked; not only this but there was the other importance factor that Alex Grieg and his crew were falling further behind as they spurred themselves on by the power of the oars alone.

Tom saw the dilemma and acted immediately, pulling away from the fray and returning to George. The others of the small contingent looked upon him briefly and with anxiousness, opening their mouths, exposing their teeth, and noisily clapping their jaw together, voicing their anger and frustration at Tom's misdemeanour in vacating his post at such a time, but no sooner had they showed their displeasure in him and they realised that this is what Tom did, this is what he was about, and nothing could be done to change him.

With sudden amazement, Tom grabbed onto the whale line with sheer exuberance and allowed himself to be pulled alone by the whale, the green boat just a few metres behind him.

The men were flabbergasted to say the least and it took several moments for them to realise what was happening.

The very implication that Tom was helping the situation was sheer ludicrous; but there it was; ludicrous to one but common sense to another, and although brain size is no indication of intelligence, in this particular situation it appeared that it did.

Tom was in fact slowing the progress of the whale to such a degree that Alex Grieg and his crew were gaining ground upon the fight and gaining ground rather quickly.

With Tom in the way, George could not manoeuvre, but if Tom were not there then the other crew and boat would not be able to advance fast enough. It called upon them all to see the picture painted clear as can be: the other crew were catching up and were soon in a position where the harpooner of the other boat was standing with his leg within the concave of the thwart and letting loose with a second harpoon. Tom released his hold upon the line and joined the others of the pod.

A lance solidly pierced the space between the ribs and the death-throes of the animal paved the way for the killer's show of exuberance. They festered in and tried to force their way into the mouth of the whale as blood flooded from the blowhole, tearing at the flesh of his lips and holding on for the feelings of glory which did follow.

The whale was putting up a hell of a fight and at one stage leapt more than five metres out of the sea with three killers still attached to his lips, a sight never to be forgotten by the men of the green boat as they looked up open-mouthed from the thwarts where their backsides remained glued.

The right whale was leasing his energy for no reward and within another five minutes the fight was over; the combined efforts of man and beast had won over another mammal of the sea.

With the whale marked in the usual, both anchor and markers attached, a second task dawned upon George as was always the case for someone so readily on their toes and willing to work. He looked over the men to give his orders as the killers grabbed the whale and took her deep, into the murky waters of the sea, out of sight and out of mind. They would do as they pleased with the whale and within twenty-four hours should be afloat and ready to be towed. But to the moment all reflected.

They had secured a kill just the other day and the whale was not far from where they were; just a few kilometres in fact. Instead of waiting for the morrow he decided that the opportunity should not be passed up and the two crews were handed the task of bringing the bacon home to fry.

It didn't take them long to find the animal as the gases had floated it as usual and on time; the only thing left now was to tow the beast back to the try-works which was some seven kilometres away. The night was pleasant though cold, the moon shone out in good quantity and it seemed that the task ahead was achievable.

The markers were pulled in and the anchor too, several ropes attached to the carcass and the men braced for the hard slog home. Their backs broke under the strain, for seven kilometres was a big ask. And to the moon George looked in wonder. The tide seemed to be with them more than not, with the moon high up and behind him. With time the satellite would make its way across the sky and to the west whereby the tide would work against them, but that was so far away that they could only think of the hot feed that would be awaiting them on their return, a return to the bunkhouse which could be just hours away, and chances were they'd be back before any substantial changes took place.

Although the weather seemed to be in their favour the work they had achieved prior to attempting the long haul had drained them of all the energy they had. There were no super heroes amongst them, just flesh and bone which was commanded over by brains and brawn, and a discipline that comes by way of the strongest motivation.

They pulled upon the oars with all their strength, continued on as best they could against the tide. The lights ahead of them showed where Twofold Bay lay but it was very far away.

After several hours of pulling the floating monster behind them they appeared to be making very little progress, their hardened hands starting to show signs of over-work and strain. Another thirty minutes and George waved the white flag... they would head on home without the cargo and return in the morning; after a good night's rest... or what remained of it.

CHAPTER SIXTEEN

It was in 1904 that the number of killer whales within the pod was to be altered by one and such an unfortunate event it was.

George held the power of the rudder in his palms and steered pleasurably out towards the mouth of the bay where a whale was buoyed and expected to have come to the surface already; all that was needed now was for the beast to be towed to the try-works where the deblubbering could commence in earnest, where the men would surrender themselves to the back-breaking work, suffering the intolerable smell and flies, the seagulls afloat the breeze pestering for whatever they could get their greedy beaks on.

One of the men in the boat was suddenly drawn to a chase and pointed it out to the others. It appeared that Jackson was chasing a grampus, gaining ground on the dolphin which sped through the surf in an all inspiring effort to escape its devastating future; the bleak and unconditional devouring which was to fall upon it.

The men smiled as they watched the chase and pulled upon their oars when fright suddenly fell upon them, an anxiousness that lasted for but mere seconds as they continued to look upon the scene so far away.

Jackson had propelled himself so well through the shallow waters that washed themselves upon the beach, and as the chase was about to meet its end the grampus moved aside and Jackson fell upon the sandy beach; high and dry, only the bottom portion of his body feeling the comfort of the sea upon him.

He thrashed about in an effort to free himself from the predicament as the grampus made its way safely beck towards the open sea and the men could see the dilemma that Jackson was in. He was too far from the water's edge to secure delivery back into his watery surrounds without the assistance of the men within the green boat. Without further ado they steered towards the killer as he continued to flap about and try with all his might to gain ground upon the retreating waves, the moon high in the sky, upon the other side of the world, pulling the tide out as it does on its journey around the earth.

The men felt that they had little time to procure a rescue, for the killer would not function well upon the beach of Twofold Bay, and even as they rowed several gulls saw this as an opportunity to flap on down and stand their ground out of harm's way, looking upon the giant killer with eyes as large as saucers, squawking as their stomachs ached to be filled, wishing with all their will to be able to peck out the eyes and given the smallest opportunity to savour what they could of this offering to them. It was then that a figure came into view, walking along the beach and towards the killer, every step deliberate and full. It was Harry Silks, homeless and obtuse; he'd seen Jackson washed ashore upon Aslings Beach; quite by accident.

The men collaborated on the man as he suddenly sprang into action, seeing George and his green boat filled with men. Silks commenced to run rather rapidly towards Jackson. He wished to be first upon the scene; but why?

The men continued upon their salvation of the killer that meant so much to them for they knew too well that Silks would not be able to move the monstrous body and blubber that was Jackson back into the surf that ebbed in and out, the white of the curling waves disappearing as they rolled upon the stretch of sand.

And that was when the horror of the situation shook them to their very foundations, where it became impossible to fathom the outcome which was about to unfold. Instead of giving aid to the whale, and in full view of a Davidson crew, Silks did withdraw a knife from a scabbard and stabbed the defenceless whale to death, followed quite quickly by his running away from the building insults and threats that were flung his way.

Several of the other killers were drawn to the sounds of the splashing flukes, where Jackson's tail was able to affect sufficient disturbance upon the water that others would rally to the scene. They too were struck hard with the horrific scene and perceived it as it should be perceived... wanton slaughter. It was then that Tom and the other killers departed the bay for a few days, simply shocked and exasperated, depressed and shattered.

What would become of the contract between man and beast? Unknown to the killer whales, Silks was escorted out of town by the local law enforcers for his own protection, never to be seen again.

A stand had to be made and Fearless Davidson undertook to repair the damage done and began legal action to have the killers protected by law by first writing a letter to the Eden Progress Association, and although the killers themselves would not know of his efforts, he himself would feel as though some form of justice had been served.

Within a few days another humpback was corralled by the killers, although there appeared to be fewer of them than before. The night was dark and peaceful and the whale was relatively easy to catch. It easily drew the men's attention to see that the killers still provided them with aid but the full devastating effect of Jackson's killing would show its face soon enough, where the pod size would be drastically reduced, fewer and fewer of their dogs would return to receive aid from the men in the capture of their lip and tongue.

CHAPTER SEVENTEEN

Stranger was dead, killed by a fisherman in Botany Bay, August 1907. She was mother to Tom and Hooky, and quite expectedly these two killers of the sea, so fond of Twofold Bay, felt the power of the separation bite them harder than anything else they had experienced in their entire life. It wasn't just the matter of fact that their mother had died, nor that the matriarch of their community no longer existed; but it was the horror of human intervention that troubled them most. Their mother had been killed by a fisherman for no other reason than to spite the species for taking away the fish that he looked upon as being provided for his net and his net alone. Of all the killer whales in the world, not a single one had ever been known, by man, to have killed a man; but of all the men in the world, plenty had knowingly killed a killer.

What was it that drove a killer whale 'not' to take the life of a man? Was it the killer's sense that a human was intelligent? Why should intelligence procure sanctity and life? The killer whale, without religion or innovation, had proved to be more human than man himself: or does being human mean that we, the human race, lack humanity.

It is not surprising, therefore, to notice that both Tom and Hooky were vacant the bay that year, to return afresh on the following, bringing with them a new invigoration and determination.

Cooper and Big Ben on the other hand, more than just friends of Stranger, found the parting to be too much to bear. They departed the pod of Twofold Bay almost immediately with Young Ben, their son. Albert, their daughter, chose to remain behind, having mothered Charlie Adgery in the spring of 1900. Shortly after further demise struck the pod, news soon arrived that Big Ben was dead, dying when stranded on the rocks at Leatherjacket Bay, and within a few months Young Ben returned without his father, to regain a little of what solace he could.

It was a terrible year for the pod of killers, affecting them all in some small or large way. First there was Jackson in 1904, and now Stranger, followed shortly after by Big Ben.

Times were changing; the vibrations and smells within the sea told them that. They were growing old and their minds were weary, full of good memories slowly evaporating to be replaced by bad.

What was to become of it all?

CHAPTER EIGHTEEN

Whaling was whaling. To the men of Twofold Bay it mattered little – other than the price they were to receive for the catch, for the amount of effort and time displaced – whether the whale caught was big or small. Equipment was important, the boats being the most blessed of all they possessed. If a reasonable catch could be secured for as little outlay as possible and with no damage dealt upon the boats then it was a good catch and one worth remembering. But one of the most remembered will be little reflected upon by history books, even though a record of the grandest proportion – which will never be broken for bay whaling is no longer practised – and that was the capture of the thirty metre long blue whale of 1910.

The sheer size made the catch a momentous occasion for those at the oars but it wasn't so much a case of capture than surrender.

The blue whale had a calf with her that measured a little over half the mother's length, a mother of a whale which totalled ninety-eight tonnes, enough oil and bone to tear the stitches of any money bag, regardless of form and manufacture.

The call of RUSHO! went out firm and loud as it had at any other time in the past, the panting of the horse from the lookout being accompanied by the flop-tailing of Tom at the Kiah. Boats were manned and the waters entered in readiness to secure another humpback, but what they met made them stare in disbelief, for it was no mere, undersized humpback.

By the time they positioned themselves in readiness to deliver their prowess, George sitting with shoulders back and ready to deliver all hell upon the blue whale, the killers had hounded the mother to such desperate levels that she breached herself upon the shore and became easy pickings; the killers had carried their task out so well that the blue whale was out of reach of them and they missed their lip and tongue, but they had their way with the calf. It was the least exciting of all the catches they could remember but one of the most satisfying.

The band of just six killers had done their job well, a small number in comparison to those that were currently not so far away and further up the coast, a task which would have taken longer to perform is further out to sea. Without the aid of the jagged shore the killers alone could not have achieved victory over the blue whale: despite having lost their lip and tongue. The sheer exuberance that the members of

Hooky's pod felt surging through them was too much to express without the show-boating of their jumping from the sea and crashing back again upon its surface, for the young one was there to sup upon.

It was a trophy to be remembered amongst the old saddle patches and the new, Kinscher and Little Jack, daughter and son of Big Jack herself, showing once and for all that skill was a lesson taught and handed down, not just a gift of chance. But what of Tom; what made him so different? What was it that drove his ambition and aptitude? What was it that founded his strong, unequivocal and unbreakable sufferance? Why did he display a heavenly allegiance to man?

Tom was a pioneer, a one and only, a creature bound by the fruits of intelligence which left the others of his species far behind in understanding. He understood, he was a freak of nature, like the 'Ghosts of the Darkness', the lions of Africa that devoured man through superior intellect and cunning, he too had unequalled knowledge and instincts of deliberation. Tom was a powerhouse of ability and procurement, a wealth of interpretation within his head busting at the seams to escape his shell and yell out to the world that he was there to pave the way to the bright light of bonding, a bonding that even Darwin, a man of generous, failed to see in full bloom.

Tom was similar to mortal man; he could feel hurt and embarrassment, fear and death, and display great courage, but above all, Tom had the ability to see beyond the makeup pasted upon a man's exterior as an astronomer sees beyond the makeup of the universe.

Jimmy fought well on this day, the day of his birth some thirty-one years before.

He'd arrived at Twofold Bay several years after the death of Typee. It was a time of upheaval when some killers departed and others strayed in, at a time the pod was still large and prosperous but had to deal with minor issues of command and structure; though little did it matter under the sway of Stranger in the years past, who for her years and with the power bestowed, stood as a strong matriarch with a long list of signals and attack manoeuvres accredited to her name.

Jimmy was quite normally a quiet mammal and far less boisterous than those like Tom. He was mated with Big Jack, a female of a line outside of that known within the pod, both her mother and father being 'offshore' variants more apt to living off fish, particularly salmon, than anything else. Tired of their life and position in the pod of seventy-odd other killers they had opted for a life of habitual change and so found their way to Twofold Bay where they stayed for several years before moving on. Jimmy, having founded a life for himself, and a mate in Big Jack, stayed on.

Big Jack had mothered two killers within the Eden pod and they were Kinscher and Little Jack, respectively a female and a male.

Over the past twelve months, Jimmy's persona in the pod of fifteen had grown quite substantially, though not because of any great feats noteworthy of praise, but because Big Jack had been recognised as matriarch since 1907. Jimmy felt more than honoured to be in the position he was in and the very idea of his being some sort of representative brought on a blossom of change in regards to effort and effect, though only to a small degree. Such an effort was accepted well by the other members of the pod for they understood well the situation he was in.

So there came a day when a humpback had been cornered once again and the familiar assaults upon the floating casket of blubber continued as they had in the past, with much effort being placed upon trying to tire the beast out and to create as much stress and horror for the humpback as was possible.

Again and again the blowhole was covered, killer after killer throwing themselves upon the back of the whale in order to impede its breathing, helping prevent the whale from sounding and turning to the open gate of Twofold Bay for an eventual escape.

The men too, were present upon the surface of the sea, prodding away with their sticks of iron, shifting their position with oars and yelling out above the noise of war to try and bring the whale to a standstill.

Several harpoons had been thrown this day and one was not well secured, though the second had done its job well and lancing had begun as usual. The whale was putting up a good fight until a last ditch effort by Jimmy saw him move in for the kill, to suffocate the whale and then rip at its flank to create further injury and insult to the humpback.

And then something went horribly wrong. With so many lines in the water and so much confusion floating about the scene of battle, Jimmy became entwined within the line and sank with the humpback. The other killers simply assisted the humpback to the bottom of the bay, initially unaware of Jimmy's predicament, and the effects of the battle upon the men was so great that they too failed to see anything amiss.

Kinscher and Little Jack were quickly alerted to the situation when Jimmy was heard crying out, unable to break free of the cumbersome mess that he had fatally attracted to himself. There was little they could do, however, and Jimmy died there within the bay he'd come to love so much, in the comfort of the love and company of Kinscher, Little Jack, Big Jack and the other members of the pod.

And so several of the pod fell to the pressures of the loss. Big Jack soon departed as she could deal with the situation no more, Walker (son of Humpy) following in her wake. Young Ben, having returned for two years after the death of his mother now departed for good, the loss of his friend weighing too much upon his mind – there had been too much death in the past. Last but not least the following turned their flukes upon the bay and left for deeper waters; Albert, Skinner and Little Jack.

The following day the carcass was retrieved by George and his crew, utterly astounded at what they found when they drew nearer the scene of the floating carcass, buoyed and anchored where they had left the humpback. Jimmy was strapped to its side as though belonging, like a baby strapped to its mother. Such a scene had never been seen before and it jolted the crew as they looked on, cutting the line away and allowing Jimmy to float away from view. They were reminded of the time Humpy had fouled the lines but she was more fortunate for the predicament was noticed prior to the whale sinking, Humpy cut from the lines and set free before death had the chance to pull the final curtain closed.

The men remembered this day as the tragedy it was, as too did the killer whales out to sea. The whalers cut a remembrance into the woodwork of Boyd's Tower, Jimmy to be remembered forever along with Peter Lia.

CHAPTER TWENTY

The Norwegians had mustered 9,500 barrels of oil from the east coast of Australia in 1913, the last for them, and they laid up their three chasers; but this was a small tally when compared to other companies of the same game. But the damage was done and the killer whale was vacant from the waters of Twofold Bay for great stints of time, but a familiar fin was seen once more as it glided through the gentle waves near the Kiah Inlet and this was accompanied by smiles upon the faces of those who knew him best. Tom was back with Humpy, Hooky, Sharkey, Brierly, Youngster, Kinscher and Charlie Adgery.

It was at these times that the cooperation between beast and man continued as in the past, with much reflection upon old times falling upon them all. Reflections of securing a 'fast fish', reflections upon the unwritten laws between the two species, and reflections upon the feeding upon lips and tongues of those slaughtered so that the killers could survive and the men upon the shore could receive the opportunity to make their blessed money.

Other killers came and went over the years, although few in number, and whales were killed as they had always been, with great cooperation and effort on the part of both man and killer of the sea. It was by no surprise that Tom and George forgot how it had been before their time when the laws were a blossoming flower, each law opening up a new beginning; but the end was near and the killers so few.

One of the more horrid circumstances to hit the pod of killers was the death of Sharkey (Jackson's partner), who in a clash with the Norwegians was slaughtered due to her attempts to feed upon the offerings of the sea. The Norwegians saw the killers as a pest more than anything else and so Sharkey bought the brunt of their anger. Brierly and Youngster then chose to depart the bay of horrors for eternity.

There was no bitterness for the crews in regards to this departure, the fact that all were growing old, both man and beast, and becoming just a little less reliant upon one another, than in past years was to be expected more than not, besides, they noticed little change overall, for the whaling industry was faltering at the head as the killer's number diminished and whaling was losing its grasp on being a way to make a good living.

And as the years progressed fewer and fewer killers returned to the slaughter grounds.

CHAPTER TWENTY-ONE

World War II was soon upon them and men disappeared from the boats to do their duty overseas. By the time the war was over only a handful of killers ever showed up at the onset of the whaling season, where winter broke upon the bay and its inhabitants, and the boats were more often than not manned by casuals rather than men of iron and full of character.

Spring came and went and then summer, autumn and winter as usual, the same game played year in and year out. On the odd occasion there were only three killers, at others there would be five, but the aggressiveness of the killer whales always remained heightened, even though individuals slowed a little in their old age; all that was except Tom who was as young as he'd ever been. And as the pod decreased in size George's own family grew and the years fell behind them all, Kinscher and Charlie Adgery leaving the pod in 1923. And George too, in all comparison with his colleagues of the sea, was as fearless as he had always been; he and Tom were peas in a pod, one and the same, a strong bond having been struck between the two.

Never before in the history of man, save the rumours of a man in the jungles of some far away country living with wolves, had man and beast performed so well together, a performance you would swear had been orchestrated well; but it was familiarity and trust that made them unique.

In the early twenties, Tom would quite often be seen to grab hold of the painter (anchor rope), it having been thrown to him, and he would grasp it and tow the boat towards a whale, more often than not several killers aiding in the antic that saw a fast approach made upon an angry whale of enormous size, speedily overtaking any opposition that might be otherwise trying to get to the whale before the Davidsons, holding dearly onto the sixty fathoms of two-inch coir rope. Tom did this in order to secure the kill, for he needed the sustenance in order to survive, and without the aid of George, Tom would have met his end all the sooner.

Eden Fisherman, Jackie Warren, even witnessed the phenomena known as Tom in 1926, where he purposely grabbed the anchor line beneath Jack Davidson's boat and towed him along the surface of the sea, not for the purpose of chasing down a humpback, but for the fun of it, and Margaret Brooks having her breathe taken away by the whales antics as Tom pulled against her father's boat the 'White Heather', tugging hard on the tow rope, trying heaven and earth to prevent him from towing a dead whale into the bay, depriving the killers of the 'Law of the Tongue': the White Heather's efforts being far from on purpose, but simply oblivious to the knowledge of propriety.

Yes indeed, they were times to remember, times that saw little evaluation in the annals of history.

Soon, however, there was only Tom and two others. Most of the others had taken to different waters to secure meals of similar and different variety, neither joining super pods nor really deviating from them, but remaining unto themselves. Several of the pod broke away and commenced their own matrilineal linkage, and some died as whales do. It seemed to Tom that his entire life had been spent with the men of Twofold Bay and it was to him a family bond of its own. They had come to rely on one another as species do in times of hardship, where bonding takes many years, if not decades, to meld into one. As for Tom's family; well, he had little to show for his merits as a male for his offspring had separated from him when their mother refused to leave her pod of transients; but he was never alone.

Year after year saw fewer whales secured and the killers were forced to pursue other means of nourishment and from other hunting grounds that had proved fruitful to their needs and desires, to the great disappointment of old friends.

CHAPTER TWENTY-TWO

So many years behind him and so many deaths. George could only be thankful that his experiences to date were vastly good and with so few filled with horror. But old memories die and new ones fill the void, in particular where devastation is the result.

George had a son by the name of Jack, and he in turn was married with three children... this is the recollection of how Tom gave a little dignity back to his friend, George in 1926:

There came a day where the small family of five, along with several other relatives, met with a horrific accident near the Kiah River and their dinghy was submerged in the freakish weather, just metres from home. Dozens of family and friends delivered themselves to the search over the coming days where two little ones – Roy and Patrician – were missing along with Jack Davidson himself.

It was a sad fact of fate that saw three deaths in one day, in a storm which lashed out its evil in more than one way. The fact of the case is as basic as one, two, three. Tom was not far from the bay but remained near Leatherjacket, more for comfort than anything else; had he been nearer to the call for aid then he would have availed himself immediately to the care of those in need. This he proved over the coming days by entering Twofold Bay and approaching the scene where many boats searched frantically for the bodies of the three that were missing.

The two children were found soon enough; the girl pulled, deceased from shallow water, and the boy's body from the sandy bottom, only his legs visible. As for Jack, nothing could be found.

Tom could see that something was amiss but didn't understand what. The men were searching for something, going over the sea floor time and time again with their boats and grappling hooks, looking for signs of something they had lost.

Tom then bombarded the area with the skills taken for granted, the signals received by his senses forming the picture clear within his mind. He could see the body of Jack beneath the surface, under the sand where the boats had searched to no avail.

For the next few days after the tragedy, the weather became beautiful and serene. Tom continued up and down in front of the bar, trying with all his presence to show the world what he knew; that he had found the remains of the one they were searching.

George looked upon his friend of the sea with great admiration, seeing Tom's presence, in this time of need, as a mark of great respect, and it suddenly dawned upon him that Tom might just be trying to tell him something. But how could that be, for the area was searched over and over, not a trace of Jack to be found.

Tom could see the expression upon George's face, the sparkle of wonder in his eyes, the methodical ticking away of the brain within his head, a brain of no comparison to his own. Tom could see without doubt that George had stumbled upon the antics of his demeanour and called for the boat to do another sweep, to search the area where Tom had indicated by his persistence, and before the hour was out they found Jack's body beneath the sand of the inlet and drew him upon the shore; Tom followed the boat in, paying his respects.

The other two had been buried just two days before Jack and now it was his turn, more than forty cars full of those wishing to pay their respects following the hearse as it drew into the cemetery at Eden and within a spy-hopping view of Tom as he contemplated the ceremony. Never before had he seen such a large congregation of men together in one spot, at one time and in complete silence, only the soft tones of the priest lifting themselves to the wind and floating down to be heard by the single killer in the bay.

Tom had completed his task and completed it well, and offered assistance to his friend which was beyond the call of duty. Tom owed this man nothing but still felt the bond as strongly as George. The bond could never be broken. To Tom, George was his family, the only family he's ever really needed. Without the bond between them both it was doubtful that Tom would have lived as long as he did.

The men had served him well, as he served them, but to Tom it was a one-way ticket of servitude for the taste of lip and tongue, the very sustenance that it offered was beyond all compare: what did he care what they did with a humpback's body after its death; it meant little to him? But the service he had paid this man of men was not forgotten, could never be forgotten, and on the conclusion of the service, George did pay a visit to the shore; not to pay his respects to jack by laying visit upon his place of death but to say a heart-felt thank-you to his true friend of the sea.

It was then that Tom turned into the bay and made way for the remainder of his pod, a humpback whale and her calf allowing themselves to be caught unawares. The fight was on and the other two members of the pod were anxious for help.

He turned and thrust his flukes, speeding through the water, slicing through the waters of Eden, and to the waiting struggle which simply had to be won, for they had been without food for quite some time, and as George had lost Jack to the ever waking sea, Tom too, lost a friend this year, for Hooky, son of Stranger, fathered by a stray, a great pod leader and easily recognised by his dorsal fin and the way in which it was bent at forty-five degrees, left Twofold Bay for all time. It was time to face the facts as they were played before them. The crew was made up of mostly new faces; they seemed inexperienced and inept when compared to the likes of those in years past, at a time before the war took the men away in droves.

The crew was one boat manned by faces that were ever changing; the sea was giving up less and less opportunities to make a kill; above all, they were growing old and weary and the times called for a substitute, a morsel of food which would be easier to quarry; less palatable but just as rewarding when considering the overall effect that a full stomach of food had on a killer whale.

And so the face of the industry, for those of Twofold Bay, was drawing to a close.

CHAPTER TWENTY-THREE

And then there was only Humpy and Tom, frolicking in the bay as they had done when they were young. But there was a difference of course; they weren't as agile as they once were and so they projected themselves out of the water with less... ambition. A stranger passing by upon the shore might look out upon them both and think how free-spirited they were; playing as though without a trouble in the world, young and looking for mischief; but to George... he knew the truth, understood it all. The killer whales were old, growing short in the tooth, age beginning to betray them.

1927 and the pod of two seemed not to have a care in the world. Once a pod of over fifty, strong in every virtue, a great repertoire of song and voice allowing them to corral humpbacks and other whales with great ease, permitting them to push the whale towards the men and their boats, to secure a meal all the sooner, but now all were different.

Humpy: older than Tom and even frailer. She was partnered with Typee and gave birth to Jackson, had heard of her son's death at the hands of Silks and his demented mind but did not understand all, for killer whales do not convey ideas like men with their patterned, slurred and slang speech. She had once led attack after attack upon whales, had ripped chunks from their lips and flank, and even once become entangled most temporarily in the line attached to a whale and then freed by George. She led a pod until 1880 and on her return in 1885 became next in line for position as matriarch after Big Jack, and was mother of Walker who had left the pod after the death of Jimmy.

Yes indeed, there was a great history here, a story to be told, a silent story which resided in the memories of Tom and Humpy. But Humpy's days were almost over.

They had both heard a humpback some distance out to sea and had followed in her wake for some time before deciding on a move against it. It was a move without the aid of man, one that they would regret. It was the same as any other, the attack launched in the normal manner... nothing different, apart from their number.

They took chunk after chunk from the whale, pressed home the stress and fear, overwhelming the whale with surging mounts of aggression, though aggression was a double-edged sword; it acted for the killers by hurrying up the cause of death, and it heightened the aggressive nature of the whale as it endeavoured to succeed in an escape, or to try and bring about a forced conclusion by causing injury to one or more of its attackers.

And so it is here, far out to sea, that Humpy received a wound to the face, an eye lost in the fight; she was now deprived of her ability as a hunter.

The whale made its escape as Tom came in close to his friend of the sea; a friend no-closer could he have been. They had succeeded in having a good fill on the blubber of the whale but this would not last them long. The line had now been drawn for Humpy. Within the week she was dead and Tom was left to compete for food on his own. No longer would he be able, nor willing, to attempt an attack upon a humpback... unless it was a calf.

CHAPTER TWENTY-FOUR

And so now there was just Tom; he died on 16th September 1930, just before midnight, the 17th unveiling the end of a legend in his own right.

A week before his death he had put chase to a grampus, taking chunks from the mammal of the sea until it died. It was a fairly quick death and a short fight, though it took a lot out of Old Tom. His teeth bore the brunt of his years, being specifically worn down in areas where he had taken the painter in his jaws, where his efforts to assist the men upon their boats had proved a devastating blow against George's opposition.

The grampus was a meal not to be forgotten, a great treat for an old warhorse, the blubber, lips and tongue taken great advantage of, a feeding fit for a king. And the spectacle drew a little crowd for it dawned upon all those of Twofold Bay that Old Tom was alone, not another killer to be seen.

Tom had remained loyal to the end, a friend of those he had come to know, and more people knew of him than he could possibly know of them. But that is where the killer whale dies and the legend lives on, for it was a week later that he was found dead after a day of frolicking in the bay, flop-tailing into the breeze as the setting sun said it's good night.

Yes indeed, he enjoyed those last hours, showing himself most temporarily upon the surface, inside the bay, onlookers seeing for themselves that something was amiss; the next day his body floated into Snug Cove in Twofold Bay, recognised without mistake by his tall and distinctive dorsal fin which had been photographed so many times in the past and even caught on camera in 1910. He died, simply, from old age in the accompaniment of starvation.

It was now, as his body lay still upon the beach that his genitalia proved once and for all that he was in fact a male, but how had he managed to live for so long is beyond anyone to fully understand... somewhere between sixty and eighty years by all comparison to realistic witness reports [as we cannot prove his date of birth].

J.R.Logan suggested that preservation was the key in order for Tom's story to remain alive and well, and such a suggestion saw to it that his skeleton was provided a home in a purpose built museum, funded for by Logan, himself.

The Eden Killer Whale Museum still exists today and puts the minds of all those that visit it into a spin over the tales that can be told or simply uncovered. No one can deny the truth, for the truth is documented so well.

Tom was a male orca, 6.7 metres long and with a dorsal fin of 1.7 metres high. He was fairly short when compared to other Orcas in other seas, but there were different casts of killers as there were races of people.

CHAPTER TWENTY-FIVE

Tom was gone and bay whaling had come to an end. George Davidson hung up his harpoon and lances in 1932, the crew disbanding to find other ways in which to support themselves and their families, but a majority of the crew were nothing more than helpers, there to assist, like the clerk of the local police station who tackles the paperwork and not the pavement.

Other orcas that were known to the bay whalers came back from time to time, laying visits upon the mouth of the Kiah River, but these visits saw little action being taken out against a humpback, for the tide was changing and whaling right across the country was dying fast.

It is strange to understand, from the human point of view, how killer whales could change their tactics of the hunt so proficiently after almost ninety years of going through the same routines, chasing whales off the coast, helping themselves to tongue and lip. But they were adverse and could turn miracles of nature when required, and the pod simply relocated to other feeding grounds, understanding full well that their easy feeding was over and that they now had to make the next best choice in where to get their meals from.

But even now as the darkness continues to fall over George and the life of the pods during the ninety years of their presence (not considering the interaction with the Yuin), where bay whaling existed for one hundred, that killer whales continue to return to Eden, and they are likely the descendants of the pods that once roamed these waters, for it is hard to change one's destiny when it's imbedded in a ninety year old tradition. And the humpback whales frequent the bay and splash around playfully, their calves by their sides enjoying the warmth of the water, feeding without a concern for being attacked by Norwegians; and George could only watch from the sidelines.

And even today, in 2008 and beyond, from the darkness of time comes a reminder of the past, for even now killer whales can be seen sporting in the waters near Twofold Bay, where the picturesque port town and with its ocean views, and forest surrounds, continues to relax all that see their playful nature, providing great delight to those that lay visit.

And here right now it is an honour to declare that science is on the killer's side, for they can confirm, quite adamantly, that they are intelligent creatures with astonishing acoustic senses, social coordination, and self-awareness. They are able to learn rapidly, are innovative and can manipulate objects. They freely interact with human beings and are a delight to work with.

CHAPTER TWENTY-SIX

To an Orca the human race is little more than a hindrance, in particular where excessive amounts of commercial blubber has continued to be exploited from the oceans and seas of the world. From right along the coasts of the countries of this world, to the open seas and the areas around the Antarctic and Arctic, whales have been openly slaughtered for the oil that they contain. However, unbeknown to the killers of Eden the International Whaling Conference of 1945, held in London, prepared extensive regulations which would see to the part-protection of species of all whales. This was followed up in 1946 by a meeting in Washington by the International Whaling Commission which drew the conclusion that international regulations should be put into place and maintained.

The conservation of the whales and their stock levels was somewhat agreed upon and passed in 1949, a solar gathering of members having come together and spoken on the maintaining of principle and the projects which included the protection of species, in particular the females and their calves, sanctuaries and limitations on the number of animals to be killed in any 'open season'.

The depletion of whale numbers has since slowed but not altogether ceased. The blatant killing over the decades was one reason of many as to why killer whales tended to deviate from their feeding routes and normal routines, but in the case of Twofold Bay the humans actually helped the killers gain food and didn't exploit them: if anything, the killer whale was exploiting man.

Twofold Bay offered much to the killers of Eden; not only was it a natural corral for which to trap baleen but it was also shallow enough to restrict a whale's escape. Leatherjacket Bay was also a natural wonder which was employed well by the killers, for the currents here, during the season of whaling, were most suited to their endeavours: the moderate current permitted the killers to swim at a leisurely pace and maintain position in particular when it came time to sleep.

It was all a matter of strategy to the killer whale. They chose the ground upon where the killing was to take place and the method by which death was to be inflicted.

CHAPTER TWENTY-SEVEN

George Davidson was dead. It is 1952 and he dies with his memories intact. He was not alone in death, with loved ones so close and Tom inside his head. The relationship between the two will live on forever. It is a slice of history of which Australia should be proud; not so much for the establishment of the relationship between man of land and mammal of sea, but for the very acts of love and affection shared between the two species.

If we look deep enough we can see how the men under George Davidson gave up much to be able to work effectively with the killers of Twofold Bay. Their equipment was of the old school; their techniques were of the old school; their foresight was of the old school.

These were not greedy men and nor were they wicked nor cruel. They had a job to do and they did it well. They did believe, however, that they were manipulating the killer whale to meet their needs.

How is it that a killer whale can put behind it the nature of the sea; the nature of the species; the torments of their world? These killer whales befriended man and used him well to gain their food. They learnt to work with man and maintained a working relationship for many decades.

If all killer whales were the same then we could assume there would be more of this cooperation; but there is not. Instead we are drawn to the reality of the situation whereby one killer, and one killer only, took a situation and manifested it to suit the needs of matriarch and pod.

The name Tom should be celebrated for he was a one and only, and such a relationship, possibly never again to be experienced by any of us living in this day and age or even the next, should be remembered for all time.

Maybe the future will behold another just like him but for George and his memories, the last fragments of peace that drift from his mind on meeting with death, Tom was simply a friend who could never be forgotten. It is to Tom's testament that George has recorded some of his fondest memories.

HISTORY

Something that may well have helped influence the killer whale activity in Twofold Bay are the factors surrounding the hunting of the sperm whale.

1712 (Sperm Whale)

It was in 1712 that the first of the sperm whales was taken from the safe harbour of its home in the sea near Nantucket, far from the waters of the Australian coast, but where several ancestors of those in the Eden pod had once frequented. The oil was considered much more valuable than that harvested from the bay whalers, shore fishing which had been a development of the Red Indians in similarity, but not in perfect union as that of the Yuin of Twofold Bay. Deep sea whaling was now an investment anxiously pursued; the curtain had been raised and the slaughter begun; an infringement of the Orca's right to feed on all that swam in any of the seven seas.

1788 (Sperm Whale)

The settlement of Australia takes hold at the same time that the South Pacific is exploited for what it holds within its parlour of delights, 1,800 souls shipped to Botany Bay as two great nations commence fishing within its waters.

1790s (Sperm Whale)

By the 1790s sperm whale fishing had spread to more favourable grounds, where they were seen to be in such large numbers that the opportunity could not be refused, hence the decimation of the South Pacific did commence, and although the killer whale tended to lay more towards the coastlines of many countries for their sustenance, routes across the great expanses of sea were patrolled.
1791 (Sperm Whale)

Many shoals were seen by members of the ship Britannia, from Van Diemen's Land to just out from the coast of Port Jackson, at approximately 15 kilometres, and the numerous sightings were recorded for the prosperity of the captain but divulged, in the end, to the governor for the Australian people and its fishing industry. The endeavours and efforts, therefore, of the human race helped dictate, within reasonable terms, that the killers did direct their attention more favourably to the coastline where migratory routes of humpback were known to exist.

Within a few short years of this sighting another was recorded to the west of the Galapagos Islands where sperm whales were seen in large quantities, copulation a common occurrence. It was now a basis of knowledge, something known by the killers for centuries, that one particular migratory route led along the coast of East Australia and out towards the islands so famous of Darwin and his findings. Not only this but the waters of the Pacific, to the north-east of New Zealand, were bountiful with sperm whales and their off-spring, so much so that the vast area, too large to contemplate, was combed by ships of many nationalities including those from Australia.

1799

Matthew Flinders stood upon the deck and saw that Twofold Bay could easily make a grand harbour, the skeleton of a right whale visible on the beach. A thought then traversed his mind where he was reminded of the days of Captain Cook, where he very nearly entered the East Coast of Australia at the point where Twofold Bay opened itself to the world, but due to bad weather was forced to the north where Botany Bay was chosen for the first settlement.

1804

It wasn't long before the commercial value of whaling hit the minds of those that continued to colonize Tasmania, where right whales (sometimes referred to as black whales) frequented the bays with their calves from June to October. This provided great opportunity to hunt sperm whale during the summer months and then the bay whales in winter, where, through the exuberance of those that lanced the whales till their heart's content, fell upon the realization that hunting from row boats was as good, if not better, than ramming home their harvest from large ships; bay whaling was now a true profession and taken up by a few bays along the coast of Australia where migratory whales tempted the greed and thirst of human desire for oil.

Sites were selected with great care as many considerations needed to take point, namely shelters for the men, cookhouse, cooperage (where casks and barrels of all description could be made and repaired, to be filled to the brim with that marvellous substance), storehouses and try-works where slabs of blubber could be easily drawn up a ramp and prepared for boiling, extracting the gold so laboriously sought.

1828

It soon became an interest, the Yuin and their exploits, and Twofold Bay made the headlines in a Sydney newspaper, bay whaling adopted soon after as more of an experiment than anything else. The spoils were so great that the opportunity could not be ignored. It was shortly after that 16 white men of a dispatch from Sydney were killed and another five years elapsed before Dr. A. Imlay secured over a thousand acres of land in the area.

The indigenous people of the region around Twofold Bay are called Yuin and had a name for the killers; they called them 'Beowas', meaning brothers or kin, they were 'transient, a social organization of killer whale which was set aside from the 'resident' and 'offshore', but with many 'resident' characteristics; they were, in essence, a 'matrilineal' organisation of killers that were, to a degree, inseparable.

As per the Romans and Greeks before them, the Aboriginals of Australia looked upon the killer whales with great respect and admiration, believing wholeheartedly that they were the reincarnation of ancestors past, where the dead took the form of a wolf of the sea. Why?

The Yuin believed that the killer whales were the returned spirits of the dead, ancestors that had come back to the world of the living and to help provide sustenance to the indigenous population. If a monster of the deep was to provide such great amounts of food for the tribe then it must be nothing less than the reincarnated spirit of a recently deceased member for their society. They were, every one, treasured as original members of the tribe and known, not only to help feed the Yuin, but also to protect them whilst in the water.

For long before the presence of any white man, the Yuin – not exploiting – made good advantage of the situation where it was quite common for baleen whales to be herded into the bay and become stranded upon the beach, whereby the strategies of the hunt become a symbolised benefit to all in the tribe and the 'Beowas' were adopted into their beliefs. It was a phenomenon that could only be explained by the belief of the 'Beowas', for why else would a killer whale home in on a humpback caught in the bay, pester and kill, to feed upon the lips and tongue, and then allow all that which remained to be shored upon the beach in order for the Yuin to feed?

Much else was also sought by the Yuin, not just food and comradery with a whale, but the more in-depth spiritual healing of infliction. It is here that rituals came into existence and all that the killer gave in jester to the people was to be used to full effect. A remedy – so it is said – evolved, where an individual so inflicted with rheumatism and the like would climb into a rotting carcase, naked and up to the neck in blubber, to gain the such sought-after relief gained by spending hours encased within the flesh and absorbing the stench and oil of the baleen's blubber.

1828 – 1830s

Thomas Raine was the first whaler in Twofold Bay in 1828, followed soon after in the 30's by the Imlay Brothers who employed several of the Yuin due to their keen ability to work hard, be reliable, and were easily skilled with the abilities of boat-handling; they were soon recognised for their talent and had good eyesight.

1838

Having sent for his brothers, Dr. Imlay undertook further exploits whereby his interest in breeding cattle continued alongside bay whaling.

1840

And at this time the sperm whale industry took precedence for the humpback whale had become increasingly available, learning over time to avoid the slaughter that occupied the bays of Tasmania, and although migratory routes were seldom changed and little voiced, it was in the interest of man to hunt where the value of the spoils could be secured in purse, hence the move from one species to the next; although, in all fair response, the sperm whale was also worth more in regards to oil.

1840s

In the 1840s, Benjamin Boyd set upon the scene and commenced to build a town in his own name; Boyd Town. It was his hope to have it grow in all aspects to one day be as big as any other city within Australia. He built a lighthouse from Sydney sandstone on the south head (Boyd's Tower) along with a little church of red brick (the spire of which could be seen from thirty kilometres out to sea), houses, storage rooms, wharves, stock-yards and the Seashore Inn which is situated on the beach and draws upon the very romance of the area, all surrounded by the lush of eucalyptus trees.

The bush itself was thick and descended to right upon the beach itself. Bay whaling was, however, not something that Boyd took too with great enthusiasm as the competition was so great, so sought to make an ambition from offshore whaling where the sperm whale could still be quarried in large numbers out to sea – for the sperm whale did not frequent the bays or the coast.

His crews were not 'overly' successful, accusingly bribed by the Imlay Brothers to miss-judge an unleashed harpoon, but the oil from the sperm whale measured Boyd's greed and filled him to the brim, his ships still much more capable of bringing home the oil than not.

Oswald Briefly, a good friend of Boyd's, who had arrived with him upon his yacht, Wanderer, made many written entries within a diary along with paintings and sketches of the activities of men and killer whales alike. It is from these accounts that the first encounter with the killers of Twofold Bay can be found, actually competing against the bay whalers that worked here as opposed to helping them, for the crews of the bay refused to allow the killers a share and frequently attacked them with the boat spades used in removing blubber from the much sought after baleen. It is here that the first of many strange incidents begins to take shape for the killers begin to show a liking towards those crews less callous in their treatment towards them.

And the men of the crews that fought the whales from upon their long and sturdy craft took little pity on the killers for their help in the hunt. The men watched as the killer whales flung themselves upon the back of the whale, charging in and taking chunks from its flanks, pestering it at every turn in order to prevent it from careering home into the depths of the open sea.

Lances continue to puncture the flesh of the humpback, the first catch in many months, but the fight isn't over just yet, for the whale must be killed and then secured, secured from the lurches of the orca as they come in for the lips and tongue. The crews endeavour to impede the killers' efforts, try with all their might to drag the dead whale away, to be deblubbered at their convenience. This is but one of the many reasons that the killers soon reside to taking their catch whilst near the mouth of the bay as opposed to within it, for the men of Twofold Bay seem to think that the whale is their just reward and should not be shared, and it was only due to the lack of a baleen plates, and little oil to quench the first of the market and merchants, that killers were not rendered into oil.

Twofold Bay was changing face, there was now Eden to the north of the bay and two other small villages to the south, separated by the Kiah Inlet. There was Boyd Town to the west and East Boyd to the east.

1843

It had become more than clear, even to those that lived in denial over the growing absence of right whales, that bay whaling in Tasmania was coming to a close. But in lieu of the bay whalers of Twofold Bay the call to boats was made, quite often, with great regularity; not by time of day, but by the appearance of whales from June and on into the long winter months. The sighting of whales in and around Tasmanian bays might have taken a turn for the worst, but the slaughter in and around Twofold Bay had just commenced.

The tides were turning and the great phenomenon was taking shape. Boyd's empire collapsed completely and the whaling gear no longer needed was sold to Alexander W. Davidson and his business partner Solomon Solomon, to sit idle for several years until the boats hit the water and bay whaling was undertaken by them.

1849

Boyd departed Australia in 1849.

1895

By 1895 sperm whaling was all but gone forever and the last unsuccessful hunt on the east coast concluded in 1896.

1955 (Sperm Whale) Norwegian

The decline of humpback numbers, not due to the killers themselves, nor even the Davidson's, for the combined number of kills were rather deplorable to say the least; but particular investments such as those of the Norwegians, where whales were taken from Australian waters, certainly aided in the rise of situations within the world such as Frenchman Bay of West Australia taking the turn it did by commencing with sperm whaling and adding infuriation upon a depleted stock.

www.ingramcontent.com/pod-product-compliance
Lightning Source LLC
Chambersburg PA
CBHW050111120726
47904CB00004B/1297